Mark Allen Smith is a successful television and documentary film producer and screenwriter. *The Inquisitor*, featuring the controversial hero known as Geiger, is his first novel. Mark's experience investigating features for the acclaimed American news magazine programme *20/20* planted the seed for his debut thriller: he was involved with a story dating from the 1970s about the remarkably brutal toture and murder of a 17-year-old in Paraguay, the last true dictatorship in the Western Hemisphere. He was further inspired to action by the shocking death of Lisa Steinberg at the abusive hands of her adoptive father; this event uncorked ongoing interest in the corrosive effect of physical and psychological pressure on children and other innocents. His journey of research convinced him that the novel was his best way to bring his story to the largest possible audience.

A long-time resident of Westchester County, Mark Allen Smith now lives in New York City's Harlem with his wife, Cathy, and a blended family of six children.

THE INQUISITOR

Geiger has a gift: he knows a lie the instant he hears it. And in his business, that gift is invaluable. Geiger's clients count on him to extract the truth. Unlike most torturers, Geiger rarely draws blood. He does, however, use a variety of brutal techniques to push his subjects to a point where pain takes a back seat to fear. Yet there is a line he refuses to cross: he will never work on a child. So when his partner unwittingly brings in a client who wants Geiger to interrogate a twelve-year-old boy, he responds instinctively and rescues the boy from his captor. But if they cannot discover why their client is so desperate to learn the boy's secret, they themselves will become the victims of an utterly ruthless adversary . . .

MARK ALLEN SMITH

THE
INQUISITOR

Complete and Unabridged

CHARNWOOD
Leicester

First published in Great Britain in 2012 by
Simon & Schuster UK Ltd.
London

First Charnwood Edition
published 2014
by arrangement with
Simon & Schuster UK Ltd.
A CBS Company
London

A catalogue record for this book is available
from the British Library.

ISBN 978–1–4448–1807–9

Published by
F. A. Thorpe (Publishing)
Anstey, Leicestershire

Set by Words & Graphics Ltd.
Anstey, Leicestershire
Printed and bound in Great Britain by
T. J. International Ltd., Padstow, Cornwall

This book is printed on acid-free paper

To Cathy

Prologue

The client sat in an eight-foot-square room staring at a large one-way mirror that offered a view into flat, smooth darkness. An audio track of a nervous laugh continually interrupted by a dry cough came through the speakers in the walls, but he couldn't hear it because he had put in the earplugs that had been left out for him.

He glanced at his watch. Eleven-twenty P.M. He'd been here three hours and was nursing a second scotch. The windowless room was old wood with a soft gray finish, and expensively appointed. The chair was an Arne Jacobsen, the rug an antique Persian. The chrome bar was stocked with expensive liquor, a pinot noir, and a Sancerre in a dewy bucket. Four conical, brushed-nickel pendants hung from the ceiling, and the etchings in the crystal scotch glasses caught their light and held it captive in brilliant, star-shaped designs. On the bar's lower shelf, a DVD recorder's face blinked with a tiny red eye.

The client was the head of security for a major U.S. electronics manufacturer. He didn't make the kind of money that allowed him familiarity with these luxuries, but the people he worked for did, and they were waiting for his call. It had taken a week of research and networking to arrange a meeting in a restaurant in Little Italy with an impeccably attired, exquisitely groomed mob boss named Carmine Delanotte, who questioned him over a bottle of Barolo and two double espressos before finally giving him the Internet code and Geiger's name, though it was understood that the name wasn't real. The code had gotten him into Geiger's website, DoYouMrJones.com, and using Delanotte as a referral had moved things along quickly. Earlier tonight the client had snatched his target — Matthew Gant, one of his company's R&D guys — from a garage and, following instructions, brought him to this bland, two-story building on Ludlow Street.

When the client and Geiger had finally met, in this room, the first thing he'd noticed was that Geiger hardly ever blinked. The client prided himself on his cool, but Geiger had put him on edge. The silky, even tone of his voice and his physical stillness added to his affect. He had elliptic gray eyes in a sharp, angular face. His body looked lean and hard, perhaps because he was a runner or a practitioner of some form of martial arts. And he had a slight tilt to his posture, as if his skeleton accommodated gravity in a unique way.

There was something truly strange about him — but then, what could you expect from someone in Geiger's line of work? The client had heard all kinds of stories. Geiger was a head case who'd done hard time; Geiger was a rogue from the NSA; Geiger was a twisted scion who didn't need the money and did it for the rush. The only common thread was that he had no equal. When they had shaken hands, the client had said:

'They say you're the best, and we hope it's

true. The specs we think Matthew stole are worth millions.'

Geiger had stared back at him, expressionless.

'I don't deal in hope here,' he'd said, and left.

For the first hour the room on the other side of the glass had been black. The only sounds were Matthew's outbursts, full of bravado and indignation. Then Geiger's hushed utterance reached the client through the speakers like a wraith come calling.

'Stop talking, Matthew. You are not allowed to speak any longer.'

It was the loudest whisper the client had ever heard. Then the lights came on, and through the one-way mirror the client saw Geiger leaning against a wall in a stark room, dressed in a black pullover and loose-fitting black slacks. The room was completely covered with white linoleum, and dozens of three-inch-wide recessed lights in the walls and ceiling made every surface glare. On the north and south walls, mounted a foot below the ceiling line, were several small video cameras. After a while the view started to play tricks with the client's vision, the room's angles gradually disappearing until Geiger seemed to be suspended in air, a sable silhouette frozen in a luminous alabaster tableau.

In the center of the room, Matthew was seated in an antique barber's chair — red leather, gleaming chrome, and porcelain. Metal-mesh belts were lashed around his waist, chest, ankles, and wrists, and when he moved bright stars of light ran across their latticework. His face was ashen, with splotches of a red flush on his cheeks. He was bare-chested and barefoot.

For a half hour Geiger stared silently at Matthew, straightening up every ten minutes to walk once around the room. He had a slight limp, but he had somehow incorporated it into his body mechanics, so it didn't look like an infirmity — it looked natural, for him. Matthew's wary eyes followed him on every circuit.

Geiger gave the barber's chair a push, starting it spinning slowly around and around. Then he left and the lights went out again. An audio track began playing a series of vignettes, each lasting a few minutes. The client heard a traffic jam with honking horns and screeching tires . . . a woman humming off-key . . . the strumming of a single chord on an out-of-tune guitar . . . a phone repeatedly ringing, stopping, and ringing again . . . and finally the nervous laugh and cough. At the start Matthew had yelled, 'Jesus fucking Christ!' but then he fell silent. Halfway through the track, the client had put the earplugs in.

Now the lights came back on as Geiger walked into the room again. Hands behind his back, he stood beside Matthew, who eyed him with undisguised fury. The client took the earplugs out.

'Matthew,' said Geiger, 'close your eyes.'

A scowl tightened on Matthew's face, but he did as he was told.

'Now. Imagine you've fallen down an empty well. It's pitch-black down there. You can't see a thing. The only sound is your breath. Your body hurts. Maybe you've broken an ankle, or a wrist.'

Geiger stayed silent for several seconds, as if to

make sure Matthew could hear himself breathing in the blackness of his prison.

'The pain puts on a light show behind your eyes. You can taste blood in your mouth. You reach out and feel around you. The walls are cold and damp, and smooth. Not a crack or a niche to get a hold of. Can you see yourself down in the bottom of that well, Matthew?'

The client felt a chill at the back of his neck. *He* could see Matthew down there.

'You try to stay calm. You start yelling for help. You tell yourself, *Someone will hear me.* But after a while you realize you're probably going to die down there. And as soon as that thought kicks in, something inside you does start to die. Not of the flesh, but the spirit. Do you know what I mean, Matthew?'

'I keep telling you, man — I don't know what you want!'

'Matthew, I said you are not allowed to speak. Just nod or shake your head. Do you remember me telling you that?'

Matthew stared at the unblinking gaze and nodded. Geiger's hands came out from behind his back with a wireless microphone and headphones. He fitted the headphones snugly on Matthew's head.

'Sennheiser 650s,' he said. 'I like them better than AKGs. It's a more textured experience. Close your eyes, Matthew.'

Matthew did, his breath catching in a ragged sigh, eyeballs nervously shifting beneath the lids.

Geiger raised the microphone and began strolling around the room while speaking softly.

5

He reminded the client of one of those self-help gurus on public television — only with an audience of one.

'Can you hear me clearly?' Geiger asked.

Matthew nodded.

'All right. Now, back in the well, Matthew. Are you there?'

Matthew swallowed, his Adam's apple bobbing up and down. He nodded again.

'Good.' The word sounded to the client like a soft prayer. 'It's important that you believe you're down in the well, Matthew, because this isn't a mind game. You are down there, and I'm your only way out. I'm the rope that can be tossed down to you and the hands that can pull you up.' He gently put a hand on Matthew's shoulder; Matthew stiffened. 'And the only thing that gets the rope tossed down is truth.'

The client leaned closer to the glass.

'It's a beautiful thing — truth. Man's only perfect creation. And I know it when I hear it. It's not that I'm particularly intuitive or perceptive, but I've heard so many lies that I can tell when the truth comes out.'

Geiger leaned down to Matthew's face, and the client could see Matthew's jaw joints flex with anxiety.

'Toscanini said he could tell if one string on one violin in a whole orchestra was out of tune. He didn't have perfect pitch, but he'd listened to so many millions of notes that he could instantly tell what was true and what wasn't.' Geiger took a breath. 'So, Matthew — don't lie to me.'

Matthew's nostrils flared like a colt's sensing

smoke. Geiger leaned closer, until only the microphone was between his lips and Matthew's.

'Did you hear what I said? *Don't lie to me!*'

The aural assault through the headphones made Matthew's head recoil with such force the client thought his neck might break. His eyes snapped open, his mouth stretched into a cavernous circle, and his howling lasted a good five seconds before it shifted down into a sucking moan.

Geiger turned his head to one side, and the client heard the *click* of cervical vertebrae. Then Geiger turned it to the other side. Another *click*. The client tried to read Geiger's face, but he couldn't discern any particular emotion in it.

'Matthew,' Geiger said, 'I need you to keep your eyes shut, stop moaning, and pay attention. Nod if you can do that.'

Matthew's groan caught in his throat. His head rose and fell in a meager, marionettic response, and his eyes closed.

'Now, there are numerous applications of pain for specific scenarios — primarily physical, psychic, and emotional pain. In those categories are many subcategories. In the physical realm, there is audio . . . '

He rapped the microphone with his knuckles and Matthew's head jerked, eyes springing open again.

'*Eyes closed!*'

Matthew howled, and Geiger gently put a fingertip on each of Matthew's quivering eyelids and closed them. Then he placed a thumb on a spot two inches left of Matthew's sternum.

'There is pressure . . . '

His thumb stiffened, and with almost no sign of effort he pushed inward and Matthew bellowed hoarsely, his face twisting in a toothy grimace. The client watched, amazed. He poked around curiously at his own ribs.

'There is blunt force . . . '

Geiger raised his arm, elbow bent at a ninety-degree angle. His forearm swung like a spring-action lever and smashed flush into Matthew's chest, driving all breath out of him, leaving him gasping, desperate to suck air into his lungs.

'And there is penetration, slicing of flesh . . . '

Geiger paused.

'But that's too medieval for me,' he continued. 'However . . . '

His hand went behind his ear and slid something out. It was shiny and silver, four inches long, immeasurably thin.

'Open your eyes.'

Matthew's lids rolled back. His brown eyes were laced with red thread.

'Do you know what this is?'

Matthew squinted at the thing between Geiger's thumb and forefinger, and shook his head. The client found himself nodding. He'd once had a slipped disc, and he'd tried everything for some relief. He knew what it was.

'This is an acupuncture needle. Its primary function is to block impulses that the brain identifies as pain from traveling up and down neural paths. But it can also create pain.' The needle glinted in his fingertips like the minuscule sword of a toy hero. 'There are ironies in my business that you can't help but notice.'

The remark was spoken without a trace of humor or menace, and the lack of both made the hair on the back of the client's neck stir. Geiger's free hand grasped Matthew by the hair. A short yelp slipped from Matthew — not a response to pain but an involuntary bark of recognition of what was to come — and Geiger deftly inserted the needle between vertebrae in Matthew's neck. Matthew didn't flinch, and his gaze never left Geiger's implacable face.

'The fact is, the human being is a remarkably vulnerable construct. This needle is lighter than a sparrow's feather, Matthew. A child's tear balanced on its end could bend it.'

Geiger wiggled the needle slightly, triggering a riff of shrill screams. Then he removed it and the yowling stopped. Tears streamed down Matthew's cheeks, his breath racing in and out of him in short, tight huffs.

'There's also manipulation of joints, application of intense heat and cold, forced ingestion of liquids. The fact is, Matthew, I could work on you for days without repeating a process.'

Geiger removed the headphones from Matthew's head and put them and the microphone on the floor. 'As for psychic pain, I think your sensitivity to physical stimuli makes that area unnecessary to explore. As for emotional pain — according to your file, you are single, unattached, an only child with no living parents, so I see no benefit in going there. You may not believe it, Matthew, but you're a very lucky fellow.'

The client wanted Geiger to pound on Matthew so he'd confess and bring this to an end. Then the client could make his phone calls and go home. But he'd sensed when he'd met Geiger that it wouldn't be like that.

'I'm not going to ask you yet, Matthew, because I can tell you're not ready to tell the truth, and I don't want to make you lie.'

'Ask whatever you goddamn want. I — I can't tell you what I don't fucking know.'

'That is true,' Geiger said. 'Irrelevant, but true.'

A thought made the client's stomach tighten. Could Matthew be telling the truth? Was it possible that someone else stole the R&D specs? Everything had pointed to Matthew, but . . .

'The well, Matthew,' said Geiger. 'You're down in the well, so close your eyes.'

Geiger's hands moved to his sides, fingers constantly flicking the air. Watching, the client wondered if there was a pattern; it almost seemed as if Geiger were playing air piano.

'All right. You've been down there awhile, and the mind is affected when the body can't move for long periods. Darkness and claustrophobia affect perception, sense of time, sense of self. They create an environment where emotional borders get fuzzy. Pain takes a backseat to fear. Hope dwindles, despair becomes a companion. Once that happens, you start to see who you really are — the depths and limits of your strength.'

Geiger knelt in front of Matthew. 'And then you're changed, Matthew, rearranged right down to the molecular level. It's the ultimate wake-up call.'

Geiger closed his eyes and massaged them with a thumb and middle finger. They were measured, precise movements.

'We'll take a short break now. You stay in the well.' He took a black silk blindfold from a pocket and tied it around Matthew's face. 'One other thing, Matthew. I've learned that once certain kinds of pain are experienced, the anticipation of further pain is almost as powerful as the sensation itself. I think in time you'll agree with me.'

Geiger walked out of view and the lights went out again. A few seconds passed, and then the door to the viewing room opened and Geiger came in. Without looking at the client, he went to the bar, poured himself a glass of water, and started drinking.

'I'm a little worried,' said the client. 'Do I have the right guy?'

Geiger nodded.

'You're sure?'

Geiger nodded again.

'How do you know?'

'I explained that to Matthew.' He put the empty glass down. 'You were listening, weren't you?'

'Yeah — Toscanini. But why hasn't he confessed yet?'

'He's not at the release point yet. He'll be there soon.'

'The release point?'

Geiger nodded once more, but looked as if he

11

didn't want to have to do it again. 'Matthew is still more terrified of what might happen if he confesses than what will happen if he doesn't. For the moment, the reality of torture is preferable to the possibility of death. But that will change.'

The client wondered what Geiger looked like when he smiled — if he ever smiled.

'We're not going to have him killed,' the client said. 'We just need to know who he sold the data to.'

Geiger stared at him with those unblinking eyes. 'But he doesn't know that.'

Geiger walked out. The client sighed and looked back to the mirror and the black abyss. The speakers delivered Geiger's gentle voice to him on quivering wings of angels.

'Matthew, are you in the well? You can answer me.'

Matthew's voice sounded like sandpaper on rough wood. 'Yes. I am.'

'Good.'

Then Matthew started to scream. The sound was so loud that it came through the speakers ragged with distortion. The angels scattered. The client turned and reached for the earplugs.

PART ONE

1

At four A.M., standing on the stoop outside his back door, Geiger watched a spider weave its web.

It was raining. The sky, ash-gray and cloudy, was gathered at the horizon like an old quilt. A drop of water clung to one strand of a new web that stretched from the porch overhang to the wooden railing four feet below. The breeze plucked the strand like a guitar string; the raindrop trembled but held fast. Then the spider came down, plump belly swaying, and began weaving a new strand.

Earlier, Geiger had been typing up his notes on the session with Matthew. As *Sgt. Pepper* came to him through the six-foot Hyperions, he felt the superb bass response, right down to the click of McCartney's pick on his guitar strings. The cat, as usual, was lying on the desk, stretched out beside the right end of his keyboard, a front paw rising and tapping at Geiger's hand whenever he went more than a few minutes without being scratched. The near rumble of his purr was loudest when Geiger scratched the scar above his missing left eye. Geiger didn't know the circumstance of the injury; the animal had looked this way when he showed up on the back stoop three years ago. Nor did he know the cat's name or where he was from — which is to say, the two were somewhat alike.

Geiger always wrote notes the same night of a session, while actions and reactions were fresh in his mind. He found that even a few hours of sleep could smudge the edges of memory. The next day, his partner, Harry, would e-mail a transcript he had made from the video of the session, and Geiger would go through it and insert comments at relevant spots.

He worked while sitting in an ergonomic desk chair, built specially for him. But he still had to get up every fifteen minutes and walk or his left leg would go pins and needles down to his toes. Over the years he'd seen three specialists about the problem — one doctor had called it 'dead-foot' — but they all said the same thing: the only recourse was reconstructive surgery. Geiger told them that no one was going to use any kind of blade on him, for any reason. Having just examined him, they understood his feelings on the subject.

Geiger had stepped out back to lose the numbness and have a cigarette. He didn't smoke inside. He found that the smell of stale smoke in a room affected his focus. Months ago, when he was new on the couch, Dr. Corley had traced that back to his father and his endless Camels. To date, that was the only picture of his father Corley had been able to pull out of Geiger — in a dream, Geiger had seen his father's stony face staring down at him, a cigarette clamped between full lips, smoke curling out of his nostrils. Geiger had remembered thinking, This is what God looks like. Only taller.

He felt the cat, which had just come out the open door, rub against his ankles. He picked the animal up and draped the furry body over his shoulder. Other than the perch on the desk, this was the cat's favorite spot.

Geiger lit a Lucky Strike and watched the spider. Full of purpose, it performed its singular task with innumerable perfect strokes. Imagine a carpenter who could spit out nails made in his gut and use his hands as hammers. Imagine a musician whose instrument was his own body. Geiger wondered, Is there any other being so diligent and artistic at creating a killing apparatus — besides man?

★ ★ ★

Geiger was an apostle, a slave to the specific. He was constantly breaking down, distilling, and defining parts of the whole, because in IR — information retrieval — the details were crucial. His goal was to refine the process to an art, which was why every single thing that happened from the moment Geiger walked into the room had its own degree of significance and required recognition. Each facial expression; each spoken word and silence; each tic, glance, and movement. Give him fifteen minutes in the room with a Jones and nine out of ten times he would know what the reaction to a particular action would be before the Jones made it: fear, defiance, desperation, bravado, denial. There were patterns, cycles, behavioral refrains. You just had to pay very close attention to see them all. He'd learned that by listening to music; he'd come to understand how every note plays a part in the whole, how each sound affects and complements the rest. He could hum every note in a thousand pieces of music. They were all in his head. In music, as in IR, everything mattered.

Still, even with the countless elements that could come into play, Geiger's view of his work was relatively simple. The client and the Jones almost always presented him with one of three basic scenarios.

No. 1: Theft. The Jones had stolen something from the client and the client wanted it back.

No. 2: Betrayal. The Jones had committed an act of disloyalty or treachery and the client wanted to learn the identity of any accomplices and the extent of potential repercussions.

No. 3: Need. The Jones possessed information or knowledge the client wanted.

Human beings are all different, but only in so many ways. Geiger's transcripts proved it time and again. Since he had started this work, he had filled twenty-six black four-inch binders, which now sat lined up on his desk. He could cross-reference the data in the notebooks by profession, age, religion, net worth, and — most important — allegation. The binders were an encyclopedia of information on response and reaction to intimidation, threat, fear, and pain. But there was no data within the pages about death. Geiger had never had a Jones die in a session — not once in eleven years. As Carmine would say, Geiger was batting a thousand.

Geiger's clients came from the private sector, the corporate world, organized crime, government. Four years ago, he'd even done a stint at a black site for some agency spooks. They believed their methods were cutting-edge, but Geiger had immediately seen that they were way behind the times; they were men pulling wings off flies while they talked of saving the world. In IR, there was no substitute for expertise. Patriotism, religion, a steely belief in what was right and wrong — these were all things to be set aside. In the end, there were lies and there was the truth, and the space between the two could be so thin that there was no room for the clutter of rectitude and conviction. The spooks at the black site had stood in the shadows observing him as he worked; to Geiger, they'd looked like cavemen watching him light a fire with a Zippo.

He was a student of the craft, and a historian. Just as the black binders contained the sum of his own work, he was a living text of the trade — its origins, rationales, methodologies, and evolution. He knew that man had been using torture without apology since at least 1252, when Pope Innocent the Fourth authorized its use to deal with heretics. Since that official sanction, immeasurable time and effort had gone into creating and perfecting methods for inflicting pain in the pursuit of what a person or group considered indispensable information or truth. The practice had no cultural, geographic, or ethnic bias. History proved that if you had rudimentary tools — hammer, saw, rasp — and basic materials — wood, iron, rope, fire — you needed little more. Add even the simplest understanding of physics and construction and you were in business.

Geiger had begun his education by studying the instincts and foundational choices of the pioneers. Certain methods and techniques were especially effective, including:

Sharpened objects. The Judas Chair proved so successful during the Inquisition that most European countries began customizing their own versions. *Culla di Giuda, Judaswiege* — by any name, it was a pyramid-shaped seat upon which the Jones, raised by ropes, was perched.

Encasement and pressure. The Iron Maiden, an upright sarcophagus, was fitted with interior spikes and apertures for the insertion of various sharp or pronged objects during an interrogation. It was also, to a degree, the ancestor of the sensory deprivation process. The buskin, Spanish Boot, and Malay Foot Press all used shrinkage and manipulation to break feet; the thumbscrew was limited to single digits, but an interrogator who carried one in his pocket could turn any place into a torture chamber.

Manacling and stretching. The rack was a technological advance, with its employment of rollers, gears, and handles, allowing one the ability to quickly increase or reduce physical pain by minute degrees.

Waterboarding was another brainchild of the Inquisition's interrogators. They understood that whereas submerging a Jones in water might prove effective over time, waterboarding triggered the gag reflex almost instantaneously, heightening the fear of death.

Intense heat had always been a staple of the torturer's trade — consider the phrase 'putting one's feet to the fire' — as had the ripping and flaying of flesh. Also useful was a wide array of tools, from the simple — such as pliers for denailing — to the complex — such as the Pear, a hinged and often exquisitely etched steel tool inserted into the vagina or anus and slowly expanded by means of a screw handle. The catalog of tools was extensive: the Wheel, the Cat's Paw, the Head Crusher, the Crocodile Tube, the Picquet, the Strappado. All these and more had been invented before the Industrial Revolution, and Geiger had come to understand that the practice of torture was not an aberration. In the cause of expedience and the quest for information, man has always been willing to trump his laws and betray his beliefs to legitimize the torture of those who do not share them.

After much study and consideration, Geiger had devised a standard operating procedure. He worked only by referral. If a company or individual was in need of his services, they were directed to his website and given the password. Harry, his partner, would immediately review the request; if he didn't see any red flags, he asked the potential client to send some preliminary information about the Jones. Then Harry started digging, and within a couple of days he put together a detailed profile. Harry was prickly, but there was no one better at what he did. He could find out things about a Jones that the spouse or best friend didn't know, the government didn't know, even the Jones didn't know. Once Geiger read the dossier, he would tell Harry whether the job was a go.

Geiger had three rules. He didn't work with children, though Harry had never received such a request. He didn't work with people who'd had coronary events in the past. And he didn't work with people over seventy-two — Geiger had reviewed studies showing that the risk of heart attack and stroke rose to unacceptable levels after that age.

But there was one gray area: the asap. Geiger's corollary to 'Everything matters' was 'A Jones is not the perfect sum of his or her parts.' So if a client wanted an asap — a rush job — Geiger would often decline. There was so much to take in: body language, verbal response, vocal tone, facial expressions, a constant stream of information that shaped his choices and decisions — and a miscalculation or an incorrect conclusion, no matter how minor, could blow up a session or even tear a hole in his private universe. Which is why Geiger preferred to work inside out and follow a game plan based on Harry's research. Some pros, like Dalton, worked from the outside in and used a more single-minded, head-on application of brutality. But with this approach, the client couldn't always be sure what shape the Jones would be in when the session was over — although in some cases, that wasn't an issue.

Geiger, like everyone in the IR business, had heard a number of stories about Dalton. The most famous one dated from Desert Storm, when Kuwaiti cops caught one of Saddam's henchmen sneaking across the border. They worked on the Iraqi for a week and got nothing, so they brought Dalton over and gave him carte blanche. That kind of session was called a 'norell,' short for 'no release likely,' meaning that it would probably be unwise to allow the world to see the Jones again after the interrogation was completed. The first time Dalton asked a question, the Iraqi smiled and Dalton sliced off a lip with a rotary knife. Then he went to work with a pneumatic nail gun — and the Jones gave Dalton what he wanted. The story may have been apocryphal, but it made Dalton's career. In IR it didn't hurt to have that reputation — that you were capable of anything — because most clients saw the Jones as the enemy and, in truth, wanted more than recompense or enlightenment. They wanted their pound of flesh.

The way Geiger saw it, politics, business, and religion were the three remaining fingers of a battle-scarred fist. Truth, meanwhile, was a weapon that even a damaged fist could still grasp and wield. It was a remarkably versatile commodity; it could be traded, or help serve an end, or produce a profit. But it was an unstable element with a short half-life, so it had to be used quickly, before it blew up in the client's face. Early on, Geiger had learned that truth was no longer sacred — it was simply the hottest thing on the market, and anyone in IR who believed that they acted within the parameters of some righteous code was at the very least deluded.

The cat jumped from Geiger's shoulder to the porch railing and went on his nightly way. Without fail, he would be back around five A.M.; the creature's clock was a nearly perfect thing.

The spider had finished its night's work. A large, striped moth was already caught dead center in the web, struggling furiously, not knowing that the more it tried to free itself, the tighter its shackles grew. Moving without haste, the spider came down from the web's upper right-hand corner. It demonstrated no sense of urgency, as if the ends were secondary to the means, the meal simply a by-product of the art that had snared it.

Geiger lit another Lucky, and as the spider reached its prize Geiger put his lighter's flame to an anchoring strand. The web, moth, and spider all went up in a puff of fire.

Geiger decided not to think about his action just now, and headed back inside. He would talk about it with Corley tomorrow.

2

Dr. Martin Corley stood at the railing of his eighteenth-floor terrace, drew on his between-sessions Marlboro Light, and frowned. Since he'd switched from the regular brand, this ritual had become the latest in a series of unsatisfying acts of self-denial intended to ward off incursions of mortality. It hadn't been the milestone of sixty that had whetted his focus and pushed him away from old habits but the aftermath of his divorce. The long marriage and its countless traditions, however threadbare and static, had provided a numbing continuity, a sameness that masked the passing of time. Since Sara had left, it was his aloneness that informed him, daily, of his age and the potential for further deterioration. First came the shift to one percent milk instead of cream in his coffee. Next came Diet Coke instead of the real thing, trading flavor for the chemical aftertaste. Then Amstel Light, which required an act of self-delusion for him to believe he was drinking beer. Now this joyless sucking of thin smoke, waiting for the hop in his pulse that no longer came. Without the attendant pleasure, smoking was unmasked for what it was — an addiction perpetuated by a mind grown too indolent to explore itself with the diligence it brought to the terrain of others.

Looking down to West Eighty-eighth Street, Corley saw Geiger come around the corner and approach the side door to his building. Geiger had called for an appointment eight months ago, after finding Corley's name listed on a psychiatric website. At their first session, he revealed the reason for his presence: two months earlier he'd had a dream of epic intricacy and drama, followed by a massive migraine. Since then, Corley had learned, the dream had been playing every two or three weeks in slightly different versions on his mind's stage, and in each case an excruciating migraine had provided the second act. In all their sessions, Geiger had been precise and devoid of guile, a provider of emotionless reportage. Corley found his new patient to be an intriguing contradiction, the equivalent of an intelligent stone.

At the end of the first session, when Geiger had decided to continue the process, he'd voiced two requirements. First, he would talk only about the dream. He would not speak about his past, or his life outside the walls of Corley's office. Second, he must be given a key to the building's service entrance so that he wouldn't have to walk through the lobby.

Corley had sat back in his chair, scratching his white-streaked beard, and asked why.

'Because I know what works best for me,' Geiger had answered.

It was the first of countless times that Corley had been struck by a tone Geiger often summoned. Though equable and uninflected, it was anchored in a certainty that made further discussion seem unnecessary, even pointless. Geiger's first rule, limiting all discussion to the events of a dream world, meant severely constricting the usual therapeutic borders, and his request for a key was far beyond the accepted rules — no patient had ever asked for one. But Corley had agreed to both. Geiger's dream, proof of some radical turmoil the man was clearly incognizant of, had been gasoline poured on the pale embers of Corley's passion. He had wanted Geiger to come back.

From his terrace, Corley watched Geiger unlock the service entrance and go inside. After dropping his cigarette in a flowerless clay pot, Corley walked back into his office.

★ ★ ★

Corley stared at the notepad on his lap. He'd started taking notes during sessions only recently. In the past, he'd jot down a few notes in between patients and flesh them out at night. Then he began to notice a slight, nocturnal stutter in his memory, a minor lag in recalling details. He'd given ginkgo biloba a try, but stopped because he kept forgetting to take it.

'So,' he said, 'the web was finished, a moth was snared, and you put a flame to everything. What do you think that was about?'

Geiger lay on the couch staring at the bookshelves on the wall. He knew the literary skyline by heart — every title, author, color, and font. In the center of the lower shelf was a framed photograph of a large, rambling house set on a rolling lawn amid majestic trees. Its strong lines and angled roof appealed to him.

27

He'd asked Corley about the house in the past and received curt responses. All Geiger knew was that it was a hundred years old and located in Cold Spring, New York, about an hour away.

'What do I think that was about?' said Geiger. 'I'm not sure. What do you think it was about?'

'Well,' said Corley, 'it could've been about control. Power.'

Geiger's fingertips tapped the couch in shifting combinations of sequence, speed, and rhythm. For Corley, the sound had become part of the sessions, a soft percussive accompaniment to spoken words. For the first four months of therapy, Geiger had called for an appointment only after a dream-migraine event, and that was the only subject discussed. But gradually the irregular sessions evolved into a weekly visit, sometimes twice a week, and lately Geiger seemed less strict about his first rule. Sometimes, as he'd done today, he would even chronicle a real-life event.

'Maybe it was about completion,' Geiger said.

'Interesting.'

'Is it?'

'I think so,' Corley replied. 'You might have said 'destruction,' which could be considered the *opposite* of completion.'

'Good point, Martin.'

Before Geiger, no patient had ever addressed Corley by his first name, in thirty years of sessions. The first time, it had sent ripples skipping across the calm surface between them, leaving the psychiatrist unsettled and shifting in his chair. It had stirred something in him, the unforced familiarity in the gesture so contradictory to Geiger's basic inscrutability. Corley had never said anything about it, and ultimately he'd embraced it as part of their unusual dynamic.

'Everything's a process,' Geiger said. 'Beginning, middle, end. That's what works best for me. You know that. Completion.'

Geiger's gaze drifted to the ceiling. Years ago there had been water damage. His eye was always drawn to the subtle change in texture caused by the repair. He knew, step by step, exactly how they'd gone about the work, because he'd done the same kind of job hundreds of times himself.

'Why do you think we're talking about the spider?' said Corley.

Geiger bent his right knee and pulled the leg slowly up to his chest. Corley waited for the familiar, soft *pop* in the sacral joint.

'The spider had finished its web,' Geiger said. 'So why did I torch it? I'm not sure. Because it's in my territory?'

'And only you decide when something's finished in your domain?'

'King of all I see?' A soft sound slipped out of him. It could have been a sigh. 'That's a line from something, isn't it?'

'*Richard the Third*?' said Corley. '*Yertle the Turtle*?'

'What?'

'The children's book.'

Corley waited, scraping fingertips down one bearded cheek and then the other. But Geiger's silence was like the sound of a door slamming shut.

29

'Do you remember any children's books?' Corley asked. 'Or songs? Does anything come to mind? Maybe toys, or — '

'No. Nothing comes to mind.'

Over time, Corley had come to think of Geiger as a lost and beleaguered boy who had somehow remained undaunted. Because Geiger's dreams were virtually the sole context in which Corley could work, he knew almost nothing about the man and could only guess at what lay beyond the borders of their sessions. Even so, Geiger's story about the spider and conversations like this one convinced him that the child in Geiger was buried beneath so much traumatic rubble that it was more ghost than real. Sometimes Corley felt like a medium at a seance trying to contact the dead.

Corley glanced at his watch. It was the last gift his wife had given him. Engraved on the back was *Where does the time go? Love, Sara.*

'We're almost out of time,' he said, 'so let me put something out there for you to think about — about the spider.' He straightened the pad on his knee and wrote, *Empathic?* 'Maybe setting fire to the web wasn't about completion or dominion.' He noticed the dance of Geiger's fingers becoming more intense. 'Maybe you didn't want the spider to kill the moth.'

Geiger's fingers came to rest, and he sat up. Corley watched the overdeveloped trapezius muscles shift beneath his shirt. Geiger's shirts were always long-sleeved, brushed black cotton, and closed at the neck.

Geiger stood up and swiveled his head left and

right. Corley heard dual *clicks*.

'Food for thought,' Geiger said. Then: 'Tell me something, Martin.'

Corley had expected the request. It had become part of the process, part of Geiger's exit ritual. It was usually *Tell me something . . .* and a question would follow, or *By the way . . .* and a seemingly insignificant bit of news would be proffered. Corley knew that these last exchanges helped Geiger manufacture a closing to a process that was, by its nature, open-ended, and so gave him, depending on the tenor of the session, a parting sense of control.

'Do you go up to your house often?' Geiger asked.

'No,' Corley said.

'Why not?'

Corley put his pad down on the desk. 'We have to stop now.'

★   ★   ★

For Geiger, the morning walk to and from Corley's office was always a sensory feast. Central Park West was a kaleidoscopic vista: taxis feinting in traffic like yellow-skinned middle-weights; sluggish, ungainly buses chugging and wheezing; dogs and their walkers sniffing and eyeing each other; joggers stretching voluptuous hamstrings at red lights as they waited to enter the park; olive-skinned men trudging through the gutters, pulling their hot dog and souvlaki carts behind them like broken penitents. It was all pure stimuli for Geiger, an assault of colors,

31

shapes, sounds, movement. Not the subtlest hue or tone or gesture went unnoticed or unheard, but no secondary, more sophisticated responses occurred. He took everything in and yet held nothing. He was both a vacuum and a bottomless pit.

He had lived in New York for fifteen years, and his arrival in the city marked the beginning of the only life he could remember. On September 6, 1996, Geiger was born an almost full-grown man of indeterminate age when a Greyhound driver shook him by the shoulder as he slept in a seat in the last row of a bus that had just pulled into New York's Port Authority Terminal, on Forty-second Street and Eighth Avenue. The boy/man guessed that he was in his late teens, but otherwise he was as much a stranger to himself as the people he passed on the sidewalks of the city. He was a scarred, aching body with an unencumbered mind, a human machine without a memory card. He ran solely on instinct.

The next day, while walking the streets of Harlem, he stopped to watch a member of a renovation crew sawing a new window frame for a run-down brownstone. A moment later, he walked through the doorless entry and asked for a job. It was a pure, thoughtless act, and when the crew chief asked if he knew carpentry he said Yes and didn't know why.

He had worked 'reno' for four years — never staying with one company for long, taking nonunion late shifts, mainly in Harlem and Brooklyn and SoHo, secretly sleeping in the basements of the buildings where he worked, saving his money. All the companies paid off-the-books cash — no ID numbers, no FICA, no paper trails. At first he'd used the name Gray, then Black. One day, passing a Barnes & Noble bookstore, he spotted a book about the artwork of H. R. Giger. The byzantine images appealed to him, as did the name with its twin g's. For visual symmetry, he added an *e* and so became Geiger.

One night, after finishing a shift in a brownstone in Williamsburg, he'd been sleeping in a crawl space in the building's basement. Awakened at three A.M. by footsteps coming down the stairs, he lay there watching flashlight beams dance between two-by-fours, listening to two men discuss their task as they went about it — installing wiring behind fresh drywall for a bug that would attempt to record incriminating conversations regarding a certain Carmine Delanotte.

'I heard Delanotte owns a dozen of these,' one of the men said.

'My brother-in-law's in real estate,' said the other. 'Says everything around here will be worth a fortune once they push the spics and the blacks out. Buy low, fix 'em up, sell high.'

'This wire's a waste of time, you know? Delanotte's too smart.'

'Maybe. But I heard they're close to turning one of his lieutenants around.'

'Yeah, well. They try and turn a lot of 'em, but most don't talk. They throw everything they've got at these guys — mindfucks, blackmail, even the occasional beatdown. The fucking guys don't talk.'

'Must be one very strange job.'

'What?'

'Trying to make guys talk. Cracking hard cases. You can't just beat the shit out of 'em, right? You got to be smoother than that, you know?'

'There are guys who know how to do it, though. Interrogators, specialists — they know how to make people open up.'

As the two men — FBI techs, presumably — continued talking, Geiger lay in the darkness and felt the birth of something. It was a weightless, free-floating thing, but it was potent enough to muster his instincts toward a direction and a course of action. He'd felt this bloom and pull once before; standing outside the dilapidated Harlem brownstone, an urge had risen up in him as if from a molecular level. He felt it this time, too, a kind of genetic calling, a sense as powerful and thoughtless as an avalanche destroying everything in its path.

3

Harry Boddicker stared up at the brightly lit, tensile webs of the Brooklyn Bridge, and then at a helicopter as it glided over the East River, humming in the indigo summer sky like a giant fire-fly.

He glanced back at the dark blue van parked beneath the FDR Drive. The Jones was in the back, gagged, tied, and taped up inside a metal trunk. He was one of Carmine's bagmen. Fifteen minutes ago, when three of Carmine's men had made the delivery, they had informed Harry that when they'd picked up the guy — they'd snatched him while he was screwing his girlfriend in her apartment — they'd had to put the hammer down hard. They'd given him two black eyes and maybe a broken nose and a couple of busted ribs.

Now Harry had to call Geiger. The last time they'd gotten a damaged Jones — a business manager from Providence — Geiger had gone on about necessary states, compromised origins, and diminished potential, his satin voice never rising or falling, and then called the job off. Because Carmine would be getting his usual discount, this gig was worth only twelve grand, but the thought of losing his share, three thousand dollars, went straight from Harry's brain to his stomach and pumped a bitter bubble of gas up his esophagus. They hadn't had a job in five days. He popped two more Pepcid Completes. Whatever they'd added to the chalky mix to make the old stuff 'new and improved' didn't seem to matter to his gut. It still roiled and grumbled as always.

He walked a little farther away from the van and jabbed at his cell phone. Geiger would pick up after the third ring. Not one or two, not four. Always three.

'What is it, Harry?' Geiger answered.

'About tonight. There's an issue. Damaged goods.'

'Details, Harry.'

Harry sighed. 'One eye's swollen shut. Nose might be broken. Ribs.'

After a brief pause, Geiger said, 'Change of location, Harry. Take him to the Bronx instead.'

'Right,' Harry said, his eyes closing with relief. Geiger was willing to take the job.

'And use propofol instead of Brevital. Two cc's.'

'Right. Propofol. Two cc's.'

* * *

When Harry called, Geiger was in his backyard doing one-armed push-ups: fifty with the left arm, fifty with the right, then forty, then thirty, the breeze drying the sweat on his naked body. The yard was a twenty-by-fifteen-foot green oasis in the midst of a dense urban sprawl of geometric concrete, brick, and asphalt. The patch of grass, backed by an oak bench and a modest Norway maple, was surrounded on three sides by a tall wooden fence that Geiger had built with over one hundred ten-foot vertical slats. The fence's longest side, opposite the back of the house, ran east-west, and Geiger had cut the top of each slat to a specific length and then shaved or carved each board so that when viewed from the back stoop the entire span was a perfect, to-scale replica of the jagged skyline of the buildings looming directly behind it.

Earlier, Geiger had studied the Jones's file and built a scenario in his head. John 'Jackie Cats' Massimo — one of Carmine's men and a hard case by any measure — was forty-two, heavyset but muscular, and comfortable with physical violence. In his younger days he'd been knifed in the chest and had taken a shotgun blast in the thigh. And he was a cat lover: he had six of them. But now Massimo was already in physical pain and might have impaired vision, so Geiger would have to rework everything — the session room, tactics, methodology. He didn't even think of canceling the job, however, because he wouldn't do that to Carmine.

Carmine had given Geiger his first job in IR, eleven years ago. The day after Geiger overheard the conversation between the FBI techs, he had gone to an Internet café and found a photo of Carmine Vincent Delanotte, reputed mob boss, as well as the address of his restaurant, La Bella Ristorante, in Little Italy. Geiger read several articles about Carmine and learned that he was something of a visionary. In the early 1980s, he had started buying run-down brownstones throughout the boroughs for practically nothing.

37

Apparently he had grasped all the possibilities — the houses provided him with a legitimate front, laundering venues, and kickback contracts — and fifteen years later a flood of cash had started coming his way. One of the articles quoted a source at the FBI who claimed that lately Carmine had been making more money in real estate than in loan-sharking and gambling combined.

That evening, Geiger had walked into Carmine's restaurant and handed the maître d' a sealed envelope.

'Give this letter to Mr. Delanotte,' Geiger said.

Perhaps Geiger's manner had an immediate impact, or perhaps the maître d' often delivered envelopes to the owner; in any case, he took the letter without a word and walked away. Geiger picked out Carmine at a table in a corner with three other men. The gleam of his blue eyes and his silver-streaked hair flashed with every tilt of his head, as if he had an alternating current running through him.

The maître d' leaned down to his boss, whispered in his ear, and held out the letter. Carmine looked at the offering, then turned his gaze toward Geiger. The cool stare measured him, and Geiger saw a flat look of nonrecognition give rise to a glint of curiosity in the man's wide, cerulean eyes. Carmine opened the envelope with a flourish of his polished thumbnail, took out the single sheet of paper, and read it. He folded the paper methodically, tore it in half, and then tore the letter a second and third time. He dropped the bits of paper into a porcelain cup on the table, lit a match, and set them on fire.

His lips moved and the words put bodies in motion. The maître d' stepped away, and Carmine's three colleagues rose and stood behind him against a blood-red brocade wall. Carmine looked again at Geiger and raised two thick fingers; flicking them, he gave Geiger an imperial command to approach.

When Geiger was three feet away, Carmine pointed at him. Geiger halted. Carmine leaned to the burning paper and blew out the flames. Smoke rose in languid puffs from the cup, and Carmine waved some of it toward his face and took in a deep, sensuous breath. Then he looked up at Geiger.

'I'm not allowed to smoke anymore,' he said in a voice that rumbled with the echo of thousands of deeply drawn cigarettes. He shrugged ruefully and sat back. 'Guys . . . ' he said. The three sentinels strolled to the bar.

'Sit down,' said Carmine. Geiger slid into a chair and Carmine poured himself two inches of Chivas. He put the bottle down in front of Geiger.

'I don't drink,' said Geiger.

Carmine raised his glass and took a small sip. 'Three years and I still can't get used to Chivas without a Lucky.' He put his glass down. 'What do you make on the late shift? What do I pay you?'

'One hundred and fifty dollars a night.'

'Cash, off the books. So it's really more like two hundred and twenty a day.'

'Yes.'

'That's more than enough to rent a room, isn't it?'

'Yes.'

'But you're sleeping in one of my houses. That's not allowed, Mr. Geiger.'

'I know.'

'Then why do you do it?'

'I save a lot of money that way.'

The corners of Carmine's wide lips tilted up. 'Are you fucking with me, Geiger?'

'No.'

'You do know who I am, right?'

'Yes, Mr. Delanotte. I've read about you.'

Carmine's lips finished their arc into a fully fashioned smile. 'Okay,' he said. 'First thing: you don't sleep in my houses anymore. Second thing: I appreciate the heads-up about the feds. I'll deal with it.' He slipped a hand inside his suit jacket and took out a taupe leather billfold. 'Five hundred sound fair?'

'I don't want your money,' Geiger said.

'No? You're so flush from sleeping free in my houses that you don't need it?'

'I have a question.'

'Ask me.'

'About your 'lieutenants.' How will you find out which one is going to betray you?'

Carmine scowled. 'Could be any one of five or six. I know a guy. He'll find out.'

'I could do it,' Geiger said.

'*What* is it you could do?' asked Carmine.

'Find out what you need to know.'

'And how would you do that, Geiger?'

'I'll ask your lieutenants questions, and they'll tell me the truth.'

'So — when you're not doing reno, you're in the truth business?'

'Information retrieval.'

Carmine's head tilted, like a dog's hearing a distant whistle. He was evaluating the tone of voice; Geiger had spoken the two words without the slightest hint of irony or sarcasm.

'*Information retrieval*,' Carmine said. 'Got it. All right — so what am I thinking right now?'

'I'm not a mind reader, Mr. Delanotte.' Geiger turned his head to the right; there was a barely audible *click*. 'But you are probably wondering if I might be psychotic — or retarded.'

Carmine's grin lurked just beneath the surface, like a shark in shallow water. 'I guess I can't really ask for a résumé, can I? You've got experience in . . . information retrieval, is it? The truth business?'

'I can tell when someone is lying. I can tell a lot about someone just by looking at them.' Geiger turned his head to the left. Another *click*. 'You're left-handed,' he said.

'That's right. How'd you know that?'

'Your eyebrows.'

'My eyebrows, huh? You gonna read my palm and tell my fortune next?'

'I don't know how to do that. But you see better out of your right eye than your left — and you had two, maybe three fingers on your left hand dislocated a long time ago. They still hurt. Probably arthritic.'

Carmine involuntarily flexed the fingers of his

41

right hand, then leaned toward Geiger until their faces were inches apart. 'Has anyone ever told you that you are one very strange motherfucker?'

'Yes. A number of people.' Geiger's fingers fluttered on the tabletop. 'Let me come to the first interrogation.'

Carmine frowned and poured another two inches of liquor. He stared at the glass, and for a moment he was absolutely still, as if listening to the sound of ten thousand hunches — his whole life, built upon them — and then his eyes started to shine with the wisdom of intuition.

'Geiger, do you own a cell phone?' he asked.

'No.'

'Get one.'

* * *

His daily regimen of push-ups done, Geiger went back into the house and stood in front of his enormous CD case. He had designed and built it himself; six feet square, it was made of flawless cherry, had ten open shelves on rollers, and held over eighteen hundred albums. He scanned the jewel cases and slid out Stravinsky's *Dumbarton Oaks*, flicked on the amplifier, and slipped the CD into the player. A tripping cascade of violins poured from the Hyperions.

He walked to a door and opened it. Inside was a small closet, just four feet by four feet, with mirrored walls from floor to ceiling. The music flowed into the closet from two mounted Bose mini-speakers.

Still naked, Geiger stared at his triple

reflections. He surveyed the cabled muscles beneath taut skin, the crooked knee-caps and pronounced bumps of the outer ankles. He turned and craned his head around to see the slight, scoliotic curve of the upper spine and the oddly flattened iliac crests at the hips. And as always, he gazed with particular intensity at the myriad razor-thin scars running in horizontal columns down his hamstrings and his calves, all the way to his Achilles tendons. They looked like patient, punctilious markings etched by an inmate on a prison-cell wall.

Geiger stepped inside the closet and lay down on his side, curling himself into a ball to fit. He reached up and pulled the door closed. He closed his eyes. As the music swirled around him, each note burst into a drop of radiantly colored light that left a dying trail like a falling star against a night sky. He could taste the sounds, too; each instrument and tone delivered a different flavor. The cello painted long, aquamarine streaks that tasted sweet and cool. The violins splashed hot red lines with hints of cinnamon.

He was in the darkness now. He needed to think.

4

Jackie Cats awakened to the sound of a cat meowing plaintively. His eyes ached, and he could open only one of them. He remembered being yanked out of bed; he remembered being taped up and forced into a large, coffinlike aluminum trunk; and he remembered, later on, some guy opening the trunk and shoving a needle into his neck. The rest was a blank — until now.

He was in a dark place and he couldn't get a sense of its dimensions. He could see that he was suspended upright in a spread-eagled position in the center of a geometric construction made of steel bars that had been bolted together at ninety-degree angles to form a hollow cube about ten feet by ten feet. He was naked, arms and legs stretched out at forty-five-degree angles, wrists and ankles tethered tightly to the upper and lower horizontal bars by leather straps. Beneath him in the floor was a round metal grille, about four feet in diameter.

His bruised body was bathed in the hard light of mini-spots shining from the eight corners of the cube. There was no other illumination, and outside the cube the black floor and ceiling merged with the darkness. He didn't know where he was, but he knew why, and what was coming. He pulled on his ties, testing them. There was no give.

The meowing dropped down into the guttural yowl of an angry feline, and soon another slow, bending yowl joined in, announcing a second cat.

Jackie Cats shouted, 'Shut the fuck up, huh?'

He couldn't believe what a schmuck he was. A dumb, fucking minchione. He'd waited years for his shot, put up with Carmine's bullshit, got the right crew together, pulled it off without a snag. Free, clear, and rich. If he'd stuck to his plan, he'd be thirty-five thousand feet up right now, six little Chivas bottles on the fold-down table, listening to *Learn to Speak Portuguese* on his iPod. But he went over to Nicki's to do her one more time, and ended up fucking himself instead. He shook his head ruefully, and it made his eyes throb.

'Fuck me!'

The yowling escalated to hisses and throaty growls, and then the unseen cats went at each other. The sound of small, thudding bodies, vicious snarls, and chalk-on-a-blackboard screams weaved into a shrill cacophony. It made him grit his teeth, and that made his eyes hurt again.

The howls stopped and he was surrounded with a thick, pulsating silence. Just past the fringe of light he saw two unblinking eyes floating in the blackness, staring at him.

'Here, pussy, pussy,' he said, chuckling. He'd made his peace with fear a long time ago. He'd looked down the barrel of a shotgun, felt a stiletto sink into his flesh, did five and a half in Attica with the beasties and the bush babies. And he had a theory about fear. It was all about regret. If you make what you want out of life and don't bullshit yourself about your choices, then there are no regrets, and a man without regret isn't afraid of anything.

Then again, he did wish that he hadn't paid that last visit to Nicki . . .

The eyes darted toward him, and something swung into the light with a *whoosh* — it was a long wooden oar — and struck him flat-sided on the sternum. His body reflexively tried to double up, but the bonds prevented it, so he shook and spasmed like a large fish on a hook, and then slowly came to rest.

'Muh — ther — fuck — er,' came out of him.

The pain crawled up into his neck and flooded his eyes with tears. Someone was standing outside the cube; he was dressed in black and wore gloves and a hood. Jackie Cats knew he wasn't dealing with Carmine or any of the guys. They'd taken him to a pro. He remembered Carmine talking about two guys in the past. One name started with a *D* — Denton, Durbin, something like that. He couldn't remember the other guy's name.

'Jesus,' he said. 'A fucking *boat paddle*?'

The oar's head smacked into the small of his back. His body tried to arch forward and the oar slammed into his stomach. The blows were wreaking havoc on his involuntary reflexes. Before his muscles could finish one violent spasm they were jolted by another. He was twisting up inside. He felt as if parts of him were being pulled from their moorings. Bile rose in his throat like volcanic magma.

'You picked a helluva way to make a living, you sick fuck. It must pay well. Don't mind if I puke, do you?'

His lunch shot out onto the floor. It occurred to him that it had probably been his last meal, and he hadn't enjoyed it. The veal had been tough. He greedily gathered air back into his lungs.

'I'm not giving anybody up, asshole,' he said.

Behind him, a soft voice said, 'I need the names of the men who helped you steal the money, John.'

Jackie Cats turned his head as far as he could. The guy was back there, but all he could see was blackness. 'You hear what I just said?' he barked.

'I need the names of the men who helped you steal the money, John.'

'Are you fucking deaf or — '

The edge of the oar met his chest with a *crack*. He howled, his head swiveling back around in time to see the oar disappear. The voice was behind him, so how could the guy be in front of him? Was there more than one of them?

'You tell Carmine — he's got his money back, and he's got me, so leave it alone. I'm not ratting. And you can suck my dick.'

He heard a click, and a stream of tepid liquid poured down on his head and shoulders, down his body, drenching him and dripping down into the grille.

'What the fuck?'

The dousing slowed to a trickle and stopped, and the mini-spots grew brighter. The stuff stung his eyes, like too much chlorine in a pool. It tasted bitter.

'It's a mixture of water and three chemical agents,' the voice said. 'Under the lights, it will start to heat up as it dries on the skin. It feels good, at first.'

★ ★ ★

For a few minutes, it did. Jackie Cats remembered lying on the tar roof of their house off Flatbush Avenue when he was a kid, the sun on his face and the heat coming up through his towel and warming his back. But now his skin was burning hot. He felt like a slab of meat on a spit. He could almost hear the sizzle.

'So how does it work?' he asked the darkness. 'You don't get paid unless I give you names? That it? 'Cuz if it is, you're doing this one pro bono. I'm telling you — you can wait till I'm fucking charcoal-broiled, but Jackie Cats ain't talking.'

'I told you what I need, John, but at the moment I'm not asking you for anything. It isn't time yet.'

'So who are you — Denton or the other guy?'

'His name is Dalton.'

'Whatever.'

His skin felt like it was shrinking, tightening on his bones. His hands had gone numb. He'd begun to feel very strange: suspended this way, he was losing the sense of where his own body started and ended. If he could just touch something . . .

'How 'bout this? One mean, crazy prick to another. Trust me when I tell you I ain't giving

48

anybody up, so how 'bout we cut to the chase and you take me out right now? Get it over with.'

He heard the *whoosh* just before the oar met his left kneecap. His bellow sounded hoarse and unfamiliar.

'Should I take that as a no?' He laughed, and that sounded different now, too. Tinny and high-pitched. 'Tell you what, then. I'm gonna explain something to you. Try and make you see why you might as well do me now.'

Another *whoosh* brought the oar smashing into his right kneecap. His teeth bit into his lower lip. He tasted blood. Harsh lights suddenly came on in the walls and ceiling. The optical shift delivered such a sensory jolt that his body stiffened as if he'd been hit again.

The room was large, about twenty feet square. There was nothing else in it except a man who stood before him just outside the steel frame. Clothed completely in black, he held the oar in his hand.

'Nice to meet you, motherfucker,' Jackie Cats said.

Geiger pulled off his ski mask. He was satisfied with how things were going. He'd used force moderately, just enough to keep Massimo's primal senses in the moment while the cube and the sodium hydroxide solution gradually did their work. Slowly the man's concrete sense of the physical self would alter and diminish, ultimately affecting his mind and loosening his sense of resolve, priorities, loyalties. Massimo was telling him how tough he was, explaining why he couldn't be broken. It was a good sign.

'Go on, John,' Geiger said. 'Tell me why we should cut this session short. I'm listening.'

'Okay then. See, the way I see things, life and death is a no-lose proposition. I've felt that way for thirty years and I'm gonna feel that way no matter what kind of shitstorm you bring down on me. You know why that is?'

Geiger started to walk slowly around the cube. The oar hung down at his side. 'Tell me, John.'

'Here's why. The way I live life in my world, somebody wants to take me out? Fine. Take your best shot and see if I go down. If I do, hey, it's cool with me, 'cuz I'm dead now and I don't give a shit. I don't care that you whacked me, or that you're fucking my wife or pissing on my tombstone. Do whatever the fuck you like, or don't. You staying with me on this, Mr. X?'

'Go on, John.'

'But if you try to whack me and I *don't* go down . . . well, you gotta know I'm coming back at you and there's a truckload of righteous retribution pulling up to your door. Because now I'm feeling like God on a long weekend with nothing to do but some really terrible fucking damage. And before I'm through with you, you're gonna tell your wife to get on her knees and suck my hose till she chokes. To make me stop your pain, you're gonna beg me to do things to her you'd never even let yourself dream about doing to the sorriest whore you could ever stick a cock in. Okay?'

Geiger knew it wouldn't be long now.

'So either way,' Jackie Cats said, 'dead or alive, I'm doing okay — see? Life and death's a no-lose proposition on a silver fucking platter. And I'm not ratting. *Not ever.*'

'I have a question, John.'

'Yeah?'

'What if you were the other guy?'

'What other guy?'

'The man in your story who you're punishing — who chooses to offer up his wife to sexual degradation in order to stop his own physical torture. Are you saying you wouldn't make that choice if you were him?'

'Fucking A right! What've I just been trying to tell you?'

'Then how are you different from him?' Geiger stepped inside the cube. This close, he could smell the residue of the sodium hydroxide solution. He'd give him a second dose soon. 'Tell me, John. What makes you different from him?'

Jackie Cats's reddened face screwed up in angry confusion. 'What the fuck're you talking about?'

'Why wouldn't you sink to those depths? What is it about you? Is it physical strength? Are you tougher?'

Geiger raised the oar and brought the edge down on the outside of Jackie Cats's right ankle with a sharp *crack.*

'Do you have a higher threshold of pain?'

He whacked the left ankle and Jackie Cats growled.

'Are you braver?'

He flipped his grip on the oar and hammered the rounded end into Jackie Cats's right clavicle. A deep gasp burst out of his bleeding lips.

51

'Or more noble — or loyal?'

He drove the oar into the left clavicle, picking spots where he would inflict intense pain without breaking anything.

'Or more loving?'

Geiger raised the oar like a spear so the bridge of Jackie Cats's nose became a bull's-eye. As he thrust it forward, Jackie Cats winced at the imminent impact — and the oar stopped an inch from him. His eyes rolled back and his head tipped to the side.

'John. What I have to say now is important, so nod if I'm coming through to you.'

'Go . . . fuck . . . yourself.'

Geiger's fingers started their dance beside his thigh.

'In this room, John, we try to deal in truth, and we stay here until we find it. Now, I do think you believe that what you just told me about yourself is true. I think that's who you think you are — but I don't agree with you.' He stepped out of the cube. 'John, my job is to retrieve information, but sometimes, in order to do that, first I have to help you become more aware of your strengths and weaknesses, what you're capable of and what you're not. Discovering your true self, John — that's what this is really about.'

Geiger walked to the wall directly in front of Jackie Cats.

'So you try to take a look at who you really are when all the poses and nicknames are stripped away. Give it a shot, John, and then you and I will talk again and see where we end up. I might even ask for the information I need.'

Geiger reached out to a black control panel on the wall, pushed a button, and another shower came down on Jackie Cats, who grunted but hardly moved. Geiger punched another button and all the lights except for the cube's mini-spots went out.

'Been there, done that, motherfucker,' Jackie Cats muttered.

The sound of the cats' hissing and yowling started again, and then Geiger's voice spoke from the dark as it had earlier.

'I need the names of the men who helped you steal the money, John.'

The sentence became an audio loop. Interweaving with the feline mayhem, the voice said the same words over and over. *I need the names of the men who helped you steal the money, John. I need the names of the men who helped you steal the money, John. I need the names . . .*

Then a noise slipped out of Jackie Cats. Even in his impaired state, the sound stunned him. It was a whimper.

5

Sipping his morning coffee and sitting at the desk in his Brooklyn Heights living room, Harry looked out at the East River. He slid his hand inside his sweatpants and felt around gingerly, his scowl like a horseshoe embedded in his unshaven face. Last night, during one of his marathon showers, he'd discovered something that made him shiver in the hot steam — a small, subcutaneous *something* in his groin. The bulge was the size of a grape and semihard.

During his years in the Obituaries department at the *New York Times*, which is where he'd worked before he met Geiger, Harry had developed the conviction that if you lived past forty, sooner or later you'd get cancer. The small percentage who didn't make it to forty — who died in a head-on or were murdered or stroked out — they *would* have gotten cancer if they'd lived longer. Now Harry was forty-four, and his body, once a brother-in-arms against the world, could no longer be trusted. He knew from all the lives he'd sifted through that within every man is his own Caesar and Brutus, and from this point on his flesh could betray him at any time. The 'Et tu' moment would come, not as a dagger in the back but as a swollen node felt while swallowing, or an enlarged pupil glimpsed in the mirror, or a grape-sized mass found by a fingertip during a shower.

At times like these Harry envied Geiger. He wouldn't change places for any price — clearly, the man had more demons than a Hieronymus Bosch painting — but that steel-trap heart and mind had a definite appeal. Nothing ever seemed out of the ordinary to Geiger. He was like some mystical engineer who'd found a way to shut down the highs and lows of happenstance and their impact. Back at the beginning of their partnership, Harry had decided that Geiger was on a mood equalizer, one of those drugs that sandpaper the rough edges off experience. But eventually Harry had changed his mind. If Geiger was on a drug, it was something he produced in his brain, and whatever that chemoneural cocktail was, Harry coveted it.

They had met eleven years ago in Central Park at three A.M. Harry was drunk, as was his nightly custom then, and he was getting his head kicked in by two skinheads. A few years earlier he had become a dreamless man — not the nocturnal variety, but a man who had let go of any notion of prospects, any promise of the new and different, any hope of *something else*. The dreams of his youth were as dead as the people he wrote about, ashes and dust, and so the arrhythmic pounding of boot toes on bones and flesh and the breath-sapping pain and the possibility of being ushered out of the world had all felt almost right. Loss had become a sidekick; it was always near, shambling along a few steps behind him. The thought of finally bidding it good-bye was stretching Harry's battered lips into a smile across broken teeth when Geiger stopped his nighttime run just long enough to lay out the punks in a blur of lethal hands and feet, and then go on his way before Harry could summon breath to speak.

Two weeks later, with thirty stitches and two new teeth in his head, Harry began a nightly vigil at the site of his humiliation. He didn't have to wait long: on the second night, in a downpour, Geiger came down the path in T-shirt and sweatpants, and Harry stepped into his route. Geiger stopped, running in place.

'What do you want?' Geiger asked.

'I just wanted to say thank you.'

Geiger's wet hair shone black as polish. Drops of rain slid down out of his brows and into his eyes, but they didn't appear to bother him. Harry noticed that he hardly ever blinked.

'My name's Harry. Harry Boddicker.'

He put out his hand, but Geiger didn't even glance at it.

'Buy you a drink?' Harry asked.

'I don't drink.'

'Well, I just thought, seeing as how you saved my life — '

'It was chance, Harry. It had nothing to do with you. If they'd been kicking a dog I would've done the same thing.'

'Then how about coffee? You drink coffee, don't you?'

For a moment, Geiger looked at Harry with his steady, unblinking eyes and said nothing. Harry suddenly felt uneasy; the man seemed to be inspecting him, judging him. Then Geiger nodded and said, 'All right, Harry.'

They went to a bar on Broadway and took a booth in the ammonia-scented shadows. While Geiger nursed a black coffee, Harry had three Wild Turkeys. Over the next three hours, Harry delivered a biographical monologue that was half an eager act of sharing and half an attempt at reaffirmation, as if the tether to his past was dangerously frayed and recounting events would buttress his place in the present.

The pace of his story picked up when he told Geiger about landing a job at the *Times*, straight out of City College, as a researcher. 'That's when I discovered I had a talent for digging stuff up. They called me 'Shovel.' Funny how sometimes it takes a while before you find out you're good at something.'

He told Geiger about nights spent sneaking into computer networks using software of his own design, about deploying those skills to unearth secrets and connect dots, about writing a major piece on racial profiling that made his reputation as a reporter.

'One morning there it was, second section, page one. 'By Harry Boddicker.' It was like, Hey, that's *me*.'

As Harry talked, Geiger said little beyond answering yes or no a few times. He nodded or shook his head to other queries, and although that was the extent of his active participation, he never had the urge to leave. He noticed that Harry tilted precipitously toward the melancholic as the alcohol settled in, and that Harry's recollections became less detailed and more scattershot as his story went on. Geiger also sensed that Harry was leaving out an important chapter: he talked about his life as if he'd lived in two distinct eras, but he never once mentioned the event that had ended one and brought on the next. At first Harry's tale was full of excitement and the pride of accomplishment, but then it veered into darker alleyways. His passion for the work waned; the quality of his stories declined precipitously; facts were smudged, deadlines missed. Drinking went from hobby to habit. After months of admonishments, the *Times* had given him one last chance and a desk in the Obits department.

'You know that sensation,' Harry said, 'when you feel like you've hit bottom, and you realize you're right where you belong?'

Harry told Geiger that being relegated to Obits had been like a homecoming — he lived with ghosts and their pasts, immersed in their deeds and declines. But it had also spurred him to create ever more sophisticated and cunning search programs. Filling in blanks, giving continuity to chaos — it became an obsession, a strange kind of resurrection.

Listening to this epic story had been a singular experience for Geiger. In those three hours, he learned more about Harry than he'd ever known about anyone, and as he ran home in the dawn light, a thought came to him as if delivered by an unseen hand. This would not be the last time he saw Harry Boddicker.

★　★　★

58

The *ding* of Harry's computer signaled a visit to the website. The sound was always a tonic. It meant work, the challenge of putting the puzzle of a person's life together, and money. Harry had discovered an appreciation for money only after he'd started working with Geiger and making a lot of it. The money was useful, of course, but it was also a salve for the shame over how he made it.

Harry had never been present at a session, but he'd come to understand that for Geiger, the work wasn't about money. God knows what it *was* about, but Harry never asked. That would be like asking Van Gogh why he painted, or asking Jack the Ripper why he went out for a stroll at night. In time Harry realized that Geiger *had* to do it, and like everything else about the man, this intrigued Harry. He dimly remembered that feeling, the thrill of a powerful undertow that could pull him out to some roiling sea. Geiger, for all his stoic strangeness, reminded Harry of what passion used to feel like.

Harry watched the website on his screen. Ninety-five percent of the hits on DoYouMr-Jones.com were Dylan fans, who found a home page with a picture of the singer, but the bell meant someone had clicked on 'password' to venture deeper into the site. The password had to be a five-word phrase extrapolated from the letters of 'melon,' Harry's favorite fruit. If they got the password right, it meant they had a legitimate referral.

Harry sipped his coffee and smiled when the

current visitor entered 'Men everywhere live on nuts.' Not bad, he thought. Of course, no one had ever matched Carmine's first log-in, in 1999. 'Minestrone, eggplant, linguine, ossibuchi, nougat.' A classic five-course Italian meal from a man whose appetite and sense of humor were as big as his sense of vengeance, who lived life the same way he wielded power — to the fullest.

The site accepted the phrase and asked for a referral. When the visitor typed in the name — Colicos — Harry recognized it. Colicos was a scrap metal baron who had used Geiger twice in the past. Harry waited while the visitor followed the instructions and provided his name, cell phone number, the identity of the Jones, and the reason why the client needed Geiger's services.

Again Harry gently squeezed the lump in his groin and considered having someone look at it. But he hated going to doctors almost as much as knowing that he had a reason to do so. Geiger had taught him how to create various false identities, but health insurance was too dicey for someone living off the grid, so he paid his medical bills in cash. He did not relish the thought of doling out large sums for exams, tests, biopsies, and all the rest.

The web page filled up with information, and then another tone signaled the visitor's exit. Harry hit 'print' and checked his watch. Lily would be arriving soon.

His gaze went to her photograph on the corner table; curled up on a couch, she looked out at him with her mischievous, 'I know a secret' smile. But his sister hadn't looked like that in a very long time. Ten years ago, he had put her in a home, and every other Sunday since then he had made the trip to New Rochelle to visit her. Sitting beside her while she stared at nothing and sang snippets of old songs, he listened to a voice that sounded ancient, as if she'd already lived a dozen lifetimes. She seemed to have become something out of a science fiction movie, a being taken over by an alien life-form, its movements awkward, its speech quaint and disjointed, its motives unknowable.

Even so, Harry was convinced that Lily maintained a firm grip on the absurdity of her life, and her persistence haunted him. Harry had tried to train himself to not think about Lily, but his sister had become a squatter in his nearly vacant conscience, refusing to be evicted. His guilt was not about the business of surrogacy — he paid a fortune to keep her in the home. Instead, he was tormented by the serrated truth that had lodged itself in him long ago. He wasn't shelling out over a hundred thousand dollars a year because he loved Lily; he was doing it because he wished she were dead. These days, six figures seemed to be the going rate for Boddicker guilt.

The downstairs buzzer sounded. Harry walked to the door and pressed the entry button on the wall. Four months ago, in a sudden act of contrition, he'd arranged to have Lily brought to his place by one of the psychiatric nurses on her day off and had found that, compared to visiting the blanched desert of her room in the home, bringing Lily to his apartment had a temporary numbing effect on his angst. Recently he had scheduled another one-night sleepover — for today.

Harry opened the door and stepped back a few feet, listening to footsteps ascending the stairs. A twenty-something woman with black, scarecrow hair, wearing green culottes and high-tops, came into the doorway's frame with a small, canvas overnight bag in hand.

'Hi, Mr. Jones.'

'Hi, Melissa.'

She turned, reaching a hand out to the unseen hall. 'C'mon, Lily. Let's go.'

A soft, satin voice spoke: 'Time to go.'

'That's right,' said the nurse, and pulled Lily into the apartment.

Drugs and madness had made his sister gray and small. She was dressed in the short-sleeved pink blouse and lilac pedal pushers he'd bought for her a few years ago. Lily's elbows, wrist bones, and cheekbones stood out prominently beneath her opalescent skin, and as always now, when Harry saw her he had to remind himself that she was six years younger than him.

'How's she doing?' he asked.

'Same,' said Melissa. 'Fine. Right, Lily?'

There was a stillness about her; hardly anything seemed to move, as if the psychosis was a cancer that had dissolved all her muscles and tendons and nerves. She looked light as air — a giant, beautiful origami figure. When her deep-set blue eyes finally shifted and settled on Harry, they gazed at him without a hint of recognition.

Harry stepped toward his sister. Her gaze was

fixed on the small hollow beneath his Adam's apple. He raised a hand and tapped the top of her head with his knuckles three times. 'Anybody home?'

Lily's lips bent ever so slightly at his touch.

Harry glanced at Melissa. 'We used to do that as kids.'

His sister walked to the wide picture window. 'I like it here,' Lily said. 'Everything moves so fast. I like seeing everything move so fast.'

The East River, barely disturbed by a ripple, carried a near-perfect reflection of Manhattan's skyline upon it. On summer days like this the city seemed to have a shining twin that lay just beneath the water.

Lily leaned her forehead against the glass and put her palms up flat against it. She began to sing haltingly in light, dancing syllables.

'*Way down . . . below the ocean . . .*'

Harry joined in. '*Where I want to be, she may be.*'

Lily seemed deaf to his participation.

'Know that song, Melissa?' asked Harry. ' 'Atlantis'?'

'Nuh-uh,' she said. 'Any coffee?'

'In the pot. Make fresh if you like.'

Harry sat back down at the desk, and his chest rose and fell with a deep breath and a deeper sigh. He took the sheet of paper from the printer. As he read, he started nodding. He liked what he saw.

'Melissa, I may have to go out for a while.'

'Okay. We'll be okay — Lily's fine.'

Harry looked up with a tilted grin. 'Yeah,' he said. 'Lily's fine.'

6

They sat at a booth in the diner on Columbus Avenue. Harry had been coming here since the 1980s, when he and his sister lived nearby. Now it was a twice-a-week breakfast place for him and Geiger. Harry would have his cheddar omelette and bacon, and Geiger would have black coffee. Harry would talk about the business — a tweak to the e-mail codec, new customized spyware, a database he'd hacked into — and Geiger would listen, sometimes responding with a one-sentence remark. Harry brought the *Times,* and when he was talked out they'd both read the paper. Harry never took the first section because Geiger read only the letters to the editor.

Harry emptied a third thimble of cream into his coffee to placate his stomach as Geiger opened the folder and extracted three sheets of paper. The first was the printout of the potential client's website entry. His name, Richard Hall, and cell phone number were followed by his request:

> I represent the owner of a private art collection. Two days ago a painting, a de Kooning, was stolen. We believe the thief is an art dealer who has served as a go-between in acquisitions for my client. My client feels that notifying law enforcement will not necessarily help recover the painting, so I have contacted you.

Harry watched Geiger's gray eyes slide back and forth. Even after working for him for more than a decade, Harry knew little about Geiger. He'd pieced together a scant profile from random remarks — not from New York, a music lover, vegetarian, didn't own a TV, lived somewhere in the city — but he had long ago stopped asking even the most casual personal questions. Whatever more particular sense of the man Harry had came from a tilt of Geiger's head while listening, the speeds and patterns of his fluttering fingers, the occasional comment about a job. Harry had come to view the nature of their bond in the simplest of terms: need. Geiger had, for reasons Harry did not understand, entrusted him with a significant part of his life, and Harry had put the task of serving him at the empty center of his own. They were the strangest of partners — joined at the hip, light-years between them.

Richard Hall's entry continued:

The man in question is David Matheson. He is 34 years old, resides at 64 West 75th Street, New York, New York, and his Soc. Sec. number is 379-11-6047. I have him under surveillance and would be able to 'deliver' him, as I am told this is how the process works. It is likely that Matheson had a buyer in place *before* the theft, so it is crucial that this be dealt with quickly. I am authorized to pay an additional $200,000 should you retrieve information leading to the painting's recovery. Please contact me by 2:00 p.m. or I will look for someone else. Sincerely, Richard Hall

Geiger put the first sheet down.

Harry grinned. 'Not bad, huh? Would you do an asap?'

'One step at a time, Harry. We have a way of doing things.'

Harry nodded and stifled a frown and a burp.

The other pages were research on both the Jones and Richard Hall. Harry had hit a dozen different veins, as he liked to call them, while digging up information about David Matheson. He'd earned an undergraduate degree in international studies and a master's in art history, and had worked for ten years as an art appraiser, consultant, and buyer. He was on watch lists in Greece and Egypt for meeting with suspected black marketeers in antiquities. He had lived in New York for thirteen years and was divorced; his only child, a son, lived with his mother in California. All Harry had on Hall was his birth date and Social, his honorable discharge from the National Guard in 1996, and thirteen years of FICA contributions from Elite Services Inc., an investigative outfit in Philadelphia.

Rita, the waitress with the bleached platinum beehive who often served them, arrived with her coffee pot. She knew not to bother talking to Geiger. With him it was always the same — black coffee, two refills, and hardly a word. Sometimes his gaze would meet hers, but there was no invitation in it. At first she'd taken his manner as coldness, but in time she'd seen her mistake: she'd interpreted his lack of warmth as the presence of its opposite, where, in truth, there was no emotion at all. She slid his cup over and poured, then slid it back and looked to Harry.

'Darlin'?'

Harry waved the offer away. 'Already over my limit, Rita, and I'm paying for it.'

'Want the usual for breakfast, Harry?'

'Nothing today, hon.'

Rita moved on. Geiger put the sheets back in the folder.

'So what do you think?' Harry asked.

'Not a lot here to work with,' said Geiger.

Harry frowned. 'I didn't have a lot of time.'

'I wasn't criticizing the effort, Harry.'

Harry nodded. There hadn't been any negative edge to the words; there never was. Geiger's neutral delivery was like an aural Rorschach test. Harry heard what he did or didn't want to hear depending on his mood. Sometimes it made him nuts.

'Chances are very good that Hall's client didn't buy the painting legally,' said Geiger. 'That's why they don't want the police.'

'That crossed my mind. Doesn't matter, though — right?'

'Did you find out if any de Koonings have been stolen or gone missing in the last fifty years or so?'

'Uh-huh. Two — in 1979 and 1983.'

Geiger's fingers danced on the tabletop.

'Harry, even if I get Hall the information he wants, there's no way we'd know if his client ever actually gets the painting back. We'd never see the extra money.'

'We could make it part of the deal. If Matheson fesses up, I could go along with Hall

67

when he gets the goods. Then we'd know.'

'No. The job is over when the session ends. We don't go past that line. Inside versus outside, Harry. You know that.'

Harry's head bobbed and his shirt-hanger shoulders hunched in a shrug.

'I know, I know. It's just a ton of money.'

Geiger picked up his coffee, blew on it, and took a sip. Harry noted, as he often had before, that even this simple action was executed with the finesse of a ballet dancer.

'Harry, how much did we make last year?'

'A million and change.'

'Twenty-five percent of that is . . . ?'

'Two hundred fifty.'

'And that's how much if you paid taxes?'

'Four hundred and twenty thousand. Okay, okay.'

Geiger held his coffee cup against his chin. In an asap scenario the Jones is more of an X factor and the clock is ticking. Ordinarily Geiger didn't like to count on luck, but when the client was in a hurry he had no choice: he was forced to hope that the Jones would slip up. Sooner rather than later, the Jones would have to show something — a weakness, a phobia, a demon — and then Geiger would play it for all it was worth. Asaps were always tricky, but they did provide their own kind of challenge.

Geiger put his cup down. It didn't make a sound.

'Tell Hall it's a go,' he said.

Harry's lips sprang up at the corners in a hallelujah smile.

'Have him snatch Matheson now,' Geiger said. 'Make the session for midnight, Ludlow Street.'

★ ★ ★

Geiger had an appointment with Corley coming up that afternoon, but first he wanted to go to the Museum of Modern Art because Harry had said there were some de Koonings there. Geiger had never been in a museum. Carmine had taken him to a gallery in SoHo once — Carmine was a serious collector — but Geiger had been unmoved. Paintings, sculpture, photographs — they weren't like music. They were unchanging images, and staring at them was a static event for him. But having an appreciation of a Jones's passion is a valuable asset in IR, so he was going to see what it was that David Matheson craved.

He walked through Central Park. The sun was a yellow decal stuck onto the sky, and softball teams were out in full regalia. The park was where he had first started studying squirrels. They were marvels of psychic economy, each reflex and movement ruled by fear. Geiger sometimes watched a squirrel stop in mid-step and freeze with its paw raised for thirty seconds as it weighed a potential threat.

Soon after he'd moved into his house, he'd started an experiment to see if he could change and control their behavior. For a week, he put a pile of sunflower seeds by the birch tree in the backyard and watched from the stoop as the squirrels ate them. Then one morning he sat down by the tree, hand open in his lap and filled

69

with seeds. He stayed absolutely still for an hour. For three mornings, a squirrel would venture within five or six feet of him, freeze, and then sprint away. Geiger realized that as the squirrels came closer, his heightened anticipation caused changes in him — pulse rate, gaze, breathing pattern — that set off their internal alarms. He would have to change his behavior to control theirs.

The next morning he sat by the tree with his eyes shut, playing a symphony in his head, denying his senses all knowledge of the external. In two days they were picking seeds from his hand; after four days they were eating while perched on his calf or thigh.

Geiger brought that experience into the session room — the ability to change his behavior to suit a scenario and to create a state of dread in the Jones while he could still function and make choices. If a squirrel's hardwiring allows a respite from fear only when it is up a tree, Geiger's goal was not to make the Jones fear that he'd never get back to the tree, but to make him forget that trees existed at all.

Recently he had told the story of the squirrels to Corley. It was one of the few times he had volunteered information about a contemporary event, and Corley had responded by asking if he felt 'disconnected from people.'

Geiger answered, 'Martin, if you've never been plugged in, you can't be disconnected.'

Geiger was aware of his differentness. Of the one hundred and sixty-eight hours in a week, he spent approximately five with Harry, one with

70

Corley, and, on average, fifteen with the Joneses. Living the rest of his life alone was not a choice. It was his organic state. The parts of himself that Geiger knew, he knew very well. The parts he didn't know, he knew not at all. Life before New York was without definition — a black room — and when he peered into it, the darkness offered faint answers. But when the dream started, it was as if a flash of lightning filled the room, and he could see that the space was endless, without borders. The dream gave him half a second's glimpse of the room's contents: countless faces, bodies, trees, unrecognizable shapes. That is where Corley came in. Geiger told him about the dream and its variations, and he used Corley's eyes to help him see into the black room and discover who he was and what he had been. Geiger did this because the more he knew about himself, the more he could bring to the job. It was all about IR.

The dream had come to him again, last night, and the aftermath had been the same. He woke up at four A.M. and saw the flashes of lights announcing the powerful migraine that was already moving like a storm front into the left side of his brain. The dream's details changed but the structure was always the same: Geiger, as a preteen boy, would rush out of someplace and try to get to a destination that was never clear. On his journey, which was filled with obstacles, he would sooner or later start to literally come apart: first his digits and then his limbs would drop off. When his head was about to fall off he would wake up.

71

When Corley first heard about the migraines, he wrote a prescription for Imitrex, but Geiger declined to accept it. He didn't take pills for his pain; in his mind, that would be attacking it from the outside. He dealt with pain from the inside, and like most of the mundane processes in his daily life, his method was uncomplicated and ritualistic.

When a migraine moved in, Geiger would put on some music, always rich and textured, and curl up on the floor of the closet. He would close the door, strap on the Sennheisers, and give himself to the blackness and sound. Then he would reach down deep and wrap his arms around the pain, and when it became all he felt, the only thing he felt, he became as strong as the pain. And that's when he would grab the pain by its throat and kill it.

Lodged in some crevice of his brain was the knowledge that there was more than one way to deal with pain. Geiger had spent much of his life traveling this road — as beast, as rider — and what few understood about pain was its dual potential. It could be used not only by the inflictor but by the receiver, and as a primal sensation it could be tapped as a source of strength. The more intense the pain, the stronger its power — he knew this. He also understood, somehow, that pain had made him who he was.

7

'I had the dream again,' said Geiger, his fingers tapping at the couch.

Corley scribbled *Increasd freq of dream* on his pad. The dream was a treasure map teeming with details; it was also a potential ingress to the inner self. Except for scattered, random images, Geiger had no memory of his life before he came to New York, but it was in the retelling of the dream and its variations that shadows of past catastrophes peeked into the light for Corley to see. The dreams were maelstroms of ambivalence in which Geiger's critical need to *act* battled his desperate need *not* to. The opposing urges created such a furious storm within Geiger that, in the dream, it literally pulled him apart. In his notes, Corley had dubbed it the 'Endgame' dream, and though he still didn't fully understand it, he had become certain of one of its meanings: as a child, Geiger had desperately sought to escape from some kind of intolerable scenario, but doing so had brought on psychological disintegration, or at least the death of that part of him capable of rejoicing in his freedom.

'It's coming more often now — the dream,' said Corley. 'Three in the last five weeks.'

'Four,' said Geiger.

Corley felt a slight, queasy shift in his chest. 'Four? The station wagon, the bike, the motorcycle . . . '

'And the skateboard.'

Corley squelched a mutter, and put pen to pad.

'I can hear the pen, Martin. What're you writing?'

'That I forgot one of your dreams. How do you feel about that?' Corley asked.

'Meaning what? Do I see you as less imperfect than anyone else?'

'Well, I think there's a certain reliance on the patient's part that I'll remember what is talked about in this room. It goes to trust.'

'Trust,' Geiger repeated. 'Do you trust me, Martin?'

The quintessential Geiger tone — smooth as a mirror, devoid of affect — forcing the listener to deconstruct the statement to try to discover the attitude within it or the intent behind it. *Do you trust me, Martin? Do you trust me, Martin? Do you trust me, Martin?*

Corley put his pad on the carpet and settled back in his chair. 'Tell me about the dream,' he said.

Geiger's fingers came to rest, his hands on his stomach. 'I'm running in a dark tunnel — old, wooden beams like an abandoned mine. There's a light ahead of me.'

'You're ten, eleven?'

'Yes. I hear the roar of a cave-in behind me. It sounds alive, like an angry beast. I burst into the light as the entrance collapses — and I've got that sense of purpose, even though I don't know where I'm going. Then I'm on a sidewalk — in New Orleans, I think — but I can't cross the

74

street because a funeral procession is going by, hundreds of people clapping and shouting, 'Hallelujah!' while a band is playing Dixieland music. The coffin comes by, small and black, on a cart pulled by four toy horses.'

'You mean Shetland ponies?'

'No, toy horses — wooden hobbyhorses on wheels. Beautifully crafted. I have to get across the street, so I hurdle the coffin, but my feet clip it, and as I sprawl to the ground the coffin tips over and this boy rolls out. My age, blue suit, polished shoes. He doesn't look like me, but I know immediately that it is me. The dead me looks so peaceful that I just want to lie there with him, but the need to get where I'm going is stronger, so I get up and run.'

Corley picked up his pad again and wrote, *Mourning for who — or what?*

'Soon I get to a river and there's a motorboat at a dock. I grab the starter cord and pull and pull. The motor turns over but won't catch. As always, my overalls are full of tools and I pull a wrench out to unscrew the engine's hood. I'm turning the bolts but the wrench won't grab hold, and then my fingers start falling off, followed by my feet and legs. My head starts to come loose . . . and then I wake up.'

Corley made another note. 'You said the cave-in sounded 'like an angry beast.' What's it angry about?'

'I guess it's angry about being buried in the cave-in.'

'All right. Could it be angry about anything else?'

'Like what?'

'Maybe it's angry at *you*.'

'Why?'

'Because you were getting out of the cave.'

'So — maybe I'm not just running out of the cave, I'm running away from the beast?'

A now-familiar heat ignited Corley's insides, the urge to soothe and comfort, to protect the little boy always trapped somewhere — in a burning building, a dark room with a knobless door, now a cave. He chafed at the nearly absurd therapeutic truth: that to free the child, he had to unlock his torment and have him live through it all over again.

Corley knew time was almost up, but he didn't want to stop.

'One thing that always strikes me about the dream is the absence of fear. You never talk about the past, but you must have experienced fear. In the dream, you go through harrowing events, but never feel afraid. You ever wonder why?'

'Because there's no longer anything to be scared of.'

'In the dream?'

'In the dream — in real life. Whichever. Both.'

'You said, '*no longer* anything to be scared of.''

Geiger's fingers skittered across the soft leather. 'We're running over — aren't we, Martin?'

Corley jotted down a final note. *What happened to Dad?*

★ ★ ★

Since Corley's divorce, weekends had acquired the feel of time in abeyance, as if impish gods had shoved wrenches in the gears of the universal clock. These two days had always been earmarked for his marriage, a chance for Sara and him to reconvene, talk, dally. Now, hours were ninety minutes and red lights took forever to go green.

He was lying on the patients' couch, reading through his notes on Geiger, which he kept in a leather portfolio. He turned on a lamp; the sun had set already, but he'd been slow to notice the darkness crowding in. He spent most of his time in this room now. The living room and bedroom, still adorned with the acquired relics of a dead union, were places he rarely visited. When Sara had announced she was leaving, she'd said he could keep everything. The declaration had been spirit-shattering — she'd made it plain that the only thing she wanted was to be gone.

Corley spent part of every weekend reading his session notes, but lately he'd become especially absorbed by his notes about Geiger. He spent hours sifting through what little information about the man he'd been able to piece together, poring over a mystery whose denouement and revelations had not yet been written. As the notes revealed, he had often gone against accepted wisdom — but not his instincts — as the therapy proceeded, largely because Geiger kept so much out of bounds. Corley didn't know where his patient came from, or where he lived, or even what he did for a living.

Outside, a shrill, nasty sound was gathering.

Corley rose and stepped onto the terrace just as a big squadron of black birds rose up from the rooftops and went into a steep dive. They were twirling and spinning, their formation changing like a kaleidoscope's fractals, perfectly conjoined. They made Corley think of Geiger. He was a crippled man-child, his psyche the handiwork of immeasurable cruelty. By sheer will, he somehow kept all his parts moving in sync. For weeks, Corley had sensed a shifting of emotional plates in Geiger, and an approaching event. He didn't think the man had an inkling that the dream was proof of defended structures giving way within him. The demon was knocking on the door, and it would not be denied entry.

Corley watched the flock of birds disappear into the leaves of the sidewalk trees. He was weary of routine, of the inexorable drift from passion to ritual, of wisdom gained at the sacrifice of optimism. He was weary of the penitents, the guiltmongers, the un-Geigers who lay on his couch addicted to their imperfections. And he was equally weary of his abetment, the fifty-minute doses of attention and patience dispensed to help them share a wan smile or shed a few tears before he sent them back out into the world.

Inside, he walked into the kitchen and flipped the lights on. The pale blue tiles above the counters still reminded him of Sara's eyes. Too many of his thoughts were prompted by memories, and the knowledge that his future would be little different from his life now weighed him down.

Corley poured himself a mug of coffee and sat down at the breakfast nook. The *New York Times* lay before him, and the headlines read like recycled slogans. 'Mass Grave Unearthed Near Kabul.' 'Suicide Bomber Kills 56 in Chechnya.' 'Bodies Discovered in Cairo Factory — Evidence of Torture Reported.' The story about Egypt was accompanied by a photograph of a windowless bunker. The floor was covered with dark blotches, and the walls were spattered with dots and arching squiggles — clearly they were the canvases of a brutal painter. Corley sipped his coffee and tried to decide whether the world had become more barbaric or if cable television, round-the-clock bloggers, and websites dedicated to whistle-blowers simply meant that less remained hidden.

I could just quit, he thought. Pack it up. He pictured the house up in Cold Spring. Of all the possessions he and Sara had accumulated, it was the only thing he'd really wanted. Since the divorce, his trips to Cold Spring had become more and more infrequent, but though he was deaf to selling, he was unwilling to consider why. Maybe he should take the rest of the summer off and spend every day in the hammock with a case of Guinness and a pack of Camels, reading novels while his gut grew and his liver and lungs went to ruin.

Corley snorted at himself. He wouldn't leave — it was foolish even to imagine otherwise. He would sit in his office with Geiger until the breakthrough came, until the psychic walls collapsed and the horror came spilling out and he tried mightily to pull the little boy from the muck and wash him clean.

A sudden, rising, angry chorus made Corley turn to the window. It was the black birds. They were leaving.

8

Harry stared out the windshield of the van at a large flock of noisy birds moving south from uptown. They tilted over the East River like a single giant wing, so black that it stood out against the evening sky, and then the flock came apart and melted into the lattice of the Brooklyn Bridge that stretched out around him.

Hours ago, when he'd left the diner, Harry had returned to Brooklyn and picked up the rental van. Richard Hall would be delivering the Jones tonight, but it was Geiger's SOP that Harry have a vehicle on hand at all sessions — another example of crossing of *t*'s and dotting of *i*'s as a way to keep the outside world's powers of chaos in check. Then Harry had stopped back home, given Melissa a dozen of Lily's favorite CDs, and spent a few hours on the couch watching his sister while she sat cross-legged in a chair, fingering a button on her blouse. He had tried a few questions — 'Lily, do you want something to eat?' and 'It's a nice day, isn't it?' and 'Do you remember my name, sis?' — but she responded only once, to his last query, saying:

'I remember all the names. I know them.'

Harry took the bridge off-ramp and headed crosstown toward Ludlow Street. He loved the feel of the city at this end. The air smelled different than uptown — spicier, more exotic.

The song of the street had a sweeter pitch, the light seemed softer, and when a job was finished he could walk just two blocks to the tiny dim sum place on Division Street and sit down to a feast for twenty bucks. Best deal in town.

Last week he'd received an e-mail informing him that Lily's nut would go up to one hundred and ten thousand a year, so tonight's asap was a godsend. He had also negotiated top dollar with Richard Hall — thirty-five grand. Geiger always left that part of the business to him and he'd gotten good at it. Who could have guessed?

On the June day in 1999 when Harry had walked out of the Times Building to find Geiger waiting for him on the sidewalk with a business proposition, Harry had no idea what he'd be getting into, and no way to make a decision based on a financial forecast. In the end, he made a life-altering choice based on his instinctive response to Geiger's matter-of-fact presentation. 'I am going into a new line of work,' Geiger had said. 'Illegal. I need a partner. You'll get twenty-five percent of the profits.' As Geiger described his vocation, Harry wondered: What was the going rate for torture? How do you build a clientele? The research part would be a snap, his forte, but the human carting might prove challenging. Forget, for a moment, the moral and legal aspects. Could he *do* it? Was that in him? He let the exhilaration in his chest provide the answer.

Harry pulled the van up to the gate of the lot next to the Ludlow Street session house and checked his watch. Hall was due with Matheson in fifteen minutes. He got out, unlocked the heavy-gauge gate, and pushed it open. As he was about to turn back to the van, he felt the presence of someone coming up behind him. He froze, and silently cursed his carelessness — why had he left the Louisville Slugger on the van's floor? Slowly he turned.

A ragged redwood of a black man stood before him, wearing a tattered New York Knicks sweat-shirt and pants of a blotched, now indistinguishable color. His clothes hung on thick, broad bones, and Harry saw the glare of mean hunger in his bottomless eyes. Harry's mind measured the steps to the van's door. Seven, maybe eight. A tricky maneuver to pull out the bat and swing for the fences. Trickier if the guy was agile — Harry never could hit a curveball. But if it came to it, he'd die trying. Nobody was ever going to beat on him again.

A hand the size of an oven mitt came out from behind the man's back. The upturned palm was desiccated and deeply furrowed.

'Gimme somethin', man,' the guy said, his voice sepulchral. 'Five bucks.'

Harry realized he wasn't breathing; he inhaled. 'Shouldn't sneak up on people, man,' he said. 'Not cool.'

'I'll send you a fucking letter next time. Now goddamn gimme somethin'.' His pupils flared with molten emotion. 'C'mon, motherfucker!'

'*Motherfucker?*' Harry said. 'Hey — do I owe you something?'

The man's great paws grabbed the lapels of Harry's sport jacket and pulled him in close.

Harry's nostrils bristled at the thick, sour smell of unwashed flesh.

'Fuck you very much,' the man said.

An airy giggle came from somewhere very near, and then a small, shiny-eyed face peeked out from behind the man's tree-trunk legs. The girl wore a soiled orange jumpsuit and sneakers with the toes wrapped in frayed duct tape, and the gap between her front teeth blinked at Harry when she grinned. She couldn't have been more than five. If Harry believed in God, he would have sworn she was an angel.

The girl looked up at him. 'Yeah,' she said. 'Fuck you very, *very* much.'

'Don't you be cursing, Laneesha,' the man said, but his eyes stayed on Harry, who was losing a battle to suppress a grin.

'What's Laneesha mean?' Harry asked.

'Fuck if I know, man.'

'Pretty name.'

'You like it? Gimme five bucks, you can have it.'

'Okay,' Harry said.

The man squinted at the answer, and let go of Harry. 'Yeah?' he said.

'Yeah. Sure.'

Harry went into his pocket and took out a money clip. He thumbed through the folded bills and frowned.

'No fives. Have to take a twenty.'

He pulled one free and held it out. The man snatched it with a thumb and forefinger, stuck it deep down in a pocket, and took a moment to reappraise his benefactor.

'Thanks.'

'Welcome.'

'You're a weird guy,' the man said. 'Cool, but weird.'

'Doubtful about the cool part.' Harry looked down at the little girl. 'You and I have the same name,' he said.

Her brow crinkled with three undulating lines of confusion. 'Your name's not Laneesha!' she said.

'It is now,' said Harry, grinning. 'I just bought it.'

She reached up and let her tiny hand disappear inside the giant's. Turning, they walked down the street. It had started to drizzle, and the streetlights threw shadows everywhere, an irregular crisscross pattern like a huge net laid down across the wet concrete.

Harry hopped back inside the van, drove into the lot, and pulled up to the wall of the session house. He parked beside the gray canvas-sided awning that extended eight feet from the building, blocking the view of the side entrance door from the windows of adjacent buildings and passersby.

Drops of rain on the windshield were momentarily set aglow by a passing wash of light. Harry turned and watched a dark green van pull up to the open gate and stop, softly idling. He got out, stepped into the flood of the headlights, and motioned the vehicle forward like an airport gate man coaxing in a jet. Then he directed the van to pull under the canvas awning. The engine died, the door opened, and a man stepped out with an attaché case and strolled toward Harry, headlights trimming the edges of his stocky silhouette with a backlit aura.

'Harry?' the man said.

'Right. Mr. Hall?'

'Yes.'

As he neared, Hall's silhouette morphed into detail. His gray suit looked off the rack. His features were middle-American bland — the face of someone sitting in a Wichita diner or an office cubicle in Des Moines. You wouldn't notice him in a crowd, but face to face Harry could see his busy eyes, always moving. Hall was one of those people who could look straight at you and see everything around you at the same time, his gaze shifting tiny degrees, scanning and rescanning the area like motion detectors getting signals from an internal command center.

He held out a ringless hand and Harry shook it. Harry's fingers felt like they were caught in a vise.

'We set?' Hall asked.

'Yeah.'

'Good. Let's do this.'

They headed for the van. Hall clearly had no interest in small talk, and that was fine by Harry. He could never ignore the absurdity of talking about the Mets or the traffic as a lead-in to torture. The worst ones were those who wanted to talk about Geiger, and what he did, and how he did it. Harry spent a lot of time building a wall around his special knowledge so he could consider himself a businessman. But the inquiries about Geiger were taps on his shoulder, whispers in his ear that made him look inward, and at those times his psychic Sheetrock couldn't hide the Medusa's head he'd grown over the last decade.

He unlocked and opened the building's reinforced side door, revealing a wide, well-lit hallway. The center of the hallway's floor was embedded with four rows of two-inch steel cargo rollers. Hall pulled out the van's sliding ramp from beneath the back doors and laid the end down onto the rollers. He grabbed the handle of the trunk inside the van and pulled it down the ramp. When the trunk slid onto the rollers, he and Harry gave it a nudge, and then walked it down to an open freight elevator at the corridor's end.

'Nice setup,' said Hall.

'Yup,' said Harry.

They shoved the trunk into the elevator and stepped inside. Harry pulled the accordion gate closed, worked the hand gear, and they slowly ascended with a jangle and rattle.

'Haven't been in one of these in a long time,' Hall said.

Harry glanced down at the silver container between them. It was the same kind he used — a six-foot, seam-welded Zarges made of a anodized aluminum. Harry had listed the brand in his prep e-mail.

'Have any problem finding a trunk?'

'No, not at all,' Hall said. He opened the attaché case and showed Harry the contents. 'Thirty-five thousand. Hundreds and fifties, as requested.'

Harry shifted the lever and eased the lift to a stop at the second floor. The room was bigger than the space in the Bronx — thirty feet square and twelve feet high, with speaker grids set into the glossy black walls and ceiling every ten feet. When Harry pushed the gate open the brassy clatter skittered off the surfaces like a handful of coins.

In the center of the room sat a motorized wheelchair, its black leather and chrome gleaming in the piercing overhead lights. Leather straps hung from the back, arms, and footrests. Otherwise the room was empty.

Hall glanced at Harry. 'A wheelchair?'

Harry nodded.

'Is he here?'

'He's here,' Harry said.

They dragged the trunk out of the elevator, and a tiny worm of thought wriggled to life beneath a rock in Harry's brain. Something was not quite right. He was about to turn the rock over and have a look when Geiger stepped into the room.

'Geiger?' Hall asked, extending a hand.

Geiger came to them, giving a single nod, hands remaining at his sides. He was dressed in a black denim jumpsuit and high-top sneakers. Hall put the attaché case down.

'Geiger,' he said, 'there's been a slight change of plans.'

Harry was perhaps the only person on earth who understood that the imperceptible shift in the muscles of Geiger's face might be a frown.

'What kind of change?' Geiger asked.

88

'Matheson slipped us. He got away.'

Now Harry turned over that rock in his mind and winced. When they'd carried the trunk into the room, it had felt light. Too light.

'Then who is in the trunk?' Geiger said.

'Someone I'm pretty certain knows where Matheson is.' Hall flicked the trunk's latches open. 'His son.'

Hall started to lift the lid, but Geiger's fingers came to rest on it, stopping its progress after a few inches.

'How old?' Geiger said.

'Twelve.'

Geiger pushed the lid back down until it closed. The action was relaxed but firm.

'I don't work with children, Mr. Hall.'

'You don't?'

Geiger's fingertips did short drum rolls on his thighs. Hall's hand went inside his jacket pocket, came out with a thick manila envelope, and dropped it on top of the trunk.

'Would another five grand persuade you to make an exception?'

'You should have let Harry know about the situation. He would have told you the policy. No exceptions.'

'You're right, of course,' Hall said with a series of choppy nods, 'but it never occurred to me that someone in your business would have any . . . exceptions.' He glanced at Harry, who was staring mournfully at the attaché case as if it were a casket. The hundreds and fifties inside it were dead to him now.

'Listen, Geiger,' Hall said. 'Seeing as how

we're here, let's talk about this for a minute. The kid has been staying with his father for a few weeks, and we're close to certain he knows where Matheson is, or where he's headed. Now, my referral gave me two names for the job — yours and a Mr. Dalton. We came to you because we understand your methods are more understated, whereas Dalton has a reputation for getting carried away. I don't want to see the boy hurt, Geiger, but I have to find out what he knows. We're really fighting the clock now. So my point is this: if you don't do the job, we'll go to Dalton. So why not take the payday?' His hands rose out to his sides, palms up, as if he'd just finished a pitch at a sales convention. 'And that includes the extra five thousand.'

Harry watched Geiger go into what he had privately coined 'dead mode' — a state that visited Geiger when he seemed to be considering something. Eyes unblinking, chest unmoving, he stood completely still for several seconds. Then a single blink seemed to bring him back to life.

'Let's get the kid in the chair,' Geiger said.

Hall's eyebrows curled into question marks, and he turned to look at Harry as if Geiger had spoken in an unknown dialect and Harry was the official translator. Harry stared back silently. He'd never delivered an underage Jones, never even considered the possibility. It had been a long time since Geiger had surprised him.

'All right, then,' Hall said. 'Great.'

He reached to the trunk and pulled the lid up. Harry bent down and caught the manila envelope as it slid toward the floor.

Geiger looked in the trunk. Matheson's son was on his side, wrists and ankles cinched together with thin plastic self-locking ties. Three strips of silver duct tape circled his head, one across his eyes and two across his mouth. His long, wavy blond hair was sodden, stuck to his forehead and cheeks like seaweed on a beach. He was dressed in a blue T-shirt, silver gym shorts, and red-and-black Nike Air LeBrons. The skin of his slender arms and legs was tanned, and his head rested on a violin case. He looked asleep, or in a coma.

'His name?' Geiger asked.

'Ezra.'

'Did you give him anything?'

'No. But he was a handful.'

Geiger knelt beside the trunk. Harry thought there was almost something of the supplicant in the action.

'Ezra . . . ' Geiger said softly, like a parent waking a child from a nap. The blinded, muted body showed no reaction to its name. 'Ezra, time to get up.'

Geiger started to straighten up, and as he did he grabbed the handle at one end of the trunk and suddenly yanked it up, standing it on its end. The boy and the violin case came tumbling out onto the floor. Harry took two involuntary steps backward, staring at the moaning body.

Geiger took hold of the plastic cable tie at the boy's ankles and began dragging him across the floor. The boy twisted furiously, like a marlin on a gaff, and muffled whimpers escaped from beneath the duct tape. At the wheelchair, Geiger grabbed the boy under the armpits and hoisted him roughly onto the seat. Then he began securing the chair's straps around the boy's ankles, arms, and chest.

Hall watched the proceedings with a hint of admiration at his lips.

'Ezra,' Geiger said as he worked, 'you're going for a ride now. You won't struggle — you'll stay completely still in this wheelchair. In a little while I'm going to ask you questions about your father, and you are going to tell me everything I need to know.' The strapping was finished. Geiger clicked his neck. Left, right. 'I'm telling you the truth, Ezra, and you're going to tell me the truth. That's why we're here. Any answer that is less than truthful — I'll hurt you. It doesn't matter that you're a child. In this room, you become ageless. That's how it works. Nod if you understand.'

A fluidal sound, something between a sob and a gurgle, came from the boy's gullet, and his head bobbed. It made Harry reflexively clear his throat.

'Good,' Geiger said. He flicked a switch on the wheelchair, and as it started across the black tiles he went to a wall and pushed a button. The low, moaning sound of a foghorn started up, rising and fading from the speakers in a random sequence. As it approached a corner, the wheelchair took a smooth left turn and settled into its route, circumnavigating the room, passing within inches of the walls. The noise presented itself to the boy as a dopplering fade, or a growing presence, or sudden sidelong blasts that made him quake in his bonds.

As Hall and Harry watched the spectacle, Geiger walked over to them.

'Harry . . . ' Geiger said, almost a whisper. Harry picked up the attaché case, stepped back into the elevator, quietly drew the gate closed, and descended out of sight. Geiger pointed toward a door beside a square mirror in a wall, and Hall followed him through. They turned to the one-way mirror and observed the wheelchair's circular ritual.

'Disorientation?' Hall said.

'Yes. The chair is on a timer,' Geiger said. 'Five minutes, then I'll begin. Something to drink?'

Hall looked to the chrome bar. 'Wine. Red.'

Geiger walked to the bar and began pouring some pinot noir.

'Does your client know you took the son?' he said.

'My client wants his painting back. How I get it is up to me.'

Geiger handed him the glass. The lights made the vermilion liquid flash. Hall took a long sip and let the wine linger in his mouth before he swallowed. He nodded with satisfaction.

'Do you know anything about him, Mr. Hall — besides what was in your report?'

'No. He lives most of the year with his mother. I've got his cell phone — two calls in the last twenty-four hours, one with a New Hampshire area code, and one with a Manhattan area code we figure is Matheson. We found the violin in his room in Matheson's apartment. I thought maybe it might be of use to you.'

'Anything else in his room?'
'I didn't notice. Does it matter?'
'Everything matters, Mr. Hall.'

★ ★ ★

Harry sat in the van's driver's seat. He had started counting the money, but he stopped as a gloominess crept in with the sticky evening air. When Geiger had spilled the kid out of the trunk it had been a pure what's-wrong-with-this-picture moment. Even if he could rig his ethical arithmetic yet another time, it was a trickier task squaring Geiger's reversal with everything he'd done in the past. Harry had become a moon in a steady orbit around Geiger, dependent on and secure in the man's gravitational force, so experiencing a shift in Geiger's axis of rules brought with it something vertiginous. Seeing Geiger do the unexpected was like watching the Statue of Liberty wink at him.

Harry sighed, and then went back to counting the money.

★ ★ ★

The wheelchair and its blind passenger continued tracing a circle, and the foghorn's sad warning came out of the walls. Hall checked the time again.

'Just a little longer,' Geiger said. 'A layman might think minors are easy to break, but it's not necessarily true. In a context of intense fear, a child is apt to go inward and shut down — or to lie, say anything, and say it convincingly.' He poured a glass of water. 'Mr. Hall, if you're that concerned about time, telling me what this is really about will make my job easier — and quicker. It's up to you.'

Hall watched him drink the glass down. 'What do you mean?'

'I mean that you're lying. That's what I do, Mr. Hall — I determine whether someone is telling the truth or not.'

Hall took a sip of his wine. 'All you need to be concerned about is doing whatever's necessary to get the kid to talk.'

'All right. Just trying to be helpful.'

Geiger looked out to the boy. For a moment, the nature of time, and Geiger's awareness of it, changed. It ceased to be perpetual and fluid and solidified into measured instants. Each brief moment had its own beginning and end, like the flickering frames of a movie glimpsed individually even as they ran together.

'I think it's time,' he said, and his right fist shot straight out, his knuckles smashing into Hall's chest an inch below the sternum, driving the breath from him in a loud, expulsive grunt. Hall stumbled back into the wall and slumped to his knees, chest heaving, hands on his quadriceps. A noise like a hacksaw cutting through copper pipe clawed its way up his throat as his diaphragm struggled to free itself from spasm and pull in air.

Geiger crouched down beside Hall. Spittle, tinted pink with pinot noir, was beginning to bubble out of his mouth. His lips opened slightly in a preface to speech.

'Uhhnff . . . uhhnff' was what came out.

The foghorn audio stopped, and Geiger rose to look through the window. The wheelchair rolled to a stop; the boy didn't move. Geiger knelt back down. Hall seemed incapable of turning his head, but his wet eyes managed to swivel in their sockets until they found Geiger's deadpan stare.

'Mr. Hall,' said Geiger.

The tears rolling down Hall's cheeks made him look deeply unhappy, as if the tough-guy persona was an act and Geiger had said something mean and wounding.

'Fffff . . . fuck,' he gasped.

'I don't know who you are, Mr. Hall — but I do know who you aren't.'

The surface of Geiger's words had a slight, gravelly patina that was unfamiliar and slightly unsettling. The unscheduled violence had ratcheted up Geiger's pulse and breathing and altered the topography of his voice.

'Do you want to tell me who you really are?' Geiger said.

Hall's head drooped, his shoulders stretching, his body searching for some physical accommodation, a way to breathe. His head levered back up; he blinked, coughed, and then blinked again, as if delivering an answer in some secret code he assumed Geiger knew.

Geiger planted his open palm tightly on Hall's face and then rammed his skull back into the wall. The crunching sound announced the crushing of some substance — wood or bone, or both — and Hall's eyes widened in further surprise before falling shut.

Geiger held Hall's head in place, observing each partitioned instant as it passed. Some kink in his optical network reduced the depth of images going to his brain, rendering them flatter than normal, like Polaroid snapshots. Finally he took his hand away and Hall slumped sideways onto the floor, revealing a grapefruit-sized dent in the wall. It was an inch deep, and moist crimson specks mingled with the mashed fibers.

The pockets of Hall's pants contained the expected: a wallet with American Express and Diners Club cards, about six hundred dollars in cash, a Pennsylvania driver's license, a State Farm insurance ID for a 2006 silver Lexus coupe. In his jacket pockets were a pack of Camels, a lighter, and two cell phones, a BlackBerry and a Motorola Droid that Geiger assumed belonged to the boy. A black leather holster clipped to Hall's belt held a Taurus Millennium Pro nine-millimeter semiautomatic.

Geiger stuck the phones in his pockets and stood up. The pulse in his eyes throbbed, producing a minuscule blip in his vision, a cambered shift of objects and surfaces. He put the gun on the bar and went through the door into the session room. He detected a hint of smoky aroma in his nostrils, and his breath was coming in long, strong exhalations, as if he were a runner pacing himself in the early stages of a marathon.

He walked over to the boy, his mind keenly aware that its moment-to-moment workings

97

were, for the first time in memory, without premeditation. Overriding all thought and feeling was the pure, unencumbered sensation of moving toward some unknown destination. It was a feeling alien to his consciousness but familiar from another domain. He knew it from his dreams.

The boy sat slack in the chair, head listing. Geiger had set the room's temperature to sixty-three degrees but the boy was sweating, his shirt and shorts flat and damp against his body, his exposed skin covered with a sheen of fear. Geiger watched the carotid artery in the boy's neck gorge and shrink to the accelerated beat of his heart.

'Ezra . . . '

The boy's body violently snapped to attention like a soldier obeying a sergeant's order.

'Ezra, there won't be any questions now.'

The boy's throat swelled with a squeaky grunt. Geiger took out his cell phone and pressed a key. Harry answered before the first ring finished.

'That was fast,' Harry said.

'Come on up — and bring the money.'

The silence on the line had a question mark at the end of it. 'The money? Okay.'

Geiger walked back into the viewing room. Hall hadn't moved; he lay on his right side in a near-fetal position. On the wall was the wet, arcing swath his wound had painted as his head had slid down from the point of impact to the floor.

Geiger heard faint music rousing itself deep within him. He saw flashes of violet and chartreuse sound begin to wave in time behind his eyes, and then the creak of an opening door and a sliver of dusty light invaded the pitch-black core of him. He felt a dull ache in his ankles. Rising up like a ballet dancer on the balls of his feet, he stretched his Achilles tendons and calf muscles. The pain and the music stopped, and then the sliver of light disappeared.

The elevator gate rattled.

'Geiger?' Harry said.

The word came to Geiger as if called to him across a canyon. He turned to find Harry standing in the doorway, bafflement breaking across his face.

'Jesus Christ. What the hell happened?'

Geiger glanced back at Hall. 'We're leaving,' he said, as if he were informing the body instead of Harry.

Harry put the attaché case down at his feet. 'Oh fuck. What'd you do to him? Is — is he dead?'

'No. We have to go now.'

Geiger moved for the door, and Harry put his hands up like a traffic cop. Geiger stopped, staring at Harry's raised palms.

'Wait a second,' Harry said. 'Just wait, okay? Jesus Christ.' He put his palms to his cheeks. 'What the hell is going on with you?'

'We have to go.'

'Can we talk about this for a minute?'

'Right now, Harry, it's more important that we leave.'

'I disagree, man. This is crazy. This is truly nuts, okay?'

'Harry,' Geiger said, 'it's probable if not certain that one of Hall's men followed him here and is waiting nearby. Wouldn't you say?'

'I have no fucking idea.'

'And that's why we need to leave — now. The longer we wait, the more complicated things will get.'

'*Complicated?* You just coldcocked a client!'

Harry looked over at the bar, at the multi-colored skyline of bottles. He hadn't had a drink since the day he took Geiger up on his offer. It had been Geiger's one requirement — that he stop drinking — and consciously or not, his sobriety had become another reason to see Geiger as his lifesaver. But even after eleven years he could still summon the taste of cheap bourbon at the back of his mouth. He was beginning to understand what the body on the floor meant, how it would likely redefine his life from this moment on, and he wanted a drink, now, to flatten the thumping pulse in his ears.

'We're going now, Harry. Out the back.'

'Going where?'

Geiger sighed. Harry was stunned; he realized that he had never seen Geiger sigh before. He couldn't have been more surprised if Geiger had screamed.

'And we leave the money,' Geiger said.

The statement sent a dull pang through Harry's chest, but somehow he had seen it coming. He nodded sadly. 'If we leave the money, you think this can all be smoothed out?'

'I don't think so.'

'Why not?'

'Because I don't think the money's important to Hall — and because I'm taking the boy with me.'

'*With* you?'

Harry looked back through the doorway. He'd forgotten about the boy. The sight of him, silent and inert, kicked an angry squall to life in Harry's stomach.

Harry turned back to Geiger. 'This is absolutely fucking crazy. You tell Hall you don't do kids, then you change your mind and say yes. And then you punch him out. *Why*, man?'

'We need a car, Harry. Go out through the alley — '

'What the fuck is this about, Geiger?'

'Take a cab to the Thrifty rental. They stay open late — '

'Geiger — '

'Get a car, bring it to the alley, back it in, and knock on the door. We'll — '

A wet cough popped out of Hall, and Geiger and Harry turned to see one of Hall's legs move, shifting from a ninety-degree angle to about forty-five. Geiger crouched beside him.

'Geiger,' Harry said, 'have you even begun to think this through?'

Geiger undid Hall's tie and began lashing his ankles with it.

'For starters,' Harry said, 'you broke your own first commandment: *Never let the outside change the inside.* I'm not saying I think you were wrong — he's just a kid — but I don't know where the hell that leaves us.'

Geiger finished tying up Hall's ankles and

101

pulled the knot tight.

'Second, maybe there's still a chance we could finesse this thing — *maybe* — but if you snatch that kid, then you've just retired yourself. Do you get that? Word gets out and we're done, man. Finished. Not even Carmine would touch us. Jesus — did you think about any of that?'

Geiger rose and faced Harry. 'No. I didn't think about any of that.'

'Well maybe you'd better — '

'Harry, listen to me.'

'I cannot fucking believe you just — '

Geiger grabbed his partner and slammed him up against the doorjamb. 'You're not listening to me, Harry. Stop talking, take a deep breath, and listen to me.'

Harry felt completely incapable of taking a deep breath, but he nodded. 'Okay,' he said. 'Okay.'

Geiger's pupils flared. They were like two shotgun barrels in a gray mist aimed at Harry.

'This,' Geiger said, 'is not about a painting.'

He let go of Harry, walked to the bar, and poured another glass of water and began to drink. Harry's shoulder blades ached from the impact with the wall. It was the first and only time Geiger had ever touched him. Clearly, this was going to be a night full of firsts — and probably lasts. He watched Geiger's Adam's apple bob up and down until he lowered his empty glass.

'Mr. Hall,' Geiger said, 'is not a private detective working for a rich man with an art collection.'

'How do you know?'

'He said he came to me because he knew I was more 'understated' than Dalton, but if I turned the job down he'd take Ezra to Dalton anyway, knowing he could end up a bloody mess, a norell. Would you do that if you were looking for a stolen painting?'

'Then who is he?'

'I don't know.' He turned back to Harry. 'But whoever he is, I don't think he's going to stop — and his job description may include murder as an acceptable option.'

'Can I ask you one more thing?'

Geiger waited, his fingers coming alive at his sides.

'What happened, Geiger?'

'What happened?'

'To you. Something's happened.'

'I don't know what you mean,' Geiger said.

Harry shook his head. 'Yeah, well . . . neither do I.'

And that's that, thought Harry. No more questions, because Geiger had no answers. There had been a massive sea change inside this room, and now Harry was in the drink, head barely bobbing above the waves, no sign of land, no sense of which way to swim, no assurance that someone wouldn't blow his head off as soon as he crawled onto the shore, if he was lucky enough to reach one. The only thing he was sure of was that if he ever did set foot on land again there'd be no more attachés full of cash waiting for him. The aftershock of that thought — that there might be a certain righting of cosmic scales at work, that some renascent sense had spurred

Geiger into an act of spontaneous grace — made him smile, sadly, as one might when cleaning out a cluttered desk drawer and finding an old photograph of someone dear and long departed.

'You're smiling, Harry. Why?'

'Not important.'

'Then go get the car.'

'Okay.'

Harry allowed himself a final glance at Hall's attaché case and walked out.

Geiger watched him step into the elevator and descend. Interacting with Harry had tightened him back up. The acts of listening and responding had been a truss wrapping around him, closing cracks and giving him a footing in time again.

Hall's limbs moved in small, lazy shifts with the gradual onset of consciousness. Geiger walked into the session room and went over to the boy.

'Ezra?'

The boy turned stiffly, as if the spell in the chair had tightened his joints and made even casual movement an effort.

'We'll be leaving soon and going someplace safe.' The boy nodded slowly. 'I'll leave the tape on until we're there.' There was no nod this time, just a brief whimper.

Geiger walked to a wall, pressed back flat against it, and closed his eyes. He felt like someone who'd been driving a road with no end. As if observing the driver from a great distance, he thought: You've been behind the wheel so long that the hum of it in your hands has numbed your senses. Your head droops, you're nodding out, and suddenly you jolt awake and hit the brakes. You pull over onto the shoulder. You look out the windshield, in the rearview mirror, out the side windows, and you discover that you're in a perfect blind spot, one where trees and humpbacked hills and bends in the road ahead of you and behind you are a veil to every perspective. You're not exactly sure when you nodded off, or for how long, but now you have no idea where you are.

You could be anywhere.

9

When Geiger got Harry's call announcing his arrival in the alley, he checked on Richard Hall; he was semiconscious but his pulse was steady. Geiger wheeled the boy into the elevator and pulled the gate closed. Through the steel latticework, he saw the violin case lying on the session room floor. He came back out, picked up the case, returned to the elevator, and went down to the basement and alley door. He'd had the door installed in case a clandestine departure was ever necessary — lockless and knobless on the outside, the door was solid steel with internal hinges, manual slide bolts, and an interior handle.

Before leaving the building, he told the boy what to expect: he'd be getting into the backseat of a car, lying down, and going for a ride that would last about half an hour. When getting in and out of the car, he was not to try to run away — there would be no punishment for an attempt, but it would be a waste of time, and time was important now.

Geiger slid the bolts back and opened the door. A Taurus four-door sat in the unlit alley with the motor running. Standing beside it, Harry's silhouette glistened slightly with a coat of drizzle.

'Can I say something?' Harry said.
'What is it?'

'We could drop him off at a police station. He's never seen us. We just keep the tape on, pull up at the station, point him toward the door, and leave.'

'Bad idea, Harry. No cops.'

'I'm just trying to help out here.'

'This has got nothing to do with you.'

Harry felt heat rise beneath his skin. 'No? How the hell do you figure that?'

'Harry, no more talking now. Go home.'

'I'm not coming with you?'

'No. Leave the van in case Hall has eyes out here, and stay off Ludlow Street.'

'What if Hall tries to get in touch with me?'

'I expect he will. I don't think Mr. Hall is the type to just call it a day. The safest thing to do is go home and stay there — until we see how this plays out. And if Mr. Hall tries to contact you through the website, don't answer.'

Geiger went back inside. Harry had the disconcerting sensation that his position in the physical world was going off kilter. Either the landscape was receding from him or he was growing smaller, shrinking.

Geiger came out leading the blinded boy by the hand. His ankle ties had been removed. Geiger opened the Taurus's back door and tossed the violin case on the floor.

'Bend down, Ezra, and lie down in there.'

Manacled arms outstretched, the boy did exactly as he was told, without hesitation or a sound. Geiger closed the car door and then the door to the building. He came around past Harry and slid into the driver's seat. He sat up straight and his hands settled gently on the wheel, precisely at nine and three o'clock. To Harry, there was something vaguely childlike about Geiger's posture. It wasn't the first time he'd had that thought.

'You're okay driving?'

Geiger's eyes scanned the dashboard displays and nodded. He turned around to look at the boy, who was curled up on his side. 'We're going now, Ezra.'

A soft, guttural cluck of understanding came from the boy.

Geiger faced forward. 'Don't call me,' he said to Harry. 'I'll call you.'

No you won't, thought Harry. He stepped back and watched the car move slowly down the alley.

★ ★ ★

Geiger drove north on Tenth Avenue. He passed two patrol cars doing slow right-lane cruises, but the traffic was light, mostly taxis. He kept his speed under thirty-five miles an hour and was making about eight blocks between red lights. He'd gotten a license five years ago, and each April since then he had rented a car and taken it out on the West Side Highway for an hour's practice, navigating the same route every time. From the rental place on Fifty-seventh Street, he would drive two blocks west to the highway's entrance ramp, drive north to the Ninety-sixth Street exit, circle under the highway, get back on the highway going south, and get off at Fifty-sixth

Street. Round and round he drove, five circuits in all. Now, on this night that had broken free of its mooring, he was actually driving somewhere, with someone, for the first time.

His distance vision was normal but his short-range focus was still interrupted by small, sporadic blips, so even though the drizzle had become a steady rain, he changed the wipers' setting from high to intermittent after a dozen blocks because their continual sweep exacerbated the anomaly. Raindrops bled down the windshield, stained with the colors of traffic lights. He went blocks at a time without seeing a soul.

As the light turned yellow at Sixtieth Street, Geiger slowed to a stop and turned around. The boy lay facing the seatback, shoulders rising and falling faintly.

'Be there soon,' Geiger said.

The boy's head moved slightly on the seat in a horizontal nod, and Geiger turned back to the wheel. He could feel his pulse echoing through his veins — not faster, but with a weighty beat instead of its usual ping. He knew that he needed to be away from the movement and sound of the world. He needed the darkness and the music to usher him back to a starting place. His life was all balance, calibration, detail. He needed to reset his internal scale.

When the light turned green he hit the gas and then saw the wet blur of a bicyclist speeding into the intersection. Geiger swerved right but heard the car's front bumper clip the back wheel of the bicycle, followed by the tinny scraping of

109

metal skidding across asphalt. He pounded the brakes, sending the boy thudding to the floor in back.

The rider had come to a stop against a parked car, pinned beneath his mangled ten-speed. He wasn't moving. Geiger turned around to check on the boy: he was wedged down sideways against the backs of the front seats, grunting through the tape across his mouth.

Geiger reached down and pulled him up onto the backseat. 'You okay?'

A loud *crack* swiveled Geiger's head to the driver's window. Outside, the bicyclist stood with a tire pump held high beside his head in a tight fist. In the misty light of the streetlamps, it was impossible to tell whether the dark patches on his glowering face were blood or grime.

'Get out of the car, motherfucker!' the rider yelled through the window.

He was tall and chiseled, ropy muscles stretching out of his T-shirt and spandex riding shorts. Both upper arms were emblazoned with tattoos of barbed helixes. After trying the door handle and discovering that it was locked, he hammered the window again with the pump. A nickel-sized spider's web bloomed in the glass.

'Get the fuck out here!'

Geiger's ears were ringing. The inside of his skull felt crowded, as if his brain had grown too big for its casing. His eyes danced forward, taking in the views of the windshield and rear-view mirror at the same time. Headlights in the rain cruised toward him.

'Are you coming out of that car or am I coming *in*?'

Geiger turned back to the bicyclist, and there, just outside the window, was a man in overalls. His wide, flat forehead shone with sweat; in his hand he held something thin and shiny. For half a heartbeat, his father stood before him. Then he was gone.

The tire pump came down on the window again, and the glass burst into a thousand tiny diamonds. The rider reached in and grabbed hold of Geiger's jumpsuit.

'Get out here, asshole!'

Geiger's right hand shot out the window frame, anchored itself in the bicyclist's hair, and pulled him halfway into the front seat. Growling in anger, the man tried to bring his arms through the opening to wage some form of attack, but the fingertips of Geiger's left hand dug into the soft cavity above the man's clavicle. The growls turned to screams.

Geiger pulled the man nose to nose. His fingers relaxed and the screaming stopped.

'Go — away — now,' Geiger said.

The man stared at him wide-eyed, breathless, raindrops beaded on his face.

'Do you understand?' Geiger asked.

The man nodded. Geiger let go and the rider wriggled his way out the window, stumbling back onto the street, hands going up to his neck.

Geiger's foot found the gas pedal and he drove off, keeping the point of the speedometer's arrow exactly between 30 and 40.

Geiger's block was quiet. Nothing moved except for rainwater in the gutters. There were few residential units on the street, and the uniform shop and bodega didn't open until six, the auto body shop and storage warehouse an hour later. Geiger's building was between a bath and shower supply outlet and an empty storefront. Constructed of tawny bricks, it was twenty feet wide, thirty feet deep, and two stories high. Its windows were boarded up and had been for a long time.

Years ago, the place had belonged to a Serb with whom Geiger had worked in renovation. When jobs were scarce, the Serb would offer Chinese food to friends and co-workers in exchange for their help in gutting the place, and before Geiger went into his current line of work he'd spent a dozen nights ripping out rotted walls and flooring. Five years later, he had gone back. Boards covered the windows, and the dumpster in the alley was filled with drywall so moldy that it obviously hadn't been emptied in months. But the Serb still lived there; he invited Geiger in and told him that he'd run out of money and the dream had died. That same afternoon, Geiger and the Serb worked out a deal, and two days later Geiger paid him in cash. He had had two-thirds of the price in hand and borrowed the rest from Carmine on friendly terms.

Geiger had done all the work on the place himself. He insulated the second floor and closed it off, upgraded the plumbing and wiring, and fenced in the small backyard. Before putting up drywall, he built a floor-to-ceiling layer of cinder blocks across all the walls and then fit every fourth block with a mixture of nitroglycerine and RDX in shaped charges that would detonate inward. He painted the walls with a soft gray he found at Sherwin-Williams called Tradewind.

Then he began creating the floor.

He had carried the design around in his head for years. Three or four days a week he made the rounds of reno sites in Brooklyn and Harlem — brownstones, small buildings, factories — searching for and buying discarded antique flooring. Sometimes he might come back with a six-foot plank of chestnut, other times a few eight-inch squares of hemlock. Employees at lumber and reclamation companies in the boroughs came to expect his biweekly visits as he sought out the more esoteric kinds of wood he needed.

Whatever the type of wood, whatever its shape or state, the process was always the same. Geiger would saw, shave, and whittle — as much by instinct as finite measure — to create the shape of the piece he saw in his head. Three lengthy sanding sessions with increasingly fine paper would take the wood down to its original, natural surface. Then, after treating all sides of the piece with a homemade concoction of beeswax and china wood oil, he would set it into the whole. One after another, the scraps became part of a huge, six-hundred-square-foot jigsaw puzzle.

He started from the outer borders and worked inward. He used more than seven hundred pieces, some as long as five feet and as wide as four inches, some no bigger than a bottle cap. The wood was teak, Brazilian tigerwood, oak, mahogany, ash, hemlock, elm, chestnut, heart pine. It took Geiger seven months to complete the fantastic mosaic, a creation a visitor would have marveled at had any seen it. In fact, the boy would be the first ever to set foot inside the place.

Geiger pulled up and parked twenty feet from his door. He looked into the rearview mirror and studied himself. He could feel his brow starting to tighten; from the far horizon of his mind, a storm had begun to move in.

He turned around and spoke to the boy, who was still stretched out on the seat.

'We're going inside now. Twenty feet on the sidewalk, then three steps up, and then we'll be in.'

He got out, opened the back door, and reached in. He took one of the boy's cuffed hands and pulled him up into a sitting position.

'Ready?'

The masked head gave a tired nod; the boy could hardly hold his chin up. The tape across his mouth had a horizontal, inward crease where his mouth had reflexively tried to suck in air for hours. Geiger grabbed the violin case and glanced up and down the block. There was no one in sight.

'We're going to walk fast now. Watch your head.'

He kept hold of the boy's hand as he slid across the seat to the door. When he swung his legs out, Geiger pulled him up and the boy immediately turned his blinded face up to the rain as if seeking some form of purification.

'Let's go,' Geiger said.

He linked his arm inside one of the boy's and ushered him toward the house. 'Three steps,' he said, and they went up without incident to the front door, which, exactly like the one at Ludlow Street, was made of heavy-gauge steel and had no external locks or knobs. On the wall beside the door was a keypad; Geiger punched in the code and a soft chirp preceded a louder click of disengaging chambers. After the door opened inward an inch or two, he pushed it open all the way and steered the boy inside. The door closed behind them, the locks clacking as they automatically reengaged.

Geiger knew that his actions had set something seismic in motion and that his place in the universe was somehow being redefined. But for a moment the silence was a palliative, a welcoming home. He put down the violin case, took a Swiss Army knife from a pocket, and cut the ties at the boy's wrists.

'I'm going to take the tape off now,' he said.

Geiger tried, with thumb and forefinger, to get hold of a corner of the tape beneath the boy's left ear lobe. Humidity and sweat had saturated the tape and emulsified the glue, and it wouldn't come loose.

'This is going to hurt.'

The boy gave a grunt that seemed to sap him

of the last of his strength, and he wobbled on his feet like a first-time drunk. Geiger took hold of him and guided him a few steps to the couch.

'Sit,' he said, lowering the boy onto the soft maroon leather. 'I'm going to get some alcohol — that will help get the tape off. And when I get the tape off, we'll talk about your mother and father.'

He walked down the hall and into the bathroom. There was a small shower, toilet, and pedestal sink with a face-sized oval mirror above it. He knelt at a chrome serving cart, knees resting on a floor inlaid with a diamond pattern of ash and teak, and reached to the bottom shelf.

It occurred to him that his voice had sounded like an intruder's. Except for phone calls with Harry and minimal exchanges with the cat, he never had reason to speak at home. The thickness in his head added to the strangeness, producing a tinny sound in his ears that seemed to trail his words like a ship's wake.

He found the rubbing alcohol, pulled a few tissues from their box, and came back down the hall. 'We'll figure things out. We need to be careful how we — '

He stared at the boy, who lay on the sofa on his side. The quiet breath of sleep ebbed and flowed from his nose.

Geiger went to the back door, unlocked it, and stepped out onto the stoop. The overhead motion-sensor light came on; twenty feet in front of him, a lone insomniac squirrel froze on the grass, primed for catastrophe.

PART TWO

10

The hot needles of the shower lanced Harry's anxiety like a boil, and helped take him away to a place where his thoughts could catch their breath and he could begin to get a glimpse of the new future.

He had walked home through the narrow, hazy streets of Chinatown and over the Brooklyn Bridge, working up worst-case scenarios. He already had seventy thousand sitting in a safe deposit box. If it came down to it, he'd have no problem selling the apartment. He'd have to do it under the radar, for cash, and most likely through Carmine, so he'd take a hit. But he was up to the minute on the asking or sale price of every two-bedroom brownstone apartment in Brooklyn Heights with a city view, so he was sure he could put another three or four hundred grand in his pocket.

That was scenario number one, based on the premise that he would never work again. He couldn't imagine himself taking another job. With no current employment record and no references, who would hire him? And what would he do — fix motherboards in a computer shop's back room? Hawk cyber software online? Drive a cab? No way, but at least he could lead an unemployed, cash-only life for seven or eight years. As far as the government was concerned, Harry Boddicker had ceased to exist. His Con

Ed and phone bills were addressed to Thomas Jones. He hadn't paid taxes in a decade. He could pretty much disappear.

And then there was scenario number two, which added his sister to the equation. Unless she finally gave up her seat on the bizarro bus or the evil bump in his groin murdered him first, in four years she would suck him dry without even knowing he existed.

When Harry had arrived home, the prospect of having to converse with anyone had made him feel nauseous. He woke the nurse, gave her an extra fifty, and shooed her out the door, telling her he'd call tomorrow when he was ready to send Lily back. A peek into the second bedroom, at the end of the hall, revealed Lily asleep on top of the bedcovers in a tucked, fetal position. She'd always slept that way.

Now Harry turned off the shower and stepped out. The Ray Charles greatest hits CD he'd set to 'repeat' was halfway through another cycle, and the soul-cleansing voice made him feel a little better. He fought the impulse to fish around in his groin while wiping himself down with one of the oversized Frette towels from Bed Bath & Beyond. He smiled wanly — he wouldn't be spending forty bucks on a towel again — and walked into the living room. He hadn't turned on the lights when he'd come in, and outside the sunrise was only a hint of the day to come, so he didn't see the figure on the couch until he was almost in front of it.

'Sit down, Harry.'

Hall's statement was one-third invitation,

two-thirds command, and his voice had the gruff edge of someone dealing with heavy physical pain. As surprised as Harry was, he was equally embarrassed by his nakedness.

'Can I put something on?'

'Sit, Harry. *Now.*'

Harry lowered himself into his favorite leather chair. It felt warm and sticky against his bare back, thighs, and ass. As casually as he could, he put his hands in his lap, covering his genitals.

'Your partner is a very strange guy,' Hall said. 'Full of surprises.'

'Tell me about it.'

'He made a big mistake, Harry.'

'Yeah. I already told him that.'

'Did he agree with you?'

'Geiger and I don't have those kinds of conversations.' Harry shifted in his seat, his damp skin making a sucking sound as it pulled away from the leather. 'Could I at least have my coat?' He pointed at his sport jacket, which was lying on the couch where he'd tossed it when he'd come home. Hall picked it up and lobbed it to him, and Harry spread it over his lap.

'I want the boy, Harry. Right away.'

'You got your money back. My guess is that's the best you're going to do.'

Hall leaned forward, his forearms on his thighs. 'I don't care about the money, Harry.' He took a deep breath, his lips spreading in a flat, wincing grimace. His hand went to his sternum and his fingertips gently explored the bruised area. 'Sonofabitch,' he muttered. 'What've you got to drink?'

'Sorry, I don't drink anymore. Sure wish I did.'

Hall stood up, walked to the window, and stared out at the East River. In the dim light, Harry could see that the back of Hall's shirt and collar had a long red stain, and the back of his head had a small white patch on it. As Ray Charles finished singing 'Georgia,' reflections of the lights on the bridge floated on the water's surface like globs of golden oil.

'Great voice,' Hall said.

'Sure is.'

'Where are they, Harry?'

'I don't know.'

'Where does Geiger live?'

'Don't know that either.'

'You've been partners for how long?'

'Eleven years.'

'And you don't know where he lives?'

'Never been to his place. Like you said — he's a very strange guy.'

Harry was doing his best to sit very still and keep his tone low-key because he was beginning to feel truly scared. It wasn't a visceral, heart-in-the-throat fear of imminent violence. But something about Hall, something about the atmosphere in the room, something about *everything* was slowly heating Harry up, gathering loose doubts and confusion like tinder and stoking the fear inside him.

'Harry, I let you finish your shower because I wanted you relaxed, thinking straight.' Hall turned back to the room. 'What's your read on me, Harry — right now?'

'You're in a lot of pain?'

'What else?'

'Running out of patience?'

'Bull's-eye. Now . . . ' Hall went into his pants pocket and took out Harry's cell phone. 'I've checked your cell — there are no sends or receiveds on it.'

'It's programmed that way.'

'Whatever, but I need you to call Geiger right now — and tell him that if he doesn't get the kid back to me asap, you're going to have a real bad time of it. Maybe I'll even take you to Dalton. Think you can do that?'

Harry felt a quick bubble of panic rise up, but then he found himself biting his tongue to keep from laughing. He didn't doubt Hall's sincerity, but the accoutrements to this little drama — his ridiculous nakedness, Ray Charles's doleful voice, the summer dawn reaching the river — all conspired to decorate the horror of the moment in a tacky wrapping that smacked of parody. Try as he might, he couldn't ignore the possibility that fate was playing his last moments on earth for laughs.

Harry took a breath and collected himself. 'Geiger won't pick up,' he said. 'He told me not to call him and said he'd call me if he needed to. Even if I left a message and told him what you plan on doing, I don't think that would change his plans, whatever they are. And I wouldn't call him anyway.'

'No? You're not just stringing this out?'

'Nope. Cross my heart and hope to die.'

As Ray Charles belted the second chorus of

'Hit the Road, Jack' — 'and don't you come back no more, no more' — Hall whirled around and marched toward the glowing red lights of the stereo equipment. He grabbed the CD player, ripped it loose, and hurled it against the wall. The housing shattered into pieces and the music died.

'I hate that fucking song,' Hall muttered.

'Me, too. Thanks.'

Hall came back to the couch and grunted softly as he settled into the cushions. Harry stared at the gun in Hall's belt holster. Harry had a gun, too — a .32-caliber Beretta Tomcat with a seven-shot clip that he kept in a holster attached to the underside of his desk. He'd bought the gun last year through Carmine, after he'd heard about a series of break-ins a block away. He'd never fired it and had only taken it out of the holster a few times to clean it, per Carmine's strict instructions.

'The thirty-five grand is in my van, Harry. Take the money and make the call.'

'Nah. It wouldn't last me very long — I've got some expensive obligations.'

'Don't we all,' said Hall. He sighed, flipped Harry's cell phone open, and punched some buttons. Harry heard it ring once, and then someone answered.

'Come up,' Hall said, and snapped the phone closed.

Harry's gaze strayed to the monitor on the desk. The Jackson Pollock screen saver glowed with a close-up of black and red blobs on a tawny surface. It looked like a NASA photo of an alien terrain. He wished he were there — he was certain that on Mars or Venus there were no trained killers waiting for a phone call to come up the stairs and put a bullet in his skull.

Hall looked at him and shook his head. 'You'd go down this road for Geiger and a kid you don't even know?'

'It's got nothing to do with them, Mr. Hall, or whatever your name really is.'

Harry wondered whether his neighbor was home. He shared the brownstone with a garrulous commodities broker who owned the bottom floor; they'd kibitzed on the sidewalk a while ago, and the guy had mentioned that he was taking the wife to Europe for part of the summer, but Harry couldn't remember when. If they were downstairs and Harry started screaming, they might very well hear him. But as soon as the idea occurred to him, he knew he wouldn't do it. He wasn't going out like a jerk, even if he'd spent too much of his life being one. For a second, he was back in Central Park, drunk in the mindless night, lying on the ground spitting blood and teeth while the muggers stood over him and asked yet again, 'Gonna give us the fucking ATM code?' He'd looked up at them and said, 'Something's happening here but you don't know what it is, do you, Mr. Jones?' They'd gone back to work with their boots, and then Geiger had come along . . .

The front door swung open. Harry and Hall turned in unison to see a tall silhouette in the dark hallway.

'No go?' a man asked.

Harry knew the voice, recognized it the way you catch a glimpse of a familiar face in a crowd but can't remember the context of your association.

'No go,' said Hall.

As the silhouette started into the apartment, Hall reached to the side table and turned on the lamp.

'Jesus,' said Harry, the word pulled from him slowly.

The panhandler he'd given twenty dollars to on Ludlow Street stood scowling at him.

'Harry,' Hall said, 'this is Ray.'

'Hi, Ray,' said Harry.

'There's a woman asleep in the back room,' Hall said to Ray. 'Go get her.'

Electric itches of dread scurried across Harry's palms. He'd forgotten about Lily.

Ray tromped toward the second bedroom and Hall turned back to Harry. 'She your wife or your girlfriend?'

'Sister.'

Ray carried Lily into the living room and put her down in a chair. Still half asleep, she listed side to side.

'Don't do this to her, Harry,' said Hall.

Harry looked back at Hall and then broke into a grin.

'What's funny, Harry?'

'Let me see if I've got this straight,' Harry said. 'You think she's your ace in the hole, right?' He stood up, tying the sleeves of his jacket around his waist to keep covered.

'What're you doing, Harry?' said Hall.

'Just watch, okay?' Harry walked to his sister and did the knuckle knock on her head. 'Anybody home?'

'Can we go for a walk?' said Lily.

'What's my name, sis?'

'Where shall we go?' she said.

Harry worked up a light, sandpapery chuckle and put it out there for them.

'Fellas, meet my little sister, Lily. She's an institutionalized, mostly catatonic schizophrenic. She hasn't known who I am for more than a decade — and at a hundred grand plus a year, she's a fucking stone around my neck.' He shook his head at them. 'I mean, I don't want to see her get hurt, but if you think that's gonna turn me around . . . ' He gave them the chuckle one more time. 'Guys, let me put it this way. Every night I get down on my knees and pray she'll die. You'd be doing both of us a favor if you broke her in half.'

Hall and Ray shared a flat look.

'Harry,' said Ray, 'she may be crazy as a fucking eight, but it doesn't mean she won't feel the pain.'

'Time for that phone call, Harry,' Hall said.

'I'm telling you — Geiger won't answer.'

'Just make the call,' said Hall. 'We'll take it from there.'

Harry could see the reflection of the rising sun crawling up the sides of two crystal buildings across the river. The earth was turning at an incomprehensible speed. *We'll take it from there*. If Hall could locate Geiger off an unanswered call from a cell phone, he had access

127

to some major-league technology.

'So,' Harry said, 'I'm thinking this isn't about a stolen painting, huh?'

'Fuck you,' said Ray. He picked Lily up and tossed her across the room. She hit the floor like a rag doll, hardly making a sound. She lay facedown, limbs askew, and then began to whimper in short spurts. Looking at her, Harry suddenly imagined that the sadness swelling inside him would crush his heart against his ribs and kill him.

Ray turned to Harry and tapped his forehead with a bratwurst-sized finger.

'*That*'s what this is about, Harry.'

'Know what, Ray? You are one shit-ass excuse for a mean motherfucker.' Ray's huge hand flashed up and grabbed Harry by the throat. 'And,' Harry croaked, 'you owe me twenty bucks, asshole.'

Ray's lips parted in a viperous grin, and for a moment Harry thought he'd take the bait.

'Stay on plan, Ray,' Hall said. 'Get her on her feet. We'll see how coldhearted big brother really is.'

As Ray let go of him, Harry took his last, best shot.

'You were real good down on the street, Ray,' he said. 'Tell me something: do you do other stuff, or does Massah Hall always have you play the homeless nigger?'

Ray's arm came up and across as if he was stepping into a perfect backhand. His forearm met Harry's skull at ear level, and the blow sent him flying.

Harry hit the floor short of where he'd hoped to, but then went into a clumsy rollover, praying it looked realistic. He came to a stop lying faceup against one of the desk's legs. He had a loud screech in his head, tears in his eyes, and a blurry but unobstructed view of the Beretta in its holster.

Hall was up on his feet.

'Jesus, Ray! What're you — a goddamn plebe? Huh?'

'Sorry,' Ray muttered.

Harry closed his eyes. His left kneecap had taken the full measure of his weight and had a ballooning throb in it now. Clusters of stars skittered across the undersides of his lids. He thought he might pass out from the pain and cursed himself for not considering that possibility beforehand. And now that the gun was in reach, he felt tiny spiders of panic crawling up and down his spine. He had no plan for how to proceed beyond this point.

Harry heard Lily whimper again and felt tears bulge beneath his eyelids. The fireworks display in his head was abruptly interrupted by a bleached-out, undulating vision. He was in their bathroom on Ninety-fourth Street, soaking in the tub and reading about the latest exploits of his beloved Green Lantern. The door opened and Lily came in — she couldn't have been more than seven. She lifted up the toilet seat and then her pleated tartan skirt, before plopping down and starting to pee. She turned to him and gave him a magnificent grin.

'Hear it?' she said. 'That's why they call it

tinkle, 'cuz that's how it sounds. Can I come in with you?'

'No.'

'Why not?'

'Because.'

'I used to.'

'I said no, didn't I? You deaf?'

'How could I be deaf if I'm answering you, stupid?' She leaned toward him and rapped her knuckles on the top of his head three times. 'Anybody home?'

Now, lying under the desk, the saddest, angriest part of him wanted to rip the Beretta from its holster and fill the room with bullets until the clip was empty and no heart among them could ever beat again.

'Harry?' It was Hall's tired voice. 'Harry, get up.'

Harry didn't move. He heard a long sigh sift through Hall's nostrils. He knew Hall wasn't interested in any of this extracurricular activity. He was all about information, precision, clean angles. He was chafing at the waste of time.

'I swear to God, Ray,' Hall said. 'If he's out cold . . . '

'I hear you,' Harry said.

'Then get up and go sit in the chair. Ray, put Lily on the couch so Harry has a good view of her.'

Harry opened his eyes. Once Ray picked up Lily he was going to pass right by him. Harry rolled over and got up onto his hands and knees, sucking oxygen to counteract his dizziness.

Harry watched Ray lean down to Lily, take

hold of the back of her blouse, and start dragging her across the floor toward the sofa. She could have been a mannequin en route to a window display.

'Rise and shine, Harry,' Ray said.

Harry's right hand rose and grabbed the edge of the desk for support. The action gave him a second's peripheral glimpse of Hall's whereabouts — he was still standing at the sofa. Harry slid his left hand under the desk and closed it around the Beretta's dimpled, hard-rubber grip just as Ray came abreast of him.

Ray paused and gave him a brittle smile. 'Show's about to start, pal.'

Harry pulled the gun free and stuck it into Ray's wide, smooth forehead. 'Move one inch and I swear to God that will be the last incredibly stupid thing you ever say.'

Harry liked the sound of that — he liked the delivery, too. He watched the lids of Ray's eyes pull back to their limits, revealing angry mahogany irises.

'Jesus Christ,' Hall said. 'I don't fucking believe this.'

Harry pushed the gun's muzzle deeper into the thin flesh. 'Hands up.'

The joints of Ray's jaw tensed and he scowled as if he'd bitten down on something very bitter. Then he let go of Lily and raised his hands above his head.

'Turn ninety degrees with me,' Harry said, 'so I have Mr. Hall in my line of sight behind you. Baby steps — and *slow*.' The two men turned on their shared axis. Now Harry could look at Ray and also have a head-on view of Hall standing ten feet away. 'Mr. Hall,' he said, 'take your gun out and toss it in the direction of the bathroom door.'

'Calm down, Harry,' said Hall. 'You sound pretty antsy.'

'I am antsy. Very.'

'Let's don't kill anyone, okay?'

'You said *you* were going to kill *me*.'

'Things happen, Harry, and things change. You make a plan, then reconfigure. So relax. You're the one with the gun in your hand.'

'Now toss yours, like I told you.'

'Harry — '

'*Do it* — before I work up enough nerve to shoot somebody!'

Hall cocked his head and smiled. 'Harry, you have a genuinely unique way of putting things sometimes.'

Hall's right hand moved to his belt holster. He gripped the gun with his pointing finger and thumb, slowly lifted it out, and tossed it through the bathroom door. It hit the tile with a sharp clatter and skidded across the floor.

'Now sit down on the couch,' Harry told him.

Hall did so, the smile still playing at the corners of his mouth.

Harry took a step back from Ray, keeping the gun aimed at the shallow gully between the man's eyebrows. They both noticed that Harry's hand was shaking.

'Scared, asshole?' said Ray.

'Parkinson's. Forgot to take my meds.' He switched to a two-handed grip on the gun, which helped reduce the trembling. 'Now get on your knees, Ray.'

Ray shook his head. 'Not happening, man. You're not gonna shoot me, and I'm not getting on my knees.'

Harry saw Hall's chin dip wearily toward his chest. 'Ray, we don't have time for this. Do what he says.'

'Not part of my job description.'

'Ray,' said Hall, '*get on your fucking knees!*'

As Ray knelt down, Harry was almost certain he saw sparks of rage leaping about in his eyes.

'Let's have your gun, Ray. Same way.'

'Motherfucking . . . ' Ray said, the rest of his thought fizzling out into a mutter as he took out a shiny snub-nosed revolver and tossed it behind Harry.

Harry couldn't keep his eyes on both Hall and Ray and see Lily, but he wasn't confident enough to take a quick glance her way.

'Lily,' he said. 'Can you stand up, Lily?'

'Sure she can,' Ray said. 'Then she'll recite the Pledge of fucking Allegiance.'

Harry's head felt lopsided and his knee was squishy and hot. For a moment he forgot that he was holding the gun.

'Know what, Ray?' he said.

'What?'

Harry stared down at him, his mind suddenly blank. He'd meant to deliver a clever rejoinder, but when nothing came he swung his arms around as hard and fast as he could. The Beretta met Ray's sneer with such force that he arched backward and landed flat on his back while his spouting blood was still suspended in the air. A wave of drops floated and then fell, dappling his pants and sweatshirt with scarlet.

Hall sprang up from the couch as the room filled with the reflexive, slurping sound of Ray trying to breathe.

Harry shifted his weapon in Hall's direction. 'Stay!'

Harry glanced down at Ray. He'd rolled over onto his side to keep from suffocating and now let out a syrupy moan. His hands were wrapped tightly around his face, but blood seeped through his fingers.

'Muhjerfushur,' Ray gurgled.

Sunlight had spread through most of the room now, and Harry let his gaze wander across it for a moment, knowing that what had been his home, his sanctum, was lost to him. But what truly hurt was the recognition that everything he'd be leaving behind had come to him because of his chosen line of work.

The sloshing sound leaking from behind Ray's palms was growing louder. He finally managed to get himself up into a sitting position without moving his hands. Harry took a step back.

'Shit,' said Harry. 'I didn't mean to do that.'

Hall snorted and sat down on the sofa again. 'Yes, you did, Harry. My guess is you've been wanting to do that for a long time. You just didn't know it till now.'

To Harry's chagrin, he realized that he had, in fact, felt a joint-loosening sense of release, a cleansing liberation. He turned and looked at Lily. She was sitting up, hands in her hair, fingers twirling and untwirling a long black hank of it in a mute, private ritual.

'I'm going to put on some pants,' Harry said.

He picked up Ray's gun and walked to the bathroom, his eyes still on Hall. He put the gun in the sink, pulled the sport coat from around his waist, and took his trousers off the toilet seat. As he stepped into them, he heard Ray spit out something thick and viscous. Harry tried not to think about what it was.

'I'm going to have a smoke,' Hall said. 'Reaching in my pocket, okay?'

Pulling on a shirt and then his sport coat while switching the gun from hand to hand, Harry came back out into the living room. 'Be my guest.'

Hall took a pack of Camels and a lighter from his pocket. Lighting a cigarette, he said, 'Why'd Geiger do it, Harry?'

'He figured if you were willing to take the kid to Dalton, then he was expendable — and so maybe we all were. I'm gonna get out of here now, with my sister. Do I need to take all the guns?'

'If you're asking whether I'm going to come out into the street running after you, guns blazing — then no, you don't have to take the guns.'

Harry stuck his feet into his loafers, grabbed a towel from the bathroom, and came back out into the living room. He was getting used to the weight of the Beretta in his hand, but he felt like a stranger in someone else's place.

He got halfway to Lily and stopped. Turning

to Hall, he held out a palm. 'My cell phone.'

Hall tossed it to him. Harry lifted Lily up and held her close. He could feel her heart beating against his chest. She started humming something very softly, stopping and starting in even, repetitive intervals. It sounded vaguely familiar to Harry, but he couldn't place the tune.

'How long has she been like that?' Hall asked.

'Too long,' Harry replied. 'I've got to ask you, Hall. Would killing both of you end this?'

'Think you could do that?'

'Strictly hypothetical. Would it?'

'De Koonings are hard to come by, Harry.'

Harry nodded and looked over at Ray.

'Hey, Ray,' he said. Ray raised his head, his large, blood-soaked hands still clamped onto his face. Harry tossed him the towel. It landed at his knees, and Ray reached down with both hands to pick it up.

Harry saw that the Beretta had done tremendous damage to Ray's face. The proud, aquiline nose was pancaked and off-center, and the plane of the upper lip was crushed and raw. The unseen teeth beneath the bloody plexus were broken if not gone.

Harry set Lily on her feet, turned away from her, and vomited. He had watched DVDs of Geiger's sessions with the keen, assiduous eye of an analyst, but this was *his* handiwork. He ran his tongue across his three false front teeth and remembered parts of him coming asunder, the searing clarity of pain and breakage, the stirring knowledge that death was an even-odds bet. He straightened up.

Ray had the towel pressed against his mouth, and his eyes held Harry like a prey in crosshairs. He mumbled something indecipherable, but the promise of vengeance was crystal clear. Harry took Lily's hand in his.

'Come on, Lily. We gotta go.'

'*We gotta get outta this place,*' she sang, '*if it's the last thing we ever do.*'

Harry started leading her toward the door, walking backward with the gun still held waist-high in his hand.

'Good-bye,' he said.

Hall nodded. 'Tell Geiger I'll see him around.'

★　★　★

Hall ached from his waist to the top of his head. He'd never had a problem dealing with the physical aspect of pain, but it made him feel stupid, because in his job, pain meant you'd screwed up. You always had the 'just in case' mind-set. You always assumed that a wrench was perched somewhere, waiting to fall into the gears. But the last twenty-four hours had rolled out a brutal trifecta: Matheson shakes them, Geiger decides to play moral relativist, a computer geek turns into Rambo. Hall took a last drag of his Camel, stubbed it out on the coffee table, and went over to Ray.

'Give me your cell.'

Ray spat out a large dollop of blood and pulled a cell phone from his pocket. Hall dialed.

'Be ready, Mitch. Boddicker is coming out — with his sister.'

'Sister?' a voice said. 'What happened in there?'

'Boddicker and Ray got into it, but later on that. I've got to get Ray's face stitched up.'

'That bad? Jesus, Richie. We're turning into the three fucking blind mice.'

'Stay close, Mitch — but not too,' Hall said. 'And don't get cute. You know he's our best bet to get to Geiger, right?'

'Wanna know what I think? I think maybe somebody who keeps making wrong choices should stop sounding all the time as if he knows what the fuck he's doing.'

Hall had wanted to punch the guy in the face for years, but he kept his sigh silent and hung up. Since the beginning of this clusterfuck, he'd been assuming that if things got much worse the three of them would end up at each other's throats, but he couldn't let it happen yet. He had another call to make, and for this one, he sat down in Harry's chair and took a deep breath, letting it out in a measured release. He dialed and the call was picked up on the first ring.

'Yes?'

'It's Hall. We have a problem, sir.'

' 'Problem' is one of my least favorite words. What is 'our' problem?'

'We lost the kid — before we were able to get any information. Geiger has him.'

'*Has* him?'

'Took him, sir.'

'Then find Geiger.'

'Yes, sir. That's the plan. But we don't know where Geiger is . . . yet.'

'Hall . . . '

'Yes, sir.'

'I'm beginning to wonder if I should start being concerned. Yesterday you said you had Matheson lined up. Now this.'

'I understand, sir, but there's no need to — '

'Find Geiger.'

'Yes, sir.'

'And keep me up to date. I don't like hearing about 'problems' after the fact. If you foresee more complications, I want to know about them before they happen.'

'Yes, sir.'

The call ended. Hall could hear the sky starting to crack, and unless he turned this job around, it would surely fall. Ray, with a loud groan, staggered to his feet and grabbed the wall with one hand to keep from falling down.

'Muhjerfushinn — '

'Ray, shut the fuck up!'

11

The boy did not sleep for long. His slumber was full of twitches and mumbled noises, and then some dream demon chased him into consciousness. Geiger sat down beside him with the alcohol and a washcloth. He put a glass of water on the floor.

'I'm going to take the tape off. Tell me if it hurts too much.'

Ezra nodded, and Geiger began slowly peeling off an end of the tape around one eye, dabbing at the newly exposed skin every quarter of an inch. The boy flinched a few times but made no sound. Once Geiger got past the first eye — the left — the rest of the tape lifted more easily. The boy's eyes were a striking shade of luminous green, the color of sea glass. There was lingering fear in them, and confusion, leaving no room for trust.

Geiger went to work on the strip across Ezra's mouth while the boy stared at him warily. Geiger carefully pulled the tape free. Ezra's cheeks and temples had two horizontal red streaks of chemical irritation. He ran his tongue across his lips a few times.

'Thirsty,' he croaked.

Geiger handed him the glass, and the boy drank it all down. They studied each other, like strangers sharing space at the start of a long trip.

'Are you gonna hurt me?' said Ezra.

His voice had a medium pitch, and Geiger heard a sporadic preteen squeak at its edges. But there also was an unexpected husky bottom to it; Geiger found the boy's voice strangely soothing, like a cello at the heart of a string quartet.

'No,' said Geiger.

Ezra dragged a hand across his clammy forehead. 'Really hot in here. Can you turn on the AC?'

'There's no air-conditioning.'

'No AC? Then can you turn on a fan?'

'I don't have a fan.'

'Don't you get hot in here?'

'Yes.'

The boy tried to read Geiger's face, looking for a hint of humor in the sharp features and stony, ash-colored eyes. He had good antennae for sarcasm. That was always his parents' tone of choice, and they'd used it for banter, scolding, small talk, out-for-blood fighting. But Geiger seemed utterly straightforward.

'Well, can I take a shower?'

'Yes.'

Ezra raised a hand, gently touched his cheek, and winced. To Geiger, the gesture, the physical presence of another person here, seemed to have a magical effect, altering the place's shape and shrinking its size. The boy's palms came to rest beside his thighs, flat on the leather cushion, as if he needed the extra support to keep from toppling over sideways. His head rested back against the sofa, and his eyelids descended.

'Why do you do it?' he asked.

'Do what?'

'Your job.' He opened his eyes again. 'That's what you do, right? Hurt people?'

Geiger took the empty glass from Ezra and stood up. Then he realized he'd had no particular place in mind to go to. He turned back to the boy.

'Ezra, do you know that this is all about your father? That they wanted to find out if you know where he is?'

'Uh-huh.'

'Do you know where your father is?'

The boy cocked his head and shifted his skinny body. 'How do I know you're not one of them? Maybe you're just pretending to be nice, so I'll tell you stuff.'

The back door was on the north wall, in the kitchen. Geiger went to it and used a keypad to unlock it.

'Where you going?' asked the boy.

'Out back, for a smoke.'

Geiger walked out off the porch, into the yard. From beyond the fence the smell of engine oil reached him as he lit his cigarette and drew the smoke deep inside him. For the length of the breath, he saw the image of his father's face above him, looking down, pearl-colored smoke snaking out of his nostrils. Until the predawn ride in the rental car, it was the only picture of his father Geiger had carried in his mental scrapbook. He knew now there would be more to come. The pages would fill up, independent of his desires or conscious powers.

'Can I come out?'

The boy was in the doorway. Geiger exhaled

and his father's face faded away.

'No,' he said. 'Stay there.'

The world outside would keep oozing in through the cracks, and the past would usurp the present, gradually taking hold. Geiger could feel his pulse pounding at his insides, a mounting internal timpani, blood and organs like hammer and anvil. He started to stroll around the yard in his singular gait, fingers in a jig at his sides.

'Hey,' said Ezra. 'Can I ask your name?'

'Geiger.'

'Like the counter?'

'Yes. Like the counter. Stop talking now. I need to think about some things.'

Geiger took one more suck on his cigarette, then let it fall and watched the butt's last plume of smoke drift southward. He wanted to light another one.

★   ★   ★

Harry pressed the pay phone's receiver tight to his ear so he could hear above the noise of the laundromat. His other hand held Lily's; she seemed to have discovered a central beat in the jumble of the washers' and dryers' competing clatter and was swaying slightly to it. He could still feel the aftershocks rippling up from his hand and through his arm from when his Beretta had smashed into Ray's face and something had given way.

'It's me,' Harry said after the voice mail's beep. 'We have to talk. Really, really important. About Hall and Matheson and the kid and the

143

whole fucking thing. I'm in a laundromat on Flatbush. Hall showed up at my place — I don't know how — with another guy, trying to find out where you are and how to get the kid back. These guys are heavy lifters. Hall has battery acid in his veins. I'm on a pay phone because Hall may have tagged my cell, so don't call my cell. It's turned off. I'll call again. Or you call me — please!'

As he hung up, he noticed that a few of the patrons had paused in their separating and folding to stare at the guy yelling into the phone. He hadn't realized he'd been shouting. He led Lily over to a line of chairs against a wall and sat down. His damaged, aching knee felt like a water balloon.

'Sit down, Lily,' he said. He gave her a little tug, but she remained standing, shifting back and forth from one foot to the other, in thrall with the motorized cacophony. Leaving the brownstone, he had dragged her three blocks before he'd been able to flag a cab. When the driver had asked where they wanted to go, Harry hadn't answered for nearly ten seconds. In a city of infinite destinations, he was struck mute by the realization that he had *nowhere* to go. Finally, he told the driver he needed a pay phone, and they cruised Flatbush Avenue silently until the harsh fluorescents of the laundromat caught the driver's eye.

Watching the machines tumble and whirl, Harry took stock. The de Kooning scenario had dipped to zero plausibility. David Matheson had something, or knew something, and Hall

144

desperately wanted it or him. Hall was obviously a wired guy, and he seemed to have access to the most sophisticated kinds of techno-tracing. Kidnapping and violence were not an issue. The man had carte blanche in an à la carte world. But Harry couldn't figure out how they had found his home. He'd made himself untraceable, unfindable. How had Hall ended up sitting in his living room, waiting for him to come out of the shower? He scrubbed the inside of his mouth with his tongue. He'd crunched two Pepcids to kill the lingering taste of vomit, but it hadn't worked.

Lily let go of her brother's hand and began slowly tracing a line on her right cheek with the tip of her middle finger, from cheekbone to jawline, up and down, like a rhythmic accompaniment as she started to sing.

'*Hello, darkness, my old friend. I've come to talk with you again . . .*'

'You're awfully talkative lately, Lil. What made you start singing that song? The bright bulbs?'

He slumped back and closed his eyes. Lily wandered off toward a little boy, three or four years old, who sat cross-legged on the floor at his mother's feet as she folded bedsheets emblazoned with a web-throwing Spider-Man flying amid large-font 'Wham!'s and 'Kapow!'s.

Harry floated through the sheer walls of memory to his University Heights apartment in the 1990s, after his sister's inner gears had started slipping and he'd taken her in and set her up in his bedroom. He would be half asleep on the living room sofa in the loneliest hours of the night, and Lily would shuffle in and hover over him and whisper, 'Harry?' It was less an inquiry than an invitation to share the fantastic adventures conjured by her devolving mind. Then the visitations stopped, and sometimes at night Harry would peek into the bedroom and find her sitting on the window seat, talking to the city beyond the glass. She'd found a new listener no one else could see.

Harry opened his eyes and was on his feet in an instant. Lily was kneeling down before the young boy, who looked up at her from the pile of plastic superheroes in his lap.

'Hi,' the boy said.

'Wonderful,' said Lily.

She stared at him like Copernicus discovering the true place of Earth in the cosmos. Harry came for her just as she reached out and took the boy's hand in hers. The mother glanced down as Harry arrived.

'Hey!' she barked.

'It's okay,' Harry said. 'She just — '

'*Aparta las manos!* No touch!' she said.

Harry grabbed Lily by the arm and pulled her up to him. Her hand remained outstretched as the boy's slipped from it.

'Sorry,' he said. 'She's a little . . . odd.'

'*Qué?*'

'*Excéntrico. Muy excéntrico.*'

The woman cocked her head, and as she studied Harry's expression her scowl relaxed into a sad, condoling smile.

He led Lily back to the chairs. He lowered his head into his hands, but it set off a hot, painful throb from Ray's blow, and he straightened up.

'What am I going to do with you, sis?'

'Wonderful,' she said, her shining eyes staring at the little boy, who had picked up his action figures and resumed the eternal battle between good and evil.

★   ★   ★

As Geiger paced in the yard, Ezra watched the odd but precise movements of the man's body. Most of the work seemed to be going on in the hips and ankles. The motion looked almost natural but wasn't; he was clearly making adjustments for some sort of injury or disease. Ezra wondered if he had been in a terrible accident — maybe a smashup in a car, or something that happened in a war.

'Geiger, I'm real hungry.'

'I'll make you something to eat.'

Geiger came across the yard and they both went into the kitchen. A black walnut counter lined two walls. There was a coffeemaker and a bean grinder, a sink and a Viking two-burner cooktop. Beneath it was a mahogany-paneled compact refrigerator. Atop one counter were a wood-block knife holder with two blades, a wooden utensils cart with two spoons, knives, and forks, and two large stainless steel bowls, one of them filled with fruit and vegetables. On a wall rack hung a cast-iron skillet and a stainless steel pot. In a corner was a combination washer-dryer. Everything gleamed beneath four hanging pendant lights. The room was handsome and minimal — there was nothing extra.

Geiger turned on the water, put some broccoli and asparagus on the counter, and took a knife from its slot.

'Weird,' said the boy.

'What?'

'You don't have any cupboards or drawers.'

The only occasion when Geiger had ever spent time in a child's presence was an afternoon years ago when he'd gone to La Bella to give Carmine his monthly loan payment and had been asked to stay for lunch with Carmine and his nephew. As always, the offer had been a smiling command presented in the form of an invitation. Geiger had sat silently while Carmine regaled him and the squirrelly boy, who had been about Ezra's age, with stories about his stints in the navy and the teamsters. Then Carmine had leaned toward him and said:

'When you walked in the door, my nephew said something. Tell Geiger what you said, Michael.'

The boy had pointed his nose down at his pasta primavera. 'I don't remember,' he said. His glance at Carmine was dark with a sullen question: *Why are you making me do this?*

Carmine's smile was benign, but then it always was. 'Michael, tell Geiger what you said.'

'I said . . . ' the boy mumbled, and looked at Geiger. 'I said you looked weird.'

'Be specific, Michael,' Carmine prompted.

The boy looked resigned to his fate. 'I said, 'Look at that guy. I betcha he's a freak job or a retard.''

148

'Good,' said Carmine, and mussed the boy's hair. He sat back, a sage preparing to dispense wisdom. 'Now, there's a reason I made you do that, Michael — it's so you won't forget lessons to be learned here. Lesson number one: Never insult someone you don't know to somebody else, because the person you're talking to might respect that person or care for him, like I do Geiger — in which case you've insulted *both* men. You see?'

The nephew nodded, his lips working nervously.

'And lesson two: Talk like that and you might end up becoming a spoiled little punk who gets his goddamn face slapped. Now go home.'

But with Ezra, there was an aura of gentleness, the kind of affect sometimes interpreted as sadness. Geiger also noticed that a stillness ruled the boy's body. Apart from actions intended and necessary, he hardly moved at all — there were no impatient gestures or childish fidgets.

With a soft meow announcing a homecoming, the cat came through the flap on the pet slot at the bottom of the back door. He stopped for a five-second, one-eyed appraisal of the visitor.

Ezra crouched down. 'Hey . . . ' He held out a hand. 'Boy, that's a bad-looking cat. He yours?'

'He lives here. He goes where he wants, but he always comes back.'

'That's a song, y'know.'

'No, I don't.'

'"The cat came back, he just couldn't stay away." You don't know that?'

The animal sprang effortlessly onto the

counter and started nuzzling his battered head into Geiger's forearm.

'What's his name?'

'Cat.'

'That's what you call him? 'Cat'?'

Geiger gave the cat a short, hard scruffing on the head, then filled the empty bowl with water. The cat settled in for a drink. The boy's lips bunched up in displeasure as he watched Geiger line up half a dozen stalks of asparagus on the counter and cut off their pale ends in one motion.

'That stuff for me?' the boy asked. Geiger nodded. 'For breakfast? Don't you have any, like, y'know — *food* food? Cereal? Munchies? Chips?'

'No.'

'Man . . . 'The boy's voicing stretched the word out into two plaintive syllables. 'Can we go get something?'

'No. No going out now. There are also apples and pears.'

'I'll have a pear,' Ezra said bleakly. He went to the bowl, picked one up, and bit into it deeply. 'Good,' he said, nodding, and took another bite without swallowing. He drew a finger softly down the cat's spine; the tail and haunches rose at the caress.

'Geiger . . . '

'Yes?'

'I think he's in the city someplace. My dad.' Geiger put the vegetables back in the bowl. 'He left me a note. He said he had stuff to do in the city but he'd try to be home later. And he told me to keep the door locked.'

'But you don't know why they're looking for him?'

'Uh-uh.' The boy shrugged, and a sigh left him as his shoulders came back down. He looked like he was deflating. 'Can I call my mother?'

'Yes. Soon. Is she at home?'

'No. She's on vacation — sorta. She's in New Hampshire, in a forest. She said it's called a 'silent word retreat' or something like that. She calls my cell at around ten every morning. Then they take her phone away from her till the next day.' He suddenly punched the counter, and the cat looked up. 'Shit — those guys took my cell!'

'No. I have it.'

Geiger took the cell phone from his pocket, turned it on, and put it on the counter. He'd wait until she made her call, then he'd get on the line. It would be tricky. *My name is Geiger. Your ex-husband is missing. Your son was abducted, he's with me now. You have to come to New York right away . . .*

'This will be hard for her,' Geiger said. 'I think it's better if we wait for her to call you — like she usually does. All right?'

'Yeah, I guess.' Ezra stroked the cat again. 'Can I pick him up?'

'Yes. Scratch his scar. He likes that.'

Ezra picked the cat up and cradled him in his arms. His pointing finger went to work on the grizzled old wound, and the animal began to purr loudly.

'Man, listen to that.'

'Ezra. How many men came to your father's apartment?'

'Two grabbed me. I think maybe I heard another one in the living room. Not sure.'

'I only met one man,' said Geiger.

'And he just let you take me away?'

'No. I knocked him out.'

The boy's eyes widened with childish awe. 'Really? You, like, hit him with something?'

'My fist.'

Geiger found the act of conversation enervating. There were so many new things on different levels to deal with: accommodating the boy's presence and voice and questions, listening and responding, focusing on what action he might take.

'One of them was a big black dude. He said he'd kill me if I screamed.'

'He was trying to scare you,' Geiger said.

The boy's voice tightened with anger, his lips crimping. 'Well, I hope he was the one you hit. I hope you really beat the shit out of him.' He turned and walked back toward the couch with his new friend in his arms.

A thought unfurled in Geiger's head like a 'Grand Opening' banner: *Nothing is as it was. Everything has changed.* He felt set loose into the world, keenly aware of something lost and left behind, like a soldier who still senses the presence of an amputated limb.

Ezra called out: 'Your cell phone beeped.'

Geiger walked to his desk. The screen on his cell phone read '1 Message.' He picked it up and punched a key. Instead of the usual 'H' or 'C' he saw '212-555-8668.' Reading the small font made the numbers' edges blur and brought a dull ache to the dark side of his eyeballs. He'd never had a call from anyone but Harry or Carmine — not even a wrong number. He chose the 'listen' option. It was Harry, the voice cutting through a background of mushy, chaotic noise.

As he listened to Harry's message, Geiger shut his eyes. He saw a sky filling with clouds, a roiling, ominous crop. He tried to visualize a god puffing up his cheeks and spewing out a strong wind that would sweep the clouds away, but none came.

'This is really cool,' said the boy.

Geiger opened his eyes and saw Ezra standing before the custom-made CD racks, exploring the rows of the vast music library. The boy tilted forward, a particular title eliciting a grunt of interest.

'That's the *Dumbarton Oaks* Stravinsky conducted, right?'

'Yes.'

'How many CDs you got?'

'Eighteen hundred and twenty-three.'

'Man, that's a lot.'

Cell phone in hand, Geiger started for the back door again. 'Be right back.'

'Can I put some music on?' asked Ezra.

'Yes.'

Outside, the mounting heat of the day was burning away the clouds and damp thickness. The opening strains of Webern's Five Movements for String Quartet reached him like a tap on the shoulder, and Geiger turned to the sound like someone encountering an old friend in an unlikely place. Then he looked down at his phone and pushed the 'call back' button. After one ring, Harry picked up.

'Hello?' Harry said.

'It's me.'

'Jeez, man. It's good to hear you.'

Even with all the background noise, Geiger could make out Harry's sigh rustling through open lips. 'Tell me what happened, Harry.'

The request was a skeleton key opening the tumblers in Harry's mind. 'A motherfucking train wreck is what happened! Jesus fucking Christ — how about guns and murder threats?' As he spoke, Harry picked up momentum, each word like a tiny hit of speed fueling him to the next. 'Bodies getting tossed around. And blood, man. A lot of fucking blood!'

'Harry, slow down. Facts.'

Geiger could see Harry talking, the familiar tone and cadence, see his scowl, his wriggling discomfort. It suddenly struck him that Harry was the only person he actually *knew*.

'Okay, facts. I walked home, took a shower, and found Hall sitting in my living room. He tells me to call you — I said no. He says he'll kill me if I don't — I still said no.'

As Harry related the story, Geiger allowed himself a momentary glimpse of its underlying import: another human being made an act of sacrifice on his behalf. He quickly pushed the thought aside.

Harry finished his account and took a deep breath. 'Jesus, man — I almost killed somebody this morning!'

'How did Hall find you?'

154

'I don't know, but he said something that makes me think he's got access to cell signal tracking. That's why I told you not to call my phone.'

'Was there a third man? The boy thinks three men came to his apartment.'

'There were only two in mine.'

Geiger's peripheral attention took note of a violin suddenly injecting a jarring melody into Webern's string quartet. It rose above the other players, but another full measure played before Geiger recognized it as a signature snippet from Mozart's Second Symphony. He ran back inside and saw the boy's cell phone on the kitchen counter. Ezra was picking it up as its Mozart ring-tone sounded again.

'Don't answer!' Geiger yelled.

The boy flinched and then turned as Geiger came at him. 'Don't hurt me! Please!' His body folded up, cowering against the counter. 'Please don't hurt me!'

Geiger snatched the phone out of the boy's hand and jammed his thumb down on the 'end' button. But the ringtone sounded again, so he hurled it at the wall and it shattered.

Geiger looked over at the boy. 'I wasn't going to hurt you.'

The boy's eyes glistened. He nodded, but tears started down his cheeks. When a sob broke from his chest, he raced out of the kitchen and Geiger heard the bathroom door slam.

'Geiger?'

It was Harry's voice. Geiger glanced at the cell phone in his hand.

'Geiger! What the hell's going on?'

'Harry,' he said into his phone, 'how do they track cell phones?'

'You know — triangulation. Cell towers are always listening to your signal, handing you off from one to another as you move around, figuring out which one will give you the best service.'

Geiger saw himself in the Ludlow Street viewing room, taking the boy's cell phone from Hall's jacket — so Hall knew the boy's number. He drew in a deep breath, trying to stem the flood of adrenaline. He heard the shower start, and it took him a few seconds to understand what the sound was, because the only time he'd ever heard it was when he was in it.

'Harry, do you have to place a call or answer one for them to get a fix on you?'

'No. As long as a cell phone is on, all it has to do is ring and they can track it.'

'How close a fix can they get?'

'Pretty tight. Three or four blocks, maybe closer.'

'What did Hall say to make you think he could track a cell?'

'He told me to call you, I said no, and then I told him that even if I did you wouldn't answer. Hall said, 'Just make the call. We'll take it from there.' What's that sound like to you, man?'

'Harry, the boy's cell phone just rang.'

'Fuck. What're you gonna do?'

'I don't know, Harry.'

The words seemed to hang in plain sight before Geiger, mocking him, a freshly coined motto for a new age. *I don't know*.

'I have to get him to his mother,' Geiger said. 'She's in New Hampshire now.'

Geiger heard Harry mutter under his breath and then say, 'Lily, come back here. Lily! Goddamnit . . . Listen, Geiger, I gotta go. I'll call you back.'

'Harry, wait . . . '

His answer was a dial tone. Geiger stood wondering what he would have said next. The quartet played on, and he walked toward the bathroom.

He rapped on the door. 'Ezra?'

The shower turned off.

'What?' said the boy.

'I couldn't let you answer the phone.'

'Why not?' The question was a plea.

'If you did, those men might have figured out where you are.'

'How'm I gonna talk to my mom now?'

'We'll figure something out.'

The door opened a crack.

'Do you have something I can wear? When I was in the trunk I . . . pissed my pants.'

The humiliation in his words hung in the air.

'I'll get you some things,' Geiger said. 'Give me your dirty clothes. I'll put them in the washer.'

'Thank you.'

One of Ezra's hands came out with his soiled things. Geiger took them to the kitchen and started a wash cycle, then went to his dresser. As he stood there, an image and echo of something rushed up from deep inside him. He was in darkness, a door was opening, and a silhouette spoke in a gruff voice:

'*Did you piss yourself, boy?*'

'*No, Pa. I held it in.*'

'*Good.*'

Geiger grabbed some underpants, a pair of shorts, and a T-shirt from the drawers and headed back to the bathroom.

12

The more Harry thought about Hall, the more his anxiety tilted toward paranoia, so when he hailed a taxi outside the laundromat and got Lily in the back with him, he told the cabbie to go into Manhattan and drop them at Seventy-sixth and Columbus, because the closest thing to a safe haven he could think of was the diner. He'd considered a hotel but decided against it. He didn't have a lot of cash on him — he'd cursed himself for forgetting to grab more before he left the apartment — and without an ATM card he'd have to nurse along what he was carrying in his wallet. Besides, front desk clerks tended to notice people when they checked in, especially if one side of your face was swollen and purple and the only luggage you had was a crazy person. But nobody noticed anyone in diners. You went in, sat down, and ate. Maybe you read the paper, or had a conversation if somebody was with you, but people watching wasn't big on the menu.

The taxi smelled of sweat and pine scent, and country music pumped out of the radio. They were halfway across the Manhattan Bridge. The cabbie's baseball cap was tilted back on his head, and he slapped the steering wheel in time with the snare drum's crisp beats, making sport of the bridge's crowded, narrow lanes.

Lily sat beside Harry. She had lost weight since he'd bought her the sky-blue blouse, and it made her look even more like a child. He realized he'd have to keep a close eye on her until he could get her back to the home. She might get hungry, for one thing. And drugs — he had no idea what meds she was on, if any. He took her hand in his.

'You always held my hand, remember?' He asked the question with no expectation of getting an answer. 'Even when we were grown up, if we were walking to dinner or the movies, you'd take my hand. Remember that?' He gave her hand a squeeze, but she stared straight ahead, fingers unresponsive to his. Still, he felt a little lighter for the memory of an old, precious bond when they were impossibly different people.

The throb in Harry's head had become a dull, flat thud. He leaned to the plastic partition. 'Hey, man. Think you could kill the radio for a while?'

'You don't like country music?' said the cabbie. His voice had an oiled, good ol' boy slide that surprised Harry.

'I just need a little quiet time. Got a headache.'

'Can do, buddy.'

The cabbie punched at the radio and the sound cut off, and as Harry leaned back Lily jolted to life, her tiny hands grabbing the lapels of his sport coat, fists tugging him back and forth with surprising force, like a child seized by a tantrum. She was mewling loudly, a tortured sound that made the driver's head whip around.

Harry gripped her at the wrists. 'Lily! What? What is it?'

'Don't do that!' she howled. 'Don't do that!'

'Lily — stop!'

'No — no — noooo!'

The sound was almost more than Harry could bear, a siren of madness and loss. 'Sweet Jesus,' said the cabbie. 'What's she want, man?'

And then Harry understood. 'Turn the radio back on!'

The cabbie jabbed at the dashboard, the bright guitar streams returned, and Lily's yowling slowed to a stop like a windup toy running down.

'Well, all right!' whooped the cabbie. 'That's what I'm talkin' 'bout!' He chuckled and gave the horn four quick taps as he headed down the off-ramp.

Harry gently pulled at Lily's wrists. Her clenched fists came away from his lapels and something fell into Harry's lap. It was a button-sized black disk, an inch across, a quarter-inch thick. He picked it up. It was made of some kind of plastic, shiny and smooth on one side and sticky on the other. Harry repositioned Lily against the seat and then settled back, rolling the tracer between thumb and forefinger like a lucky coin.

'Son of a bitch,' he whispered to himself.

A scene flashed in front of him like a three-second cut in a movie trailer. Nighttime. Ludlow Street. Ray in his homeless person guise getting in Harry's face, then grabbing him by the lapels and pulling him close.

Harry turned over his lapels and spotted a small circle of gummy residue on the fabric of

161

one. He nodded with admiration and astonishment. That's how they'd found his place so easily. Ray had planted the thing on him. A whole production before the session, the little girl included, just in case something went wrong later on.

Harry took the tracer and stuck it on the back of the seat in front of him.

At the bottom of the ramp from the bridge, the cabbie stopped as the light changed to yellow at Canal Street. He turned around again and gave Lily a smile. He had a ruddy scrub brush of a mustache, and the gap between his front teeth amplified the good ol' boy aura.

'You okay now, honey?' he said.

Lily's head was turned to her window. Outside, a bus idled beside the taxi, rattling and snorting. She said nothing.

Harry reached out and pushed her hair back from her eyes and let his fingertips caress her cheek. She took no notice of the gesture.

'I'll tell you something, buddy,' said the cabbie. 'You're a good man, the way you look after her. The world today — folks don't treat their own like they used to.' He took off his cap and ran a hand through his thick tangerine hair. 'They talk that stuff 'bout global warming? Well, it seems to me the warmer it gets on the outside, the colder we get in our hearts. Hell, look at me. I got a sister, too — she's divorced, lives down in Baton Rouge — and I ain't seen her in four years.' He turned back to the windshield. 'I'll tell you, buddy, you bring the shame up in me. When I go on break, I'm gonna give her a call.'

Harry turned around and squinted out the back window at the long line of vehicles idling in the drizzle behind them. Farther back, the cars and cabs melted into a stubborn river fog. Harry felt as if the world had suddenly become very small.

He turned back to the driver. 'Hey, I got a question.'

'Shoot.'

'For an extra twenty, can you step on it, zig and zag, shave a couple of lights?'

The cabbie chuckled. 'Somebody following you, buddy?'

'I don't know. Maybe.'

'Well, whatever. You want the hammer down, you got it.'

The light turned green and the cab lurched forward and veered sharply into the next lane. A horn blared in their wake.

Harry closed his eyes. 'De Kooning, my ass.'

★　★　★

Ezra opened the bathroom door. Geiger's shorts almost reached his knees, ballooning around his legs. His bare chest and arms had half a dozen purple bruises from the previous day's man-handling, and the stripes on his face were redder now.

'I'm sore all over. Can I have some Advil?'

'I don't have any,' Geiger said.

'Tylenol?'

'No. I don't take drugs.'

'Drugs? Advil's not cocaine, you know?'

163

He pulled Geiger's T-shirt on, wincing from the effort. Its hem came to rest halfway down his thighs. The getup made him look even younger, like a kid playing dress-up with his father's clothes. He sat on the toilet seat and started putting on his sneakers.

'What happens now?' he asked, his head bent to the task. 'If you aren't one of them, then what're you gonna do with me?'

'Do you have any relatives nearby?'

'Uh-uh.'

'No grandparents?'

'Dead.'

'Uncles, aunts?'

'No.'

Geiger watched him lacing up, the long fingers working systematically, making precise knots and matching loops.

'Dad knew, didn't he? He knew when he left that those guys were after him, right?'

'I don't know, Ezra.'

Geiger stepped aside as Ezra stood up and came out. Then he followed the boy back toward the couch.

'This really sucks, man. I mean, I don't want to be here. I want to be home with my mom and sleeping in my own bed.' He looked over at the pieces of his cell phone strewn on the floor. 'Mom's gonna freak.'

'We'll call her. We'll find a pay phone and call her cell.'

'Why can't you just call her now on your cell?'

'I can't let her know my number. I can't let anyone know that.' Geiger could imagine her standing somewhere, dialing Ezra's number again, growing a little anxious.

Ezra sat on the couch and put his head down in his hands. Webern was rising to a powerful, melancholy arc, and Ezra's fingers came alive at his temples, wiggling along with the violin, coaxing the notes out of the air.

'This is great, right here where it climbs,' he said. 'Sounds like crying, doesn't it?' He hummed along, his voice cracking at the summit of the melody, and then his focus shifted and he leaned closer to the floor, as if noticing it for the first time. He reached down and ran a fingertip across the ornate design.

'Man, this floor is cool. Where'd you find something like this?'

'I made it.'

Ezra tilted his head at Geiger as one might at an idiot child. 'You made the floor with your *hands?*'

Geiger nodded, feeling as he did the muscles at the back of his neck, stubborn and ungiving.

Ezra got up and began to prowl across the shining surface, studying the network of designs, the stars and disks and crescents, shaking his head as if encountering an impossible creation. 'This is amazing,' he said. 'People've told you that, right?'

'You're the first person to see it.'

The boy looked up. 'Like . . . nobody's been in here?'

'No.'

'Never ever? How long have you lived here?'

'Almost seven years.'

'You don't hang with anybody?'

'No. That's what works best for me. Being alone.'

Ezra's smile bloomed for the first time. It came out slowly, wistful and melancholy. It unsettled Geiger to see it on such a young face.

'Yeah,' the boy said. 'I'm not Mr. Cool either.'

There was a continual stutter in Geiger's experience of things — in sound, sight, and action. It was as if he were reading a book, a story about Ezra and himself, and every few seconds it all paused — balanced for a moment on a temporal cusp while he turned the page — and then the story resumed. He was aware that the sensation bled into his physical state as well, a minute hesitation in his breathing and heartbeat accompanying the stutter.

Every few feet, Ezra stopped his tour of the floor and turned around to view the masterpiece. 'It changes,' he said. 'When you move to a different place, it looks different.' He leaned against a wall and folded his arms. 'Know what it's like? It's like a kaleidoscope.'

'Yes. It is.'

'My dad would really like it. He knows a lot about art.'

'He buys and sells art?'

'Uh-huh. Goes all over the world. That's why Mom got me in the divorce, 'cuz he isn't around a lot — which is sort of why they got divorced in the first place, I guess.'

His shrug was almost lost within Geiger's shirt. He looked like some woeful survivor from a disaster — the oversized clothes, the discolored

166

flesh on his face and arms, the solemn look of shock. A slow flush started to rise on the boy's face like an infusion of dye.

'Why didn't he call me?' Ezra asked. Anger screwed his voice into a wounded sound, as if invisible hands had hold of his throat. 'Where *is* he? Why didn't he *call*?'

The boy's yelp buzzed inside Geiger's ears like the whine of insects. He swiveled his neck to the left but the click wouldn't come. He needed it. He needed the sound and sensation of realignment, of pieces sliding into their proper place. He turned his neck to the right. The vertebrae refused to obey.

'I *hate* him!' Ezra smacked the wall with his palms, and the action seemed to recharge him and propel him unsteadily toward Geiger. 'He left me behind. That's what he did, right?' He stopped inches from Geiger, his outrage already dying out, doused by a heavy sadness. 'How could he do that?' It was not a question born of confusion or disbelief but a statement of wonder. He went back to the couch, sat down, and stared at the patterns in the floor, 'I can't believe how bad I feel,' he said. 'I've never felt anywhere near this bad.'

Ezra had known different degrees of betrayal: a friend turning cold and distant, a music teacher stinging him with an insult, a bully humiliating him in a locker room. The divorce had been a dual betrayal — in the end, neither his mother nor his father loved him enough to put him before their own discontent — but he was in new emotional territory now.

167

The cat came to Geiger, got up on his hind legs, and started using Geiger's pants as a scratching post. Geiger picked him up by the scruff of the neck and perched him on his shoulder. The boy smiled in spite of himself.

'He likes it up there, huh?'

'Ezra, do you want to go to the police?'

'You'd take me to the police?'

'I can't go in with you, but I'll take you there if you want. There's a precinct nearby.'

'What'll the police do with me?'

'They'd take you somewhere and look after you until your mother got here.'

Images of cramped rooms with cots and men with handcuffs on their belts crept into the boy's mind. He saw windows with dark bars.

'Somewhere like what?'

'Somewhere for children. Someplace safe.'

'I'm safe here, aren't I?'

'I think so.'

'What do you mean? Do they know where you live?'

'No,' said Geiger, 'they don't. But what I'm trying to say is' — he struggled to line up the words — 'I don't know who those men are. I don't know what they're capable of finding out.'

To the boy, the statement shimmered with menace. He'd had only a second's look at one of the men, but it was enough. That morning, his father had already gone when he'd awakened. His father had left a note: 'Got early meeting. Keep door double-locked and put chain on. I'll call later. Dad.' He'd had an Eggo waffle, gone back to his room, and started practicing his

168

violin. He'd forgotten about the chain and was so absorbed in his music that he hadn't heard them jimmy the door. He'd gotten just a glimpse of the black man lunging at him before the duct tape had blinded him.

Everything about the event had felt unreal, as if he'd suddenly become a character in one of those stories where someone is plucked from this life and flung into a magical realm where the enemies of goodness use their superpowers to unleash evil in the world. He remembered that when the men put him in the trunk he thought he was going to die — not immediately, but soon. That idea was utterly new to his mind, and it had changed him.

'I want to stay here — with you — till Mom comes.'

'All right.'

'Can we get something for pain?'

'Yes. What?'

'I don't know. Anything.'

'All right. But you stay here. I'll go.'

Geiger took the cat from his shoulder and dropped him on the couch, and he curled up in Ezra's lap and closed his eye. Geiger checked his pockets for cash and went to the door.

'I'm going to set the locks, so don't touch the keypads. You could . . . trigger things.'

'Like what?'

'Just don't touch anything.'

'Okay.'

'Promise?'

'I said okay, didn't I? I'm not going anywhere. Can I watch TV?'

'I don't have a TV.'

'You don't have a TV? For real?'

'Yes. For real.'

'And when you get the medicine, get some *food* food, okay?'

'All right, some food food, too.'

★ ★ ★

When Harry met Geiger at the diner for breakfast, it was usually earlier in the day. Now, as he and Lily slid into a booth, he noticed that the sun was higher in the sky and that its rays followed a more direct route through the large windows. His stomach felt like it was the site of a rugby scrum on a muddy field. The smell of food commanded various juices to start flowing, and as he sat with Lily beside him, his stomach's rumblings were so loud that the two teenage girls in the next booth giggled at the noise.

His roiling gut was playing havoc with his concentration, making it hard for him to focus on the Butch-and-Sundance question: who *are* those guys? He also had no idea what they were really after, which made it all the harder to know how to outsmart them. He did have one consolation, though: right now Hall was watching a blip on a screen as it crisscrossed the streets of New York. The tracking device riding around in that cab ought to keep him busy for at least a little while.

Lily was looking out the front window, locking in on one passerby after another, her head swiveling as she followed them out of her field of vision. When the two of them used to come here

170

on weekends armed with the *Times*, Lily would read Harry's obits aloud as if they were Shakespearean soliloquies, adding her own touches of passion and drama.

Harry put a hand on her shoulder. He could feel the rounded bumps of bones under her thin skin. He leaned to her ear.

'Hey, Lily. You remember this place? Remember reading — '

'Jesus! What happened to you?'

It was Rita, putting steaming coffee down in front of Harry as she gawked at his swollen, livid temple. Harry was so distracted he'd forgotten about the battle wounds.

'I'm okay.'

'Sure you are — and I'm still a natural blonde.' Rita leaned in closer. 'Really, Harry, what the hell happened? And don't tell me, 'You should see the other guy.''

Harry grinned, which made him wince. 'Actually, that's right on the money, doll. Swear to God.'

'You need some ice on that.'

'Okay. And have you got some Advil?'

She nodded and went back behind the counter. Harry put a hand up to his face. It didn't feel like his, and now that he thought about it, very little of his body and brain felt like the *him* he'd lived with for so long — from his throbbing head and sore groin to his dulled focus and softening heart. He felt in between lifetimes, afloat in some shifting temporal goo. He dumped three doses of cream into his coffee, sucked the vapors in, and took a grateful sip.

Rita held an ice-filled ziplock baggie and a container of Advil out to him. 'Here.'

'Thanks.' He put the bag against his face. It felt wonderful.

'And who've we got here?' she asked, nodding toward Lily.

'Lily. My little sister.'

'Nice to meetcha, hon,' said Rita.

When Lily didn't respond, Rita raised an eyebrow. But then a memory surfaced and a look of astonishment came into her eyes.

'Your *sister*? The one you used to come here with way back?' She took a closer look. 'Yes, yes, I remember. *Lily*.' Her cheeks tightened with sadness. 'Oh my — Harry, what happened?'

'She broke,' Harry sighed, 'and her warranty had run out.' He popped five pills into his mouth and washed them down with more coffee. 'She doesn't really talk, and she's been in an institution a long time.'

Rita clucked and shook her head. 'Poor thing.'

'I've, uh, got her for the day.'

'Gonna take her to see the fireworks tonight?'

'Jeez — July fourth. Forgot all about it. Nah, we won't be watching the fireworks.'

'You eating?' Rita asked.

'Until I pass out or throw up.'

'Charming. And sis?'

'I don't know. I'll try and feed her.'

Rita's nose crinkled up, and she leaned closer to Lily and sniffed. 'I think she needs to go to the bathroom, Harry. She gone lately?'

'Uh-uh.' He sniffed too. 'Jeez, I didn't even notice.'

'Does she — go by herself?'

172

Embarrassed, Harry shrugged. 'I don't know.'

'Jesus, Harry — you don't know a helluva lot. Didn't they give you a list or something?'

'Who?'

'The home.'

'Oh. No, I — I was in kind of a hurry. Rita, could you do me a favor and check the ladies' room to see if the coast is clear, so I can take her in there?'

'You can't go in there, Harry. That place has more traffic than the Holland Tunnel.'

They both looked at Lily. A sparrow had landed on the windowsill outside and Lily was watching it watch her. Every time it cocked and recocked its tiny head, Lily did the same, as if conversing in a silent avian language.

'Christ,' sighed Rita, 'I'll take her.'

'You're a lifesaver, Rita.'

Harry grabbed Rita's hand and gave it a tight squeeze. Holding her hand felt good, and abruptly he realized that he might start weeping. He had no idea why.

'Harry,' Rita said. 'I can't take her unless you let go of me.'

'Sorry.' Harry let go of Rita and took Lily by the wrist. 'C'mon, kiddo.' He stepped out of the booth and helped Lily stand up.

'The birds . . . ' she said.

Rita wrapped her arm around Lily's waist. 'Let's go, sweetie.'

As she steered Lily toward a narrow hallway, Rita hollered to the counter. 'Manny! Gimme a chedlette, bacon crisp, nuke the homeys. Carla, watch mine for a minute.'

Rita and her ward disappeared into the shadows, and Harry sat back down. The coffee was beginning to pacify the ache in his head, so he tried to unscramble his thoughts by making a mental list of the issues he needed to sort out.

One: Hall had gotten past the firewall on the website. He didn't think that this was possible without a legitimate in, so maybe he should try to contact the referral for some dope on these guys. But Hall had used Colicos, the scrap metal guy, as his reference, and it would be a major hassle getting to him.

Two: *Could* Hall track people by cell phone signal? If he had somebody inside Verizon or Sprint or wherever, he could get that kind of information for a price.

Three: What the hell was he going to do with Lily? He didn't have the cash to pay for a rental car or a cab to drive her all the way back to the home in New Rochelle, and he didn't have the nurse's number so he could call and tell her to come pick Lily up. For now at least, it would have to be a brother-and-sister act.

'Mission accomplished.'

It was Rita. She eased Lily down in the booth and put a plate of food in front of Harry.

'She was wearing a diaper, so now she's not,' Rita reported. 'You might want to think about picking some up for her. And Harry — she said something.'

Harry picked up a forkful of eggs but before eating said, 'Yeah, she likes to sing songs.'

Rita shook her head. 'No, she *said* something. She said, 'Tinkle.''

The past and all its lighter-than-air dreams closed in on Harry like a force field. He put his fork back down on the plate and stared into his sister's dark, wishing-well eyes.

'She said that? 'Tinkle'?'

'Yeah. You know, when she was on the toilet peeing.'

Harry felt Rita's hand on his shoulder and then realized that tears were sliding down his cheeks. He reached across and rubbed his sister's arm softly.

'Jesus, Lily. You're still in there somewhere, aren't you?'

Rita gave his shoulder a squeeze and said, 'I'm gonna tell you something, Harry. You're a good man. The way she is? Not every guy would take care of a sister like this.'

Harry sat back and wiped the tears away with his palm. 'Not true, Rita, but thanks.' He picked up his fork. 'Funny, though — you're the second person to say that today.'

'That makes it two against one, Harry, so I must be right.'

'Yeah, how can I argue with you and a cabbie from Louisiana?' He shoveled some eggs into his mouth, but even before he finished the bite he stopped chewing. That cabbie: suddenly he heard the driver's drawling voice say, *I got a sister, too.*

His senses ping-ponged from uncertainty to paranoia and back as he replayed the scene with the taxi driver in his head. Almost immediately he was sure: he had never told the cabbie that Lily was his sister.

He and Lily didn't look anything alike now,

but could the driver have overheard some part of their conversation and made a reasonable deduction about who Lily was? Or — more likely — had the cabbie known who Harry and Lily were before they got into the cab? Geiger said the boy thought there had been *three* men. Harry had to swallow hard to force the food all the way down his throat.

'Rita, is there a back way out of here?'

'I thought you were starved.'

'I am. Is there?'

'Yeah, down the hall. Goes out to the alley.'

Harry stood up and got Lily to her feet, took a few bills from his pocket, and put them on the table.

'If a guy with red hair and a mustache comes in, you didn't see us. He might have a southern accent, too.'

'You're giving me the creeps, Harry.'

'That makes two of us.'

Harry suddenly grabbed Rita's startled face in his hands and gave her a hard, quick kiss.

'See you,' he said, and pulled Lily toward the hall.

Out in the alley, the morning heat was cooking the pavement's patina of garbage scum. Harry took hold of Lily's skinny forearm, pinned her behind him, and peeked out from the corner like a mouse checking out cat-ruled terrain. Cars sped by playing beat-the-light, power chords roared out of the apartment window of some heavy-metal freak, and two women tottering on silver stiletto heels walked their little foo-foos on rhinestoned leashes. Everything was loud and busy and moving, but Harry picked out a taxi parked half a dozen cars in from the corner on the opposite side of the street. The shade of the trees turned the profile of the driver inside into a smudged silhouette. The head was moving — talking, or bobbing to the radio, or chewing something — but Harry couldn't tell if it was the good ol' boy or not.

He leaned back out of view and turned to Lily. She stood against the wall with her eyes closed.

'So what do you think, sis?' Harry said. 'Your redneck buddy one of the bad guys?'

'*I see you, baby*,' she said, her eyes still shut. She smiled.

Harry sighed so deeply he heard himself do it. ' "Tinkle." I can't believe you said that.'

A stoner came down the sidewalk, nursing a butt and scratching his patchy attempt at a beard.

'Hey, kid,' said Harry.

The teenager turned. His T-shirt read, 'Blow it up and start over.'

'Yeah?' he said.

'You want to make twenty bucks?'

The kid's middle finger sprang up. 'Fuck off, perv.' He flicked his cigarette at Harry and kept walking.

'Hey, wait, it's not like that! *Thirty* bucks!'

The stoner stopped and looked back. 'To do what?'

'See that cab parked up there? I need you to cross the street, get a look at the driver, keep going to the corner, come back, and tell me what he looks like.'

'Who're you? James Bond?'

'That's right. I'm James fucking Bond. Deal?'

'Fuck yeah.'

As the guy started across the street, Harry gave him a loud whisper. 'And don't be too obvious.'

The stoner nodded and walked toward the taxi. Harry watched as the kid took out a cigarette and then leaned right down into the window of the cab. The driver's darkened profile turned to the stoner; a moment later, Harry saw a flash of amber light.

'Jesus,' Harry said. He leaned back behind the wall and waited for the kid to return. When he didn't show, Harry peeked out again and came nose to nose with him. He flinched and felt a hot zap of pain slice through the side of his face.

'Hey, Double-oh-seven,' the stoner said. 'How ya doin'?'

'What'd he look like?'

'Cash first.'

Harry pulled his wad out, peeled off three tens, and put them in the kid's outstretched palm.

'So?'

'Red hair. Nice thick 'stache. Baseball cap.'

Harry felt an odd satisfaction — his hypothesis was right — and it amused him to think of the button-sized tracer stuck to the cab's backseat. But he also felt a nasty tingling in his hands. He wanted them around the cabbie's neck.

'Is he the guy you're looking for?' the stoner asked.

'Thanks for the help, kid.'

'Sure, man. Rock on.' He flashed a peace sign and went on his way.

Finding the answer to one question only triggered an avalanche of others. He still had no idea who he was dealing with; he didn't even know how many people were after him. But all that could wait. For now, only one thing mattered. He put his arm around Lily and started her down the alley.

'C'mon, sis. We got to find Geiger.'

*   *   *

Mitch had parked a quarter of the way down the block so he could see the front of the diner but couldn't be seen from inside the place. As he waited for Boddicker and his sister to emerge, he occasionally glanced down at the blinking blue light in the center grid of a black, PDA-sized instrument on the seat beside him.

His cell phone rang and he picked up. 'Yeah.'

'Still got him, Mitch?' It was Hall.

'Yeah, still in the diner.' His molasses drawl was gone. 'Where are you?'

'Upper West Side. We're cruising. They got a hit on the kid's cell.'

'How's Ray doing?'

'He's stitched up. Overall, I'd say he looks much better. He's got that harelip thing going on — ladies're gonna love it.'

Mitch took note. Mean, dead-on sarcasm meant that Hall was worried. Not just stressed out but wired in a big-picture way. It was bad to hear but good to know.

After Hall hung up, Mitch continued watching the entrance to the diner. His mind, meanwhile, was building a bracket of strategic configurations in case the job went south. A week ago it had tasted like a piece of cake, but not anymore. Although Mitch thought the odds were still in their favor, at this point he had to work up plans for worst-case scenarios. He called it his 'fuck or be fucked' mode, and the key to it was staying a couple of steps ahead of the enemy, whoever that might be. Ideally, Hall would continue to run the show — the man was smart, resourceful, and ruthless. And Mitch had always worked well with Ray, who would walk through a wall before he'd go around it. But if this operation completely blew up and it came down to a body count, then so be it. He'd be the one doing the counting.

13

The place was otherworldly, more hell than heaven. Blaring, combative colors fought against a grab bag of aromas and a shifting mélange of sounds. Shiny oranges and reds and browns, voices and music and mechanical buzzes, scents of oil and cinnamon and fish and meat all collided and intertwined.

Geiger stood just inside the doorway, stunned by the onslaught. He'd never been in a Burger King or any other fast-food establishment. He'd been in Carmine's restaurant and the diner, but this, in every way, was a different experience. He moved a few steps closer to the counter and its three lines of customers. Looking at the wall-mounted array of menus dense with words and numbers and pictures was like trying to decipher a map of the galaxy.

'Hey, man. Are you on line or what?' A head poked into Geiger's view from behind him; it was a white kid in a do-rag wearing half a dozen cheap chains heavy with gewgaws.

Geiger looked blankly at him. He felt suspended and seized up, as if he'd forgotten how to breathe. His hearing seemed affected as well — he was having trouble locating the sources of sounds.

'Visit this planet much, man?' said the kid as he moved past Geiger toward the counter.

Geiger took his place in one of the lines and

repeated Ezra's order to himself while he waited.

Finally it was his turn. 'What do you want?' said the woman behind the counter. The brim of her BK-emblazoned baseball cap had a thumb-sized stain at the left edge where she had tugged on it with greasy fingers a thousand times.

'Just get me a burger, and fries, and a Coke.'

'Then you want a meal?'

'Yes. I want a meal.' Geiger studied the woman's frown. Why else would he, or anyone else, be in here?

'Which one?'

'A burger. Fries. Coke.'

'Which *meal*, mister?' Her thumb pointed at the backlit menus above and behind her. 'One? Two? Three? Which?'

'I don't care,' Geiger said.

'Then just pick one,' she said.

'Meal number one.'

'Okay. Mustard-ketchup-pickles-onions?'

'What?'

'On the burger. Mustard-ketchup-pickles-onions?'

It was spoken as a mindless recitation, a litany as automatic as a blink or a breath. But to Geiger it made the surface of things ripple absurdly. Mustard-ketchup-pickles-onions. He couldn't put it out of his mind. It became an audio loop, a Mobius word strip, a child's nonsense rhyme. Geiger became aware that his jaw was as tight as a bear trap.

'What'll it be, mister?'

'Everything,' Geiger said. 'I want everything.'

* * *

182

Ezra sat in Geiger's chair, at Geiger's desk. The cat lay in his favorite spot, just to the right of the keyboard, his gray silken stomach exposed. He prompted Ezra's hand with a tap of his paw whenever a minute had passed between scratchings.

Ezra stared at the long row of black three-ringed binders before him. They were labeled chronologically, starting with 'Jan-June 1999' and running right up to the present. He felt as if the binders were calling out to him, all of them whispering, 'Open me.' He slid the keyboard to the side, pulled one of the binders toward him, and laid it on its side. Nearly two dozen tabs jutted from the stack of pages. His fingers randomly found one, and then he opened the binder and began to read.

- <u>DATE/TIME</u>: 5-22-2004/3 A.M.
- <u>LOCATION</u>: Ludlow St.
- <u>CLIENT</u>: NYPD detective
- <u>REFERRAL</u>: Carmine/ASAP
- <u>ISSUE</u>: Detective's 24-year-old daughter missing
- <u>JONES</u>: Daughter's ex-boyfriend, 25
- <u>DATA</u>: Daughter missing 3 days. Detective has 'real bad feeling' about ex-boyfriend, and rather than arrest him he went to Carmine for a favor.
- <u>SETUP</u>: Jones strapped in barber chair, clad only in boxer shorts. Muscular. Shaved head. Room fully lit. Portable cart w/aerosol spray, straight razor, blindfold.

Ezra turned a few pages, scanning them. This time, the word 'razor' caught his eye. He went back to the top of the page and read more slowly again.

G: Do you know where Lisa is, Victor?

Jones: I told you, man — I don't know where she is! You think I messed with her just 'cuz she broke up with me?

G: Victor, I know what you told me, but I think you are lying — and I'm usually right about these things.

————G *takes straight razor from cart, swivels blade out of sheath.*

G: Victor, pay close attention to what I'm saying now, because it's crucial that you understand what is to come. I've honed this razor to such a sharpness that precise cuts barely cause any pain.

Jones: Oh man, this is so fucked.

————G *takes vial of aerosol freeze spray from cart.*

G: Victor, this works immediately and wears off quickly.

———— G *takes one of Jones's fingers and sprays the tip. Jones flinches, stiffens.*

Jones: Motherfuck — that shit's cold!

————G *puts down aerosol, then cuts tip of Jones's middle finger*
with razor. Blood brims from cut.

Jones: Fuck, man! You cut me!

G: But it didn't hurt. Did it, Victor?

————G *prepares to make another cut.*

Jones: No, it didn't fucking hurt!

G: Victor, you're only here to tell me the truth. Nothing else. I'm going to blindfold you and ask you again about Lisa — where she is, if she is still alive — and then I'm going to start slicing parts of you —

———*Jones becomes more agitated.*

Jones: No, no, no, man. That's totally not —

G: — but I'm going to apply the spray first, and that, along with the blade's sharpness, means you will feel the pressure of the blade, but no pain.

Jones: Jesus, are you fucking crazy, man?

G: Victor, blood carries oxygen through the body. If blood loss is gradual, you can lose up to twenty-five percent of it — about one and a quarter liters — before your organs start to shut down from oxygen deprivation —

Jones: Jesus Christ, man! Don't cut me!

G: — so the heavier the bleeding, the less time it takes to die. But you won't know how much you're bleeding, or how long you have to live.

———*G takes a blindfold and ties it around Jones. Sprays Jones's face, chest, arms, groin. Jones flinches, whimpers.*

G: I'm going to start cutting now, Victor.

Jones: C'mon, man. Wait. This is fucked. Don't do it!

———*G folds blade back inside sheath and draws blunt edge of sheath across Jones's left arm. Jones struggles in straps.*

Jones: Oh fuck!

G: Victor, where is Lisa?

Jones: I told you, man! I don't —

G: You're wasting time and blood, Victor.

185

———G pulls down Jones's boxer shorts.
Jones flinches wildly.
Jones: No, no! Fuck, man, no! Not my —
———G grabs Jones by the throat.
G: Next question, Victor. Do you want to be cockless or heartless?

Ezra slammed the binder shut, as if locking in a monster before it could reach out and grab him. The cat jumped up and leapt from the desk.

Ezra slumped back into Geiger's chair. He would spend the rest of his life with this day tucked into a pocket of his memory, and over time it would become a yellowing receipt itemizing the cost of what he'd lost in the past twenty-four hours. And scrawled at the top would be the question he now uttered aloud:

'Why did you save me?'

⋆   ⋆   ⋆

Amsterdam Avenue was a tangle of noises. Geiger felt vulnerable, almost defenseless, and he was still trying to absorb not only his encounter with Burger King but also his visit to a drugstore. He had never been in one of those, either, and the experience of confronting a palisade of brightly colored containers in the 'Pain and Sleep' aisle had been nearly paralytic. There seemed to be curatives for every sort of pain and dosages for every person and situation. It had taken him ten minutes to decide on a small bottle of Children's Advil.

He turned down his block. Up ahead on the

186

sidewalk, sitting in his folding chair with his scarred crutch at his feet, was the man everyone in the neighborhood called Mr. Memz. The last thing his right foot had ever stepped on was a land mine in a jungle in Vietnam, and he'd come home without half the leg. His sanity was often questioned by those who walked by, but his ability to memorize vast amounts of text had made him a local legend.

To supplement his disability checks, Mr. Memz sat at his outpost and took wagers from passersby on whether he could recite, verbatim, a page from any of the half dozen books he had on display on a portable card table. The bettor would declare the size of his wager, pick a book, choose a random page, and read the first four words of a sentence aloud. Mr. Memz would then begin his recitation, ripe with the drama, humor, or passion that the selection, in his estimation, called for. He almost never made a mistake, and even then most of his customers rarely pointed it out.

As always, Mr. Memz was dressed in military-issue camouflage, and as Geiger approached he was stubbing out a Newport.

'How you doing, BT?' said Mr. Memz. 'BT' was the nickname he had bestowed on Geiger years ago. It stood for 'Big Talker.'

'I don't have time today,' Geiger said as he went by.

'Whoa,' said Mr. Memz, grinning. '"I don't have time today." Shit, man — that's five whole words. I don't think you've ever said three words in a row. You keep running on at the mouth and

I won't be able to get a word in edgewise.'

Geiger stopped. He had seen something on the table, and the image pulled at him like a harpoon in his back. He returned to Mr. Memz's station.

'So what's it gonna be today, BT?'

'Two dollars.'

'*Two dollars?* You think I live on Twinkies? You know what a GI with stumps gets from the government every month? And have I ever told you what 'Nam Vet' stands for?'

'Yes.'

''Not a motherfucking vacation ever taken.''

'Okay, five dollars.'

'Now, that's a number a man could get to like, BT,' said Mr. Memz, and his fingertips scratched at his granite beard.

Geiger put down his Burger King and drugstore bags, and picked up a well-thumbed copy of Jack London's *The Sea-Wolf*.

'Nice choice, BT.' Mr. Memz stretched back in his chair. 'Give me a smoke.'

Geiger took out a pack of Luckies and nudged one out. Mr. Memz stuck it in his lips as Geiger brandished his plastic Bic lighter, but Mr. Memz waved it off.

'Shit, man, have a little self-respect. Gonna kill yourself, do it with style, huh?' He picked up his worn chrome Zippo from the table. 'This baby's been with me since Nam. I used it in-country forty times a day. Worked every time, even in that endless, motherfucking rain.' He flicked it open and grinned at the singular *click*. 'Great fucking sound.'

Mr. Memz talked more than any person Geiger had ever met, but Geiger liked listening to his recitals. And he liked watching the way Mr. Memz moved, how he'd refashioned his approach to a world created for two-legged men. Decades of whiskey and smoke had worn away the edges of his voice, making it a gruff foghorn. Sometimes, when there was bourbon in his blood, Mr. Memz would tug on his ponytail and talk about the friendship between physical pain and his body, and Geiger would pay close attention. The man knew all about pain.

Mr. Memz lit his cigarette and left it smoldering in his lips. 'Let's go.'

Geiger paged through the book. Without understanding how, he knew what he was looking for, and though the small letters shifted on the paper like jittery ants, he found the passage almost immediately.

''He sprang for me with a half-roar, gripping my arm,'' Geiger read, still unused to the rolling tumble of his voice inside his ears. Mr. Memz's eyes looked up into his, and he began to speak, words and smoke coming out of him like a salvo of shots.

''He sprang for me with a half-roar, gripping my arm. I had steeled myself to brazen it out, though I was trembling inwardly . . . ''

★   ★   ★

'' . . . though I was trembling inwardly,'' the nine-year-old boy read aloud from the book.

The boy's father sat before the stone hearth,

189

his thick body clothed in faded denim overalls. His right hand pulled at his dense clipped beard. He drew deeply on his cigarette, and as he exhaled the smoke turned pale amber from the fire's light.

The cabin was the work of a master carpenter. The walls and cathedral roof were made of massive split logs. Windows were set high, so the view from within was only of lush treetops and infinite sky. The floor was an astonishing work of art, a detailed re-creation of Bosch's Garden of Earthly Delights, the thousands of inlays a testament to virtuosity and obsession.

''He had gripped me by the biceps with his single hand, and when that grip tightened I wilted and shrieked aloud. My feet went out from under me. I simply could not stand upright and endure the agony.''

'Stop now, son. He is overcome with pain, but the question is — why?'

'Because . . . because he is weak?'

'Weak, yes — but not of the body. True strength has nothing to do with muscles. His mind is weak because he doesn't know pain — and what we don't know, we fear. And it is fear that makes us weak.' He sucked on his cigarette. 'Watch now.' He blew on the tip, sending the loose ash drifting away, revealing the hot orange flush. He lowered the cigarette and ground it into the top of his hand without a flinch or a sound.

'You see, son? Not the body. The mind.'

⋆ ⋆ ⋆

Geiger became aware that Mr. Memz had finished his recitation and was now sitting back in his chair. With his eyes on Geiger, he flicked his butt away and offered up the smile of a charming lunatic. Geiger took a five-dollar bill from his pocket and held it out to Mr. Memz, who took the money and kissed it.

'Question, BT.'

'What?'

'During my splendid performance, you weren't looking at the page and following along. So how do you know I got it right?'

'I've read it before. Many times.'

'Why didn't you say so, man?'

'Because I'd forgotten.'

He started away. It was a downhill journey, and the spinning earth tugged at him. The heat rising off the street turned the view into a rippling, molten curtain. Two men at the entrance to the auto body shop wielded clamorous pneumatic tools, loosening bolts on the wheel hubs of a jacked-up, blood-red Magnum. The sun made the sweat on their bare mahogany backs a glistening polish.

A flash of light pulled at Geiger's eyes. He turned and saw a silver Lexus with tinted windows cruising slowly up the street. Geiger crouched down behind a parked car and watched the Lexus pass by and then pull over at Mr. Memz's post. The driver's window came down and smoke drifted out from inside the car. A hand came out holding up a six-inch square card, its glossy surface glinting in the sun. Mr. Memz leaned forward in his chair and looked closely at the card. His lips moved, but Geiger couldn't hear what he said.

The dark glass slid up and the Lexus pulled away. Geiger remembered that Hall's insurance card said he drove a Lexus, but he couldn't remember what color. His memory wouldn't give up the information. He watched the car turn onto Amsterdam and drive out of sight, and then he moved quickly to Mr. Memz, leaning down to his ear from behind.

'Mr. Memz.'

The vet seized up in a flinch as if someone had hollered, 'Incoming!' He twisted around.

'Fuck, man! Don't be coming up on me like that!'

'I need to ask you something,' Geiger said.

Mr. Memz's back rose and fell with a deep breath. 'BT, I think I liked you better when you kept your mouth shut.'

'The Lexus. What did the driver want?'

'He showed me a photograph of somebody who looked a lot like you. Asked if I'd seen the guy around and said his name was Geiger. That your name, BT? Geiger?'

Where did they get a photograph of him? Geiger felt his ruptured seams being tested again. The more the world poured into him, the wider they stretched.

'What did you tell him?'

Mr. Memz's thumbnail raked his beard. ''I will give no information or take part in any action which might be harmful to my comrades.''

'What?'

'Article Four, man. Code of Conduct. You

192

don't give up your own.' Mr. Memz smiled. 'I told the guy I'd never seen you.'

As Geiger rose, he saw a double image of Mr. Memz that was gauzy at its edges. He knew what it meant, and what was on the way.

'Thank you,' he said, and headed for home.

'Hey, BT,' Mr. Memz called out. 'Dude's got sniper's eyes! I know 'em when I see 'em, man, so watch your skinny ass!'

* * *

As soon as he entered the code to the front door lock and stepped inside, Geiger saw the boy sitting at the desk. Three of the black binders were spread open before him.

Ezra slowly turned to Geiger, his eyes ablaze. 'This is what you do? *This?*'

The pressure in Geiger's head was almost unbearable, but he had the presence of mind to reach for the keypad and punch in the interior code.

'What's *wrong* with you?' cried the boy, rising from the chair. He was frantic, panicky, his body swaying and his arms waving, like a jack-in-the-box set free of its coil. The boy's movements left stuttering trails across Geiger's vision.

'Don't talk now,' Geiger said. His voice reached him from somewhere far away. The visitation was very close now; the tiny lights had come calling. The textbooks called it the 'aura' — a rare, warping prognostic of the migraine.

'If this is what you do, then why didn't you do it to *me?*'

193

The boy was yelling now, the volume ramping up the pitch of his voice and whetting it. His words cut like a knife.

'Don't . . . talk,' Geiger said.

Geiger started toward him, but the movement triggered a vertiginous light-headedness and he stopped. He heard his own gathering breath; it roared in his ears as if coming from a stranger standing behind him. He dropped the bags and turned for the CD rack. He'd need the music before he went into the closet. He tried to focus on the countless shimmering jewel cases, but the slightest shift of eye in socket rendered the titles on their spines indecipherable. The aura's magnitude was beyond his past experiences — the degree of distortion, the recasting of light into barbed stars, the conversion of symmetry into chaos and flux. When he reached toward a shelf, the assault began, an incendiary device going off in his skull, near the crest, sending white-hot tendrils down toward the backs of his eyes.

But Ezra, his fear running wild, was not finished. '*Why did you save me?*' he shouted.

'*Stop!*' Geiger yelled, and then the migraine hit him full force. He howled and fell to his knees as if smitten.

Ezra stumbled back against the desk. 'What . . . what's the matter with you?!'

Swaying, Geiger grabbed hold of his temples. He made a noise that might have been a word.

'I'm sorry!' said the boy. 'I'm sorry! Please don't flip out on me!'

Geiger started crawling for the sanctuary of

194

the closet, his fingers feeling the smooth marquetry, his eyes shut tight to keep the light at bay. He extended his right hand until it brushed against the closet door, then turned the cold brass knob and dragged himself inside. He pulled the door closed and let the darkness come.

Gradually he became aware that Ezra was calling to him.

'Geiger! Say something!'

'Music,' Geiger croaked. 'Put on the music.'

He lay in the dark, his right forearm a pillow for his head, his left arm holding his knees up close to his chest. His brain was on fire. Something had been breached. The pain was breathtaking, and now it had a face. Geiger could see it: a phantom gaining flesh and blood.

Then he heard music. A single strand of it — elegant, melancholy, consoling. He closed his eyes. He could see the colored puddles of sound, taste the notes, feel them falling on him like a cold rain, cooling the fire in his mind.

★ ★ ★

When Ezra had heard Geiger's plea for music, he had dashed for the CD rack but then swerved to the couch when he caught sight of his violin case. Now he stood at the closet door, his trembling fingers drawing the bow across the instrument's strings. Nestled beneath his chin, the violin was more than a comfort; it felt like crucial ballast, the weight of something known and good that could prevent him from being tossed about by the maelstrom all around him. He closed his eyes, and as he played, there came a flicker of understanding — he, too, needed the music to ease the pain and take him to his own place of peace.

14

Harry had always steered clear of Internet cafés. He didn't want somebody sitting next to him, craning a neck. And he didn't trust these places — even if they had online security, it would be useless. But desperate times called, so here he sat at a counter in Charlotte's Web Café, at one of its six laptops. Lily sat to his left, her spindly fingers picking walnut crumbs off a scone, holding each up close to her eyes like a forty-niner admiring a shiny, newfound nugget.

Outside, the sun was a shimmering white wafer turning the city into a skillet. It was the kind of heat that turns a driver's honk into an insult, a frown into a threat. But the café was well air-conditioned, which made Harry inclined to forgive the low-fat jazz that simpered from the wall speakers. And the coffee he'd bought from the Asian guy working behind the counter wasn't bad either.

Harry rolled a sip of coffee around in his mouth and thought about how to word his plea to Geiger. He had logged on to AIM as Stickler and checked out the status of GGGG. Geiger was active. What should he write? How about 'I'm about to lose it, man. I hurt all over and I've got a crazy person in tow and those fuckers are following me. Just tell me your address.' How had it come to this? He didn't even know where the one person he considered a comrade lived.

He'd thought about calling Carmine and asking for help or at least a place to lie low, but the man gave him the creeps. He'd last seen him a year ago, at a session. The Jones had been supplying Carmine with bathroom fixtures for some town-houses, and Carmine had been tipped off that, as he'd put it to Harry, 'the prick likes to spell 'refurbished' N-E-W.' The Jones had caved within minutes while Carmine watched, sipping Chartreuse VEP Green that cost one hundred and eighty-five dollars. After Harry had repacked the Jones for transport back to one of Carmine's safe houses — an oxymoron if Harry had ever heard one — Carmine had come to him, squeezed his shoulder, and said:

'Harry, Harry. Our boy's a thing of beauty, isn't he? It's like watching a chess match in a boxing ring.'

'Nicely put, sir.'

'Kasparov and Ali rolled into one. He's a genius, our boy.'

Harry still remembered the chuckle that had finished the exchange; it was as smooth as the perfectly folded silk handkerchief that peeked from Carmine's suit pocket. Carmine served as a reminder to Harry that some people did exactly what they pleased and got everything they wanted, usually because they had eyes in the back of their heads, a seemingly endless supply of aces and dirks up their sleeves, and no qualms or guilt about using them.

Right now, the only person who seemed knowable to Harry was Geiger. Even though yesterday's bizarre act had sent Harry's world off its axis, Geiger was still his only hope, the one hand that could pull him out of free fall. Geiger was all he had left.

Harry's fingers went to the keyboard.

★ ★ ★

Ezra was still so frightened he couldn't sit still. He wandered through Geiger's loft, staring at the intricate floor as a way to control his panic. Geiger had been in the closet long enough for the CD player to finish a Honegger sonata and get halfway through Fauré's Sonata in E Minor. But Ezra had no idea whether the music was helping. The attack had come so suddenly and looked so violent that to him it seemed entirely possible that death would be the final result.

Ezra opened the closet door. Geiger's fetal position made it difficult to tell if he was breathing, so Ezra gently nudged Geiger's shin with his sneaker's toe. Geiger's left arm instantly pulled his knees in tighter against his chest; he curled up like a pill bug expecting an imminent attack.

'Are you asleep?' Ezra whispered.

He took a step inside and sat down beside Geiger. Leaning back, he stared at himself in the mirrors. That was what his father was: a visible but untouchable reflection. He was a two-weeks-a-year presence, or a voice on the phone, or an IM partner. A burst of heat ran down Ezra's back, equal parts anger and fear. He wondered where his father was. He wished he was dead; he prayed he was safe. He hated him for his selfishness. It had put Ezra in this closet, and now monsters prowled the streets, searching for his scent.

Ezra rose. Careful not to jostle Geiger, he went to the desk and sat in Geiger's chair in front of the computer. The AIM icon at the bottom of the monitor beckoned him. He clicked it, signed in as Guest, and set up a message to BigBossMan, the name on the account his father used for their sessions.

Ezra glanced over at Geiger's dark, tucked figure, and then typed:

GUEST: Its EZBoy. Where are you?

He clicked 'send' and sat back, staring at the boarded-up windows before him. No light made its way through, and only ghosts of the street's shrillest sounds crept in past the soundproofing.

The *ping* of an incoming message straightened Ezra's spine. He took a breath and leaned toward the screen. The upper right-hand quadrant displayed the message in a small, sans-serif font.

STICKLER: hey. its me.

Stickler? Ezra sank back into the soft leather. Who was Stickler? The greeting seemed personal, even intimate. Ezra's hands reached out to the keyboard but only hovered there, his concentration failing him. For a moment he felt almost nauseous with fear — for himself, for his father, for the man in the closet. If Geiger didn't

200

wake up, what then? Ezra had no idea where he was, but he did know that he was locked in from the inside.

Ezra took a long breath and let his fingers fall to the keys.

★　★　★

Harry stared at the message.

GGGG: who are you?

This was absurdity of a new sort, the kind of cosmic joke only a petty God with too much time on his hands would stoop to pull. Harry was so astonished, he spoke aloud without realizing it.

'What the *fuck*?'

Heads all around the café rose, eyes swiveling to locate the boor. Even Lily looked up from her scone project, licking her fingers like a cat cleaning its paws. Harry ignored the gawkers and started typing.

STICKLER: who am i? who are you?
GGGG: this isnt geiger. im ezra.
STICKLER: the kid that got snatched?
GGGG: yes. who are you?
STICKLER: harry, geigers friend, where is he? go get him, right now.
GGGG: hes sleeping.
STICKLER: wake him up.
GGGG: im scared to. something happened to him. something bad.

201

STICKLER: whats that mean?
GGGG: he was really freaky, he had a kind of fit.
STICKLER: fit?
GGGG: screaming and stuff, on his knees, in terrible pain, sort of blinded, then he crawled into a closet and went to sleep on the floor.

Harry stopped. Had Geiger had a stroke? A heart attack? An epileptic seizure? But even as he wondered what had happened, Harry realized that he wasn't shocked at the thought that Geiger might have had a meltdown. The episode at the session room and the decision to take the kid with him had only been a preview. For years he'd thought of Geiger as a man whose enormous strength was matched only by the massive weight of his burdens. Had they finally brought him to his knees? At the first rub of the question, Harry knew he'd been waiting for this moment for a long time.

Harry started typing again.

STICKLER: ill come there then. where are you?
GGGG: what do you mean? im at geigers.
STICKLER: i know. <u>where</u> is that?
GGGG: i dont know. I was blindfolded when he brought me in and all the windows are boarded up. i cant see outside. how come you don't know? i thought you were his friend.

Harry rummaged around in the place where he kept his meager stock of patience, but the cupboard was almost bare. He was stretched thin, fed up with his own trespasses more than anyone else's. And dealing with kids always gave him the heebie-jeebies. Their transparency made him feel clumsy, artless. He was going to have to walk a tightrope to the boy.

> STICKLER: listen, kid. i know youre scared. i dont blame you. but i am his friend. ive just never been to his place. remember there was another guy there when he put you in the car? that was me.
> GGGG: okay. but how are you going to find me? i dont know where i am and im locked in here.
> STICKLER: ill think of something.
> GGGG: hurry.

Frustrated, Harry slammed his palm down on the counter, sending a loud *whomp* rolling through the place. Lily twitched and heads bobbed back up.

'Jesus Christ!' he growled.

The Asian counter guy arrived, hovering at his side, espresso-stained fingers tugging at the beard surrounding his frown.

'You're making too much noise, mister,' he said. 'Much too much.'

Harry said nothing, his eyes locked on the screen.

'Hey, mister? Hear me?'

Harry looked up, molars fused. One word escaped through his teeth. 'Yeah?'

'You're making too much noise.'

'Was I? Sorry.'

'So no more yelling,' said the counter guy. 'People don't want to hear that. Okay?'

Harry placed his palms on the counter and

took a shaky breath.

'I heard you,' he said. 'No more yelling. I got it.'

'Okay,' said the counter guy, and then he leaned toward Lily, who sported a coating of crumbs from her lips to her lap. 'And please, lady. Can you try and be a little neater?' His finger directed her nonexistent attention to a sign on the wall that read, PLEASE KEEP FOOD OFF THE COMPUTERS. He nodded at her. 'Okay, lady? Thanks very much.'

Harry rose from his chair and came nose to nose with the counter guy. He was suddenly so angry that he felt as light as a feather, almost giddy with malice.

'Listen, man,' he said. 'I'll finish soon as I can, without another sound, and then we'll leave. But do *not* talk to her.'

The counter guy framed his response with a faint, inquisitive smile. 'Are you threatening me?' he asked. 'Because, mister, you don't look like you should be threatening anybody.'

Harry's hand went up to his face — he'd forgotten about its battered state. His rush died away instantly, replaced by a wave of confusion and shame.

The laptop called to him with another merry *ding*.

GGGG: you still there? huh?

Hearing the computer's chime, Lily started singing. '*Jingle bell, jingle bell, jingle bell rock . . .* '

204

As she sang, only her wide, pale lips moved, and her frozen stare and immobile body were bizarrely at odds with the lyric.

The counter guy looked at Lily and then turned back to Harry. 'What's wrong with her?'

'I said never mind her, okay?'

But some synapse in Lily was misfiring, and she began singing louder. As her volume rose so did she, standing up with a touch of a wobble.

'She high on something?' asked the counter guy.

'Yeah, high on life,' said Harry. 'Now I'm just going to finish up the IM and then get out of here, okay?'

Lily, still singing, came to the end of the song and raised both arms high. '*That's the jingle bell rock!*'

This last burst took something out of her, and, reeling, she flapped her hands for balance. They came down on the counter, spilling Harry's coffee and spraying the laptops.

'Okay, that's it!' said the counter guy. 'You've both got to leave.'

As the man hustled away for a rag, Harry grabbed Lily and shoved her back down on her stool.

'Stay! Don't move!'

⋆　⋆　⋆

Frantic with worry as he waited for Harry's response, Ezra stood up and stepped away from the computer. He wanted to stomp his feet and

205

yell, but if he did he might wake the monster in the closet. Ezra didn't believe Geiger was a monster, but he was certain there was one living inside him. Ezra had felt its wrath when he'd watched it bring Geiger to his knees, and he didn't want to rouse it again.

Trying to contain his panic, Ezra wandered away from the desk and spied the two bags lying where Geiger had dropped them near the CD racks. He picked up the bag with the Burger King logo, stuck a hand inside, and took out a burger. In two bites he'd devoured half of it, and his head drooped with narcotic pleasure. Then he snapped upright and gave a eureka cry.

'Receipt!'

He tore the Burger King bag apart, French fries flying everywhere.

'Receipt . . . c'mon, receipt!'

But there was none. He snatched up the drugstore bag and shook it upside down. The bottle of Advil fell out, and behind it came a small white slip of paper, drifting slowly toward the floor. Ezra snatched the receipt out of the air and scanned the printed data.

'Yes!'

He lunged for the desk.

★ ★ ★

The counter guy started soaking up the mess with a cloth.

'I said leave, didn't I?'

'Give me a break, man,' said Harry. 'Five minutes. That's all I need. She won't do it again.'

206

'Leave.'

'Three minutes.'

'*Now*,' the counter guy said, and to put an exclamation on the command, he sent a pointed finger down toward the laptop's power button. Harry's hand closed around the guy's forearm and stopped him. He knew he was a clenched fist from disaster.

The counter guy stared at him open-mouthed. 'Let go of my arm or I'll call the cops.'

'Let me send one more IM, man,' Harry said. '*One* more.'

'Just get the hell out of here — and take Miss Jingle Bells with you.'

The guy was practically yelling now, but his words were punctuated by a cheerful *ding*, as another message appeared on the laptop.

GGGG: im near la vida discount drugs at 1474 amsterdam!

Harry reached for the keyboard, but now the counter guy's finger found its mark and landed on the power button. The screen went black.

'Out! Both of you!'

Harry took Lily's hand and pulled her off the stool. They started for the door, the hobbled leading the helpless. But Harry was elated; he had an address, a place to go.

★   ★   ★

Ezra stood at Geiger's desk, reading the IM's new declaration.

207

STICKLER has signed off and cannot receive messages
offline.

He retrieved the half-eaten burger and sat
down again. The cat came by and curled up in
his lap. Ezra fed himself with one hand, stroked
the cat with the other, and refused to cry.

15

Mitch's coffee was cold. He drank coffee day and night, but he hated it cold. When the heat was gone, something happened to the milk and three sugars that left a coating on his tongue, making him scrape it back and forth against the edges of his front teeth.

He poured the coffee out the window and checked the trace locator. Boddicker and his sister were still in the diner, setting a record for the world's longest breakfast. Or maybe Boddicker was spiking his coffee and getting an early start on happy hour. From the look of him, he'd taken a few hits when he'd gotten into the ring with Ray.

Years ago, when Ray had first come aboard, Mitch had sized him in five minutes: big dick, tiny brain, no rearview mirror whatsoever. If you cracked his skull open you'd find IRREGULAR stamped on his frontal lobe. But Mitch had no problem with Ray — the guy had the instincts of a fart, but he knew how to do what he had to do.

Though Mitch trusted his read on Ray, he still found Hall baffling after all these years. Mitch looked at life as a game of football, X's and O's on a chalkboard, and he read people's actions the same way an offensive or defensive coordinator tries to decipher and react to the other team's schemes. With Hall, the X's and O's said one thing, but they didn't always tell the truth. As often as not, the whys of Hall's behavior and decisions completely eluded him.

Hall was not the sum of his parts. He was far from a tight-ass, but he dressed like one, button-down head to toe. He told a great joke, but rarely laughed at anyone else's. He usually went by the book, but he showed obvious contempt for it. He always had your back, but he clearly resented having to watch it. And he was very good at his job but seemed to dislike doing it. Hall was the anti-Ray, and to Mitch that meant he couldn't be trusted.

Mitch reached into a knapsack on the floor, took out a Nitro-Tech protein bar, and started to nibble. He never went anywhere without his Nitros. In his business you could never count on getting a meal, and who knew what'd be in it when you did? There was too much shit in the world — in the food, the water, the papers, the movies, people's bodies and heads. Mitch worked hard to eat right and stay lean. Half a dozen times a day he'd grab a pinch of flesh at his waist with his thumb and forefinger just to see if he was getting soft.

Now he wished he hadn't tossed his coffee. The Nitros went down a lot easier with it, and sticky nuggets were clinging to the walls of his throat. Mitch could see a food cart on the corner at Columbus Avenue. If he walked over to it, he was almost certain that no one looking out the diner's windows would have a line of sight to him. He had to have something to drink. He eyed the dot on the tracer's grid, got out of the cab, and headed for the corner. With a glance across the street at the diner's sun-glazed

210

windows, he racewalked for a few steps and arrived at the food cart. The swarthy proprietor's dense beard and forehead glistened with sweat from the steam billowing up from some cooking apparatus. Mitch took up a position where the cart hid him from the diner's vantage point.

'Bottle of water,' he said.

'Got no water today, mehster. They scroot me at pehkup place.'

Mitch nodded. The *i*'s coming out like *eh*'s meant Mideastern. A Ranee, or Rocky, or a Leb. Maybe even an Izzy. Not that it made any real difference.

'Tough work, huh?' said Mitch.

'S'okay. Back home, they scroot you worse. 'Bout every-theng.'

'Yeah? Where's home?'

'Damascus.'

Mitch nodded again. He liked being right. 'Gimme a Red Bull.'

'Yes, sehr — one Red Bull.'

He dug his hand down into an ice-filled drum and came out with a can of Red Bull. Mitch paid him, popped the can, and took a sip. He had a decent view of the diner's interior. He could see about three-quarters of the booths and tables and their denizens — but he couldn't see Boddicker or his crazy sister, and now it wasn't the Red Bull's megadose of caffeine that was starting to pump up his pulse. He was getting that tight pinch of stress in his temples.

He glanced at a minivan parked across the intersection, directly in front of the diner. A delivery truck was coming across Columbus;

211

Mitch used it as cover as it passed by and hustled across the street. Peering through the minivan's windows, he could see straight into the diner without being seen himself.

'Fuck me,' he said. He pulled out his cell phone and punched two buttons. There was an answer halfway through the first ring.

'Yeah?' It was Hall.

'They're loose,' Mitch said.

The silence on Hall's end was potent. Then: 'How long?'

Mitch's cheeks crimped in a wince. 'Don't know.'

'Three questions,' Hall said, 'just so we're on the same page.'

Mitch knew that the three questions would actually be statements, each meant to clarify the parameters of a negative situation. But, in classic Hall fashion, the questions would also be designed to point out that Mitch had screwed up and was, in truth, an idiot unworthy of the continued inhalation of oxygen.

'One,' Hall said. 'Targets were in a diner having breakfast?'

'Right.'

'Two. You were parked outside, watching the trace?'

'Right.'

'Three. Then how did they walk?'

'I dunno,' Mitch barked. 'The trace has them right fucking here!'

Hall's voice shifted into low gear and became a purr. 'Mitch, where are you?'

'On the corner of Seventy-sixth and Columbus, standing in front of the diner.'

'I thought you were in the car with the trace.'

'I just came out to get a fucking Red Bull! I've been out of the car for two minutes and I never took my eye off the diner.'

Mitch's cell phone screen might as well have had a video feed. He could see Hall sitting behind the wheel, tapping it with a finger. He was probably smoking a cigarette, the butt locked in his scowl. Ray would be beside him, listening, exchanging looks.

'Go back to the car,' Hall said, 'and check the trace.'

'I'm on it,' Mitch said, and started away in a jog, cursing Hall's dark heart. The only thing he hated more than feeling clueless was sounding that way. He slid into the front seat and checked the locator's display.

'It's still dead on,' he said to Hall. 'Sonofabitch might as well be sitting in my lap. I don't get it.'

'Go in the diner, ask a question or two, then call me back.'

'Where are you guys?'

'West Side, the One thirties.'

'Any more hits on the kid's cell?'

'No.'

'On Boddicker's?'

'No.'

'The kid's mother?'

'No.'

The line went dead.

'Fuck you,' Mitch muttered. 'And fuck each and every one of us.'

Rita saw the red hair and the mustache as soon as the cab driver came to the door. She strolled over as Mitch stepped inside.

'Sit wherever you like, hon.'

'Thanks, but I'm just looking for somebody.'

Rita noted the good ol' boy drawl and watched him scan every corner of the place.

The cabbie turned back to her. 'I let a guy and a gal off here a while ago, and I think he dropped some money in the back when he paid me. Two twenties.'

'Jesus,' Rita said, 'an honest cabbie.' She gave him a grin. Mitch returned it with an 'aw, shucks' shrug. She prayed she wasn't overdoing it.

'He's maybe forty or so. Thin, kinda washed out. And the gal was dressed in purple — kinda odd.' He tapped his forehead.

Rita's heart was tap-dancing. She put her hands behind her back because she wasn't sure if they were shaking. There was something genuinely sinister coming off the guy.

'Hmmm,' she said, pausing. 'No, I don't think I saw them. Must be your lucky day.'

She forced herself to meet his stare. She had no idea how she was coming off, and the guy's expression wasn't giving her a hint.

'Well,' he said, 'guess you're right. Okay if I use the head?'

'Sure, hon.'

She poked a thumb over her shoulder and held her smile in place as he walked away. She felt a little light-headed from the adrenaline buzz. She let a few seconds pass and then glanced back. The guy had gone into the hallway, out of sight.

* * *

Mitch stood in front of a door with a big Hollywood-type star and the name Angelina painted above it. He gave it a double rap, then turned the knob and opened it enough to stick his head in. Unoccupied. He moved down to the door with a star and Brad on it, put an ear to it, then walked inside. Someone had left the water running in the sink. He crouched down to peek under the door of the stall. It was empty. He turned the faucet off and looked in the mirror. He was sure the waitress was lying, but it didn't matter — Boddicker was gone. The guy was sharp. He'd trumped Hall and Ray, and now he had Mitch standing in a bathroom staring at himself.

Mitch went back out to the hall and saw what he was looking for — a back door — and stepped into the alley. A copper-skinned dishwasher was leaning against the wall having a smoke, his dark eyes empty of interest.

'*Ha visto un hombre y una mujer vestidos de morado salir de aquí?*' Mitch asked.

The dishwasher shook his head, and Mitch headed across the street for the cab. Boddicker had made him and played him — and Mitch didn't know how.

* * *

When his cell rang, Hall pulled over on Amsterdam. The back of his head and his sternum ached, the wolfed-down Egg McMuffin shifted at the bottom of his stomach like a shipwreck on the ocean floor, and he was furious — not at Mitch, not at Ray, but at himself. He'd thought his prep for this job had been impeccable. He'd followed Worst-Case Scenario six ways from Sunday, but he'd misread everyone:

Matheson, for being cold enough to run and leave his son behind.

Boddicker, for being a lot more than the sad sack he looked like. When they'd first met, Hall hadn't felt a thing coming off the guy, and now he'd chumped them twice.

And Geiger, for having a genuine soft spot.

He answered the call. 'Yeah?'

'They're long gone,' said Mitch. 'So where do you want me now?'

Hall glanced at Ray, who was fishing an orange plastic pill container out of his pocket.

'C'mon up here. We're at One thirty-third and Amsterdam.'

'On my way.'

Hall sank back into his seat. If the three of them ended up sharing a toilet for the rest of their lives — or just got disappeared if the wrong guys found them first — it would be on him. His biggest mistake had been misjudging Geiger. Hall had originally settled on Dalton for the job — the man was a psycho, but what you saw was always what you got — but to his surprise the image of a boy strapped to a chair spitting blood from a mouth that had one lip missing had made

216

him change his mind. Now it occurred to him that, at least in one way, he and Geiger might have something in common — and that in the end, this weakness could put the dagger in both their backs.

Hall turned to watch Ray jiggle two pills into his palm and bring his hand up to his horror-movie mouth. A groan and wince followed immediately. Ray's brain was telling his jaw to open, but his muscles were balking in protest because the task was too painful. Ray stared at the pills and then looked over at Hall. Words leaked out of his lips like soup too hot to swallow.

'Help . . . me . . . out,' he said, and his free hand pointed at his grisly mouth.

'Jesus fucking Christ,' Hall said, shaking his head.

Ray's swollen, purple-circled eyes narrowed into slits. He looked like a huge, angry raccoon.

Hall snatched the pills from his partner's hand, grabbed Ray's jaw, and yanked it open. An ursine growl came out of the open maw. Hall shoved the pills into Ray's mouth and pushed his jaw shut.

Closing his eyes, Ray swallowed. 'Thanks,' he muttered.

16

When the pain first came, Geiger's mind shut down like an engine sensing overload. Time stopped. The world, the universe, ceased to exist. There was only nothing. Then the void was filled with a visitation from the past. It was not so much an act of memory as an encounter in the present. His mind straddled then and now.

★ ★ ★

His father, holding a candle, led him to a door. He had finished building the space that day. He swung the door open: the room, if it could be called that, was four feet square.

'You'll sleep here from now on,' he told the boy.

'But, Father . . . it's so small.'

'Go inside and lie down.'

'I don't want to be alone, Father.'

'You are not alone. You'll have the music with you.' His father lifted the candle into the space. A cassette recorder and half a dozen cassettes lay on the floor.

The boy stepped inside. 'Sleep' his father said, shutting the door. Now nothing existed but blackness and the boy's trembling breath.

Groping blindly, he gathered up the cassette player and tapes. He lay on his side, curled tight into a ball. The soles of his feet pushed against one wall, his spine and scapula against another,

218

the back of his head against a third.

He waited for whatever came next.

$$\star \quad \star \quad \star$$

Geiger opened his eyes to see Ezra staring down at him.

'Hi,' the boy said, and then walked out of Geiger's field of vision.

Geiger sat up. He had a sense of the floor and walls accommodating his efforts, as if surfaces were solid but somewhat malleable. He stood up and waited while equilibrium gradually returned, and then stepped out of the closet. This had not been sleep, and his involuntary loss of consciousness and suspension of control were new and unsettling to consider. The rules of his migraines had been broken. The dream had always been the trigger, but this time the migraine had come on its own. Now, Geiger realized, he could at any moment be attacked from within and rendered helpless.

He started down the short hall toward the living room, hands up and out at ten and two o'clock, like a man making his way in the dark. He took a slow, careful detour to the desk. Ezra was settled on the couch, arms wrapped tightly around bent legs brought up against his chest.

'Why do you do it?' he asked.

'I get people to tell the truth. I retrieve information.'

Geiger shook loose a cigarette from its pack, turned to the boy, and saw the violin on the couch beside him.

'Was that you playing while I was in the closet?'

Ezra nodded. 'I thought maybe you died.' He sighed through his mouth and a soft 'Ohhhh' came out with it. 'Thanks for the food. And the Advil.' He was greatly relieved that Geiger was awake, but the man was just so strange. How could he be both his protector and a professional torturer?

Geiger stood before him silently.

'What's wrong with you?' Ezra said.

'I don't know.'

'You're not going to have another fit, are you?'

'It's not a fit.'

'What is it?'

'A migraine. A very powerful headache.'

'Boy, it sure didn't look like a headache to me. Maybe you should see a doctor?'

'I see a psychiatrist.'

'Really? And he, like, knows what you do?'

Ezra tried to picture Geiger sitting in a room, talking with a psychiatrist about his work, but his mind drew a complete blank.

When Geiger didn't reply, Ezra went on: 'I went to a shrink when Dad moved out. Mom took me.' His bony shoulders jerked in a shrug. 'It was pretty lame. The shrink kept asking how I felt — you know, about the divorce — and I hardly talked. So Mom did most of the talking — about wanting to move to California and taking me away from my violin teacher and that kind of stuff. She'd ask the shrink, 'Was that selfish?' And the shrink would say, 'Do *you* think it's selfish?' And she'd say 'What do *you* think?'

220

So we'd sit there and they'd just ask each other questions.'

'I'm going to have a smoke,' Geiger said. He walked to the back door, punched in the exit code, and stepped out into the yard. The lawn flashed in the sun like filaments of green glass, and he had to squint before his eyes could accept the sharp light. His legs felt rubbery, but there had been no trail of echoes chasing the boy's voice, no visual ghosts lurking at the edges of his movements.

He sat down against the tree and lit up. He was thinking about the boy's mother, trying to envision the future so he could figure out a way to get there. Too many things felt beyond his control. Hall was close by and, as Harry feared, he clearly had technology on his side. Trains and planes and buses felt like too much of a risk — the possibility of stakeouts seemed real — and the prospect of driving a car seemed unwise, given his current state. Geiger was accustomed to being the master of his mind and body, but now he was more like a slave to both. To believe that there wouldn't be another ambush from within was foolish, so it would be reckless for him to attempt to bring the boy to his mother. The mother would have to come to the boy. In the meantime, he and Ezra would have to leave this place. He needed to get help.

Ezra came to the doorway and watched Geiger sitting utterly still beneath a tree. He reminded Ezra of the miniature Buddha his mother had put in the garden, and that set off a pang of longing. He saw her sitting at the piano, teeth

221

biting her lower lip, struggling bravely to keep up with him while playing a duet for piano and violin, trying not to curse aloud at her flubs while he tried not to laugh. He always felt closest to her at those moments. The wordless flow, the weaving of a musical tapestry, the sharing of sounds.

'Can I come out?' Ezra asked.

'Yes.'

Ezra went down the two steps, stood just beyond the stoop's awning, and turned his face up to the sky.

'Feels good,' he said. 'So, what happened to the guy I read about? Victor, I think his name was. Did you . . . slice him up?'

'No. But he thought I did, so he told me the truth. The girl was tied up in a basement.'

'So you saved her life?'

'I got the truth. What happens after that isn't my concern. It's not part of the job.'

'Do you always get them to tell the truth?'

'Yes. You can make anyone do almost anything.'

Geiger's almost offhand delivery of the statement underlined its brutal truth. Ezra wondered how you learned to be a torturer. Were there books to read? Videos to watch? A school where you took courses?

The cat came out and jumped up on the railing. Ezra made little circles on his head with his pinkie.

'You should give him a real name,' he said. Then he grinned. 'Hey, you could call him Tony, after Tony Montana.'

'Who?'

'Tony Montana — you know, Al Pacino in *Scarface*.' He cocked his head at Geiger's blank expression. 'Get it? *Scarface*, the movie?'

'I don't go to the movies.'

'Well, you ought to name him something. 'Cat' is kinda dumb.'

'We're leaving,' Geiger said. He stood up and went inside.

Ezra followed him in. Geiger was filling a glass with water from the tap.

'Are we gonna try and call my mom?'

'Yes. But we have to call from a pay phone.' He chugged the water down. 'And then we won't come back here.'

The sentence grabbed at Ezra with an icy, unexpected undertow.

'Why not?'

'Because the men who are looking for you are close by. I saw them driving around when I was outside.'

The cold tug of fear grew stronger, and then Ezra remembered his IM episode with Harry.

'Oh shit — I forgot! Your friend . . . '

'My friend?'

'Harry. He's your friend, right?'

'What about Harry?'

'I IM'd with him when you were in the closet. He wanted to come over.'

'He doesn't know where I live.'

'I know, but I sent him the address on the drugstore receipt. I don't know if he got it or not, because he signed off.'

Geiger bent to the washer-dryer, took Ezra's

223

clean clothes out, and brought them to him.

'Get dressed.'

'What about Harry?'

Geiger pushed the clothes into Ezra's hands. 'Get dressed.'

As Ezra headed to the bathroom, Geiger went to his desk. Harry's IM was still on the screen. He scrolled it back and started reading.

When he'd finished, Geiger clicked it off, revealing Ezra's attempted IM session with his father still beneath it on the screen.

GUEST: Its EZBoy. Where are you?

But now there was a reply to Ezra's question. It had come at 1:06 P.M., fourteen minutes ago.

BIGBOSSMAN: you're not on your own laptop? where are you?

Geiger's fingers started tapping at the sides of the keyboard. Then he began to type.

GUEST: matheson, answer now

He could feel pieces of the world, fluid and energized, sliding toward each other as if driven by nature. Harry and Hall on the same path, searching for him; his father's visitations; Matheson finally showing himself. Geiger felt like some sort of black hole, drawing everything toward him, past and present, the outside and the inside.

The IM came to life.

BIGBOSSMAN: who is this?
GUEST: we have your son
BIGBOSSMAN: please don't hurt ezra
GUEST: for ezra's sake we hope you still have what we want and are still in the vicinity
BIGBOSSMAN: I have it and im still in the city

Geiger tried to keep a firm grip on his mind, but it kept slithering away. He felt as if he were both car and driver, trying to steer as he read the road signs that gave him directions to the unknown place he must be bound for.

His fingers began typing again.

GUEST: type your cell number. we will call you in a short time to tell you where to meet us. we will only call once and if you don't answer we will kill the boy
BIGBOSSMAN: 917 555 0617. i'll do whatever you say. please don't hurt my son

Geiger grabbed a pen, scribbled the phone number on his palm, and signed off. He heard Ezra come out of the bathroom and walk up behind him.

'So what're we going to do?'

'I'm going to change my clothes and then we're leaving.'

'What about Harry?'

'We can't wait for Harry.'

'What about the cat?'

'The cat goes where he wants to go. Say good-bye.'

* * *

225

Outside, Geiger walked up to Mr, Memz and handed him his pack of Luckies.

'Who's the kid?' Mr. Memz threw a look toward Ezra, who stood in the shadows of the entrance to the check-cashing store ten feet away, violin case in hand.

'I'm keeping an eye on him,' said Geiger. He had changed into a black pullover and khaki pants. 'I need you to do something for me. I'll pay you.'

Mr. Memz shook out a cigarette, lit it, and sat back in his chair. 'Your buddies keep coming by. Every half hour or so — they're on a route. This about the kid?'

'Yes,' Geiger said. He took a folded piece of paper out of a pocket. 'Somebody else may come looking for me. His name is Harry. Skinny, brown hair, scar on his forehead. He might have a woman with him. He'll probably look lost, like he doesn't know where he's going.'

'You sure got popular in a hurry, BT. Who woulda thunk?'

Geiger handed the paper to Mr. Memz, who unfolded it and looked at the information. It was an address, written in neat block letters.

'If you see him,' said Geiger, 'would you tell him to meet me there?'

'Uh-huh.'

Mr. Memz flicked his lighter to life, lit an edge of the paper, and watched the flame consume it.

'You'll remember it?' Geiger asked.

Mr. Memz glanced up at Geiger, then pointed a big-knuckled finger at his own face. 'Who am I — and what do I fucking do?'

Geiger glanced down the street. 'I have a question.'

'Shouldn't you be getting out of here?'

'One question.'

'Yeah?'

'Are you in pain all the time?'

Mr. Memz cocked an eyebrow. This was a subject dear to his battered heart and brain.

'There's all kinds of pain, man.'

'I meant your leg.'

'Shit, man — my *leg?*' He grabbed his shirt and yanked it up. The right side of his torso was a thicket of scars. 'Shattered. Every bone on this side. When I roll over in bed, I sound like a bowl of Rice fucking Krispies.' His foot started to thump the pavement. 'Pain's not the thing, man. It's just the *messenger* — the thing that makes you remember *why* you hurt. Understand what I'm saying?' He stared at Geiger, head atilt. 'Yeah, I think maybe you do. Now get your ass going before your pals come back.'

Geiger turned and waved at Ezra. The boy stepped forward, and the two of them headed up the block to look for a cab.

'*Semper fi,* kid,' said Mr. Memz.

Ezra looked back at the one-legged man.

'Who's that?' he asked Geiger.

'Mr. Memz.'

'Memz?'

'Like in 'memorize.' He knows entire books by heart.'

'For real?'

'For real. Walk faster.'

Mr. Memz watched them go up the block. They had almost reached the corner when he heard a soft voice singing, '*Sally, go 'round the* roses . . . ' It was not much louder than a whisper, like a lullaby sung to a baby. '*Sally, go 'round the pretty roses . . .* '

The music made him smile. He knew the song immediately: the Jaynetts, 1963. He turned to find the singer a few feet from him on the sidewalk. A fawn of a woman, she was staring up at the sky and holding a man's hand. The man looked lost.

★　★　★

Hall stopped at the red light at 133rd Street and looked over at Ray, who was nodding out. His eyes were shut, and his chin kept dipping until his head snapped back up and then slowly started down again. The meds and the pain had made him half of what Hall needed him to be. Hall had thought about the implications of Ray's disability while he'd watched the doctor stitch him up.

'Wake up, Ray!'

Ray's eyelids rose to half-mast.

'Ray, I need your eyes, goddamnit!'

Ray sat straight and stared out his window.

'I'm up, I'm up.'

★　★　★

Harry froze when he heard someone call his name.

'Hey, are you Harry?'

When he and Lily had gotten into the taxi outside the internet café, Harry had told the cabbie to drive until the meter read ten dollars. He had thirteen bucks left and figured he'd better hold on to a few, so at 116th Street the driver pulled over, and Harry walked the last eighteen blocks with Lily in tow. His knee was so swollen he thought he could hear it swish with each step.

'Harry? Geiger's Harry?'

Harry turned around. 'Yeah?'

Mr. Memz jabbed a finger toward Amsterdam Avenue. 'He's up there. On the corner. Better double-time it, man.'

Harry looked up the block and saw Geiger stepping off the sidewalk toward a cab that was pulling up next to him. Geiger opened the back door, and Ezra hustled over and climbed inside.

'Geiger!' Harry shouted, as Geiger slid into the backseat and closed the door. '*Geiger!*'

★ ★ ★

Geiger gave the address to the cabbie's reflection in the rear-view mirror. 'And take Convent to Morningside. It's faster.'

'Wait,' Ezra said. 'Listen.'

The boy jabbed at the window button. The glass slid down and he tilted an ear.

'I thought I heard . . . '

'Heard what?'

There it was again, faint but clear.

'*Geiger!*'

'That!'

Geiger stuck his head out the window and peered down the street. Two figures were trudging up the sidewalk toward them. He got out of the cab.

Harry, pulling Lily up the slight hill, was a third of a block away, limping, hollering, and waving. Geiger watched them move into the street to cut down the angle to the cab and then saw a silver flash behind Harry at the bottom of the hill. A car had turned onto the street.

'Stay here,' Geiger told Ezra. He started down toward Harry, moving faster with every step.

'Come on, Harry,' he said. 'Move!'

Harry saw Geiger and stopped. He bent over, hands on thighs, panting heavily. Geiger arrived in a jog and picked Lily up in his arms.

'It's Hall, Harry. Run!' Geiger started back to the cab with Lily.

Still bent over at the waist, Harry swiveled and looked behind him. The Lexus was coming up the street at a crawl.

'Fuck . . . me.'

He pushed all the air out of his lungs and lifted himself upright.

★ ★ ★

Mr. Memz, watching the show, saw Harry start hobbling forward as fast as he could. Then he turned west and observed the slow advance of the silver Lexus.

'Jesus H. Christ, here we go.' He tugged at his ponytail, his head swiveling back and forth, gauging distances. 'C'mon, man,' he shouted at Harry. 'Faster.'

Halfway to the corner, Harry's knee buckled and slammed into the asphalt.

Mr. Memz winced and then looked back at the

Lexus. 'He's never gonna make it,' he muttered.

Grabbing his crutch, Mr. Memz stood up.

★ ★ ★

If Ray hadn't slipped back into a semi-nod, Hall wouldn't be driving so slowly. But as he worked his way up the block, he had to check both sides of the street. Finally he reached over and hammered Ray's chest with a backhanded fist. Ray's bloodshot eyes sprang open.

'Stay awake! I mean it, Ray. Drop your end and I will send you to your fucking reward. Got it?'

Ray grunted in reply.

Hall saw them just as Geiger deposited Lily in the cab and turned back for Harry, who was twenty feet short of the taxi. Hall's foot pounded the accelerator as his hand felt for the gun in his belt. With a rich growl, the powerful car sped up the hill.

Hall's mind quickly scanned scenarios. Run them over? Pull up between them and the cab? Make a big show with the gun? And if a cop shows up?

He glanced at Ray. 'You're on Geiger. I go for the kid. He's got to be in the cab.'

Ray nodded. The car's speed and the scent of vengeance had kicked him into a higher gear. 'And I want Harry, too,' he said.

As Hall turned back to the street, he saw a figure dressed in camouflage step out from between two parked cars. Leaning on a crutch, standing not a hundred feet away, the man

231

turned toward the oncoming car and seemed astonished to see it.

Hall slammed on the brakes. Ray, unbelted, went thudding face-first into the dashboard. His howl was almost as loud as the shriek of rubber clawing at asphalt as the Lexus held its line, barreling head-on for Mr. Memz.

'Motherfucker!' shouted Hall, practically standing on the brake pedal.

At the last second, Mr. Memz fell backward, his crutch clattering, just as the Lexus came to a halt.

Hall was looming over Mr. Memz before he could catch his breath.

'You *blind*? Huh?'

Hall bent down and grabbed Mr. Memz by an arm.

'Get up! *Up!*'

Mr. Memz pulled his arm free. 'Back off, Jack! I think maybe I broke something.' He let out a loud moan and snuck a look uphill.

★ ★ ★

'Go,' Geiger said to the cabbie from the front seat. 'Fast.'

The driver hit the gas, and they bolted into traffic. Harry closed his eyes and took a few deep breaths to even out the pain. Then he leaned forward and looked across Lily at Ezra.

'You're Ezra.'

'Yeah.'

'I'm Harry. We've met, sort of. This is Lily, my sister. She doesn't really talk.'

Ezra nodded. Nothing seemed strange to him any longer. 'Hi, Lily,' he said.

Lily turned to him, one child's gaze meeting another's.

'I know lots of songs,' she said. 'Do you?'

'Well, I . . . ' Ezra paused. 'Yeah, I know lots of songs, too.'

'That's because we're all born with a million songs inside us — and we know them all by heart.'

Harry turned to her, his mouth opening as if to say something, then closing again.

'But as we get older,' Lily continued, 'we forget them. Every day we forget some, and every day we get a little sadder. But children haven't forgotten too many yet.'

She closed her eyes and settled her head on Ezra's shoulder.

17

When he opened the door, Corley was startled to find not only Geiger but also a boy of eleven or twelve with symmetrical pink stripes marking his face; a skinny, bedraggled man with a discolored contusion on his left temple; and a delicate woman whose unfocused, darting gaze immediately suggested that she suffered from significant psychological problems.

'We need to come in,' Geiger said.

The gathering at his door was so bizarre, and the wash of despair and weariness coming off them so strong, that Corley didn't know how to respond.

'Geiger,' he said. 'Who are all these — '

'Martin, we need to come in.'

Geiger's voice was unsettling: the timbre of it and the crests of inflection were slightly different from the smooth, nearly atonal speech Corley was accustomed to hearing. He looked more closely at Geiger and saw it in his eyes. Something had happened.

'Come in,' Corley said, opening the door wide and waving at the two oversized leather chairs and the two beige sofas in his living room. 'Please, sit down. Anywhere.'

Ezra chose a chair. Harry planted Lily on a sofa and collapsed beside her with a groan. Geiger remained standing.

Corley followed his guests into the room. 'I'm

234

Martin Corley. I'm a psychiatrist.'

Harry's head snapped upright. 'Wait a sec. You're Geiger's *psychiatrist?*' He looked at Geiger. 'You see a shrink?'

'This is Harry,' said Geiger, 'and Ezra and Lily, Harry's sister.'

'Well,' said Corley, 'this is certainly a very unusual situation. I think we can all agree on that.'

'Doc,' said Harry, 'I should probably tell you that Lily's been institutionalized for fifteen years, so she won't be agreeing on anything.'

'I see.' Corley noted her collapsed posture as she sat on the sofa. 'Clearly you've all been through a bad time. Harry, you look pretty banged up. Are you all right?'

'Far from it, Doc. You got any Advil?'

'Yes, I'll get you some. Can I get anyone else something? Food? Something to drink?'

'Could I have a soda?' asked Ezra.

'I have some Diet Coke. That okay?'

'Yes, thank you.'

'And you know what?' said Harry. 'I'll have a *drink.*' Feeling Geiger's stare, Harry glanced at him. 'What? I quit drinking for the job — and the job's over, man. You got any bourbon, Doc?'

'I think so.'

'No alcohol for him, Martin,' Geiger said.

'Come on, man — I'm not going on a bender. I just want a drink.'

'No.'

Corley was mesmerized by the exchange. Geiger the interacter. And what else? A protector, too. There was something appreciable to witness here.

235

Corley turned to Geiger, who was leaning against a wall, staring at something very far away from the room. 'Geiger . . . '

Geiger followed him into the kitchen. Corley turned to him as he came in.

'I need to know what's going on, Geiger. Especially with you.'

'It's very complicated.'

'All right, but at least give me the short version for now.'

'Martin, there is no short version.'

★   ★   ★

Corley listened as Geiger told him the story. It came out in brief sentences, heavily edited, with minimal pauses. The boy was being hunted — never mind by whom. Geiger had rescued him — never mind how. The bad guys were still looking for them — never mind why. Geiger's plan was to get Ezra back to his mother.

'And something happened to me,' Geiger said. 'I had a migraine. And now I'm having . . . visions. Flashbacks.'

'Of what?'

'My father.' Geiger put a hand up. 'The rest will have to wait, Martin. I have to go somewhere.'

'Where?'

'I won't be long.'

'You've brought me into this, Geiger. I really need more information.'

'Right now, what's best for *you* is no more information.'

There it was again: the inflection in his speech, the use of emphasis to underline his meaning. Corley marveled at it.

'Martin, you can't tell anyone what you don't know. Down the line, if the police were to get involved with — '

'Let's talk about the police, Geiger. Why don't we call them? The boy is safe here.'

'Discussing this with the police would not be good for Harry and me.'

Corley's cheeks puffed out in frustration. 'This is unacceptable.'

'I'm going to go now, Martin. I will try to get in touch with Ezra's mother, and then I'll see someone, and then I'll be back. Then we'll find a way to meet the boy's mother and that will end it.'

'You have it all worked out?'

'No. But I'm certain I'm going in the right direction. It's like the dreams, Martin. It feels just like the dreams.'

Corley hesitated at voicing his next thought but decided it had to be said. 'You never get to where you're going in the dream — and you fall apart at the end.'

Corley watched something happen to Geiger's face; the muscles shifted ever so slightly. He'd never seen it before. It looked almost like an appreciation of a dark irony.

But Geiger said nothing and then walked back into the living room. Corley followed. Lily and Harry were asleep, heads resting against each other at a tilt.

'I'm going out,' Geiger said.

Ezra hopped out of the chair. 'What do you mean?'

'I'm going to call your mother.'

'Then I'm coming, too.'

'No. You can't be out on the street.'

'But I don't want to stay here alone.'

'You're not alone.'

Corley watched Ezra take three quick steps to Geiger's side.

'I want to stay with you,' Ezra said. A wet glaze coated his eyes, and he grabbed Geiger's hand.

'You'll be all right here,' said Geiger. 'Martin's a good person. I'll be back soon.' He glanced over his shoulder at Corley.

'It's okay, Ezra,' said Corley. 'If Geiger says he'll come back, he'll come back. You know that, right?'

Ezra's eyes hadn't left Geiger's. 'Promise?'

'I promise,' Geiger said.

Ezra looked at Geiger for another moment and then let go of his hand.

Geiger nodded at Corley and went to the door. He left without looking back.

* * *

Mulberry Street at three o'clock in the afternoon was a narrow stretch of commerce on the verge of gridlock. Even so, it never stopped moving. Delivery boys made their rounds by van and foot, shoppers walked past with bags of cured meats and pastas, old men sat on stoops chewing on dead cigars. A dense efflux of aromas rode waves of heat and the shifting breezes. More

238

than once, Carmine had told Geiger, 'If heaven smells, it smells like Mulberry Street.'

Outside the Mulberry Deli, Geiger fed some change into a pay phone. He had never used one before. He listened to the ring. Once, twice, and then a woman answered.

'Hello?'

'Mrs. Matheson?'

'Not for a while. Ms. Wayland. Who is this?' Her voice had a 'shoot first, ask questions later' edge.

'Ms. Wayland, my name is Geiger. Try not to be alarmed. This is about your son.' He could hear the sudden intake of breath.

'Oh God, I knew something was wrong when he didn't answer. What's happened?'

'Ezra is all right. And he is safe.'

''Safe'? What does that mean?'

'Yesterday your son was kidnapped by men trying to find your ex-husband, who is hiding — '

'*What?*'

'Please, Ms. Wayland. I need to finish as quickly as possible.'

'Where is my son — and who the *fuck* are you?'

Geiger stared at the handset, which felt unwieldy and strange. 'I took Ezra from the kidnappers. He is safe now.'

'Where is he?'

'In a safe place. He — '

'Listen to me, you bastard. If you — '

'*Quiet!*'

Heads on Mulberry Street turned. Geiger

239

clicked his neck and took a breath. 'Ms. Wayland, if this was a threat and I wanted something from you, I would have said so. Take a moment to think about that. I want to get Ezra back to you. That's the only reason I am calling.'

He heard a sob, and then a sniffle. 'Go on,' she said.

'You need to get on a plane to New York. Please don't try to contact the police. It will only make things more difficult. You will just have to trust that I am telling the truth. It is possible the kidnappers have your cell phone number, so when you arrive in New York do *not* use your cell phone or they may be able to locate you. Go to a pay phone and call my cell phone. They don't have my number. When you call, I will tell you where to go.'

'But how — '

'Write down this number and repeat it to me: nine-one-seven, five-five-five, four-seven-seven-eight.'

'Hold on.'

Geiger closed his eyes. There was too much of the world around him. He could feel the weight of every sound, sight, smell, and molecule of air pressing on him.

'Okay,' Ezra's mother said. 'I wrote it down.'

'Repeat it to me.'

'Nine-one-seven, five-five-five, four-seven-seven-eight.'

'I know this is difficult, but do not tell anyone about this call. Do not share any of this information with anyone. Make up an excuse to leave, and leave.'

'All right.'

'I'm going to hang up now.'

'Wait! Will you . . . ' She paused and seemed to gather herself. 'Will you please tell Ezra I love him?'

'Yes.'

After hanging up, Geiger walked to Mott Street. La Bella was halfway down the block. Carmine had a cell phone and Geiger had the number, but Carmine didn't talk on the phone. It didn't matter whether it was business, or pleasure, or something dark and desperate. You didn't call Carmine Delanotte. You went to La Bella.

*　*　*

The maître d' looked up and gave Geiger his composed smile.

'Mr. Geiger. How are you? Haven't seen you in a while.'

'Is Carmine here?'

'Of course. Let me tell him you're here.'

Geiger smelled garlic and oregano, and heard the Stones' 'Beast of Burden' playing on the restaurant's sound system. La Bella wasn't a throwback to an old-style Italian eatery with water-color murals and a nonstop loop of Frank Sinatra and Jerry Vale. It wasn't a front or a laundry, either. The floor was covered in six-inch-square, hand-painted tiles from Bologna, the lighting was provided by angled pin spots, and the walls were adorned with black-and-white photographs of Italy that could have been from a MoMA exhibit. The waiters moved unobtrusively around the room wearing Armani vests and slacks. Carmine was forward-looking in everything he did, and his obvious pride in what he'd achieved was a product of action, not arrogance. As he liked to say to Geiger and his many associates, 'Never make believe you know everything, but make sure you find out.'

The maître d' returned and gestured toward the door in the back wall. It was flanked by two bodyguards.

'Mr. Geiger — the office, please.'

Geiger followed the maître d' to the back of the restaurant. The sentries gave silent nods, and one of them opened the door. Geiger stepped into a living room-style office of cool gray walls, thick carpets, and bird's-eye maple and chrome furnishings. Geiger had borrowed the style when he'd designed his Ludlow Street viewing room.

Carmine put aside the *Wall Street Journal*, rose from the couch, and took off his reading glasses.

'Here he is.' He grinned. 'The man from IR.'

Carmine was, by nature, a hugger of both men and women. But he'd learned that Geiger preferred minimal physical contact, so he waved a hand at a large, silk chair.

'Sit,' Carmine said.

The maître d' stood waiting in the doorway. Carmine didn't have to look to know he was there.

'Kenny, a double X for me, black coffee for Mr. Geiger. No sugar.'

The maître d' nodded and closed the door

softly. Both men sat down. Geiger was silent; he knew not to rush things.

'Strange times, my friend,' said Carmine, and patted the *Journal* with an elegant hand. 'The economy tanks and business has never been better. I picked up three houses on Staten Island last month, dimes for dollars. In a few years I'll turn them over threefold. Very strange — but very profitable.'

When you went to see Carmine, it was for one of two reasons: you had something to tell him that you believed he would consider worth knowing, or you needed a favor. In either case, you followed Carmine's lead and waited for the moment when he asked why you'd come.

There was a knock on the door.

'Come,' said Carmine.

The maître d' walked in and put the double espresso and coffee on the table between the two men.

'Thank you, Kenny.'

As the maître d' left, Carmine picked up his cup. He winced, and then smiled and shook his head.

'Goddamn fingers.' He took a sip of the espresso, smacked his lips with satisfaction, and put the cup down. He flexed his fingers and opened and closed his hand into a fist three times. 'They've really been bothering me lately. Remember the first time we met, when you told me about the feds, and you said I had a couple of bum fingers?'

'Yes.'

Carmine took another sip of his drink. 'I ever

243

tell you how it happened?'

'No.'

'Funny story.' He sank back into the cushions. 'Summer 1970. I'm in the navy. We're in Boston, waiting to go overseas. Ever been to Boston?'

'No.'

'You ought to go. Great town. So we get a night ashore, and I have the best lobster fra diavolo I've ever tasted. But you don't eat seafood, right?'

'No, I don't.'

Carmine pointed at the table. 'Drink your coffee while it's hot. Why do I always have to tell you that?'

The answer was that Geiger didn't like La Bella's coffee, and he never drank it unless prompted by Carmine, which was every time. He picked up the cup and drank.

'So I end up walking around Cambridge, and I hear someone talking on a microphone, so I walk through this arch in a brick wall and you know where I am?'

'No.'

'I'm in a courtyard in Harvard University. There's a rally going on. Anti-war stuff. Vietnam. A sea of tie-dyed T-shirts and long hair. Before your time. A guy on the steps of a building with a microphone is talking about the war. I'm at the back of the crowd, and this kid just in front of me turns around — Jesus in jeans — and looks me over. I'm in my crackerjack whites, flat hat at my John Wayne angle, and he says, 'What the fuck are you doing here?' And I said, 'I'm listening. It's a free country, isn't it?' And the kid spits on my shoes. He *spits* on my *shoes*. Do you know how much time I spent, every day, polishing those shoes?'

Geiger took another sip of coffee.

'So I throw a punch, but before I can land it he jumps up and kicks me in the chest and puts me on my ass. Karate, kung fu, whatever — it was just like in the movies. He's all of a hundred and forty pounds soaking wet and he puts me on my ass. I get up and load up my left, swing it all the way back for a knockout — and smash it into a lamppost. Wham! I'm howling and the kid walks away. I never even got to hit him. But you know what? Now I had two dislocated fingers, just like you said, and a crushed knuckle, and my hand is in a cast when the rest of my guys go off to Nam. I never went over. That little Harvard prick kept me out of the war.'

Carmine drained his cup. Geiger had another swallow from his.

'So what's new in IR?'

Geiger put his cup down. This was the time. His temples drummed.

'I need your help with something.'

'Business-related ?'

'I need a gun.'

The blue eyes flashed. 'For what?'

Geiger didn't want to tell him the whole story. His focus was starting to fuzz again on the edges. 'It's just a precaution.'

'Have you ever fired a gun before?'

'No.'

Carmine noticed a tiny piece of lint on the front of his tailor-made shirt and flicked it off.

'Eddie!'

One of the bodyguards came inside and stood motionless, hands clasped at his belt buckle.

'Geiger needs a piece. Not too big. He's never used one before. Let's keep the recoil down.'

The guard nodded. As he turned and walked out the door, he left a trail of images in Geiger's vision.

Geiger reached for his coffee and knocked the cup over. The spill started running off the table's edge, onto the carpet, and he watched each drop fall in slow motion.

'Don't worry about it,' said Carmine. He sighed and flexed his fingers again.

Groggy as Geiger was, he caught the pang of rue in his benefactor's voice. He wondered what had been put in his coffee.

Carmine stood up and ran a hand through his silver mane. 'I don't get you, Geiger. I'm a very smart man, but I don't get you.'

Carmine knelt down directly in front of him, reached out, and patted his cheek affectionately. 'I have to ask you something while you can still answer me. Can you understand me?'

This was another new sensation for Geiger — a drug-induced slide out of consciousness. He felt a spread of prickly heat from the neck up, but he didn't care. 'Right,' Geiger said.

Carmine reached out again, but this time he gave Geiger a firm slap across the face.

'Why did you do it? What the hell could you possibly have been thinking?'

'Right,' Geiger said.

'You think I'm happy about this? I'm not,

Geiger. You're my boy.'

Geiger's head started to loll. 'Right,' he said again.

'I wish there was a choice here, but I do business with these people. Remember when you told me the feds bugged my house? That was my fucking invitation to them. You gave it to me. You're the one who hooked me up with them! We talked. We made a deal. I help them out once in a while, give them a name, do them a favor — and they leave me alone. Jesus, Geiger. It wasn't Colicos who sent Hall to you. It was me.'

'Right.'

'You know who you've been fucking with? These guys are contractors — and I don't mean the kind who do renovation. They're *government* contractors. Understand? They're the guys who do the stuff nobody's ever supposed to find out about, and they don't play by the rules, because they don't have to. They're all ex-commandos and mercenaries, fucking cowboys! And most of them are crazy, because if you do this stuff long enough, that's what it does to you — it makes you crazy. Bottom line, they do anything to get the job done, because they know they're gonna get *disappeared* if they don't. These guys don't retire with a pension and health benefits. Capiche?'

Carmine tugged at his jacket sleeves, as if he'd suddenly decided they were too short.

'They called this morning and very politely said that if you should happen to come by . . . So now do us both a favor. Just tell them what they want to know. I know he's just a kid — but be smart.'

'Right.'

Carmine grabbed Geiger's face in his hands. 'And I'm gonna tell you something else, Geiger — about life. All your 'outside versus inside' stuff? It's bullshit! Life owns your ass — from day one, cradle to grave. You don't get it, Geiger. You think you can *choose* whether you're in or not, but you can't. If you come out of this alive, you remember that.'

'Right . . .'

Just before Geiger blacked out he had a thought, and even in his deeply muddled state, the irony did not escape him. He had never felt so good in his whole life.

PART THREE

18

'Geiger. Wake up.'

The voice was behind him. He could feel the restraints at his wrists, ankles, and chest. He was lashed tightly to something. He opened his eyes and quickly went down a checklist of his senses. Sight, sound, touch — they all seemed to be in working order. No fog, no fuzz, no delay.

He was in his own place — the Ludlow Street session room — strapped into the barber's chair, wearing only his white jockeys. The air-conditioning was off. It was hot. He was already sweating.

'I'm awake,' he said.

A man stepped in front of him. Very thin and well over six feet tall, he was dressed in loose beige khakis and a gray sweatshirt. He wore round glasses, and his lightbulb-shaped head had only a few tufts of sparse, graying hair. To Geiger, he looked like a praying mantis. He held a pair of disposable white latex gloves.

'My name is Dalton,' the man said. 'It's a pleasure to meet you, though who would've thought it would happen like this?' His voice had the tranquil, measured tone of a high school teacher who knows every teenage trick in the book. He pulled one of the gloves on. The *snap* bounced around the room. 'I like the lightly powdered,' he said. 'What do you wear?'

'I don't. I don't like the way they feel.'

251

'You don't worry about infection? Aids, Hep C . . .'

'There's hardly ever any bleeding with me.'

Dalton put the other glove on. *Snap.* Geiger looked to the one-way mirror. Who else was here? Hall, certainly. Carmine? Probably not, but he heard the echo of his words: *I do business with these people. You know who you've been fucking with? They're government contractors.*

Dalton followed Geiger's eyes. 'You have a wonderful place here, Geiger. You've got a real eye for the little things, the special touches. And the viewing room — beautiful.' Dalton walked behind Geiger, out of his sight, then came back around pushing the wheeled cart. 'I brought some of my own things and picked out a few of yours, too.'

On the cart's top shelf were a handheld butane torch, a box cutter with the grip wrapped in duct tape, an awl with a wooden handle, an aluminum baseball bat whose upper portion was encased in a four-inch layer of blue rubber foam, and Geiger's antique straight razor. The bottom shelf of the cart was stocked with half a dozen white hand towels, a roil of gauze, a roll of adhesive tape, and a neatly folded khaki wind-breaker.

'It must be very strange, being on the other end of this,' Dalton said.

Geiger looked at Dalton's loose, oversized clothes; he couldn't get a sense for whether the man's body was in good shape. His face was sallow and free of wrinkles. He looked to be about fifty.

'How long have I been out?'

'About forty-five minutes.' Dalton took off his glasses and began polishing the lenses. 'Now, first things first. I'm out of the loop on this. All I've been told is that they want to know where the boy is. So . . . where is the boy?'

Geiger remembered that he'd written Matheson's cell number on his left hand. The hand was extended just past the end of the chair's arm, palm facing the floor.

'That Jones in Iraq,' said Geiger. 'Did you really cut off his lips?'

Dalton's smile reminded Geiger of a dog baring its teeth just before it growls.

'Sorry,' Dalton said. 'I never kiss and tell. But let me ask you something.' He put his glasses back on. 'Do you know what they call you?'

'Who are 'they'?' Geiger asked.

'Some of our mutual . . . *friends.*'

'No,' said Geiger. 'I don't know what they call me.'

'They call you the Inquisitor. What do you think — you like it?'

Geiger was monitoring his pulse. It was slow. He considered the moniker: *The Inquisitor.* The royalty of torture. The CIA loved their code names.

Dalton looked slightly disappointed at Geiger's apparent lack of interest. 'Well, I like it. Very elegant.'

Geiger remained silent, waiting Dalton out.

'They're in a real hurry about this, Geiger,' Dalton said, pulling the sleeves of his sweatshirt up to his elbows. 'So I'm not going to bother with any head games — not that head games are

253

my strong suit, and not that they'd work on you in any case. No, I'm going straight to the pain. That's my humble expertise — that's what I do.'

Dalton turned to the cart, and Geiger slowly rotated his palm so he could see it. The skin had a moist sheen. He stared at the number: 917 555 0617. He recited it silently, committing it to memory.

The door to the viewing room swung open and Hall barged out. Dalton turned at the disturbance.

'His hand!' Hall yelled. 'He's got something on his palm!'

Geiger clenched his hand into a fist, rubbing his fingertips against his palm, working at the skin, until Dalton grabbed the hand with both of his and pried the fingers open. Hall arrived as the palm was revealed — a smudged but still legible 917 5 was followed by a smear of blue ink.

'It's a phone number,' said Dalton.

'I can see that,' growled Hall. He glowered at Geiger. 'Don't make this hard. You're smarter than this.'

Geiger nodded. 'How is your head, Mr. Hall?'

Hall ignored him. As he headed back to the viewing room, he spoke over his shoulder to Dalton: 'Get to work on him — now!'

The door slammed. Dalton reached toward the cart and picked up the awl and the butane torch. The awl's steel needle was four inches long and a sixteenth of an inch thick, and the wooden grip was darkened from the sweat of countless uses. The torch fit perfectly in his hand.

'As I was saying. Expertise . . . '

His thumb pressed the torch's ignition button, and a thin, two-inch-long blue flame shot out of the nozzle.

'It's always seemed to me the most egalitarian of assets,' Dalton said. 'Anyone can have an expertise. You don't have to be smart, or rich, or clever. You don't need a degree. There's no privilege involved, no genetic lottery. You can be a ditchdigger and have an expertise. A shoe salesman, a dishwasher, a garbageman . . . '

He brought the needle of the awl into the flame and kept it there.

'I've always felt that you can tell a lot about a person if they have a genuine expertise. If they do, you know for certain, without knowing anything else about them, that they are dedicated. They have applied themselves, they have a passion for something that has driven them to a point well beyond where most people would ever go. That says a lot about a person, don't you think?'

The awl's needle glowed red. Dalton turned off the torch and put it on the cart. Geiger stared at the incandescent needle; it looked like the nucleus of a hearth's fire compressed into a single, lucent filament. He felt the past being awakened by it.

Dalton studied the needle's tip, then brought it close to Geiger's left cheek with an unwavering hand. He grabbed Geiger's hair with his other hand to immobilize the head.

Geiger didn't move. 'You don't have to do that,' he said.

'Where is the boy?'

Geiger shut his eyes. A single piano note cascaded down into a full chord, and luminous puffs of clouds bloomed, laced with streaks of bright, falsetto-fueled lightning. *They say everything can be replaced. They say every distance is not near.*

Very slowly, Dalton pushed the hot needle into Geiger's cheek until Geiger felt the tip break through the inner side and poke at the edge of his tongue. Dalton wiggled the probe.

So I remember every face of every man who put me here.

'Geiger, where is the boy?'

As Dalton had intended, the torture delivered a dual sensation: the searing burn of the hot steel and the sharp pain of the piercing of flesh. Geiger's brain had a moment to form a critique. Heating the needle was, ironically, counterproductive, since it produced something of a desensitizing effect on the skin, diminishing the intensity of the invasion.

Dalton adjusted the awl's angle slightly downward and jabbed it in farther, into the soft, connective tissue beneath the tongue.

'Where is the boy?'

Any day now, any day now . . . The high, sweet voice weaved toward the hot blast of pain and, like a viper, wrapped itself around it and strangled it . . . *I shall be released.*

Dalton shoved the awl in deeper. Its point came up against something solid. Bone. The pain was molten. Geiger was inside the sun.

'Geiger . . . where is the boy?'

Geiger opened his mouth and spat blood. Dalton shook his head and pulled the awl out. The heat had created a circular pink flush on the cheek, and a crimson bubble of blood began to grow in its center. Dalton picked up one of the hand towels and began wiping off the instrument with short, measured strokes.

'I'm curious,' he said. 'Professionally speaking, on a scale of one to ten, how much did that hurt?'

Geiger's eyes opened, and when they swiveled to Dalton light flashed on their wet surfaces. 'How much did *what* hurt?' he said.

Dalton looked up from his cleaning ritual. He had heard the stories for years: about the boy wonder who'd brought a new style to the trade, about the wizard who at one point even had the CIA singing hosannas, about the master who could draw out the truth without drawing blood. But the man in the chair was not what Dalton had expected. He was too . . . But Dalton couldn't complete the thought, couldn't quite put his finger on the qualities that set the real man apart from the legend.

Dalton put the awl down and picked up the bat.

'Now, this takes me back,' he said, and took two short checked swings. 'You like baseball?'

'I never played.'

Dalton swung and hit Geiger flush on the left pectoral. Dalton's grunt was almost as loud as Geiger's, whose lips twisted and seemed to pull the rest of his face inward, like an eddy sucking in debris. The physical agony ballooned inside his chest, and the army of angels' voices in his head sent a volley of high-arcing arrows raining down on the pain. *I see my light come shining* — piercing it, puncturing it, deflating it — *from the west down to the east.*

'Tell me where the boy is, Geiger.'

When no answer came Dalton swung again, hitting the top of the sternum at the nexus of the clavicle. The force of the blow caused the trachea behind it to seize up, and the result was a combined feeling of choking and asphyxiating. Geiger's ears filled with a high-pitched whine that drowned out the music inside him; he struggled reflexively against his bindings, his chest heaving.

Dalton grabbed him by the jaw and rammed his head back against the headrest. The thrust actually helped Geiger gulp some air.

'Listen to me,' Dalton said, leaning in very close. His breath smelled of peppermint. 'I like my work, but I'm not enjoying this. It's weird, you being who you are. So I'm going to tell you something. Call it a professional courtesy. This job is in effect a norell — hear me? *No release likely.* You may as well be at a black site. They'll have me turn you into a Cobb salad before they tell me to stop. So don't do this — stop being whoever you think you're being, because that's not who you are. And because if you don't, you will probably die in this chair.'

Dalton straightened up and rubbed the back of his neck. 'Now, was there any part of that you didn't understand?'

Geiger was finally able to swallow.

'What's a Cobb salad?' he asked.

Dalton brought the bat down hard, smashing it across both quadriceps.

* * *

The loud clap of the blow and the wild twisting of Geiger's torso made Hall, watching through the one-way mirror, grimace.

''What's a Cobb salad?'' he repeated. 'That's very funny.' He turned to Ray, who was sitting on the couch with a glass of ice pressed to his face. 'Considering his situation, that is a great line.'

'Tell Dalton to start cutting him,' said Ray. 'He'll talk. And make sure he tells us where Harry is, too.'

Hall poured himself some Clynelish.

'Hey, me too,' said Ray.

'No alcohol.'

'I'm feeling better, you know.'

Dalton had found some lidocaine in Geiger's medicine cabinet and given Ray a shot in his lower face. The pain had lessened, and Ray's vitality was increasing.

'Ray, Harry didn't give Geiger up. So what makes you think Geiger will give Harry up?' He raised the glass to his lips, then stopped and put the Scotch back down. 'Listen to me, Raymond. The job is Matheson. That's it. After that, I don't ever want to see Geiger or Harry again. Ever. We clear?'

'After this is done, my time's my own,' Ray said.

Hall could see Ray's brain squirming inside his skull like a mutt in a cage. That would be all they'd need — to find Matheson, escape from this mess clean, and then have Ray go after Boddicker and leave a bloody, mile-wide trail. He was beginning to wish Harry had shot the sonofabitch in the head.

Hall turned back to the viewing window. Dalton was focused on the cart, eyeing his options. Geiger — red welts spreading on his chest, bleeding from his cheek — sat in the chair with his head bowed. The two men looked like deep thinkers considering a serious point of debate. Geiger was breathing through his mouth, cheeks puffing slightly with each long exhalation. Then he looked up, staring directly at the glass as if he could see right through it.

'What's your story?' said Hall, as if Geiger could hear him, too. 'You in the market for a little redemption? That what this is? Sorry, man — ain't gonna happen. You're going to hell, just like the rest of us.'

Hall's cell phone rang, and he answered.

'You in position?' he asked.

'Yeah,' said Mitch, 'I'm here. Right downstairs, across the street.'

'Stay put.'

⋆   ⋆   ⋆

Dalton turned to Geiger, hands behind his back, head bobbing in a slow, satisfied nod, as if he had figured out some especially difficult riddle. Mr. Chips in a chamber of horrors.

'What do you do with it?' Dalton asked.

Geiger, his head inclined again, shifted his jaw slowly, searching for a position that would allow him to talk with the least discomfort.

'Do with what?' he mumbled.

'With the pain. I read all the studies. Do you do that 'put it in a box' thing? Or do you go Zen and rely on mind over matter? Which is it? I'm fascinated — honestly. I saw the backs of your legs when we stripped you down, and clearly you've had plenty of chances to practice. So what do you do with the pain?'

'It's my . . . ' The last word was difficult for Geiger's battered mouth to form, so it came out a slushy mutter.

Dalton bent down. 'It's your *what?*'

Geiger's head slowly rose until his eyes met Dalton's. Their faces were just inches apart, so close that Geiger could see his reflection in Dalton's glasses.

'My ex — per — tise,' Geiger said.

Dalton's hands came out from behind him. They held Geiger's antique straight razor, and Dalton saw the shift in Geiger's eyes and the tightening of his chest muscles. The movements were minute but unmistakable. Dalton's feral smile reappeared.

'This is a real beauty, Geiger. Where did you get it? Is this an old friend?' He admired the ornate handiwork on the mother-of-pearl handle. 'And the backs of your legs? You know, the way you deal with the pain tells me that maybe the two of you know each other very well.' He pulled the blade out from its sheath. There was an

261

inscription etched into the polished steel. ' "To Ben, with love, from Paula.' Mom and Dad? Am I right?'

A smoke-spewing train came chugging through a tunnel in Geiger's memory, barreling toward the moment. He sensed what cargo it brought, and the train's clatter and roar set his eardrums vibrating.

'You got cut for years, huh? Was it Mommy or Daddy? I'm thinking it was dear old Dad.'

Geiger saw a glimmer of something new in Dalton's eyes, but it wasn't sympathy.

'You had a very bad time of it, didn't you, Geiger? Sorry, but now you and I are going back there.'

Dalton ran his gloved thumb gently up and down the blade's finely honed edge. The latex split open.

'A little too sharp, I think.'

Geiger watched him start tapping the razor on the cart's metal railing, creating a serrated design the length of the blade's edge. The train kept coming, its Cyclops eye burning fiercely.

'Where is the boy?' Dalton said.

★   ★   ★

'*Are you ready, son?*' said the voice inside Geiger's head.

★   ★   ★

'I'm ready, sir,' Geiger replied.

Dalton turned, smiling quizzically.

262

'No need to be so formal,' he said. He examined the blade and then laid it down on Geiger's left quadricep, four inches above the knee joint. 'We'll work upward. I think that's what your father did. When I reach the groin — if we get that far — I'm going to cut off your testicles.'

Dalton pressed the blade down evenly. The entire length of it sliced into the flesh.

★ ★ ★

The boy lay facedown, naked, on a bench in the great room. The music played softly. 'I see my light come shining . . .'

His father stood over him, holding the pearl-handled razor.

'What do we know, son?' he said.

'Life makes us ache for the things we think we need, and the pain makes us weak.'

'So what must we do?'

'Embrace the pain, a little each day, and grow strong.'

★ ★ ★

Behind his glasses, Dalton's eyes narrowed as he examined his handiwork. The altered razor left a puckered, four-inch incision whose jagged edges sent the blood flowing in different directions across Geiger's thigh.

'Tell me where the boy is, Geiger.'

★ ★ ★

Geiger's father laid the blade down on his upper thigh.

'Steady now, boy.'

It had been years since he had flinched or made a sound during the ritual, but his father still prompted him each time.

'Say it with me, son,' he directed, and they chanted together softly.

'Your blood, my blood, our blood . . . '

★　★　★

'Your blood, my blood, our blood,' mumbled Geiger.

Dalton, about to make his third cut, had stopped to wipe Geiger's blood off his gloves when the slurred words slipped out.

'What did you say?'

He slapped Geiger across the face, smearing his cheeks with his own blood.

'Geiger, you said something. What did you say?'

★　★　★

Geiger's father drew the honed edge across the flesh, opening a thin, wet, red crevasse. The boy stayed rock-still. He was watching the music inside his head.

'Did it hurt, son?'

'It didn't hurt, Father.'

'The truth?'

'Yes.'

'Good. In a world of liars, pain will always bring the truth. When I'm gone, that may serve you well.'

264

Dalton bent down and rested his hands on Geiger's knees.

'Tell me where the boy is.'

Geiger's lids fluttered and rolled up. Dalton peered at him; it was like looking into the windows of an abandoned house.

'It didn't hurt, Father,' said Geiger.

Dalton looked to the viewing room. 'Hall! I'm not sure what we've got here!'

The viewing room door opened.

'What the hell is that supposed to mean?' Hall said.

'The light's on but nobody's home. See for yourself.'

Hall moved toward Geiger. He was becoming increasingly aware of a heavy weariness — not some existential burden or crisis of conscience but a palpable weight, like a ball and chain trailing from an ankle. He'd put in almost twenty years. Nothing got simpler; everything got more complicated, more opaque. No one really knew anything anymore.

Hall stopped beside the barber's chair.

'I'm not going to bullshit you,' said Dalton. 'I don't really know where he is.'

'Where he *is*?'

'I've never seen anything like this before. Believe it or not, I'm not sure he's feeling this.' Dalton adjusted his glasses. 'It's like he feels the pain, but it . . . '

'But it *what*?'

'It doesn't hurt.'

'Cut him again. Let me see what happens.'

Dalton made another cut. Geiger's pupils and nostrils flared, his hands balled up, and the muscles in his forearms visibly hardened. But he made no sound and showed no other response.

Hall grabbed him by the sides of his head with both hands. 'Do you want to die? Is that it?' He bent down and spoke directly into Geiger's face. 'Have you ever seen someone bleed out?'

Geiger shook from the rumble of the churning steel roaring toward him. It was nearly on top of him now.

'Because I have, man — and you wouldn't want a rabid dog to die like that. You hear me?'

But what Geiger heard was a different voice calling to him. And as his eyelids fell, the memory train plowed into him, shattering his view of Hall and the room around him, revealing another, more vibrant world beyond.

★   ★   ★

'Son! Come here, son!'

The boy came out of the cabin and headed up the side of the mountain. It was dark, but there was a good moon and he could make his way through the woods without much difficulty.

'Son! Where are you?'

His father's voice, higher-pitched than usual, seemed to be bouncing off the dense trees, but he had a general sense for where it was coming from.

'I'm coming, Father!'

Something made him start running. It had

266

been raining all week, and his shoes sank into the wet ground with each step.

'The truck, son! Do you see the truck?'

The boy ran a bit farther and then spotted the pickup's dim silhouette about fifty feet away. Leaning downhill, the truck looked like a bull with its head lowered, ready to charge. He could see that its bed was filled with freshly cut four-foot sections of a tree.

'Yes — I see it!'

'Come to the truck! Come around!'

His father lay on his back, pinned beneath the left rear tire, which rested on his thighs. The upper half of his father's body was visible in the moonlight, but his lower legs were obscured by the truck's wheel. To the boy, his father looked like some mythological creature, a half man who must have angered the gods.

'I can't move, son. The truck got stuck. I was trying to jam some wood under the tires when the brake slipped.' Rising from the waist with a growl, he pushed against the tire but couldn't free his legs. He lay back down, his chest rising and falling violently. 'Come pull me out.'

The boy moved behind his father, crouched down, and put his arms around his chest.

'Now pull, son, on three — pull hard! One, two, three!'

With a roar, his father shoved against the tire again and the boy pulled. But his shoes slid from under him in the mud and he fell.

'Again, son. Try again.' The boy got back up, arms tight around his father. 'One, two, three!'

They pulled and pushed, but the result was

the same. His father flopped back into the boy's lap. Exhausted, they huffed in unison, drizzle tapping at their faces.

'What are we going to do, Father?'

'Find some rocks and branches and jam them under the other three tires. Then try and drive the truck forward. Remember how I taught you?'

The drizzle was turning to rain again. As the boy went about his task, he tasted the autumn decay in the air and felt it underfoot beneath the leaves and twigs. He shoved his gatherings beneath the tires and then got into the truck. He had to slide down in the seat so that his feet could reach the gas and brake. He could see his father in the side-view mirror.

'I'm ready, Father!'

'Turn the key — but don't touch the gas yet.'

The boy worked the ignition, and the engine hacked to life.

'Put the stick on 'D,' and then press the gas gently. When you feel the wheels turning, press just a bit harder. Go ahead — do it!'

The boy pushed down on the gas pedal slowly, and the truck began to shudder. He could feel the tires starting to turn, but the truck did not move forward. A low growl began to claw its way out of his father. The boy watched him in the side-view mirror, fists dug into the mud.

'Don't stop!' his father shouted.

The boy pressed harder and the tires began to spit mud, splattering the mirror. His father's torso twisted in its prison, but the truck would not budge.

'More! Harder!'

The boy had to tighten his grip on the wheel as the vibrations increased. His father's growl rose to a bellow. The boy checked the mirror again and saw bits of bright red mixed into the specks of mud.

He jumped from the cab, ran to his father, and knelt beside him. His father lay coated with muck and blood, ragged breath coming from open lips.

'No more, Father — you're bleeding! The wheel is tearing you up!'

'We'll wait till the rain stops and try again.'

'Father, let me go down the mountain. I could find someone and bring them back.'

'No! You will not leave this mountain. It's not time yet.' His father paused to catch his breath. 'There's a rifle in the truck. Bring it to me, son.'

'Why?'

'Wolves, and the bears. They know when things are hurt. And they can smell blood. Now bring me the rifle and then go home.'

'I want to stay here with you.'

His father's eyes found his. Raindrops had cleared thin, meandering paths down his father's dirty face.

'Father . . .' The boy was silent for a moment. 'Does anyone know I'm here?'

'The world knows nothing of you. That is my gift to you.' He coughed, and then spat blood. 'You are no one.'

Something started to tighten in the boy's chest. His head ached, and he felt his heart pounding.

'Father . . . ' he began.

269

But his father would not let him continue. He reached up and grabbed hold of the boy's jacket.

'You're my son, and I've given you what you needed.' He walloped the boy across the face, but the boy did not cry. His father pulled him chin to chin. 'You see? No tears. Remember: better to be strong than to be loved.'

His father closed his eyes and turned his head away. The boy got to his feet, walked to the truck, and climbed inside.

⋆ ⋆ ⋆

Ray entered the session room and came over to join Hall and Dalton.

'Jesus, what the hell is going on?' Ray asked. 'Is he asleep?'

'I wouldn't call it sleep,' said Dalton. He turned to Hall. 'Should I try and bring him out of it?'

'No,' said Hall. He put a cigarette between his lips, lit it, and winced at his strong inhalation. 'Give him a few more minutes. Let's see what happens. Maybe we can use it.'

⋆ ⋆ ⋆

The boy shot up awake in the truck. The sudden burst of screams mixed with guttural grunts jerked his eyes to the mirror, and he saw dark shapes thrashing about near the back wheel. He grabbed the rifle and jumped out. The grunting stopped; two pairs of copper eyes flashed at him, and then the wolves went back to work, heads jerking violently as teeth ripped flesh. His father's

270

howling began again, his arms flailing, his fists useless. The boy raised the rifle and fired. The blast sent the wolves running, and the recoil kicked the boy down on his back. He lay there for a moment, breathless, staring up at the huge, scarred moon resting precariously on the tops of the pines. Then he sat up and moved to his father's side.

The boy watched his father's chest rise and fall very slowly, as if a great invisible weight lay upon it. With each ascent, parts of him caught the moonlight and glistened dark burgundy; with each descent came a soggy gurgle, leaking life.

His father's right arm rose at the elbow, beckoning. The boy leaned closer and saw that the wolves had torn away his father's coat and taken parts of his shoulders and arms. His left cheekbone gleamed white beneath the moon. His mouth opened and blood trickled out.

'The pain,' he gasped.

'What can I do, Father?'

'Where is my knife? Give it to me.'

The knife lay in the mud. The boy put it in his father's hand. His father's arm rose, but there was no strength in him, and his fist, clutching the blade, fell feebly upon his chest.

'Help me.' His eyes wandered in their sockets until they found his son. 'Help me.'

'How? I don't understand.'

His father's forefinger rose an inch and tapped at his chest. 'Here.'

The boy shook his head rapidly back and forth. 'No!' he said, his voice a whimper. 'No, I won't do it!'

'Do as I say, son.'

The boy was crying now. 'Father . . . please!'

*　★　★　★*

Geiger's audience leaned forward at his muttering.

'What did he say?' Hall asked Dalton.

'He said, 'Father, please.''

'Look,' Ray said, pointing. 'He's crying.'

Tears leaked from the corners of Geiger's closed eyes, sliding down his cheeks and turning pink when they mixed with his blood. Suddenly he began to shudder violently, his body quaking in its restraints.

'Wake him now?' asked Dalton.

'No,' said Hall. 'Not yet.'

*　★　★　★*

His father eyed the boy's tears, and then his face twisted into a mask of disgust.

'Is this what I've made of you? A weeping, useless little boy? Then go. Get out of my sight! Leave the rest to the wolves. I don't want your face to be the last thing I see.'

The boy felt a surge of hot, viscous blood in his chest, and then an unstoppable force rose up from a dark hole and rushed through every part of his body, making him shake violently.

'I hate you!' he shouted.

His father found the strength to shake his head. 'No, you don't. It takes strength to hate. All my work — for nothing.'

272

The boy saw the bloody lips move again, but now he could not hear the words above the roar in his ears. For a moment the world went black. It's the moon, the boy thought; the moon must have fallen down.

Finally he looked again at his father. 'Where?' he asked.

His father's fingertip settled on a point just to the left of his sternum. 'Here,' he said, a grim smile pulling at his ruined lips.

The boy placed the knife's point next to the finger and wrapped both his trembling hands around the hilt. Slowly, he pushed the blade down into his father's heart.'

★   ★   ★

Geiger's mind was sent reeling away from the dark forest, defying the vision's gravity and seeking refuge beyond it. But what came before him was a floating curtain, and then, as the curtain parted, it revealed the long shelf carrying all his session books: the black binders, the hundreds of Joneses, the thousands of pages filled with strategies and methods, reactions and conclusions. Geiger could see the faces of his subjects, he could hear every epithet and plea ever uttered, every sound a human can make in fear or pain. Confronting him was a compendium of the darkest of man's arts — and a garish portrait of a monster that now, for the first time, he recognized as himself.

A sudden wave of nausea rolled over Geiger, and he began to retch. He hadn't eaten since the previous day, and dry heaves racked him.

Hall waited until the first wave seemed to pass. 'Go back to work, Dalton. Right away — now!'

'Don't cut me anymore,' Geiger said between gasps. 'Please.'

Dalton, Hall, and Ray shared a stunned glance. 'No more pain. Please, no more.'

'Then tell me where the boy is,' Hall commanded.

Another surge of nausea rose up, and the retching consumed him again.

'Jesus Christ, Geiger! Where is the kid?'

'Still at my house,' Geiger sputtered.

Hall felt a hot spike of adrenaline, but he quickly throttled the rush. 'You left him alone?'

'Harry needed a doctor. I needed a gun . . .'

Hall was shaking his head. 'Don't fuck with me, Geiger. That long a trip, you wouldn't leave him alone.'

Geiger's head rose, a fine thread of blood-tinged spittle drooping from his lips. 'He isn't alone,' he said.

While the words hung between them, Hall felt a singular sensation: if only for a moment, chaos, chance, and strategy all seemed to be joining hands. 'Matheson is with him?' he said. 'How?'

Geiger spit out another dollop of blood. 'They IM'd — from my house.'

'Does he still have what we want?'

'I don't know. I don't know what you want.'

'Address?'

'Six eighty-two West One thirty-fourth Street. Tan building.'

'Right. Boarded windows. I saw it.'

274

'You need the code.'

'What is it?' Hall said, patting his pockets for a pen.

'Seven-three-two-two-three. Easy to remember.' He looked Hall full in the face, his stare cavernous. 'It's 'peace' on your phone.'

For a moment, Hall was unable to look away from Geiger. Something was missing from his eyes, something that had been there yesterday. Hall had seen it happen before: the bottom gives way, and the heart of a man drops out of sight like a body through a trapdoor. Hall felt a brief quiver in his gut.

'Clean him up,' he told Dalton. 'Stop the bleeding. He stays in the chair till we come back. Come on, Ray.'

They went to the elevator and stepped inside. Hall pushed the gate shut and they descended.

★　★　★

Dalton tried folding the razor back into the sheath, but the dented blade didn't fit anymore.

'Sorry about your razor.'

He tossed it onto the cart and started wiping Geiger's wounds with a hand towel and applying pressure. There was a lot of blood.

'You have a talk with your old man?'

Geiger stared back, barely conscious.

'That was very intriguing. But it was a little disappointing at the end, when you came to. I thought you'd take it farther down the line — I was sure you would, actually — which is why I think you may be lying.'

275

Geiger's voice was a whisper. 'Why didn't you say so?'

'My job is to make you talk. It's Hall's job to figure out whether you're telling the truth.' He reached back to the cart and picked up a roll of gauze. 'If you are lying, then either you're buying time or they're walking into something.'

Dalton started wrapping the gauze around Geiger's mauled thigh, raising the limb every cycle to push the roll under and back up.

'In case they do come back, I'm not going to tape this up — I'll just tie it off for now. You want some water?'

He looked up. Geiger's head hung to the side, his eyes shut, a slow drip of scarlet blood creeping from the corners of his lips, down his jaw.

★ ★ ★

Driving up 134th Street, Hall was pleased to note that Mr. Memz and his sidewalk office were gone. He slowed the Lexus at Geiger's door — they would need to be as close as possible so they could quickly get Matheson into the car. But there were no empty spaces, so he double-parked with the engine running.

Hall turned to Ray. 'How do you feel?'

'I'm all right,' said Ray, nodding. 'Face is just kinda numb.'

Hall looked his partner over. 'Let's go.'

They stepped out. Ray headed up the steps as Hall glanced down the alleyway.

'Hold up,' Hall said. 'Let me see if there's a back door.'

276

He jogged thirty feet to the dumpster at the end of the alley and climbed up. Peering over the top of the wooden fence, he saw the stoop's overhang and the back door beneath it. He climbed down and walked quickly back to Ray.

'There's a back entrance. You go in the front, I'll take the back. When I get to the back door, I'll call your cell. We stay on the line, and on my signal we punch in all but the last number of the code. When I say, 'Go,' we enter the last digit at the same time and go in — guns in hand, but just for show. Got it?'

'Yeah.'

'The code is seven-three-two-two-three.'

'Seven-three-two-two-three. All set.'

'We grab him, leave the kid, and go out the front. Okay?'

Ray nodded, and Hall ran down the alley. Back up on the dumpster, he vaulted over the fence and landed in a crouch on the backyard grass. He took out his cell and dialed as he walked up to the back door.

'Ready?' he whispered into his phone.

'Yeah.'

'Okay. Start now.'

Through his cell Hall heard the front door panel's chirps as Ray began entering the code. He started doing the same on the back door's panel.

'Okay,' Hall whispered. 'Last number. Ready?'

'Yes,' said Ray.

'Go,' said Hall, just as two loud gunshots put him in a one-eighty spin. His gun came out, searching for a target. Then he heard two more shots — *Pop! Pop!* — and realized that it was a pneumatic tool spitting air bullets at the body shop up the street. Hall pocketed the gun and let out a deep breath mingled with a muttered 'Fuck.' Turning back to the panel, he entered the last number but the back door didn't click open. He jabbed at 'cancel' and reentered the code. Nothing.

Hall pressed the phone to his ear. He thought he could hear Ray moving through the house.

'Ray, talk to me. You inside?'

'Yeah.'

'I can't open my door. There must be a shutoff in the system after one door accepts the code.'

'Well, stop trying. There's nobody here except a goddamn one-eyed cat.'

'What?' Hall's temples began throbbing. 'You check everywhere?'

'There are only two inside doors. Closet and bathroom. That's it. Nobody's fucking home!'

Hall turned and leaned back against the door. It struck him that Geiger had a very nice backyard, and that no one would ever suspect that the house had one — which was very much Geiger. In lying, Geiger had been buying time, and every minute bought was a minute Hall lost. Hall would have to call Dalton and tell him to start in again — he had no other play — but he was beginning to think that Geiger would never talk, and Matheson would win the game, and then there would be hell to pay.

He ended the call with Ray and tapped in Dalton's number.

'Yes?' Dalton's voice said.

'Put him on. Put me on speaker, so you can both hear.'

★ ★ ★

Dalton knew voices. He could read them like a surgeon reads an X-ray, and he was surprised to hear more temperate resignation than fury or resolve in Hall's words. It was the voice of someone who had become deeply weary of his task, its tone as flat as a mortician's.

Geiger's head was at half-mast, a rose-hued bubble at the center of his lips. When Dalton tapped him on the shoulder and he stirred, the bubble popped.

'It's for you,' said Dalton. He pushed the speaker button and held the cell phone to Geiger's ear.

'Yes,' Geiger said, his voice a hoarse whisper.

'Dalton is going to go back to work now,' Hall said.

Geiger said nothing. Dalton raised one eyebrow, then pulled a new pair of gloves from his pants pocket.

'Geiger,' Hall continued, 'I need to know that you understand what I just said.'

'I understand what you said. Where are you?'

A corrosive chuckle leaked into the session room from Dalton's cell phone. 'Where *am* I?'

★ ★ ★

Standing on Geiger's back stoop, Hall answered his own question: 'We're at your place, but there's no one here except your cat.' He strolled down into the yard. He wished now that he'd had that Scotch. 'Okay. So you bought Harry and the kid some time. I get it.'

'No, Mr. Hall. I don't think you do.'

A new smoothness in Geiger's tone surprised Hall, and then he flinched at the sound of Ray's fist hammering the inside of the back door.

'Hey!' Ray called. 'I can't get out!'

'You're locked in, Mr. Hall.'

Ray pounded the door again. 'Hear me, Richie? The doors won't open! The fucking code doesn't work!'

Hall sighed. Another nail in their coffin. 'And we need the exit code to get out,' he said.

'That's right, Mr. Hall.'

Hall watched two squirrels race halfway down the tree, each chasing the other, round and round. Clearly neither wanted to catch the other — it was the chase that gave them pleasure.

'How many times have you entered the code to try and get out?' Geiger asked.

Hall's mind almost ticked past the obvious — 'You're locked in, Mr. Hall' — and then made a U-turn. Geiger thinks he has *all three of us* trapped inside the house, Hall thought. Score one for the bad guys.

'Can I ask why?' said Hall.

'Because you can't leave without putting in the exit code — and if you enter an incorrect code twice, the system becomes armed.'

'Armed,' Hall said. 'Go on.'

'There are twenty directional explosive charges behind the drywall, Mr. Hall. If you enter an incorrect exit code a third time, they will detonate — and the house will implode.'

'Implode? Like those old casinos in Vegas?'

'Yes. And Mr. Hall — it's best you don't try to remove the window bars, either.'

'Right,' Hall said, looking back toward the house. 'Geiger, hold on a sec.' Hall muted the cell. 'Ray!' he shouted. 'How many times did you enter the code?'

'To get out? Uh . . . twice!'

'Well, don't touch the security panel again! You got that?'

'Why?' Ray called.

'Just don't! Don't touch *anything*!'

Hall sat down with his back against the tree. He took out a cigarette and flicked his lighter. But instead of lighting up, he just stared at the flame. He had to start shifting his focus, put on a new lens. If they didn't get Matheson, he would need to have a way out, because there would be no going back for a sit-down with the man to explain his failure. There would be no favors to call in, and no helping hands, either. That meant Ray and Mitch would be on their own, too. But they'd never been the Three Musketeers, anyway — there'd been no buying into the 'all for one and one for all' crap. If need be, Mitch would drive the bus while Ray threw him under it.

Hall lit his cigarette and punched Geiger back up on the cell. 'Okay. So you've got three fuckups locked in your house.' He allowed himself a sliver of a private grin. 'What now?'

'Dalton releases me, and when I'm safely away I'll call you back and give you the exit code.'

'How about you give me the code now, and

when we get out I tell Dalton to let you go?'

'I like my idea better, Mr. Hall.'

Ray began banging on the back door and shouting again.

'Hey, Richie! What the hell is going on?'

Hall rolled his eyes. 'Geiger, give me a minute, okay?'

'Sure.'

Hall muted the cell and walked across the yard and back up the stoop. 'Ray,' he called through the door, 'we've got a problem here. The house is one big bomb!'

'*What?*' Ray said. 'Well, maybe we oughta, y'know, call somebody!'

'Yeah? Tell me who we should call and I'll give them a ring. Want me to call the fire department? Or how about the cops?'

'Fuck you.'

'I'm dealing with this, Ray — just hang on for a few minutes.'

Hall sat back down against the door. With a thumb and forefinger, he pressed on his eyes so firmly that he saw white phantoms crawling on the insides of his lids. When had he slept last — thirty-six hours ago? Probably more.

Something brushed against his arm, and Hall opened his eyes to see a cat coming out the pet door. The cat glanced at him — Hall saw that it was missing an eye — and then walked into the yard.

The encounter gave Hall an idea. 'Ray,' he called. 'Tell me something about the inside of the place.'

'Huh?'

'Tell me about something in Geiger's house that caught your eye.'

'Well, he's got a great CD rack. Custom-made.'

Hall brought the phone back up and turned the mute off.

'Okay, Geiger,' he said, 'your way. Dalton — you there?'

'Yes,' said Dalton.

'Let him go.'

'I heard you, Mr. Hall — but just repeat it one more time so we're clear.'

'Let Geiger go. Release him.'

'All right.'

'How long before we get the code, Geiger?'

'About half an hour,' Geiger answered. 'Fifteen minutes to stitch up my thigh and get out of here, and another fifteen minutes after I leave.'

'I'll be waiting. And by the way, Geiger, this is a real nice CD rack you got here. Can I put on some music without blowing us up?'

'Feel free, Mr. Hall.'

* * *

The line went dead and Dalton clicked off. He put the cell on the cart, picked up his jacket from the bottom shelf, and took a Ruger LCP .380 pistol from one of its pockets.

Watching him, Geiger said, 'I'm not going to do anything to you.'

'Strictly precautionary,' Dalton said, his voice without inflection. 'I'm going to undo your right wrist, then you do the rest. Don't begin until I've stepped away or I'll shoot you. Understood?'

'Yes.'

Dalton kept his eyes and gun on Geiger's face while his free hand found the wrist restraint and popped its clasp open. He took four steps back, snapped his gloves off, and dropped them onto the floor. Geiger noted the precision of Dalton's movements: he was meticulous to the last gesture, sweatless, unruffled. His gun still had Geiger's forehead for a target.

'Go ahead,' Dalton said.

Geiger raised his arm. The initial sensation was of extreme lightness, but then, as he reached down, the feeling inverted, and the bone and flesh felt so sodden that his arm might have dragged him out of the chair and down to the floor if he hadn't been bound at the chest. He undid the chest strap, and his ribs lifted and his lungs swelled like bellows. The air streaming in felt cool and dense.

Dalton chuckled drily. 'Geiger, this has been fascinating. When I write my memoirs it will be one of the highlights.'

Geiger reached down and undid the left ankle restraint. 'You're going to write a book?'

'When I retire. I've already chosen a title: *Dalton: My Life as a Torturer*.'

Geiger freed his other ankle.

'But not to worry, Geiger, I'll change your name.' Dalton let out a short *hmmm* of a laugh. 'I guess I'll have to include an author's note: 'Some names have been changed to protect the *guilty*.''

Geiger's fingers closed on the last binding at

284

his other wrist and he pried it open. He looked up at Dalton, his body suddenly feeling lighter again. 'I'm going to stand up now and go into the viewing room to stitch myself up and get some fresh clothes.'

'Go ahead.' Dalton nodded, waving Geiger on with the gun.

Geiger rose from the barber's chair. His first steps were hesitant, and he held his arms out slightly at the hips for balance. The lower half of him felt newly weighted, as if parts of his insides had come loose and slid below his waist before settling in his legs and feet. The loosely wrapped gauze around his thigh, soaked with blood, began to droop. As he shuffled forward, the gauze came unwound and trailed behind him on the floor.

Dalton followed him through the door and stopped as Geiger opened an armoire at the far end of the viewing room. On one side were shelves of medical supplies, on the other drawers of clothes. Geiger took out packets of absorbable traumatic sutures, a pair of scissors, and rolls of gauze and adhesive. He considered lidocaine spray but decided against it; the wounds were jagged and thus would be tricky to sew up, and the pain would help guide him so that he could achieve a tight stitch.

He pulled pants and a black pullover from a drawer and limped to the couch. He let himself drop back into the cushions, but his mind and body were out of sync, and the back of his head smacked hard into the wall before he finished his descent.

'Ouch,' said Dalton, and lowered the weapon.

Geiger held the needle and thread in front of his nose, and in trying to marry them struggled with a frequent shift between foreground and background, as if his brain were a camera lens searching for a focal point. On his third pass Geiger found the needle's eye with the suture.

Dalton pulled a bottle of Rémy Martin off the bar and poured some into a glass. Sipping the cognac, he watched Geiger sew first one cut and then another, his stitches like those of a master tailor. He didn't see Geiger flinch even once — the man had the tolerance of a bull.

'Where'd you learn how to do that?' Dalton asked.

'My father taught me.'

Geiger had been working at spreading out the pain — taking the waffling burn in his chest, the dull throb in his mouth, and the sharp, barbed pangs in his thigh and sending them throughout his body until the pain was everywhere, making each stab and tug of the needle more a part of a whole rather than an individual assault on his flesh.

'Is he a doctor?'

'A carpenter. Was — he's dead.'

Geiger pulled the last stitch, snipped it with the scissors, and knotted the end, then sat back and rubbed his palms against the cushions to rid them of his blood. 'May I have a drink, please?' he said.

'What can I get you?'

'Anything.'

Dalton put down his cognac, examined the

bar's selection, and poured an inch of vodka into a glass. His gun nosing up, he walked the drink over to Geiger.

'Here you are. Left hand — nice and slow, please.'

Geiger's eyelids dropped. A long breath blew out of his open mouth. 'Give me a second — I'm in a lot of pain.'

'Take your time.'

'You're very good at what you do, Dalton.'

'Praise from Caesar.'

Geiger's hand drifted up for the glass. When Dalton's gaze moved to it, Geiger's good leg snapped up and smashed into Dalton's groin. Dalton doubled over, his spectacles falling, and Geiger's forearm swung into his jaw with such force that two teeth shot out of his mouth. As Dalton went to his knees, Geiger swatted the gun out of his hand. Dalton held there for a moment, swaying, and then toppled over onto his stomach, one cheek to the floor, huffing like a beached fish.

'There was no praise intended,' said Geiger.

Geiger moved carefully off the couch and straddled Dalton, holding Dalton's left arm high up on his back and pinning the other arm to the floor at the wrist. Geiger's blow had rattled Dalton's skull with such intensity that several blood vessels in his right eye had burst, covering it with a spidery hemorrhage.

'Make a fist with your right hand,' Geiger said.

'A fist?' Dalton said, gasping.

'Yes, make a fist.'

'Why?'

'Because you're not going to do this anymore.'

Dalton shook his head. His chest was heaving, but he managed a wolfish grin. 'No. I don't think I will. I want to see Geiger the Great in action. A once-in-a-lifetime opportunity, you know?'

'Sorry. You're about a day too late.'

Geiger pushed Dalton's left arm higher up his back, and Dalton squealed with pain. 'Dalton, for most of my life I've wondered what it would be like to kill someone. Say no again and you will give me one less thing to wonder about.' He kept cranking Dalton's arm higher. 'Make a fist.' And higher still. '*Do it.*'

A muffled syllable signaled concession, and finally Dalton's right hand curled into a ball against the floor. Geiger made a fist of his own and sent it smashing down on Dalton's, whose scream nearly drowned out the sound of his fingers breaking. Then Geiger grabbed Dalton's left hand and swiftly jerked four of the fingers back until the bones snapped. Dalton's howl was lower this time but longer, and soon it became a rough, growling whir. His hands, resting on the floor with the fingers splayed, looked like two crabs someone had stepped on at the beach.

Geiger got to his feet and fell back onto the couch. He took a deep breath. 'Early retirement, Dalton. Teach yourself to type with your toes and you can start writing your memoirs.'

Geiger picked up his pants and pullover and considered the least torturous way to put them on.

19

'That's it,' said Harry, turning from a window back to the living room. He sighed. 'That's the whole story.'

After Geiger had left, Corley had put out an assortment of finger food, and once Harry and Ezra had gorged themselves, he'd sent Ezra into the bedroom to watch television and then demanded that Harry tell him exactly what was going on or he would call the police. In telling the tale of Ezra, Harry at first tried to skirt the details of what he and Geiger actually did for a living, but early on it became clear that everything would have to come out. It was the first time he had ever told anyone about his work, and the undertow of the loathsome truth pulled at him.

As Harry talked, Lily sat next to him on the couch, her fingers twisting the ends of her hair in a secret ritual. Corley, sitting across from them, seemed lost in a world of his own, his eyes locked on the tightly spun gold-and-blue swirls of the living room's Oriental rug. In truth, Corley's eyes saw nothing in the room. His vision was pointed inward at the countless pieces of Geiger's psychic puzzle.

'Doc?'

Corley was shaken by the revelation about Geiger's work, and by his blindness to it. Torture. Was this how Geiger's hidden past had been expressing itself all these years? A tiny, sharp-toothed beast started gnawing at Corley's insides. Should he have seen it — or at least sensed something?

'Doc?'

Corley looked up. 'Yes?'

'I'm sorry this ended up on your doorstep. I really am.'

Corley waved away the apology but then gave Harry a narrow look. 'Putting aside, for the moment, what you two have been doing for the past decade — you do realize that this is kidnapping, a serious federal crime?'

'Yeah, but we didn't kidnap him. We're the . . . un-kidnappers.'

Harry took a sip of ginger ale and fisted a burp. He put a piece of sourdough pretzel up to Lily's lips, but she ignored the offering.

'Eat something,' he said.

'I can't remember,' she said, her eyes darting from side to side.

'Remember what?'

'There are so many words, and so many different meanings, and they all have to be in the right place. Where's Harry?' she asked.

Harry gave Corley a quick glance. 'Jesus, she said my name.' Then he turned her face to his. 'Right here, Lily. Hey, it's me, Harry.'

Corley got up and came over, crouching in front of her. He studied her eyes' movements, noting the extended frozen stare that was interrupted by sudden zigs to the left and right.

'You said sometimes she comes out with a lyric as a response to things?' Corley asked.

'Yeah. Sometimes it feels like a connection to

something, sometimes not.'

Corley leaned in close to Lily, his face just inches from hers.

'Lily?' he said. Suddenly he smacked his palms together. Harry flinched in surprise, but Lily remained unmoving. 'Lily!'

'I want to go,' she said.

'I want to go, too, Lily,' said Corley. 'Where shall we go?'

Lily half-sang, half-spoke: '*Way down below the ocean . . .* '

'See?' said Harry. 'That could mean something — or nothing. She loved that song, and you just said, 'Where shall we go?' It can really make you crazy.'

Corley returned to his chair. 'There is something going on inside. Whether it's reactive, responsive, or random, I don't know. But there's a process at work, and at the end of it, she arrives at some kind of decision — for lack of a better word — and she sings.' He shook his head. 'Sometimes I think it takes superhuman strength to construct and maintain the kinds of walls that keep the horror locked up and the world at bay. Is she on medication?'

'Yeah, I think so, but I don't know what kind.'

'Well, we're going to need to keep a close eye on her. What was she like, Harry? Before.'

'A little spacey, but very smart. Funny, too, in a goofy-funny way.' He shook his head ruefully. 'And for so many years now, I haven't been there for her.'

'Harry, you know what someone once said about guilt?'

'What?'

'If a man didn't feel guilty, he'd probably think it was his fault.'

Harry's shoulders dipped. 'Doc, it's appreciated, but I don't need a shrink. I know who I am.'

They eyed each other, Harry's account of the day's events once again floating between them, invisible but magnetic.

'He's been gone a long time, Doc,' Harry said.

Corley glanced at his watch. Almost three hours. Worst-case scenarios were starting to fill his head.

'I'm sure he's all right,' said Harry, but his lack of confidence in the statement was clear to both of them. Harry tried to grin. 'I mean, he's a big boy, right?'

Corley craved a cigarette. He wondered if he had any regular-strength Marlboros stashed anywhere.

'No, Harry,' he said. 'He's a very *little* boy.'

★   ★   ★

Geiger, carrying a small gym bag, walked for three blocks before he found a café with an empty booth shadowed enough to obscure his presence. He had taped a two-inch square of gauze over the hole in his cheek, but nothing could hide his stark pallor. There was much to do, but at the moment he needed black coffee and a few minutes to sit in relative solitude. He knew what Corley would say: Don't let these memories slip away, don't lock them back up.

292

They're part of you. Keep them alive and carry them with you.

The waiter put his iced coffee down, 'Anything else?'

'No.'

The waiter, a kid of no more than twenty, made no effort to hide his staring at Geiger's face. 'You okay?' he said.

'Yes.'

Geiger heard the hollow chafing in his voice and saw the dubious look in the kid's eyes.

'Yes,' he said more firmly. 'I'm okay.'

The waiter clearly wasn't convinced, but he wandered off.

Geiger took a long drink from his glass. He had wanted the coffee hot, but he knew that heat would encourage more bleeding from the wounds in his mouth. He swirled the chilled liquid around in his cheeks for twenty or thirty seconds before he swallowed, and then sank back into the booth's cushions.

He knew that inner scars had given way and old wounds had opened. For years, he'd been vigilant about keeping the outside from getting in. But what he'd really done was seal in the demons that dwelt in his darkest places. Now he was turning inside out, and he didn't need to summon Corley's spirit to understand that what had been dead was exhumed and alive again.

You're my son. I've given you what you needed.

*   *   *

Hall finished dragging the bench from Geiger's yard to the alley-side wall. He stepped up and climbed over the fence, then jumped onto the dumpster and down to the alley. He called Ray on his cell as he walked toward the street.

'Yeah?'

'I'm in the alley, going back to the car.'

'Fucker better call soon.'

'He said half an hour.'

'And if he doesn't?'

'I think I'm starting to understand Mr. Geiger. He'll call.'

'And if he doesn't?'

Hall slid into the Lexus. 'I don't know, Ray. I haven't gotten that far.'

'Well, get there, man,' Ray said, and hung up.

Hall adjusted the seat so he could stretch out. He had that tingle in his fingertips, usually a harbinger of inspiration. He didn't believe in luck, but he did believe that sometimes chaos threw all its pieces to the wind and when they fell back down to earth they fit together. It was the 'put a million monkeys at typewriters and someday you'll get a masterpiece' scenario, and Hall's instincts told him that this shambles could still turn out to be his *Hamlet*. As he lay back in the Lexus, he saw it clearly, right there in front of him: his one last shot.

* * *

Mitch picked up his cell phone and called Hall.

'Yeah?'

294

'I'm on him,' Mitch said. 'He's coming out of a café.'

Mitch watched as Geiger limped to a pay phone on the corner. Earlier, he had spent almost two hours parked down the block from Geiger's Ludlow Street place. When Geiger had hobbled out, he'd looked like a shell-shocked vet hitting the street for the first time since a mortar had put him down. For three blocks, Mitch had crawled behind him in his cab, and then he had parked again, half a block from the café.

Now, observing Geiger as he picked up the pay phone's handset, Mitch was starting to feel pumped. He had the come-to-Papa buzz in his pulse that kicked in when things were looking up and chance finally decided to get with the program. Sometimes you could just sit back and watch it all come together and grin.

Mitch sipped his coffee. It was cold, but he didn't mind. It tasted just fine.

★　★　★

Geiger held the phone to his ear but kept a finger on the cradle's release. He was trying to resurrect Matheson's phone number: 917-555-0 . . . His mind's eye squinted at the murky vision of the numbers he'd written on his hand after their IM session: 061 — what? 8?

He dialed the number. It rang once.

'Hello?' said a man's voice.

'Matheson?'

'Who?'

'Matheson?'

'There's no Matheson here,' said the voice.

Geiger hung up and let his forehead rest against the booth's siding. He was managing the pain and the loss of blood, but doing so required nearly all his resources, and very little energy remained for focus and recall. He tried to see himself writing the number on his palm: 061 . . . 7?

He dialed again. Someone picked up before the first ring finished.

'Yes?' a man said.

'Matheson?'

'Yes.'

There was blood in Geiger's mouth. He swallowed. 'Listen carefully.'

'Where is my *son*?' Matheson said, his voice vibrating with fear and anger.

'Matheson, do not speak. Your only part in this conversation is to listen. This is not a negotiation. You will go where I tell you to go and bring what I ask you to bring. If you don't, your son will not survive your recklessness. So please, listen carefully . . . '

⋆ ⋆ ⋆

Geiger got out of the cab and headed into Central Park. He felt light-headed as he walked, and he was aware that some people stared at him as he made his way toward the quadrangle of ball fields. All four fields had games in progress, and because of the July Fourth holiday, there were so many spectators that a person could easily become an anonymous part of the crowd.

Geiger had told Matheson to sit on a bench behind the westernmost field with a *New York Times* rolled up tightly on his lap, but even without the setup he could have picked the man out of a mass of strangers. He had seen this sort of extreme fear so many times: the raccoon eyes from sleeplessness, the high-strung shoulders, the anxious, bouncing heel. Matheson's gray suit needed pressing and his handsome, stone-cut face needed a shave. Geiger could see that under less stressful circumstances he would look very much like a thirty-four-year-old Ezra.

Geiger came up behind him.

'Matheson?'

He tried to talk out of the right side of his mouth to minimize the pain, and it made his words oddly slurred. Matheson started to turn, but Geiger planted his hands firmly on the other man's shoulders to stop the maneuver.

'Don't turn around. Just watch the game.'

'Where is Ezra?'

'You have something for me, yes?'

'You get it when my son is sitting right here.' Matheson patted the bench. 'Where is he?'

'You've lost the right to be with your son.'

'*What?*'

'From now on, it will be Ezra's decision whether you see him or not. You have no say in it.'

'What the hell are you — '

He started to turn again, and this time Geiger dug his fingers into the hollows above his clavicle. Matheson froze with a soft yowl.

'Do not try and turn around again. If you do,

I will break your neck.'

Matheson felt something tug at his brain. It was the *voice*. He'd heard it somewhere before.

★ ★ ★

Hall shot up straight in the driver's seat at Mitch's news.

'Matheson? You're sure?'

'Yup,' Mitch replied, his voice coming through the cell. 'I followed Geiger's cab to the park, and now I'm about fifty feet away from them. Matheson's sitting on a bench and Geiger's standing right behind him. Goddamn fucking jackpot, man!'

Hall's lips held their tight, hard line. He wasn't ready to celebrate just yet. 'But the kid's not with him?'

'No. No kid.'

'Then what the hell is this about?' Hall's fingers did a drum roll on the steering wheel. 'What are they doing now?'

'Nothing. Talking.'

Hall stared at his cell. He would have to make another status call soon, and he wondered how long he could put it off before the man on the other end of the line decided to not answer his call.

★ ★ ★

'Who are you?' Matheson said.

'Not who you think I am.'

'Meaning what — that you're not one of

298

them? So why won't you give me Ezra?'

'Because right now, you're as much a danger to Ezra as they are. Whatever you're peddling, you brought your son into it. You made him a target, and a victim.'

'Peddling? I'm not — '

'So here is what is going to happen. You're going to give me whatever it is they're looking for — let's just call it the package. Then I'm going to take Ezra to his mother — '

'Julia? She's here?'

'And once Ezra is safe, I'm going to contact the men who are after you. I will tell them that I have the package, and assure them that as long as they stay away from Ezra they won't have to worry about it ever seeing the light of day.'

'You don't know who I am,' Matheson said, 'or what this is all about, do you?'

'And I don't care, either.'

'Have you heard of Veritas Arcana?'

'The whistle-blowers?'

'Yes. That's who I am. But Veritas Arcana isn't an organization — it's only me and a few committed volunteers. And now you're asking me to bury something the world needs to know about. Except it doesn't belong to me — or you.'

'And you'd put Ezra's life up as collateral?'

'No. I love my son — I would never do that.'

'You don't understand, Matheson. You already did.'

Matheson started to say something, then stopped. He brought one hand up to his face, bowed his head, and covered his eyes. 'Christ,' he said. 'I had no idea they were so close. I just

299

needed six or seven more hours. Just . . . ' He sighed deeply and went silent.

A batter approached the plate, doffed his cap to the crowd, and patted his substantial belly. There were as many laughs as cheers.

'Two crucial points, Matheson,' said Geiger. 'One: as much as anything, luck is the reason that your son isn't already dead. And two: they won't stop. Not as long as they feel there is the slightest chance they can accomplish their task. That's what they do. They don't stop.'

Something scratched at Matheson's mind again.

'I know your voice,' he said.

'No, you don't.'

The cost of his conversation with Matheson was making Geiger tremble with exhaustion. It was time to get what he came for and go.

'Matheson, hand the package over — now.'

Matheson nodded at the ground, then reached inside his jacket. He took out a manila envelope and held it up. Geiger took the envelope and slipped it into his bag.

Matheson sighed again. 'Would you tell Ezra I love him — and that I'm sorry?'

★ ★ ★

'Matheson just gave him an envelope,' reported Mitch. 'Manila, about four by ten.'

'Fuck.' Hall had a cigarette going and took a deep drag. 'Why would Matheson give it to him?' He was asking himself more than Mitch. 'And how could Geiger even know what it is?'

'Maybe he doesn't. Maybe it's not our stuff. Maybe it's money and Geiger is holding Matheson up before he gives the kid back. Jesus, Richie — who cares? This is our chance. I'm fifty feet away. I could steamroll 'em and grab — '

'No! You're in a crowd in Central Park, for chrissake. Since 9/11 every fucking New Yorker wants to be a hero. You'd have a dozen people jumping on you before you know it.'

'Okay, Richie, but now Geiger's leaving. Who do I stick with?'

Hall turned on the Lexus's emergency flashers, and for a moment he watched them blink on and off. Did they even need Matheson anymore?

'Matheson or Geiger? C'mon, Richie!'

Hall punched the flashers off. 'Geiger,' he said. 'Geiger's got the stuff now. Stay on him.'

Hall ended the call and drove up the block. After taking the turn onto Amsterdam, he pulled to the curb at the corner. He kept the motor running and got out. Leaning against the car's warm steel, he stared back down the street at Geiger's place. A few people strolled the sidewalks. The sun was just starting to go down, and shadows had begun to roll themselves out like black wallpaper on the sides of the buildings.

Hall took a deep, slow, pleasing breath. He felt better now. Every job had its detours and dead ends, and he'd been on plenty of cakewalks that had turned hellish. But he still got a rush watching calamity get put in its place.

He looked again at Geiger's building. Now it was time to deal with Ray.

The thought occurred to Ray while he was sitting on the toilet in Geiger's bathroom. For more than twelve hours, his brain had been overheated — dealing with pain, saturated with medication, deprived of sleep — but the heaviness was moving away. His inner skies were clearing.

He had always been aware that in his partners' eyes he was the 'dumb one' of the trio, and that was fine, because he'd learned that when crunch time came around, knowing how others saw you was as good as being smart. So what came to him now, with his pants down around his ankles, was that if Geiger didn't call with the code, Richie wouldn't go out of his way to get him out of here. And if the whole operation fell apart, Richie and Mitch were going to be checking airline schedules to destinations without extradition treaties and not giving him a second thought.

Ray knew the 'you're fucked' monster had just taken a seat at the table, fork and knife in hand. But he wasn't about to become the monster's next meal without insisting on some company.

* * *

'So what the fuck, Richie? Huh?'

Hall had been watching the foot traffic on 134th Street when his cell rang, and he immediately noticed that the edge in Ray's voice was returning. The lidocaine must be wearing off.

'Hang in, Ray. Mitch has got him covered. We just talked.'

'Yeah? I'm happy for both of you. What about me?'

'Ray, Mitch is on him. He's gonna snatch him any minute now, and then we'll get the code. All right?'

'I want out of here,' Ray said, 'or fuck everyone and everything. I do not go down solo on this. Hear me?'

Leaning against the car, Hall studied the glow of his cigarette for a moment. 'Ray, have I ever *once* not had your back? *Ever?*' He listened to silence, and then flicked his butt away. 'That's right, Ray, I have *always* been there for you — and now you want to give me this hard-case bullshit? Jesus, man.'

Ray was silent for a moment. 'Yeah, okay. I hear you.'

Hall heard a *beep* on the line. 'That's better, Ray. Now hang on while I put you on hold for a minute — Mitch is calling again.'

Hall switched over to Mitch's call. 'What's happening?'

'He's on Eighty-eighth just off Central Park West. He's stopped at a side door to 281 CPW. He must have a key, because now he's going in.'

'You where you can see both the side door and the lobby entrance?'

'Uh-huh.'

'Stay put. I'm on my way.'

'Where's Ray?'

'Still locked up,' said Hall. 'We'll get him later.'

Before switching back to his call with Ray, Hall looked down the block at Geiger's front door. He had been waiting for the stretch of sidewalk in front of Geiger's building to be clear of people, and now it was.

He clicked Ray back on.

'Ray, I've got the code. Mitch squeezed it out of Geiger and just called me with it.'

'Great! How'd Mitch get him to give it up?'

'I believe he stuck a gun in his mouth and said, 'Please.''

'Amazing what a little good manners will get you.'

Hall glanced at his cell. 'Okay, ready? Here it is: five-six-eight-three. Got it?'

'Five-six-eight-three,' Ray repeated.

'Right. That's 'love' on the number keys. L-O-V-E.'

'Peace and love — I get it.'

'Okay, Ray. See you in a minute.'

'Right.'

Hall clicked off his cell and stared at its face. 'Good-bye, Ray,' he said.

When it came, the sound was not what Hall expected — it was more a muffled *foomph!* than an explosive roar. Hall watched the building fold in on itself like a house of cards, and when the cloud of gray dust settled, it revealed the collapsed structure as a pyramid-shaped pile of rubble, with no damage to its neighbors on either side. Geiger had installed the directional charges perfectly.

Cars screeched to a stop, heads popped out of windows, people came rushing out of doorways. Hall slid back into the Lexus and drove away.

The *clank* of the service elevator coming to a stop jolted Geiger awake. He had nodded out during the ride, and now he felt his damage more keenly, the forty-five-second gap in consciousness allowing the pain to win back territory. He was like a diver coming up from sunless depths, punch-drunk from the pressure, but still aware that he had to keep his ascent slow so he didn't black out on the journey to the surface.

Geiger picked up the gym bag. Moving carefully, he walked into the stairwell and through the door into the hallway. Everything around him had to be perceived and measured; he would need to constantly realign himself so that he could efficiently manage every expenditure of energy.

He knocked on the door — it took less effort than finding the buzzer with a fingertip — and when the door opened the look on Corley's face further informed Geiger about his state.

'Jesus!' said Corley, taking Geiger's arm gently and bringing him inside.

Harry shot unsteadily to his feet and stared at Geiger. 'What the fuck happened to you?'

Corley led Geiger to one of the leather chairs, and Harry hobbled over to help him down into it.

Geiger felt the chair's cushion under him, but he didn't allow himself to relax into it. 'Harry,' he said, 'Hall's a hired gun — either for the CIA or someone like them.'

'Oh, man,' Harry groaned. 'We are in the deep stuff. You know where Hall and the others are now?'

'Locked inside my place.'

'And what the hell did they do to you?'

'Not now, Harry. Too much to do.'

Corley was trying to get a read on Geiger's mental state, but he couldn't make it past the physical spectacle: the bandaged cheek, the bloodless, ghastly face, and the suggestion from the way Geiger composed his body in the chair that there was more damage beneath his clothes.

Ezra's voice called out: 'Geiger? You back?'

The boy ran down the hall toward the living room but stopped short when he saw Harry and Corley looming over Geiger's chair, which had its back to him.

'What's wrong?' Ezra said.

'It's all right,' said Corley.

But Ezra knew better, and when he rushed around the chair and came face to face with Geiger, he gasped. Against the black pullover, Geiger's face looked nearly white, and his eyes were red and glassy.

'Geiger!' Ezra said, putting a hand on Geiger's leg. 'Are you okay?'

Geiger's face tightened with pain. Ezra instantly pulled his hand away and put it on the chair's arm.

'Yes, I'm okay,' Geiger said. 'Your mother's coming for you.'

'She is? When?'

'Getting on a plane. Right away, She said to tell you she loves you.'

Ezra tried to smile but failed. Geiger slowly reached out and covered Ezra's hand with his own. 'It'll be okay, Ezra.'

As small as the gesture was, Corley was staggered by its power. He had never heard Geiger speak of anyone with affection, much less show it. Whatever had happened to Geiger in the past few hours, Corley knew it had changed him.

Geiger turned to him now. 'Martin,' he said.

Corley crouched down before the chair, 'Yes?'

'We can't stay here. We need to go someplace else.'

'Why?'

'I don't know how it will play out when Ezra's mother shows up.'

'What do you mean?' Ezra asked.

'I mean your mother could be upset. She might want to speak to the police.'

'But you saved me.'

Geiger smiled wanly at Ezra and then looked again at Corley. 'Martin, we need to go someplace where there aren't doormen, neighbors down the hall, security cameras in the elevators, witnesses everywhere. Your house in Cold Spring — she could meet us there.'

'Well, I suppose so,' said Corley, masking a sigh. It probably was the right move, but the prospect of it pained him. The house was a haven for memories of a happier time in his life.

'Do you have a car, Martin?'

'Yes. We could be there in an hour and a half.'

'Not 'we', Martin. Harry, do you think you can drive?'

'Yeah, I guess so,' said Harry. 'It's my other leg

that's pretty banged up.'

Corley stood up. 'Hold on a second, Geiger. What are you — '

'You're not coming, Martin.' Geiger looked up at him. 'That way we can still keep you out of this.'

'Keep me 'out of this'? I think it's a little late for that.' Corley studied Geiger for a moment and then gestured for him to get up. 'We need to talk, Geiger. Come into the office — just for a minute.'

Corley walked into the kitchen and continued on into his office through a door in the kitchen's back wall.

Geiger gave Ezra and Harry a look, and then pushed himself up out of the chair, He rose by increments, dozens of muscles realigning to accommodate his damage, his mind pushing the corporal into the background. Gathering his strength, he walked through the kitchen and into the familiar office. He wanted to focus all his energy on completing what he had started, whatever form that might take.

Corley closed the door softly and turned to him. 'Geiger — '

Geiger held up a hand. 'Martin, the best thing is for you to stay here. You have no place in what happens once we leave.'

'No? I'm sorry to have to play the shrink, but let's look at what's occurred here, at what you did. *You came to me.*'

'It was necessary, Martin, But you're not going anywhere now. And I don't have time for this.'

It suddenly struck Corley that Geiger might

not set foot in this room again, that they were taking part in some sort of finale. Since his divorce, the only true commitment Corley had made had been to Geiger. Now something had happened to Geiger, quite possibly the event that Corley had long been waiting for, the catalyst that would finally reveal the source of all the cruelty and the damage. But if Geiger left and never returned, Corley would never know what Geiger had finally understood.

'Martin,' Geiger said, 'I need you to give me the keys and the directions.'

Corley tried to keep the anxiety out of his voice. 'Harry told me everything, Geiger — about what you do, about information retrieval. But even if every person you dealt with was guilty or corrupt, even if they were all serial killers or Hitlers or Bernie Madoffs — '

'I'm getting out of the business, Martin.'

'Jesus, Geiger, it's not that simple, and you know it. We need to talk about this.'

'But not now, Martin. Not until this is over.'

'Then this is how it has to be,' Corley said. 'We *all* go to Cold Spring.'

Geiger shook his head, 'No, you're not coming.'

Corley gave a soft chuckle. 'What are you going to do, Geiger — tie me to a chair?'

'That won't be necessary, Martin. Just do as I say.'

Corley stared at Geiger and saw another man gazing out from behind the hard slate eyes — the Geiger he'd known nothing about before Harry told him of Geiger's extraordinary, terrible skills.

And as he looked into the eyes of this man who always persuaded people to give him what he wanted, Corley's breath snagged on something inside him. He had to straighten his spine to jar it loose.

'I feel like I haven't done enough, Geiger. I . . . '

Corley trailed off into silent thought. All the walls we build . . . how the mind makes its own bricks and mortar to save itself. All the things we carry within ourselves . . . how they are far heavier than any burden we might put upon our backs.

'Martin,' Geiger said. 'Do you trust me?'

Corley remembered Geiger asking the same question just yesterday. Then it had seemed like another one of his inscrutable offerings, but this time Corley understood that it sought to measure, and test, and possibly even define what they were to each other.

'Yes,' Corley replied.

Geiger slowly nodded, his eyes softening a little. 'Good-bye, Martin.'

20

Mitch's surveillance gaze was on full power, toggling back and forth from the building's entrance on Central Park West to the side door around the corner on Eighty-eighth Street. While he waited for Geiger to make his next move, Mitch listened to a show on talk radio that always got his juices flowing.

'And so here we go again,' the host said. 'Have you seen these photos of the supposed 'torture chamber' in Cairo? It looks like a dirty basement to me, but the so-called enlightened liberals — otherwise known as morons — are at it again, whining about human rights and due process for terrorists. And on this day of days, July Fourth, let me ask you something: do you think they have loved ones fighting to protect their freedom in Iraq and Afghanistan? Well, forgive me if I answer my own question. No! They don't! And that's why they can't understand what democracy really means — because to understand that you have to sacrifice something *meaningful*, maybe even lose something precious and dear — and I don't mean having the waiter tell you they're out of your favorite sushi!'

Mitch pounded the steering wheel. 'Right on, dude! That's the Independence Day spirit talking!'

Mitch's attention turned to a garbage truck that was pulling up alongside a line of parked cars on Eighty-eighth Street. The truck's street-side door opened and a man in a DSNY jumpsuit hopped down. He walked to the heap of black plastic bags at the curb, but he took his time about it. Even with the sun low on the horizon, it was still hot.

Mitch took a moment to watch the guy as he started grabbing bags and heaving them into the mouth of the truck.

'Poor sonofabitch. Gotta be a hundred inside that suit.'

⋆ ⋆ ⋆

In the building's garage, Corley stood a couple of feet away as Harry turned the ignition of the old Chevy Suburban. The engine hacked a few times before catching and achieving a rumbling idle. Ezra, violin case on his lap, sat in the second row; Lily sat next to him, her head on the boy's shoulder. Geiger sat utterly still in the last row, eyes shut, hands clasped in his lap.

Corley came closer and spoke to Harry through the open window. 'It hesitates when you give it a lot of gas, so be careful about passing somebody on the highway.'

'Gotcha,' said Harry.

'And the radio and air-conditioning don't work.'

'Not a problem.'

Corley poked his head inside. 'Everybody all right?'

'I'm good,' said Ezra.

'Geiger?'

312

There was no answer.

'I think maybe he's asleep,' said Ezra.

Corley sighed and straightened up. He had never felt so old, or so useless.

'Take care, Harry.'

'Thanks, Doc — for everything.'

'And bring him back safe.'

'That's the plan.' Harry turned and smiled up at Corley. 'You okay, Doc?'

'Yes, I'm fine.'

'Well, okay then. Here we go.'

Harry shifted into drive, and as soon as the car began to move Corley turned and headed for the elevator. He didn't look back.

★ ★ ★

The clouds that had been gathering for the past couple of hours were teases, refusing to let loose and rain. Every few seconds, a couple of drops hit the windshield, but Mitch didn't bother with the wipers. As his eyes went from mark to mark, he registered the fact that the building's garage door was opening, and he saw an old Suburban begin to pull out. But at first he didn't flag it as a significant event.

Meanwhile, the talk-show host was on a roll. 'You know when debating interrogation techniques became irrelevant, my friends, if not absurd?'

'On 9/11, dipstick,' Mitch answered.

'September eleventh, 2001, when Islamo-fascists slit the throats of eight American pilots and proceeded to murder over three thousand

American civilians — *that's* when!'

Mitch eyed the Suburban again, and this time he gave it his full attention. It was hard to get a good look at the driver through the car's windshield, but something about the silhouette seemed familiar.

⋆ ⋆ ⋆

Harry pulled out across the sidewalk and stopped. A garbage truck was blocking his way. He eyed the remaining garbage bags and sighed. 'We're going to be here all night.'

He watched the garbageman for a minute. Aware that he had an audience now, the guy began mixing in some pretty slick dance moves as he worked. Harry laughed, then stuck his head out the window.

'Hey, man,' Harry called out. 'I need a favor. Could you back it up maybe five feet so we can get by?'

⋆ ⋆ ⋆

Mitch's eyes were locked on Harry now, and as the garbage truck began backing up, he punched in Hall's number.

'Yeah?' Hall answered.

'We got movement. Old Chevy Suburban. Harry's driving.'

'Harry?'

'And — bingo — Geiger, the kid, and Harry's sister are all with him. Where are you?'

'Ninety-eighth Street. Follow them — and run

the plates so we know whose car it is. Call back with your loke and I'll catch up.'

'Okay.'

With the garbage truck clear of the driveway, the Suburban pulled out into the street and drove west.

'All this crap about waterboarding and wall slamming?' the talk-show host continued. 'Tsk tsk, oh my — and let's be sure Abdul gets due process, too. Habeas damn corpus, my ass!'

'You got that right, dude,' said Mitch, and turned off the radio. He pulled a laptop out from beneath his seat, placed it on the passenger seat, and gently hit the gas.

★ ★ ★

An hour north of the city, Hall was driving up the Saw Mill River Parkway past woods broken up by sheer gray walls of rock. The holiday traffic wasn't bad going in this direction.

Mitch came back on the speakerphone. 'Okay, I got the car's owner. Martin Corley, MD. Lives in the building. Divorced. No kids.'

'Do a cross-ref — maybe he's got a place north of the city. Check property, electric, and phone records. Where are you now?'

'Route Nine, coming up on the Bear Mountain State Parkway.'

'I'm near Ossining, so not far behind you.'

Looking across the parkway's divider, Hall saw the American Dream creeping south, bumper to bumper. Cars with families on their way home from a day in the country — radios blaring, dogs with their heads out the window, bicycles on racks, sleepy children in backseats with sunburned cheeks and taffy melting in their pockets. What a country: fifty thousand miles of highway helping people find a little peace somewhere.

Hall put the cell on mute and turned on the radio. He wondered what peace would feel like to him after all this time, and thought he knew the answer. It would be a moment where he wasn't thinking three moves ahead — better yet, a moment when there were no more moves at all.

He didn't have to wait long for a report to come on the radio.

'This is WCBS with breaking news. We've got more on the building explosion at West One thirty-fourth Street in Manhattan. Rich Lamb is at the site. Rich?'

'David, the building was a two-story structure, believed to be a private residence. The fire department, NYPD, hazmat crews, and federal authorities are all here, but no one is saying very much. I can tell you this: it looks more like an *im*plosion than an explosion. The place seems to have collapsed in on itself, leaving everything around it untouched.'

'Could this have been a terrorist act, Rich?'

'Investigators will have to consider that possibility. This place could have been either a target or a bomb factory where something went wrong. And, of course, the cause of the explosion could have been something less sinister, like a gas leak. Commissioner Kelly is due to make a statement soon. Until then, we'll — '

Hall turned off the radio and unmuted his cell. It was time to play the string out.

'Mitch?'

'Yeah?'

'I think Geiger's place blew up.'

'*What?* With Ray in it?'

'It's on the radio. A building on West One thirty-fourth.' He paused for effect. 'Leveled. Nothing left.' Hall fashioned a sigh. 'Jesus . . . ' he said.

'Oh man,' said Mitch. 'The poor fucker.' He let out a sigh that matched Hall's. They were kindred spirits, each critiquing their own performance while studying the other's.

Hall counted off an appropriate pause, then held on to his somber tone. 'Anything new on Corley?'

'Just came up,' Mitch replied. 'Corley owns a house in Cold Spring. Twenty-nine River Lane. Maybe fifteen minutes away.'

'Satellite it.'

'Already did. It's outside of town, closest neighbor at least a quarter of a mile away. He's got a dock on the river.'

'Boat?'

'On the dock. Looks like a rowboat. This is a helluva lot better than an apartment on CPW, huh?'

Hall smiled. The million monkeys were typing away, and one of them seemed to be on the verge of producing something quite extraordinary.

'Yeah,' Hall said. 'It's perfect.'

317

21

'Geiger . . . '

Geiger opened his eyes to see Harry staring at him from the driver's seat. Otherwise the Suburban was empty.

'We're here,' Harry said.

'Where is here?'

'Corley's house in Cold Spring.'

Geiger opened his door, leaned out, and spat blood. 'I have to get some ice.' He picked up the bag and got out of the car.

Harry met Geiger as he began walking slowly up a flagstone path. He reached out as if to help him, but Geiger shook his head.

'I'm all right.'

'No, you're not.'

Geiger turned to face him, his eyes brimming with a hard light. 'Yes, Harry, I am.'

As Geiger continued on toward the house, Harry looked around. To the west, the grounds stretched in a smooth, downward slope toward the water, untended and wild. Between the meadow and the river stood a dense line of trees; old firs and beeches, their trunks thick and knobby, spread crooked branches that cast long shadows in the fading sunlight. Ahead of Harry, the house — a two-story gray colonial — rested on the highest point of land, its eight-foot first-floor windows and wraparound porch providing a soaring view of the Hudson and the hills on its far side.

318

Bordered by tall, spike-topped ground lamps, the flagstone path led to the front entrance, and as Geiger and Harry neared the steps, Ezra and Lily appeared in one of the first-floor windows. Standing side by side, they were only dimly visible, the glass's thick film of dust making phantasms of them, as if they were in the world but not of it.

From inside Geiger's bag came the ring of his cell phone. Halfway up the steps, he stopped, took out the phone, and answered.

'Ms. Wayland?'

'I'm here — at JFK.'

'Are you using a pay phone?'

'Yes. Let me speak to my son.'

'In a minute, but first you're going to talk to someone who will give you directions. You need to rent a car. We're at a house in Cold Spring, New York.'

Geiger handed the phone to Harry.

'Hi,' he said, 'this is Harry.' He took Corley's directions out of his pocket. 'Here's where you're going. Got a pen?'

Geiger reached the top step and rested for a moment. The front door opened and the boy stood before him, gazing at him with a quizzical expression.

'That's your mother on the phone, Ezra. Go talk to her.'

Ezra was silent for a moment. 'They beat you up trying to get you to tell them where I was, didn't they?'

'Yes.'

'But you didn't tell them.'

'No.'

'What did they do to you?'

'You don't need to know that.'

'Okay.' Ezra gave him a last look and then went down the steps.

Geiger entered the house. Beyond the foyer, a long hall ran straight to a back door; off to the right, a stairway led to the second floor. The living room, immediately to the left, had a high unfinished-wood ceiling and was dominated by a hearth of uncut stone that took up half a wall. Lily stood before it, her fingers tracing the crooked lines of fitted rock.

'It's a great big puzzle,' she said.

Geiger moved into the room and sat down on an overstuffed couch. He had often stared at the photograph of this house in Corley's office and wondered what its interior looked like. He leaned over, reached past the edge of an old Persian rug, and ran a fingertip across the wide-plank floor. Old pine. The wood needed oil; linseed would be best, with a touch of tung. He sank back in the cushions. He could hear Ezra outside, walking the porch with a fresh step, talking to his mother on the phone.

'No, Mom,' the boy said. 'No first name. Just Geiger.'

Harry hobbled in and handed Geiger a glass full of ice cubes, then sat down beside him with a groan. He glanced at Geiger's pants; the fabric against his thigh glistened.

'Thank you,' said Geiger, and sucked a few cubes into his mouth.

'So who worked you over?'

'Dalton.'

Harry cocked his head. '*Dalton?*'

'Yes. It was his farewell performance.'

'Meaning what?'

'I broke all his fingers.'

'Jesus . . . '

Harry marveled at the speed with which violence had invaded their private world. Torn flesh and shattered bone were becoming commonplace.

'Harry, we need to find out if there's a TV and DVD player here.'

'Why?'

'Just have a look around, okay?'

'Will do.'

★ ★ ★

Cold Spring's Main Street slid down a hill to its end at a railed stone promenade. For decades, the owners of many of the street's elegant two- and three-story buildings had faithfully kept the nineteenth-century architectural pedigrees of their properties intact. The colorful brick façades and wrought-iron railings that fronted the town's galleries, bistros, and antiques stores looked almost painterly in the twilight, and the sidewalks were thick with people, all of them heading downhill toward the water for the July Fourth festivities.

Hall and Mitch sat in the Lexus, parked at the top of the hill across from the village green.

'So what's it gonna be, boss?' Mitch said.

Hall magnified the satellite map on his

laptop's screen and put his finger to it.

'Here's where we are, and here's Corley's place. Once it starts getting dark, we go north about six blocks and then turn left here, on River Lane. After about half a mile, we pull into the woods and go on foot from there. Looks like a walk of about a quarter of a mile.'

'Then?'

'We split up, here, at the tree line.'

'And?'

Hall sat back. 'We go in front and back, and then see what happens.'

'Go in with the house lights on or wait till they're off?'

The questions were all relevant, but Hall knew Mitch was doing more than asking. He was measuring response time, poking for soft spots. Hall glanced at Mitch's flat, impassive face. Over the years more than a few people had made him for a classic ex-jock, a plain can-do guy, but Hall knew better. Mitch was as introspective as a copperhead, but he had a knack for the quick read and an uncanny memory for crucial details about everyone he had ever dealt with. In the past, that had always made him a valuable asset. Now it made him dangerous.

'Lights on,' Hall said. 'No reason to walk into walls.'

'Okay.'

'There's Harry, the kid, the sister — and Geiger.'

'A lot of people,' said Mitch.

Hall turned the laptop off. 'That's why we make the big bucks, right?'

Harry discovered the machines in the first-floor guest bedroom, across the hall from the living room. They sat under a sheet atop a dresser — a twenty-three-inch Samsung monitor and a JVC disc player.

'Found 'em,' he called out, pulling the sheets off the other furniture in the room. 'In here.'

Geiger limped in, put the gym bag on the four-poster bed, and sat down in the wicker rocking chair beside it. He ignored the steady thudding in his carved-up leg.

'Lock the door, Harry.'

Harry did so and then pushed the power buttons on the two machines. He turned to Geiger. 'Feel free to tell me what's going on anytime you like. Just jump right in.'

'In my bag. The envelope.'

Harry reached in and pulled out the package. 'This?'

'Yes. Matheson gave it to me.'

'And how the fuck did — '

'I met him this afternoon,' Geiger interrupted, 'after finishing with Dalton. Questions later, Harry. Let's just do this.'

'Okay, all right.'

From the envelope, Harry took out five jewel cases, all carrying shiny black minidiscs.

'These are what this has all been about?' He took the mini-disc out of the case marked '1' and held it up. 'Doesn't look like a de Kooning, does it? CD or DVD?'

'Let's find out.'

Harry slid the disk into the JVC's slot, hit 'play,' and took a seat on the edge of the bed.

The blackness on the screen shifted and a razor-thin silver line appeared at the bottom. The lower right corner displayed the running time and a date: '2/16/2004.'

Harry pointed. 'The silver line at the bottom? That's a digital lock. The disk can't be copied without decoding.'

A man's voice spoke with a thick Middle Eastern accent in a barely audible whisper. 'Video twenty-seven. February sixteen, two thousand four.'

The monitor bloomed with an image of a brightly lit, windowless room, shot from a camera placed in a high corner.

'Well, it's not a greatest hits album,' said Harry. He pointed at the screen again. 'See how the edges of the feed are irregular? Hidden camera — it's wedged in somewhere behind the walls.'

A metallic clattering came from offscreen, an uneven but rhythmic rotation of sound. Geiger leaned forward.

Two men with buzz cuts, wearing standard-issue khakis, came into view wheeling a rickety gurney to the center of the room. Lying on it, strapped to the rails at the ankles and wrists, dressed only in soiled boxers, was a tightly muscled bearded man in his thirties, swathed in a coat of sweat. His face was stamped with a rash of purple welts and blood-encrusted cuts, as were his chest and upper arms. The harsh lighting played up the dark hues of the inflicted damage.

'Jesus,' said Harry, 'what is this?'

A man in a short-sleeved white shirt and khaki shorts walked into the frame and stepped up to the gurney. He stroked his manicured goatee for a few moments, then tapped the fettered man on the shoulder and spoke in flat, slightly nasal English. He was obviously American; to Harry, the accent sounded midwestern, farm belt.

'Morning, Nari,' the goateed American said. 'It's a new day, my friend.'

'*Allahu akbar,*' croaked the man on the gurney.

'Yeah, I know,' said the American. 'God is great, and America is the great Satan.'

'Wait a minute,' Harry said. 'Nari? As in Nari *Kaneesh?* Oh man . . . '

Geiger rose from the chair and grasped one of the bedposts.

'Nari,' the American said. 'Do you want to talk to us today?'

'This is unjust. I — I have done nothing . . . '

'I'll take that as a no.'

'I have told you. Each time they came to the hotel room, they knocked on the door and told me to put the blindfold on before they came in. Then — '

'I know. They drove you somewhere, you spoke with two men, and they drove you back to the hotel and told you not to remove the blindfold until they had gone.'

'Yes, this is so. I never saw any of them.'

'I know, Nari, I know. It's just that — we're still not sure you're telling the truth.'

'I was acting for *good,* to make a *peace* . . . '

'And we believe that. But we still think maybe

325

you saw the faces of the Qaeda operatives you met with, maybe even saw where they brought you, and that you just need some help remembering.'

Nari's head started shaking side to side in fervent denial. 'No, no, no,' he said, the gurney rattling.

'Jesus Christ,' said Harry. 'It *is* him.' He turned to Geiger. 'This guy is the Egyptian minister who secretly met with al Qaeda and then disappeared.' Harry thumped his thigh with his fist. 'This is fucking *huge*.'

Geiger's eyes never left the monitor.

The American pressed a button on the gurney and raised it to a sixty-degree vertical position. 'So you've been telling us, Nari — which is why we decided to bring in someone new, someone who might encourage you to be a little more forthcoming.'

'This is wrong!' cried the prisoner. 'I am an elected official of an ally of the United States!'

'Yes, you are,' said the American, 'and that should help you see the nature of the situation — which is that we will do whatever we have to do to protect our interests. So if you don't cooperate with the new interrogator . . . Well, you know what they say: Mess with the great Satan and you end up with his pitchfork up your ass.'

The American looked out of the frame and gave a 'come in' wiggle with his hand. 'Nari, meet your new friend — the Inquisitor,' he said, and stepped out of camera range.

The man who now stepped up to the gurney

was dressed all in white — white T-shirt, loose slacks, sneakers. It was Geiger.

'Holy shit,' Harry said, standing up. 'Where?'

'Cairo,' Geiger answered. 'Black site.'

The video Geiger put two fingers to his new charge's neck to measure his pulse rate.

The prisoner's eyes smoldered as he spoke. 'I cannot tell you any more than I already — '

Geiger's hand shifted, grabbing the man's neck tightly, his thumb and forefinger digging deep into the flesh beneath the corners of the jaw. Nari choked down into silence.

'You're right, Nari,' said Geiger. 'You will not tell me anything — now. Later you will, but it isn't time yet. For now, it's best that you don't speak at all.'

Nari's eyes registered surprise and confusion. 'But peace is what I was trying to — '

Geiger's grip tightened, rendering the man mute. 'Not a word, Nari.' His fingers dug deeper, and the prisoner's grimace stretched so wide it looked like a smile. 'Nod if you understand me.'

Nari nodded.

Geiger leaned toward the DVD player and pressed the 'pause' button. Then he went back to the chair and sat down, as frozen as his image on the screen.

Harry remained standing. He started nodding as the pieces began to fall into place. 'Black site. CIA. Cairo. Someone hides a camera behind a wall and secretly records the sessions. Does the CIA know? Maybe, maybe not.' He frowned. 'Probably not. The stuff sits somewhere for years. Someone digs it up and gives it to

327

Matheson. Or he finds it himself — whatever. But why Matheson?'

'Because Matheson runs Veritas Arcana.'

'The outfit that leaks all the classified stuff? That's him?'

'Yes.'

'Okay — that works. So Matheson gets ahold of the discs, but before he can break the digital lock and get them online, Langley or someone else in Washington finds out he's got them and then lets the dogs loose. Hall and friends go to work — and we know the rest. Okay, I get it. So what's in the videos, Geiger?'

Geiger looked at Harry impassively for a moment before answering. 'I used applied pressure — a lot of it. Acupuncture, headphones, audio loops, deprivation — neither of us slept for two days. Before he broke, there was a lot of . . . howling and screaming.'

'Geiger, Nari Kaneesh was the number two guy in the Egyptian Parliament!'

'Harry, keep your voice down.' Geiger spoke without heat. He was staring at the freeze-frame, recalling his countless acts of cruelty, his pragmatic embrace of violence. He could feel the muscles in Nari's throat constricting beneath his fingers. He could feel the flesh of hundreds of other victims in his hands, tightening in fear and flinching in pain and yielding in despair . . .

Harry leaned toward the DVD player and hit 'eject.' He took the disc out of the tray and gazed down at the piece of plastic.

'Put it back in the bag, Harry.'

'We're not destroying them?'

'No. I'm going to do what I told Matheson I would do. I'm going to call Hall, tell him I have the discs, and promise that as long as they leave Ezra alone, no one will ever see what's on them.'

Harry blinked. 'You're out of your mind, Geiger. You hold on to these and you'll have to spend the rest of your life in a cave. Even if they leave Ezra alone, they'll come after you — and like you said, they don't stop.'

Geiger took a deep breath. He could feel his whole body expanding with it, millions of molecules drawing strength from the oxygen. Then, slowly, he let the breath out and nodded.

'I know.'

★   ★   ★

The kitchen was the heart of the house, with entries from the central hall and living room and two round skylights. Harry found an unopened box of Ritz crackers and a jar of peanut butter and began making miniature sandwiches on the speckled granite counter, piling them on a plate.

Lily sat at the oval oak table, hands clasped before her, humming softly. Ezra sat next to her, one brow tilted up.

'I like her,' Ezra said. 'I never met a . . . you know, a crazy person before.'

'No?' said Harry. 'Well, take your pick. You got a house full of 'em.'

Harry brought the plate to the table and put a hand on Lily's shoulder. She tilted her head, as if she'd heard a sound instead of felt someone's touch.

'Who's there?' she asked.

'Me. Harry.'

Ezra grabbed a handful of the cracker sandwiches and popped one into his mouth.

'I know something,' said Lily. Her voice was like fingertips on satin.

Harry grinned and sat down beside her. He took her hands in his. 'Okay, sis,' he said, 'so what do you know?'

'I know why Harry's sad.'

Her soft declaration pushed him back in his chair. He let go of her hands.

Lily reached over to Ezra and closed a hand around his wrist. 'Let's sing,' she said.

'Okay, sure,' said the boy.

'*Rock-a-bye baby, in the treetop . . .* '

Ezra joined in: '*When the wind blows the cradle will rock.*'

The song rang in Harry's ears like a mournful bell. 'Ezra,' he said. 'Stop. Don't sing.'

The boy stopped singing but gave Harry an uncertain look.

Lily continued: '*When the bough breaks the cradle will fall . . .* '

'Lily, be quiet now.'

'*And down will come —* '

'Lily!' Harry shouted.

Her lids dropped shut, and a tear slipped out of each eye.

'Harry,' Ezra said. 'What's — what's going on?'

'Nothing. She's crazy, remember?'

'But she's crying. Why's she crying?'

Wearily, Harry got up from the table. 'She's

crying about a girl,' he said, and walked out of the room.

* * *

Upstairs, Geiger stood in the shower, head bowed, palms flat against the wall. He had run the water cold to inhibit fresh bleeding, but as the water circled the drain it had a light pink tint. The shower tiles were a bilious green, and Geiger idly wondered if Corley had chosen the color, or acquiesced to someone else's desire, or declined even to take part in the process.

Geiger stepped out and dried himself carefully with a towel. In the oval mirror above the sink, he could see a full-length glass on the door behind him. He turned around to his reflection.

The extent of the damage made it difficult to take in the whole body at once — the separate wounds all competed for his eye's attention. The garish red circle with the central puncture in his left cheek; the ugly welts across his chest and quadriceps; the trio of long, stitched gashes in his thigh, their puckered edges already gleaming with fresh blood. His gaze bounced from one to another, and a hot sweat pushed its way up through his pores.

Growing dizzy, he found the sink with a wavering hand and lowered himself onto the toilet seat. The mechanism of memory was turning slowly, grabbing moments from his mind's black room and hauling them up into the light: a fire-lit blade in a swollen fist, droplets of blood on a rough-hewn floor, lupine silhouettes

331

ripping flesh from bone . . .

For a moment, Geiger focused all his energy on the tile floor's mosaic of small octagons. The maze of black lines held fast, anchoring his sight, and the maelstrom faded away.

★ ★ ★

Hall found a spot where he could turn off the road. He pulled fifty feet into the woods, cut his headlights, and turned off the engine. He and Mitch pushed their window buttons and the dark glass slid down with a hum that was instantly overridden by a wave of cicada whirs and cricket chirps. A hoot came down from a nearby branch.

'Jesus,' said Mitch. 'When was the last time you heard a fucking owl?'

Hall reached into the glove compartment, took out a silver earbud with a two-inch-long stick mike, and fit it in his left ear. Mitch dug into a shirt pocket, pulled out his bud, and did the same. Then they took out their guns and checked the clips. Hall ran down the to-do list in his head and nodded.

'Okay, once things take off, you follow my lead.'

'Right.'

They slapped their clips into place, got out of the car, and headed west.

'When we go in, guns out,' said Hall. 'But no triggers unless we have to.'

'Right.'

They walked through the woods in silence. As

they approached Corley's house, they came to a clearing and stopped. From this point on, it was comparatively open ground — a meadow two hundred feet in diameter dotted with a dozen trees and large bushes, and the house perched in the middle. Light from the windows and the ground lamps leading up to the front entrance created an apron that stretched thirty feet from the house.

'Okay,' said Hall, and pointed. 'Phone lines come in the back. Get them before you go in, just in case.'

'Right.' Mitch winced and smacked his neck. 'Fucking mosquitoes.'

'Let's make sure the buds work before we go. Stay put.'

Hall headed off, staying inside the tree line. While sitting in the car, he had made up his mind about how to play this. He would walk right up the front steps. If the door was locked, he'd ring the bell. No tough stuff, no gun — better to keep the temperature down, at least at first. He'd tell Geiger to get everyone together, and then he'd ask for the discs; they were stolen property, and he needed them back. And if this didn't fly, well, there was always Plan B.

He waved off a mosquito. 'Mitch, you hear me?' he said softly.

'Crystal. You hear me?'

'Just fine. Okay, when you take out the phones, let me know and I'll move.'

'Right.'

'Go tree to tree, Mitch. There are a lot of windows.'

'Richie, I've done this kind of thing before, you know?'

'Go.'

Hall watched Mitch slip from the trees and start for the back of the house in a crouch, moving across the clearing from one isolated tree or bush to the next. Hall took his earbud out, put it in his shirt pocket, and closed his eyes. He wanted to bring his pulse down before he made the call, so there would be no bumps in his voice, not even a ripple of concern.

He pulled out his cell and dialed a number.

'Yes?' said the voice.

'It's Hall, sir.' He took the silence as a prompt to continue. 'We're on target. An isolated house in Cold Spring, New York. I'm looking at it now. The discs and four people inside. We're about to move in. We'll have the discs very soon.'

Hall felt a chill before he understood why. As he spoke, he'd heard a faint echo of his own voice coming back at him through the line, meaning that the phone on the other end was on speaker. The man had others with him in the room; they were listening in, most likely because he wanted them to advise him about a decision he was mulling. Hall knew that couldn't be good.

'Four inside?' asked the man.

'Yes, sir. Four.'

'This started as a single-target event, Hall. You've turned it into something very different. You've got five in the mix now, including Matheson. That's a big number.'

Hall stared at the house; its many windows

were growing brighter as the night grew darker. 'You're right, sir.'

'Five X's walking around when this is done,' said the man. 'That's too many. Everything has to finish clean on your end tonight. No loose ends. And then we'll find Matheson. Understood?'

Hall saw Mitch dart across open ground to an unkempt bush near the house. 'Yes, sir.'

'And, Hall . . . if there *are* any loose ends, that makes you one, too.'

'Yes, sir.'

The call cut off. Hall put his cell away and stuck his earbud back in place. He could hear Mitch's huffing, but it was almost drowned out by the thumping of his own pulse at the base of his skull.

They wanted everyone in the house dead.

⋆ ⋆ ⋆

Geiger and Ezra leaned on the porch railing. In the west, beyond the river, the sky just above the darkened hills showed a faint trace of coral where the sun had disappeared. Geiger had found a pair of Corley's gray sweatpants in a bedroom dresser and put them on. Ezra looked down at the row of ground lamps beneath the porch. Mosquitoes and moths spiraled around the spikes, smashing themselves into the bright glass.

'Ezra,' Geiger said. 'I saw your father today.'

Ezra jackknifed up straight. 'When? Where?'

'Just before I came back. In Central Park.'

'How did you — ?'

'It's a long story. But he's all right.'

'Did he ask about me?'

'Yes.'

'Then why didn't he come back with you?'

'He wanted to see you. I wouldn't let him.'

'Why not?'

'I told him that from now on he couldn't see you without your permission. That it was up to you.'

'You did?'

'Yes. So when this is all over, you'll decide when you want to see him — *if* you want to see him. Okay?'

'Well . . . ' Ezra shook his head. 'Okay, I guess.'

'And something else.'

'Yeah?'

'I have what those men are looking for. In my bag. They're discs. Videos. I got them from your father. No one's going to bother you now that I have them.'

'Videos like what?'

'It doesn't matter. But just so you understand, Ezra, your father left you alone because he felt the videos were very important, and didn't want Hall to get them. He had some extremely hard choices to make. Okay?'

'Okay.'

'I have to make a call,' Geiger said, and started down the steps.

★   ★   ★

336

Hall watched from the woods as Mitch ran to a huge beech tree and then disappeared behind its massive trunk. The tree's heavy shadow stretched to within a few feet of the house's back door.

'See me?' Mitch whispered.

'Yes.'

Then Hall saw Geiger walking down the steps and into the front yard, dabbing at something in his hand.

'Geiger's out of the house,' Hall said. 'Front yard. I think he's making a call.'

Hall's cell vibrated inside his pocket, against his upper thigh. 'Jesus,' he whispered, 'I think he's calling me.'

'Don't answer,' Mitch said.

'No, I'm going to — we can use this. Hold on.'

Hall took out his earbud and pulled his cell from his pocket. 'Hello,' he said.

'It's Geiger.'

'You're taking your sweet fucking time with the exit code, Geiger. You said you'd call me in half an hour, remember?' Hall watched Geiger walk in a tight circle, two hundred feet away.

'I met with Matheson. I have the discs.'

'Go on,' said Hall.

'I'm going to keep them.'

'Unwise, Geiger. Very.'

'The boy is going to meet his mother soon. After that, as long as Ezra remains safe and unharmed, no one will ever see what's on the discs. That is the deal.'

'I don't do deals, Geiger. That's not part of my job. Now, when do I get the goddamn code so we can get out of your fucking house?'

'I'll call again.'

Hall watched Geiger jab his phone, and the call ended.

* * *

As Geiger came back into the house Harry was walking out of the first-floor bedroom, shaking his head.

'You find her?' Harry called out.

Geiger heard footsteps above them, and Ezra appeared at the top of the stairway.

'Nope, she's not up here,' the boy said, coming down the stairs.

Harry glanced at Geiger. 'She's gone.'

'How long?'

'I don't know. You two were outside, and I closed my eyes for a few minutes . . . '

'Ezra,' said Geiger. 'Go look for a flashlight in the kitchen drawers.'

The boy hurried off, and Harry slumped against the door-jamb.

'She hasn't gone far, Harry,' Geiger said. 'You take the front yard, I'll go out back.'

'No,' said Harry, looking down at Geiger's leg. 'You stay here. Ezra and I can look.'

'I'm all right, Harry.'

'Are you serious, Geiger?'

'I'll go slow and — '

Harry's fist suddenly swung out and hammered the wall. '*Stop!* Just — stop, okay? I don't need you falling down out there and blacking out. Looking for one train wreck in the dark is going to be hard enough, all right?'

Geiger stared back at him, and then slowly nodded.

★ ★ ★

Hall was waiting for the click, that moment when everything merged — situational prep, timing, intuition, adrenaline flow.

'Go ahead, Mitch,' he said. 'The phone lines.'

Mitch came into sight from behind the beech, a charcoal phantom that stopped just short of a pool of light around the back door.

Hall's gaze skidded left; Harry was coming down the front steps, flashlight in hand.

'Lily!' Harry called.

'Christ,' said Hall.

'What's wrong?' said Mitch.

Hall's eyes swiveled again as the back door opened and Ezra walked out. Mitch became a statue, standing in the black shadows not twenty feet away. Ezra turned, his back to Mitch now, and peered into the night.

'Lily!' the boy shouted.

'He doesn't see you,' Hall whispered. 'Go back. *Go.*'

Mitch stepped away from the door, and the shadows swallowed him back up.

'Now do not fucking move.'

Hall shifted his focus again. Harry left the light cast by the front windows and the ground lamps, his flashlight's beam carving a funnel in the darkness and moving off toward the woods.

'Fuck,' said Hall. 'Geiger's still inside. We need them all in one place.'

Ezra was slowly turning around, toward the beech tree.

'Lily!' the boy called.

The sky exploded with brilliant, sparkling stars of red, white, and blue. Hall flinched and then looked toward the river. A second later a loud boom knocked a hole in the night. Faint echoes of a crowd's cheers reached them as the stars descended, splashing the lawn with muted light.

'Un ... fucking ... believable,' whispered Hall.

With Ezra looking skyward, Mitch slid sideways toward the cover of the tree trunk. But as the fireworks faded, Ezra turned back toward the beech. Then he stepped forward and stood just under the spread of the fifteen-foot branches.

'Lily?'

'He's coming toward you, Mitch,' whispered Hall. 'Do what I say. Not before.' He watched Ezra approach the trunk. 'Coming on your right. Wait.'

★   ★   ★

Standing with his back to the tree, Mitch heard the boy stop a few feet from the giant trunk.

'Lily?' Ezra said softly. 'You there?'

Mitch heard the boy take a few more steps.

'He's at the base of the tree, Mitch,' Hall whispered in his ear. 'Starting to peek around the trunk. Take one full step left — now.'

Mitch moved his back off the bark but kept his fingertips anchored. He took a step.

'Don't be scared, Lily. It's just me, Ezra.'

Hall whispered again. 'He's going a step at a time. He doesn't want to spook her. Get ready to take another step left . . . Go.'

Mitch moved. He almost laughed aloud: a dozen years of hard work had come to a game of hide-and-seek with a twelve-year-old. He heard a buzz and felt a mosquito land on his cheek; he stayed perfectly still as the proboscis dug into his skin and started to feed.

'Get ready,' Hall said. 'Left one step. Go.'

Mitch took another single side step.

'Lily?' Ezra said.

Mitch heard the boy sigh, and then his steps sounded like they were moving away.

'Okay,' Hall whispered, 'looks like he's leaving.'

Mitch let out a deep breath, leaned back against the tree, and took particular satisfaction in crushing the mosquito on his cheek.

But then he heard more movement, steps coming back toward the tree.

Hall was suddenly alive in Mitch's ear. 'Fuck. Mitch, he's coming — '

'Lily?' Ezra's head peeked around into Mitch's view. 'Are you — ?'

Mitch grabbed him by the collar and slammed him up against the tree. His other hand clamped down tight over his mouth.

'Not one sound,' he hissed.

'Easy, Mitch!' Hall said in his ear.

Even in the dim light under the tree, Mitch could see Ezra's eyes shining with fear.

'I mean it, kid. One sound and I'll break your

neck. Understand me?'

Mitch felt the boy nod beneath his hand.

'All right, Richie,' Mitch said. 'It's chicken salad time.'

'Don't hurt the kid,' Hall replied. 'I'm on my way.'

★ ★ ★

Lily came out of the trees. The night was alive with sound and light. She slipped off her shoes and felt the high grass underfoot, the blades working their way between her toes as she walked. She stopped at the bank of the river. She could hear it as it ran past.

The sky suddenly roared and gave birth to a new moon. Fully grown, beaming, the moon sent its children flying into the night, a thousand of them, singing, laughing, racing one another down to the water.

Lily could hear her own voice singing — young, silky, wrapping itself around her like a caress.

'*Way down below the ocean . . .* '

She watched the lights floating on the swift surface of the river, shining up from the city below. That's where the children were going. They were going home. She sat down. She could still hear them, their song rising up from beneath the water, a bubbly, sweet canticle.

'*Way down below the ocean, where I want to be, she may be . . .* '

★ ★ ★

Hall arrived beneath the beech's canopy, panting.

'Nothing I could do,' said Mitch.

Hall looked at Mitch in the darkness, thinking he heard a smirk in his voice. 'All right,' said Hall. 'We move fast — before Harry comes back. We use the kid as a chip. I go to the back door and get Geiger to come out. Then we all go inside, get the discs, and go.'

'Okay,' Mitch said.

Hall crouched down to Ezra's eye level. He was surprised to find as much fury as fear in the boy's gaze.

'Ezra, do this right and we're done in five minutes, and then everybody goes home. When Mitch tells you to, I want you to call to Geiger. You shout, 'Hey, Geiger, c'mere. I'm out back.' You say it nice and cool, like you just want to show him something. I know you're scared, so take a few breaths and calm down. Think about how soon this can all be over. I'm not going to hurt you or Geiger, kid. I just want to get back what your father stole.'

Hall stood up and turned to Mitch.

'Wait on me.'

Hall stepped to the shadows' perimeter and then raced to the back door. Flattening himself against the wall, he took out his gun.

'Now, Mitch,' Hall whispered.

* * *

Ezra could smell Mitch's sweat as the man leaned in close. It was dense and sour, the odor

343

of something that had grown in darkness.

'Okay, kid. This is all on you. You screw up, a lot of people get hurt.' His hand came away from Ezra's mouth. 'Say it. 'Hey, Geiger, c'mere. I'm out back.''

Ezra felt a swirling in his head that made him feel like he was going to faint. He tried to fix his eyes on the blooming fountain of fireworks behind Mitch, but the image kept sliding away.

'Say it, kid,' said Mitch. 'Call out to him — now.'

Ezra shook his head.

Mitch's hand grabbed Ezra's face and slammed the back of his head against the tree. '*Do it.*'

The wet glaze of Ezra's tears turned each falling, pyrotechnic spark into a five-pointed star. It was a galaxy of pain, but again he shook his head.

Mitch stood up straight and turned toward Hall. 'The little prick won't do it.'

★ ★ ★

Hall tried to envision a one-on-one with Geiger inside the house. Did he have guns in there? Unknown, but doubtful. And Geiger had to be hurting; the fact that he hadn't come out to join the search party confirmed that. Still, Geiger seemed to be immune to adrenaline and fear, so who knew what he was capable of? Hall had already guessed wrong — twice.

He decided to go into the house alone. If things got hairy, he didn't want Mitch turning his encounter with Geiger into the O.K. Corral. He sprinted back to Mitch and Ezra.

'All right. Hold on to him, Mitch. Stay out here — I'm going in alone. Wait for my signal.'

Mitch clearly didn't like the sound of this. 'Why?'

'Because I've decided that this is the right way to play it.'

Mitch shifted his grip on Ezra and moved closer to Hall. 'Well, seeing as how every decision you've made about how to handle Geiger has been wrong, maybe we should — '

'Do what I tell you, Mitch.' Hall leaned in until his face was inches from his partner's. 'That's your job, okay? Now just shut the fuck up and do what you're told.'

A crashing *boom* made all three flinch. After it passed, Mitch looked at Hall and nodded.

'Okay, boss,' he said. 'Go ahead. Me and sonny boy'll watch your back.'

Hall ran back to the door and pulled his gun out. He gave himself a moment and then swung the door open and stepped inside. He started down the hallway.

'Geiger!' he shouted. 'It's Hall!'

★   ★   ★

Geiger had dozed off in one of the living room chairs, and the voice cut into him like slashing teeth. It was Hall. How had he gotten out, and how had he come here?

'You've got the discs, Geiger, and we've got Ezra! Let's do this!'

Geiger stood up. He felt a fiery stab of pain in his thigh, but it didn't matter. And it didn't matter how Hall had found them — he, Geiger, had brought him here. He had put Ezra and everyone else right in Hall's crosshairs.

'Come on, Geiger — let me see you!'

Geiger's gaze drifted through the room. There were two ways out: into the hallway and into the kitchen. He saw a wrought-iron poker standing against the hearth, its barbed spike covered in dust. He picked it up.

Hall's voice seemed to be coming from somewhere near the back of the house. Geiger waited for him to call out again.

'We can finish this while no one else is here, Geiger! Nice and clean!'

Geiger cocked his head, tracing the sound. Now he was sure: Hall had come in the back door and was in the hallway, moving toward him. He was perhaps twenty feet away.

It was a given that Hall had a gun. Geiger shifted his grip to the midpoint of the poker's shaft and held it like a spear. He raised the weapon, took a stance, and rehearsed a throw, pivoting on his left leg as he would have to do when he threw it. The leg quaked and burned, but the stitches held.

Hall had gone silent. By now, he must have moved past the hallway's entry to the kitchen. Geiger slipped noiselessly through the living room's doorway, into the kitchen. Did Hall have Ezra with him? He didn't think so; it was too quiet.

Geiger stepped over to the kitchen's rear

doorway. Hall had to be in the hallway off to the right. Geiger raised the poker shoulder-high, stepped silently into the hallway, and turned.

Hall was ten feet away, alone, up near the entry to the living room. His back was a bull's-eye, but if Geiger could get closer he could use the poker as a club. He waited, watching Hall creep toward the living room doorway.

When fireworks lit the sky again and were followed by a spate of crackles and pops, Geiger started forward, using the sound as audio camouflage. Hall was leaning around the entry's molding.

Now just three feet away, Geiger slid his grip down to the poker's handle and raised the weapon high.

'Geiger!' barked a voice behind him.

*   *   *

Hall whirled around and blindly backhanded his gun into the side of Geiger's skull. Geiger dropped to his knees. The fireplace poker clanked to the floor.

Hall glanced up at Mitch, who stood just inside the back door. His partner's gun was pointed at Geiger's head, and the boy was muzzled and firmly in Mitch's grasp.

Hall glared down at Geiger. 'There's no more time, Geiger — I want those discs!'

Geiger had trouble making out some of Hall's words. There was an ocean's roar in his right ear.

'Let the boy go,' he said, his voice barely a whisper.

Hall shook his head. 'The discs — now.'

Geiger swung his head slowly and looked down the hallway at the boy. Then he turned back to Hall. 'They're in the bedroom,' he said, pointing to the doorway on the left.

Hall took a quick look inside the bedroom and saw a gym bag sitting in the middle of a four-poster bed. 'Okay, let's go — you first, Geiger. Mitch, wait in the living room with the kid.'

Geiger rose to his feet and walked unsteadily toward the entry to the bedroom.

Hall waved him inside with his gun and then pointed at the bag. 'Open it.'

Geiger pulled the bag to him and took out an envelope. He turned it upside down and the minidiscs fell onto the bedspread.

An adrenaline mule kicked wildly in Hall's chest. He sucked in a lungful of oxygen to neutralize it.

'So,' Hall said, 'did you look at them?'

'One of them. For a few minutes. Do you know what's on them?'

'No.'

'Black site interrogations. Somebody shot the sessions with a hidden camera. And I'm in the videos.'

Hall gathered up the discs and put them back in the bag. 'Tell me something, Geiger. How'd you get so good at your job?'

Geiger looked directly at him. His left temple was bleeding, and Hall could see that his eyes were having trouble focusing. 'You could say I was born to it,' Geiger said. 'It's in my blood.'

For a moment, Hall turned the words over in his mind, thinking of how much time he'd spent in the devil's den over the years. Geiger was right: it was in the blood. The virus, the incurable human virus.

He pulled the bag's zipper closed. 'That's it, then,' he said.

'Let the boy go.' Geiger's voice was still a whisper.

Hall motioned at the doorway with the gun. 'Into the living room.'

'Let him go, Hall. His mother will be here soon. Don't — '

'Move!'

Geiger stepped into the hallway, and Hall trailed him as he moved slowly into the living room. Mitch, his gun in his lap, sat with Ezra on the couch.

Hall raised the bag. 'Got 'em.'

'Halle-fucking-lujah,' said Mitch, and stood up. 'Let's go.'

Hall didn't answer or move. His gun stayed on Geiger, and he saw Mitch read his eyes.

'No?' Mitch said. 'We're not done?'

Hall shook his head.

'Is this from the top?' Mitch asked.

Hall didn't respond. He turned toward the open front door, listening, and then suddenly raised his gun and shoved Geiger against the wall beside the doorjamb. Leaning back, Hall took a peek through the door and watched Harry limp into the apron of light around the front of the house.

Harry stepped onto the flagstone path and ascended the steps, his face sweat-streaked and dark. Anguish and guilt had swallowed him. In most ways Lily had left him years ago, but now he sensed that she was truly gone — and it was his doing.

Harry was one step inside the front door when he felt the barrel of Hall's gun at the back of his skull.

'Walk with me, Harry,' said Hall. 'Baby steps to the sofa.' Hall steered him into the living room. 'Sit.'

Still standing, Harry turned around slowly. He stopped when the gun rested on his nose. He gave Hall a smile, though it looked more like a gash than a grin, and sat down. Hall backed up a few steps, keeping the gun pointed directly at Harry.

'Well, well,' Harry croaked, hoarse from all his yelling. He glanced over at Mitch, whose gun was pointing at Geiger. 'We've got Moe and Larry. Where's Curly?'

'Dead,' said Mitch.

'That right? Bummer. Curly was always my favorite.'

Harry took a quick look at Geiger, who stood with his back to the wall next to the front door. No immediate help there: Geiger's eyes were glassy, and one side of his face was covered in fresh blood. Harry tried to catch Ezra's eye, but the boy was sitting on the other side of Mitch, his head down. He looked as if he'd been crying.

Harry didn't know how long he could stall, but he knew he had to keep talking. He turned back to Mitch.

'So tell me something, Bubba,' Harry said. 'How long did you sit in the cab at the diner playing with yourself before you figured out that I'd made you for a fucking idiot?'

Mitch didn't flinch. He stared at Harry impassively, all business now.

'Stop talking, Harry,' Hall said.

Harry stabbed a finger at the windows. 'You know what, Hall?' he said. 'My sister is out there lost, or worse, because of you — and you don't give a shit.' Then he noticed the gym bag in Hall's hand. 'Got your de Kooning, huh?'

Hall nodded.

'So why are you still here?'

One look at Hall and another at Geiger gave Harry his answer. He stood up.

'Sit down, Harry,' said Hall.

'*Fuck you.*' Harry put his whole body behind the invective, and Hall releveled the gun.

'Harry, I'm gonna tell you one more — '

'Let's say I came at you,' Harry said. 'You know — so I could rip your fucking heart out. Would you shoot me, Hall?'

'Sit the fuck down!'

Harry took a quick glance out the front windows: nothing. 'And what if while you were shooting me, Geiger went for you? I guess one of you would have to shoot him, too, right? And then there's the kid . . . '

Hall's face had turned to stone.

'Oh, and don't forget Matheson,' said Harry.

351

'That makes four. You won't let him walk around and make life miserable for you, right? So how about it, Hall? When does it get hard to kill people? When you've taken out a dozen? Two dozen?'

Harry checked the windows again, and this time he caught a glimpse of something. Relief flooded him. He had almost run out of things to say, but now he could stop talking.

'You know what, Hall? Forget it — don't worry about it.' Harry pointed at the windows. 'Worry about them.'

Hall pivoted and looked outside. Far away, two pairs of headlights had just turned into the long driveway.

Harry shrugged. 'I decided to call the cops and get them to help look for Lily.'

'Motherfuck . . . ' said Mitch, springing up from the couch. His gun still on Geiger, he moved to the windows — and then Harry bull-rushed him, shoulders down, arms outstretched. Mitch's arm swiveled around with the gun, but Harry rammed him chest-high, wrapping his arms around him. His momentum carried them crashing through a window onto the porch, where, locked in Harry's embrace, they did a clumsy, backward two-step until they hit the railing, broke it apart, and fell out of sight.

Hall's gaze followed the two men for half a second too long, and Geiger forced his battered body into motion. It was a graceless, lopsided endeavor — one hand grabbing at Hall's gun wrist, the other going for his windpipe — and when Hall turned in response, it became entanglement and struggle more than focused violence. For a few moments, Hall seemed to have the advantages of balance and strength, but then Geiger slammed his forehead into Hall's and they fell to the floor, Hall's gun skidding across the pine boards and stopping against the front door's saddle, the gym bag dropping onto the living room's dusty rug.

Geiger turned back toward the couch, his eyes searching for the boy. 'Ezra — run!'

The boy took two steps toward the door before veering right and reaching down for the bag as he ran. Darting around the two fallen men, he raced outside and was gone.

Too weak to overpower Hall, Geiger fought like a wrestler in defensive mode, his twisting limbs doing whatever it took to keep Hall tied up. But then one of Hall's hands found Geiger's maimed thigh, and Hall dug his fingers deep into the wounds. The pain was a firestorm, and Geiger's grip gave way as a howl rose in his throat.

Hall scrambled to his feet, grabbed the gun, and turned on Geiger, who lay sprawled on his back. The weapon came up; Geiger waited for the kill but saw Hall pause and reconsider: the proximity of the police made a gunshot out of the question.

Hall tucked the gun into his belt and gave Geiger's wounded leg a fierce kick.

'And stay down, Geiger!' he hissed, before disappearing from view.

Geiger lay motionless, his blood seeping into

the rug as the music flooded him. Turbulent, discordant choruses of brass and strings shook him — tasting bitter and pungent, they were potent, chromatic, rousing. His mind took hold of the music, wielded it like a club, and pummeled the pain flat.

Slowly, he got up, first to his knees and then to his feet. He moved heavily toward the open front door and leaned against the jamb. He did his best to perform an internal inventory, trying to measure what he had left and guess how far it would get him. The left leg of Corley's sweatpants was turning dark red, sticking to his burning thigh.

Geiger saw the headlights coming up the driveway, close now, and he moved out onto the porch. Holding the broken railing, he looked down and saw Harry lying on top of Mitch, belly to belly, both as still as corpses.

Geiger started lumbering down the steps. 'Harry?'

Harry's head stirred, and then he rolled off Mitch, onto his back. The spike of one of the ground lamps protruded from Mitch's sternum, and his dead eyes were open.

Harry's chest shone with blood, but he looked up at Geiger and raised an arm. 'I'm okay,' he said, pointing toward the river. 'That way — both of them.'

★   ★   ★

Ezra stopped when he found a tree that looked thick enough to hide him. He stood with his back against it to make sure, then slid down its trunk to the ground. He had been running blind and so had lost all sense of bearing. The night was alive with sound: the continuing explosions in the sky, the far-off cheers of the crowd, the mosquitoes buzzing nearby. And he could swear he heard the perpetual rush of the unseen river.

Given the mayhem he had left behind at the house, it was impossible for him to guess who might have survived or who might be coming to look for him.

He clutched the bag and waited.

* * *

Hall moved silently through the trees. A night mist gave the woods a soft, smudged look, like a drawing in charcoal on gray paper. But every few minutes, a new hail of fireworks lit the sky, and suddenly the forest seemed alive with shadowy ghosts.

As Hall made his way toward the river, new possibilities came into sharp focus. Once he found the boy and retrieved the bag, the way forward was simple, clean, doable. He had the laptop's satellite picture in his head; the dock and its rowboat were due west through these woods, about a hundred yards away. He would row out to the middle of the river so that no one could spot him from the shore, then float south with the current for a few miles. At the next town downriver, he'd row back in and find a way to get back to the city.

He knew the boy was near. Hall hadn't been

that far behind him, and he hadn't seen anything move since he'd reached the trees. The boy was hiding someplace, scared to death, and it was almost a sure thing he wouldn't budge. An adult might get wired by the adrenaline and make a move, but a kid would almost certainly be frozen by his fear. Hall didn't expect to see any movement — he would have to coax the boy out.

* * *

'Ezra?'

The boy was drenched in sweat. Even so, the faint but distinct call of his name chilled him. It was less than a shout, more than a whisper. He couldn't tell who was out there or how close the person was, but he was too frightened to peer around the base of the tree. Had Geiger come to rescue him, or was Hall hunting him down? He waved a hand at the swarm of mosquitoes that danced around his head.

The voice came again, closer this time. 'Ezra? Where are you?'

This time he was almost sure it was Geiger's voice. But something stopped him from answering. What if he was wrong? He pulled the gym bag tight to his chest. He didn't know what was on the discs, but he felt as if he held his father's life in his arms.

A new burst of fireworks exploded. His back reared up against the tree trunk, and a wave of panic hit him. The woods went quiet for a minute, and then the voice came again.

'Ezra? It's *me*.'

The promise in that final word so unnerved him that something finally came apart in the boy. Some tether, stretched beyond its limits, broke, and he began to weep. His sobs came in short, ragged bursts and would not be stemmed.

★ ★ ★

Hall had been weaving through the trees in a sideways two-step, calling the boy's name. When he heard the noise he didn't stop but veered twenty degrees west. There was no question — it was a human sound, and its source was very close by.

Hall slowed to a stop, staring at a pine tree thirty feet away whose impressive girth claimed a larger perimeter than its neighbors. He understood the sound now. It was the boy, and he was crying.

Moving counterclockwise, Hall closed in, and soon he saw the murky profile of a figure huddled at the base of the pine. He crept forward using a slow heel-to-toe step, but the soft crunch of a twig made Ezra flinch. Without a backward look, the boy started away in a frantic crawl and then rose to his feet, sneakers digging for traction. But Hall was quicker, and Ezra's sprint lasted only five strides before Hall grabbed his ankles and sent him tumbling onto his chest.

Hall flipped the boy over and straddled him, clamping a hand over his mouth.

'Listen very closely, Ezra: I am *not* going to hurt you. No one else has to get hurt. I'm taking the bag, and you won't see me again. When I go, don't call out for Geiger. Just wait a few minutes, then get up and head that way, back to the house.' He jerked a thumb over a shoulder. 'Okay?'

Hall lifted his hand up. The boy swallowed and then spoke.

'Yes.'

'Good.' Reaching for the bag, Hall stood up and gazed down at the boy. 'Tell your father I might be in touch.'

A shout filtered through the woods. 'Ezra!'

Hall dropped to his knees and his hand muzzled Ezra again. Even with the trees batting the sound about, Hall could tell Geiger was near. The man just wouldn't stop.

'Ezra — tell me where you are!'

Hall leaned down and spoke into the boy's ear.

'Sorry, kid,' he whispered. 'Change of plans. You're coming with me down to the river, just in case he shows up. And remember — I've got a gun and he doesn't, so if you make a sound, you're killing him. You do understand that, right?'

He stood up, pulling Ezra to his feet, locking the boy's hand in his.

'Okay, now we run.'

They bolted through the woods, toward the river. Twice the boy began to fall behind and Hall had to yank him back alongside him. Soon they saw dark gray space beyond the legion of trees, and a moment later they stepped out into the open. The Hudson rolled before them. Another splash of fireworks lit the sky, allowing

Hall to spot the dock jutting into the water only a hundred feet north. He saw a hump at the dock's end: the row-boat.

Hall broke into a run, half-dragging the boy in his wake. As they raced onto the dock, the warped, loose planks beneath their feet clattered loudly, sounding like a volley of muskets. Hall came to a quick halt, freezing Ezra beside him, and looked back toward the house.

Nothing moved along the tree line. Turning, he pulled the boy quietly down the dock.

* * *

Sitting on the grassy riverbank just north of the dock, Lily looked up from the lights in the water when she heard the sound. The musical tones played by wooden planks beneath dashing feet called up a vivid picture in her mind: she saw tiny mallets in a child's hands tapping on a toy xylophone. Then she turned and saw two figures sprinting magically across the river. She smiled.

* * *

Every time Geiger came down on his left foot, a fireball went off in his ravaged leg. Soon after he had entered the woods he'd felt his stitches giving way, so he'd taken off his shirt, torn a sleeve loose, and used it as a tourniquet to wrap his upper thigh above Dalton's cuts. Now an off-kilter, rolling walk was the best he could do, and with each step the world wobbled and shook. His brain made the necessary calculations

359

to maintain balance, but it was becoming harder to crystallize thought. An unknown voice spoke to him from somewhere: *You can lose up to twenty-five percent of your blood before your organs start to shut down* . . . Then he realized it was his own voice, reminding him of a biological truth he had passed on to others countless times.

He called Ezra's name as he went — the darkness didn't answer — but then a clattering noise pulled his head in the direction of the river. He knew it wasn't fireworks; it was the sound of bodies in motion.

A green nova bloomed in the sky, and its thousands of shards showed Geiger a path just ahead of him that sloped gently down through the trees. He used a deep, purging breath as a trigger to get himself moving. Suddenly he thought of Corley and knew the dream was alive within him. But this time it was different: he still didn't know his destination, but for once he was certain he could reach it. He felt a powerful surge, a purity of purpose that carried him forward along the path.

★ ★ ★

Ezra sat folded up on the dock, his arms wrapping his knees. He prayed Geiger would come; he prayed Geiger would be too late.

Hall was three feet away, on his knees, untying the second of two ropes that secured the inverted boat to two metal cleats. Ezra watched him dig at the petrified knot with his nails, and eyed the gun and gym bag lying next to Hall on the weathered planks. He wondered how heavy the weapon was — would it take two hands to hold up?

'What're you gonna do with me — after?' Ezra asked. 'I mean, when you're ready to go?'

Hall ignored him. When he finally pulled the knot loose, he stood up and turned the boat over onto its hull. He put the oars that had been stowed under it in their locks, tied its six-foot tether line to one of the cleats, and pushed the boat into the river. Caught by the current, the rowboat swung downstream with its bow pointing toward them.

The thought of going down the river with Hall was too much for Ezra to bear. Should he try to run away? If he did, he'd lose the bag and the discs forever . . .

Reaching down, Hall picked up the gun and stuck it in his belt. Then he grabbed the bag. For a moment he looked at Ezra silently, finally meeting his gaze.

'You scared?'

Ezra nodded.

'Good,' said Hall. 'Stay scared.'

⋆   ⋆   ⋆

Geiger came through the trees. The riverbank was directly ahead of him, and from it a dock stretched into the dark water. He could make out two figures at the end of the dock, one standing, the other sitting.

Geiger started onto the dock, the old planks rattling beneath his feet. The standing figure turned and raised his arm, pointing something at him.

'Geiger,' Hall called out. 'Stop.'

'Let Ezra go.'

'Get off the dock, Geiger.'

Ezra got up on one knee. 'Do what he says, Geiger. I'll be okay!'

'Geiger, just get off the fucking dock and we're good. If not — I take him down the river with me.'

Geiger kept coming. The dream had always had a beginning and a middle, but it had never had a real end. Now he had finally reached the last part. Completion waited.

'All right then,' Hall said. 'Fuck it.' He put down the bag, reached for the tether line, and pulled the boat up against the dock's end.

'Get in the boat, Ezra,' Hall ordered, waving toward the rowboat with his gun.

'Don't do it, Ezra!' Geiger was halfway along the dock now, and he could see the pale oval of Ezra's face as he turned to look at him.

'Get in the goddamn boat,' Hall shouted. 'Now!'

Ezra jumped down into the boat, and Geiger heard the oars rattling in their locks. 'I want the boy, Hall — and the discs.'

'Can't do it, Geiger,' Hall said, letting go of the boat and allowing it to ride on its tether again. He picked up the bag. 'They wanted all of you dead, all the loose ends tied up nice and tidy. But now *I'm* a loose end, and so when I disappear I'm going to let them know that if they come after me, Veritas Arcana gets the discs back. Now the discs are *my* insurance policy.

That's how this ends, Geiger. Now back off!'

Geiger, now only twenty feet from the end of the dock, could see Hall's eyes flashing in the night. 'Not possible, Hall.'

Hall brought his gun up level with his shoulder. 'I don't get you, Geiger — I really don't. Why are you doing this?'

'Let's just say that it's what works best for me.'

'Geiger, I *will* put you down.'

'No, you won't. Not with the police so close — they'll hear the shot.'

Above them, the fireworks' big finale erupted. A new burst exploded every two or three seconds, filling the night with brilliant stars and deafening *booms* and *bangs* and *crackles*.

'No, they won't,' said Hall. He fired.

The impact knocked Geiger sideways and flung him down onto his back. He lay on the dock staring up at the umbrella of bursting lights. In the midst of the careening, raucous universe, he was drifting away on a warm, soft bed of silence. He saw nothing, felt nothing. He knew only that he was leaving.

He heard a voice calling his name. It was Ezra; the boy was very insistent about something, his tone pleading and urgent. Geiger couldn't make out the words, but then there were no words. There was only a howl.

★   ★   ★

The water was alive with light, and the city of children was so dazzling now that Lily imagined it could illuminate the world. But when she

363

heard a long, anguished scream, she rose to her feet. She knew what it was: the children were crying. They were scared, and they were calling to her from their home beneath the water.

★ ★ ★

Hall stared at Geiger's body, fifteen feet away. He had aimed for the upper right quadrant, the best way to achieve maximum impact without causing lethal damage. But he couldn't tell if his aim had been true. Geiger wasn't moving — he could be bleeding out or dead. Hall had wanted to stop him, not kill him, but in the end it hardly mattered, as long as he could finally be on his way.

He pulled the boat back in. Ezra sat on the rowing bench, his head down on his knees. As the boat came to the dock, the boy looked up at him. Something about his face surprised Hall. It was his eyes: they were dry, and instead of tears there was a bright hatred that shone like cold starlight. Again Hall wavered about letting the boy go. He didn't want to harm him, but if he left him behind, Ezra would tell the police about the boat and point them in his direction. Then the cops would stake out the shore and maybe put a chopper over the river.

'Have a seat in the back, Ezra. Time to take a ride on the river.'

Ezra stared at him for a moment but then moved to the stern. Hall stepped down into the rowboat, put the bag at his feet, and reached up to untie the tether line from the cleat. He glanced up to dock level and saw Geiger stumble to his feet, the right half of him shining and wet.

'Jesus Christ . . . ' muttered Hall.

He pulled the rope free of the cleat, and the boat started drifting away. Hall stood in the boat, shaking his head and watching Geiger shuffle slowly forward, his shoulders slanted crookedly, like tipped scales. Geiger came to an unsteady, stuttering halt at the end of the dock.

Hall made a megaphone of his hands. 'It's over, Geiger! Just let it go!'

★   ★   ★

At first Geiger wasn't sure what he was seeing. Perhaps it was the hallucination of a blood-starved mind, or maybe he was now fully in the grip of the dream's embrace.

Two hands rose from the river like pale aquatic creatures and grabbed the rowboat's gunwale. A head broke the water's surface; Geiger saw the mad eyes of a savior, the open mouth of a child seeking its own kind, a body pushed by fear and exhilaration beyond its limits — and then Lily tried to lever herself up out of the river.

With her added weight, the boat abruptly listed forty degrees, causing Hall to rear backward and send the vessel into a full capsize. He, Ezra, and Lily all disappeared beneath the upturned boat without a sound.

Geiger knew he would finish the dream now, awake and in the world. There would be no coming apart.

He heard a voice behind him, a hoarse and desperate shout:

365

'Geiger!'

But he knew the call came from outside the dream, so he dove off the dock's edge, slamming down on the water, and began swimming for the boat. The coolness of the river was both a stimulant and an anesthetic, pricking the mind and numbing the flesh.

As he neared the boat, he dove under. Geiger swam forward through the blackness, and then desperate hands found him, clawing, grabbing. They pulled him into the thrashing madness.

★　★　★

Harry staggered down the dock. The river churned with unseen violence around the rowboat. Flailing, anonymous limbs broke the surface, then disappeared beneath it, as if the river had staked a claim to them. Then the commotion ceased.

The last pyrotechnics painted the sky with a majestic facsimile of the American flag. As the lights gradually dispersed and winked out, the flag dissolved, leaving only a few stars shining modestly in the blackness. The distant cheers faded to silence.

Harry watched the boat drift down the river, looking for any sign of life around it, desperately fighting against the pull of grief. Then he saw a figure surge up from beneath the river.

The swimmer started for shore, obviously exhausted. One arm slapped the water; the other dragged something behind. Harry raced off the dock and ran a few steps along the river-bank. Looking out across the black water, he still couldn't tell who it was. When he reached a spot opposite the swimmer, he jumped down to the stones and mud. The skinny figure crawled the last few yards and collapsed on the shore, coughing, heaving. The gym bag lay beside him.

Harry knelt beside Ezra and gently put a hand on his back. Ignoring the shouts and the skittering flashlight beams coming from behind him, he slowly rolled the boy over.

Ezra looked up at him and hacked up some of the river.

'Easy,' Harry said. 'Easy.'

He saw the question in Ezra's eyes before it was asked. 'Geiger?' said the boy.

Harry shook his head, and Ezra began to cry, a silent, abyssal outpouring.

★   ★   ★

They sat on the top front step of Corley's house — Ezra, wrapped in a blanket, and Harry, his chest bandaged from shoulder to waist, with his arm around the boy. They shared the same flat stare of fresh grief.

The lights of two police cars and an ambulance drew shimmering patterns of color on the yard. Earlier, sitting in the living room, a first round of questions had been asked of each of them, eliciting answers intended to confound instead of clarify. Theirs was a mystifying tale of a home invasion by two strangers who had attacked them for inexplicable reasons, resulting in one dead body and three people missing in the river. In all the drama and confusion, the gym bag had been tossed onto the kitchen counter, unexplored. At a break in the questioning, Harry had excused himself and paid a visit to the bathroom, where he had emptied the bag of its contents and hidden the discs in the toilet's tank.

Now, as they sat on the step, Ezra finally turned to Harry and told him about what had happened in the river's black turmoil. The boy had been no match for the strength of other hands pulling at him and grasping for control. Then someone had pried him free from the tangle of bodies, shoved the gym bag into his midsection, and pushed him up toward air and life. But the cost of his survival felt unbearable.

'I'm so sorry,' Ezra said, shaking his head.

Harry turned to him. 'For what?'

'This is all because of me.'

Harry pulled him closer. 'No, it's not, Ezra. It's just . . . ' He was desperate for more words, for something wiser or more soothing to say to the boy, but nothing came.

A car drove out of the woods, and a policeman jogged forward and stood in front of it, his arms up. The car stopped, and a tall, lanky woman got out. The cop approached her, a ten-second conversation took place, and then she shoved him out of the way and marched forward.

'Ezra?'

The boy looked up, startled by the sound of a familiar voice. Harry, smiling, gave Ezra's shoulder a squeeze.

The woman caught sight of her son and started to run.

22

Business was bad. A dog days heat wave had driven people from the street, and it didn't help that the city had started hauling away the wreckage of Geiger's house. A storm fence with a gate had been put up in front of the lot, and the demolition crew had cordoned off a strip of the sidewalk.

Mr. Memz took a half-smoked cigarette from his pack, flicked his Zippo, and lit up. When the skinny guy with the cane stopped at his table, it took Mr. Memz a second or two to place him. But then the scene came back to him, and he remembered the name, too.

'Harry, right? Yeah, Geiger's Harry. The cane threw me off for a sec.'

Smiling faintly, Harry raised the dark cherry cane and showed Mr. Memz its carved handle.

'Distinguished, huh?'

'Wish I could use one. It's a nice look.' Mr. Memz glanced up at Harry hopefully. 'Hey, Harry, you got a smoke?'

'Nope, sorry.'

'Damn. Hardly anybody smokes anymore.'

Harry scanned the street, his new habit. 'So how's business?'

'Shit, man — *what* business?'

A loud *crunch* made them both turn. A tractor had just dropped a load of debris from the ruined house into a dump truck.

Turning back, the two men looked at each other.

'He's gone, man,' Harry said.

''Gone' as in gone away?'

'No — drowned. Upstate, five weeks ago.'

Mr. Memz's lips twisted into a dark grimace, and he shook his head. 'Was it that July Fourth thing I heard about, the one on the river?'

'Yeah.'

For a moment Mr. Memz sat utterly still, but then he growled and slammed a fist onto the table. His books jumped.

Harry sighed. 'I just wanted you to know.'

Mr. Memz said nothing. The growl had become a hollow mutter.

Harry tapped his cane on the sidewalk. 'I gotta go now, okay? I gotta be somewhere.'

'Okay.' Mr. Memz nodded, his eyes blank. 'See ya 'round.'

'Probably not, actually.'

'Okay. Won't see ya 'round.'

Harry put his hand inside a jacket pocket, brought out an envelope, and dropped it on the table. 'Just tying up some loose ends.'

Mr. Memz glanced at the envelope. 'What's that?'

'Just something to hold you over till business picks up. I really gotta go, man. You take care.'

Mr. Memz watched Harry walk off toward Amsterdam Avenue, and then his gaze came back to the envelope. He picked it up and pulled its contents halfway out. He slowly fanned twenty five-hundred-dollar bills with his fingertips.